EIGHT-THIRTY KYOTO TIME: FOUR-THIRTY IN CHICAGO.

Alex Hunter reached Ted Blankenship, his top Chicago operative.

"Ted, I want you personally to go to the dead-file room and pull everything we've got on Lisa Chelgrin. I want that file here in Kyoto as soon as possible. Wrap it up and give it to one of our junior fields ops."

"Alex, does this mean the case is being . . . reactivated?"

"I'm not sure."

"Is there a chance . . . I mean, do you think you might have found her after all this time?"

"I really don't know, Ted. More likely than not, I'm just chasing shadows and nothing will come of it. So I expect you not to talk about this, not even to your wife."

"Alex . . . if you've found her it's very big news, isn't it?"

"Very big."

The Key to Midnight

Leigh Nichols

PUBLISHED BY POCKET BOOKS NEW YORK

Another *Original* publication of POCKET BOOKS

POCKET BOOKS, a Simon & Schuster division of
GULF & WESTERN CORPORATION
1230 Avenue of the Americas, New York, N.Y. 10020

ISBN: 0-671-80915-6

First Pocket Books printing June, 1979

10 9 8 7 6 5 4 3 2 1

CONTENTS

PART ONE

JOANNA

A sound of something;
The scarecrow
 Has fallen down of itself.
 —Bonchô, 1670–1714

· 1 ·

In the dark, Joanna Rand went to the window. She stood there for a long while, naked, trembling.

Wind from the distant mountains pressed coldly against the glass in front of her, rattled a loose pane.

At four o'clock in the morning, the city of Kyoto was quiet, even here in Gion, the entertainment quarter with its nightclubs and geisha houses. An incredible city, she thought, a thousand years old yet as new as a fresh idea. Kyoto, the spiritual heart of Japan, was a fascinating hodgepodge of neon signs and ancient temples, plastic gimcrackery and beautiful hand-carved stone, the worst of glossy modern architecture thrusting up next to palaces and ornate shrines that were weathered by centuries of hot, damp summers and cold, damp winters. It was a metropolis that, by some mysterious combination of tradition and popular culture, gave her a renewed sense of man's permanence and refreshed her sometimes shaky belief in the importance of the individual.

The earth rotates on its axis, revolves around the sun; society continuously changes; the city grows; people create new generations; and I will go on like them, she told herself. That was always a comforting thought when she was in darkness, alone, unable to sleep, morbidly energized by the powerful yet indefinable fear that came to her every night.

Calmed somewhat but not anxious to return to bed, Joanna dressed in red silk robe and slippers. Her slender hands were still shaking, but they were no longer uncontrollable.

She felt violated, used, and discarded, as if the creature in her nightmare had somehow attained a physical

3

form and had repeatedly, brutally raped her while she slept. A remembered ache pulsed as steadily as if it were a real wound in the moist juncture of her thighs.

The man with the steel fingers reaches for the hypodermic syringe . . .

That single image was all that she retained of the nightmare. It had been so vivid that, at will, she could recall it in unsettling detail: the texture of those metal fingers, the sound of gears working in them, the way the light had shone off the edges of them.

She switched on the bedside lamp and studied the familiar room. Nothing was out of place and the air contained only her own familiar scent, but she wondered if she truly *had* been here alone all night.

She shivered.

• 2 •

Joanna came out of the narrow stairwell into her ground-floor office. She flicked on the light and stood for a moment just inside the door, studying this room as she had those upstairs. The soft glow from the brass lamp cast purple shadows across the bookshelves, rattan furniture, and rice-paper paintings. The lacy branches of potted palms were transferred in silhouette to the wall opposite her. Everything was in order.

The desk was littered with paper work that needed to be done, but she wasn't in a bookkeeper's frame of mind. She needed a drink.

The outer door of the office opened on the plushly carpeted area around the Moonglow Lounge's long cocktail bar. There wasn't complete darkness in the club: two night lights burned above the smoky blue mirrors behind the bar, and eerie green bulbs shone at each of the four exits. She could see the barstools as well as the main room beyond, where sixty tables and two hundred chairs faced a small raised stage. The nightclub was silent, deserted.

Joanna went behind the bar and fixed a glass of dry sherry over ice. She sipped it, sighed—and became aware of movement near the open office door.

Mariko Inamura, her live-in secretary and assistant manager, had followed her downstairs. Mariko was wearing a bulky brown bathrobe that seemed two sizes too large for her, modest as always; and her black hair, usually held up by a pair of ivory pins, spilled to her shoulders. She came to the bar and sat on one of the stools.

"Like a drink?" Joanna asked.

Mariko smiled. "Some water would be nice."

"Have something stronger."

"No. Just water."

"Trying to make me feel like a lush?"

"You aren't a lush."

"Thanks for the vote of confidence," Joanna said. "But I wonder. I seem to wind up here at the bar every night around this time. And not to get a drink of water." She put a glass of water on the counter.

Mariko picked up the glass and turned it slowly in her hands but didn't drink from it. Joanna watched her admiringly. Mariko had an inborn grace that turned even the most common act into a brief piece of theater. She was quite pretty, around thirty years old, Joanna's age, with big dark eyes and delicate features. She seemed to be unaware of her beauty; and her humility was perhaps her most graceful aspect.

She had come to work at the Moonglow Lounge one week after opening night. She'd wanted the job as much for the opportunity to practice her English with Joanna as for the salary. She'd made it clear that she intended to work at the club a year or two, thereafter to obtain a position as an executive secretary with one of the large American companies that had branch offices in Tokyo. But six years passed, and she apparently no longer found Tokyo appealing, at least not by comparison with the life she now enjoyed.

The Moonglow, Joanna thought, has worked its spell on Mariko too. It's the main interest in her life now as surely as it is the *only* interest in mine.

Besides, an unexpected sisterly affection and concern for each other had developed between them. Neither made friends easily. Mariko was warm and charming —but still surprisingly shy for a woman who worked in a Gion nightclub. A part of her was like the quiet, retiring, soft-spoken, self-effacing Japanese woman of another age. Joanna was the opposite of Mariko in temperament, vivacious and outgoing. She could be at ease with nearly anyone—but she found it difficult to allow that extra degree of closeness that transformed an acquaintance into a friend. Because friendship was not an easy thing for her, she'd done what she could to keep Mariko. She'd given the woman an ever-increasing share of responsibility for the management of the Moonglow as well as a larger salary every year; and Mariko had reciprocated by working very hard. They had decided, without once discussing it, that separation was neither desirable nor necessary.

But why Mariko? Joanna wondered. Of all the people I might have chosen for a best friend, why her? Well . . . because there is absolutely no danger that Mariko will ever get nosy, no danger that she'll try to find out too much about me.

That thought surprised Joanna. She didn't understand herself. What could Mariko possibly find out? What was there to hide? She had no secrets.

Glass of sherry in hand, she came out from behind the bar and sat on a stool.

"You had that nightmare again," Mariko said.

"Just a dream."

"A nightmare," Mariko insisted. "The same one you've had a thousand other nights?"

"Two thousand . . . three. Did I wake you?"

"It was worse than usual."

"No. Same as always."

"Do you think you can fool me?"

"All right," Joanna said. "It was worse than usual. I'm sorry I woke you."

"I worry about you," Mariko said.

"No need to worry. I'm a tough girl."

"You saw him again . . . the man with the metal fingers?"

"I never see his face," Joanna said wearily. "I've never seen anything at all but his hand, those godawful steel fingers—or at least that's all I remember seeing. I guess there's more to the nightmare, but it never stays with me after I wake up." She shuddered and drank some sherry.

Mariko put a hand on Joanna's shoulder, squeezed gently. "I have an uncle who is—"

"A hypnotist."

"Psychologist," Mariko said. "A doctor. He uses hypnotism—"

"I've heard all about him a dozen times before," Joanna said. "I'm really not interested."

"He could help you remember the entire dream. He could help you look into your past and find the cause of the nightmare."

Joanna stared at her own reflection in the blue bar mirror and finally said, "I don't think I ever *want* to know the cause of it, my friend."

• 3 •

Alex Hunter realized that if his employees back in the States could see him eating dinner at the Moonglow Lounge, they would be astonished at his behavior. They knew him to be a demanding boss who expected perfection and quickly dismissed workers who couldn't deliver it, a man who was at all times fair but never more than that, a man who only occasionally offered mild praise but was very often given to sharp and accurate criticism. In Chicago, he was known to be a silent man, too silent, one who rarely smiled. He was widely envied and respected but certainly not well liked. His office staff and field investigators would be disoriented if they saw him now, for he was chatting amiably with the waiters and smiling continually.

He did not appear capable of murder, but he was. In fact he had committed murder twice. He'd pumped six bullets into the chest of a man named Ross Baglio. On another occasion he'd stabbed a man in the throat with the wickedly splintered end of a broken broomstick. Both times he had been acting strictly in self-defense. Now he looked like nothing more than a rather elegant business executive on vacation.

This society, this depressurized culture, so different from the American way, had a great deal to do with his high spirits. The relentlessly pleasant and polite Japanese inspired a smile. Alex had been in their country just ten days, but he could not recall another period in his life during which he had felt even half so relaxed and at peace with himself as he did now.

Of course the food contributed to this effect. The Moonglow Lounge maintained an excellent kitchen. Fine Japanese cuisine changed with the seasons more than any style of cooking with which Alex was familiar, and here was a chef who fully understood that. It was also important that the color of each food should complement the item next to it, and that everything be served on china that was, both in pattern and color, in harmony with the food it carried. Tonight he enjoyed a dinner suited to the cool late-November evening. A delicate wooden tray was placed before him and upon it stood a bone-white china pot that contained thick slices of *daikon* radish, reddish sections of octopus, and finally *konnyaku,* a jellylike food made from devil's tongue. A fluted green bowl contained a fragrant hot mustard in which each delicacy could be gingerly anointed. There was also a large gray platter with two black and red bowls, one containing *akadashi* soup with mushrooms floating in it, the other holding rice. An oblong plate offered raw sea bream and three garnishes along with a cup of finely grated *daikon* for seasoning. It was an ideal winter meal: the food hearty and of the proper somber colors.

But when he had finished the last morsel of bream, Alex Hunter admitted to himself that it was neither the hospitable Japanese nor the quality of the food that made him feel so well. His good humor was primarily the result of the eager anticipation with which he awaited Joanna Rand's appearance on the small stage.

Promptly at eight o'clock, the house lights dimmed, the stage curtains drew back, and the Moonglow Lounge's band opened with a rich rendition of "A String of Pearls." It wasn't the equal of any of the famous orchestras, not a Goodman or a Miller or a Dorsey band, but surprisingly good for house musicians who were born, raised, and trained many thousands of miles and a couple of decades from the origin of the sound. At the end of the song, as the audience began to applaud enthusiastically, the band swung into "Moonglow," and Joanna Rand entered from stage right.

His heartbeat quickened; his pulse gained sudden strength in his throat and temples.

How deeply am I going to get involved with this woman? he asked himself. It was a pointless question, for he already knew the answer.

Slim and graceful, she was one of the loveliest women Alex had ever seen. Although she had a sinuous, exciting body, her face was far more alluring than her legs and buttocks and breasts. She was not beautiful in any classic sense: Her nose wasn't thin or straight enough, her cheekbones not high enough, her forehead not wide enough to satisfy the arbiters of beauty at *Vogue*. Her chin was feminine but strong, lips full, blue eyes several shades darker than the washed-out fuzzy blue of the models who were in demand for magazine covers and television commercials. Her complexion was fashionably flawless but not fashionably pale. She was golden; her thick hair was golden; she seemed to glow with good health. The skin was slightly crinkled at the corners of her eyes, and she looked thirty years old, not sixteen; but that made all the difference. Her beauty was not plastic; it was enhanced a hundredfold by the experience and character that was evident in her face.

She belonged on a stage, not merely to be seen but to be heard as well. Her voice was superb. She sang with a tremulous clarity that pierced the stuffy air and seemed to reverberate within him. Although there was a full house and everyone had been drinking, there was none of the expected nightclub chatter when she performed; the audience was polite, attentive, rapt.

He knew her from another place, another time, although where and when eluded him. Her face was hauntingly familiar, especially the eyes. In fact, he felt he'd not just met her before but had known her well, even intimately. But that was ridiculous. He wouldn't have forgotten a woman as beautiful as this one. So it had to be wishful thinking. Still, it nagged at him.

Tense, motionless, Alex Hunter watched and listened. He wanted her.

· 4 ·

When Joanna Rand finished her last song and the applause finally faded, the band swung into a dance number. Couples crowded onto the shallow dance floor. Conversation picked up again, and the room was filled with sporadic laughter and the musical rattle of dinnerware. As she did every night, Joanna took a moment to survey her domain from the edge of the stage. Pride bubbled within her: She ran a damned good place.

In addition to being a singer and restaurateur, Joanna Rand was a practical social politician. At the end of her first hour-long act, she did not disappear behind the curtains and wait in a dressing room until the ten o'clock performance. Instead she stepped down from the stage in a soft swish of pleated silk and moved slowly among the tables, acknowledging compliments, bowing and being bowed to, stopping to inquire if dinner had been enjoyable, greeting new faces and chatting at length with regular customers. Joanna knew that while good food, romantic atmosphere, and quality entertainment were sufficient to establish a highly profitable restaurant, more than that was required if the club were to be a legend in its own city, in its own time. That extra degree of success was what she wanted. She knew people were flattered to receive personal attention from the owner, and the forty minutes she spent here between acts each night was worth thousands of dollars in repeat business.

She saw that the handsome American with the neatly clipped mustache was present for the third evening in a row. The previous two nights they had exchanged no more than a dozen words, but Joanna had sensed they wouldn't remain strangers for any length of time. At every performance he sat at a small table near the stage and watched her with such single-minded intensity that she had to avoid looking at him for fear she would become distracted and forget the words to a song. After each show, as she mingled with the customers, she knew without looking at him that he was watching her every move. She imagined she could feel the pressure of his eyes right now, and she felt as if she were under a microscope. Although being scrutinized by him was creepy, it was also curiously pleasant, and she was more than a little pleased to see him again.

When she reached his table he stood and smiled, a tall, very broad-shouldered man who managed a

European elegance in spite of his awkward size. He wore a three-piece, gray-black Savile Row suit with blue lining, what appeared to be a hand-tailored Irish linen shirt, and a pearl-gray tie. He said, "When you sing 'These Foolish Things' or 'You Turned the Tables on Me' . . . well, I'm reminded of Helen Ward when she sang with Benny Goodman."

"That's forty years ago," Joanna said. "You're not old enough to remember Helen Ward."

"I admit I never saw her perform. I'm only forty myself. But I have all her records, and I think you're better than she was."

"Oh, she was wonderful," Joanna said. "You flatter me too much."

"I'm merely stating a fact."

"You're a jazz buff?"

"Swing music mostly."

"So we like the same little corner of jazz."

"Apparently," he said, looking around at the crowd, "so do the Japanese. I was told the Moonglow Lounge was *the* nightclub for transplanted Americans and discerning tourists. But ninety percent of your customers are Japanese."

"They have a greater respect for native American music than most people back in the States do," Joanna said.

"Swing is the only music I've ever developed a lasting enthusiasm for." He hesitated, then said, "I'd offer to buy you a brandy, but since you own the place I don't suppose that would be proper etiquette."

"Besides," she said, "I wouldn't permit it. I'll buy you a brandy." He pulled out a chair for her, and she sat down.

A white-jacketed waiter approached, bowed to both of them.

Joanna said to him, "Yamada-san, *burande wo ima onegai, shimasu.* Remy Martin."

"Hai, hai," Yamada said. *"Sugu."* He hurried toward the bar at the back of the room.

The American had not taken his eyes off her. He

said, "You really do have an extraordinary voice, you know. Better than Martha Tilton, Margaret McCrae, Betty Van—"

"Ella Fitzgerald?"

He appeared to consider it, then said, "Well, she's really not someone you should be compared to."

"Oh?"

"I mean, her style is so utterly different from yours. It would be like comparing oranges to apples."

Joanna laughed at his diplomacy. "So I'm not better than Ella Fitzgerald. Good. I'm glad you said that. I was beginning to think you had no standards at all."

"I have very high standards," he said quietly. "And you more than meet them."

His dark eyes were instruments of power as effective as jolts of electricity. His unwavering stare sent an extended series of shocks through her. Good God, she thought, I'm responding to him as if I'm a sixteen-year-old girl with glands rampant! She felt not only as if he had undressed her with his eyes—men had done as much every night that she'd stepped onto a stage—but as if he had undressed more than her body, as if he had stripped her mind bare as well and had discovered, in just one minute, everything worth knowing about her, every private fold of flesh and thought. She had never met a man who concentrated on a woman with such intensity, as if every other human being on earth had ceased to exist for him. She felt again that peculiar combination of uneasiness and pleasure at being the focus of his undivided attention.

When the two snifters of Remy Martin arrived, she used the interruption as an excuse to look away from him. She sipped the brandy and closed her eyes, as if to savor it without distraction. In temporary darkness, she realized that while he had been staring into her eyes he had transmitted some of his own intensity to her, for she had lost all awareness of the noisy club around her: the clinking of glasses, the laughter and talk, even the music. Now all of that returned to her

with the gradualness of silence reasserting itself in
the wake of a tremendous explosion.

Finally she opened her eyes and said, "I'm at a
disadvantage. I don't know your name."

"You're sure you don't?" he asked. "I've had this
feeling . . . that we've met before."

She frowned. "Not that I recall."

"Perhaps it's just that I wish we'd met sooner. I'm
Alex Hunter."

"From the United States."

"Chicago, to be exact."

"You work for an American company here?"

"No. I work for myself."

"In Japan?"

"I'm on vacation for a month. I landed in Tokyo
eight days ago."

"How long will you be in Kyoto?"

"I planned on two days, but I've been in town longer
than that already. I've got three weeks left. Maybe
I'll spend them all in Kyoto and cancel the rest of my
schedule. *Anata no machi wa hijo ni kyomi ga arimasu.*"

"Yes," she said, "it is an interesting city, the best
in Japan, to my way of thinking. But the entire country
is fascinating, Mr. Hunter."

"Call me Alex."

"There's a great deal more to see in other parts of
these islands, Alex."

"Maybe I should come back next year to take in
all of those places. But at the moment it seems to me
that everything I could possibly want to see in Japan
is right here."

She stared at him, braving those insistent dark eyes,
not certain what to think of his approach, his style.
He was quite the male animal, showing his colors,
making his intentions known. For as far back as
Joanna could remember, she had been a strong woman,
not merely in business but also in her personal, emotional life. She seldom wept and never lost her temper
or self-control. She knew the meaning but not the
experience of hysteria. She was obsessively self-reliant.

Always, she was the dominant (though never domineering) partner in her relations with men. She preferred to choose when and how a friendship with a man would develop, and she liked to be the one who decided when it would begin to be more than friendship. She had her own ideas about the proper, desirable pace of romance. Ordinarily, she wouldn't have liked a man who was so unromantically, unimaginatively direct; however, in Alex Hunter a frank, no-nonsense, stylishly aggressive approach was inexplicably appealing.

Nevertheless, because she didn't know how to respond to a man who took charge with such swiftness and self-assurance, Joanna pretended not to see that he was considerably more than casually interested in her. She glanced around the room as if checking on her waiters and the happiness of her customers, then sipped the brandy and said, "You speak Japanese so well."

In acknowledgment of the compliment, he bowed his head an inch or two. *"Arigato."*

"Do itashimashite."

"Languages are a hobby of mine," he said. "As are fast European cars and fine restaurants. And speaking of fine restaurants, do you know of one in this neighborhood that serves lunch?"

"There's a place in the next block," Joanna said. "A lovely restaurant built around a garden with a fountain. It's called Mizutani."

"That sounds perfect," he said. "Shall we meet at Mizutani for lunch tomorrow?"

She was startled by the question but even more surprised to hear herself answer without hesitation. "Yes. That would be nice."

"Noon?" he asked.

"Yes." She took another sip of her Remy Martin, trying to keep her hands from trembling. Joanna knew, by intuition or an even stranger sixth sense, that whatever happened between her and this man, whether it was good or bad, would at least be entirely different from anything she'd experienced before.

• 5 •

The man with the steel fingers reaches for the hypodermic syringe . . .

Joanna Rand sat straight up in bed, soaked in perspiration, gasping for breath, clawing at the unyielding darkness for a moment before she got control of herself and switched on the lamp.

She was alone.

She pushed back the covers and got out of bed with an urgency sparked by some deep-seated fear that she could not understand or even begin to identify. She walked unsteadily to the center of the room and stood in a familiar confusion that she'd known on a hundred other nights.

The air was cool, sharp, *wrong.* She smelled a combination of harsh odors, a blend of several strong antiseptics that simply didn't belong in this room: ammonia, Lysol, alcohol, lye soap, Listerine, an unpleasantly fragrant stew of germicidal substances. She drew a long breath, then another, but the pungent vapors faded as she attempted to pinpoint their source.

When the odor was gone altogether, she reluctantly admitted, as she had on other occasions, that the stench hadn't actually existed. It was left over from the dream, a figment of her imagination or, perhaps more accurately, a fragment of memory. For although she had no recollection of ever being ill or injured, she half believed she *had* been at one time in a hospital room that was absolutely drenched with an abnormally powerful odor of antiseptics. Most important of all, she felt that in the hospital something awful had happened to her, something that was the cause of the repeating

16

nightmare about the absurd but terrifying man with steel fingers.

She padded into the white-and-green bathroom, poured a glass of water. She returned to the bed, sat on the edge of it, drank the water, then slipped under the covers and turned out the lights.

Outside, in the predawn stillness, a bird cried. A large bird, a piercing cry. She heard the flutter of wings. The bird fled past the window, feathers brushing glass with a sibilant sound, then sailed off into the night, its thin screams growing thinner, fainter, ever fainter.

• 6 •

Suddenly, Alex recalled where and when he had first seen the woman. Joanna Rand wasn't her real name.

Alex woke at six thirty Thursday morning in his suite at the Kyoto Hotel. Whether vacationing or working, he was always up early and to bed late, needing less than five hours of rest to feel refreshed and alert. He was grateful for his uncommon metabolism because he knew that by spending fewer hours in bed he was at an advantage in any dealings he had with people who were even greater slaves to the mattress than he was. To Alex, who was an overachiever by choice as well as by nature, sleep was a particularly detestable form of slavery, insidious, each night a temporary death to be endured but never enjoyed. Time spent in sleep was time wasted, surrendered, stolen. By saving three hours each night, he was gaining eleven hundred hours of life every year, *eleven hundred hours* in which to read books and see films and make love, more than forty-five "free" days in which to observe, study, learn—and make money. It might be a cliché, but it was also true that time was

money. And money, in Alex's philosophy, was the
only sure way to obtain the two most important things
in life: independence and dignity, either of which meant
ten thousand times more to him than did love, sex,
friendship, praise, and religion combined. He had been
born poor, raised by a pair of hopeless alcoholics to
whom the word *dignity* was as empty of meaning as
the word *responsibility*. He had made up his mind
when he was a child that he would discover the secret
of the wealthy. And he had found it while still a boy:
The secret of the wealthy was *time*. Having learned the
lesson, he applied it with fervor. In twenty years of
judiciously managed time, his net worth had increased
from five hundred dollars to more than four million.
He believed that his habit of being late to bed and
early to rise, while half at odds with Ben Franklin's
immortal advice, was a major factor in his phenomenal
success.

Ordinarily, he would shower, shave, and dress within twenty minutes of waking, but this morning he made
a concession to his vacation and allowed himself the
routine-shattering luxury of reading in bed; and it was
there, with a book in his lap, that he realized who
Joanna Rand was. While he read, his subconscious
mind, loathe to squander time, apparently had been
occupied with the mystery of Joanna, for although he
hadn't been consciously thinking of her, he suddenly
made the connection between her and a face out of
his past.

Since his junior high school days, he'd talked to
himself whenever he'd needed to work out an answer
for a personal or career problem. Now he put down
the book and said, "Good God Almighty, it's her. Has
to be her. Joanna looks like her but ten years older.
And sounds like her . . . ten years later."

He got out of bed, took his bath, shaved. He stared
at his smooth cheeks in the bathroom mirror, then up
at his own eyes. "Slow down, old boy. Maybe the
resemblance isn't as remarkable as you think. It's been
ten long years since you've even seen a photograph of

Lisa Chelgrin. Once you have pictures to make a comparison, Joanna Rand might turn out to look as much like Lisa as a giraffe looks like a Shetland pony."

He dressed and sat at the desk in the suite's sparsely furnished drawing room. "Besides, isn't everyone in the world supposed to have one or two Doppelgängers, unrelated twins, floating around? Yeah. So the resemblance here could be pure chance. Yeah. Think about that."

For a long while he stared at the telephone in the center of his desk blotter, then said, "Yeah. Only thing is, I never did believe in pure chance." He had built and come to own the second-largest private security and investigation firm in the United States by having little or no respect for coincidence, by digging for more than happenstance in events that seemed to be related by pure chance. He pulled the telephone closer, picked up the receiver, and placed an overseas call through the hotel switchboard. There were delays, a lot of routing problems, broken connections that had to be restored more than once, but he finally reached his company headquarters at eight thirty in the morning, Kyoto time—four thirty in the afternoon, Chicago time. He spoke with Ted Blakenship, his top man in the office. "Ted, I want you to personally go to the dead-file room and pull everything we've got on Lisa Chelgrin. I want that file in Kyoto as soon as possible. Wrap it up and give it to one of our junior field ops who doesn't have anything better to do, and put him on the first available flight in the right direction."

Blakenship chose his words carefully, slowly. "Alex, does this mean the case is being . . . reactivated?"

"I'm not sure."

"Is there a chance . . . I mean, do you think you might have found her after all this time?"

"I really don't know, Ted. More likely than not, I'm chasing shadows and nothing will come of it. So I expect you not to talk about this, not even with your wife."

"Of course."

"Go to the dead files yourself. Don't send a secretary. I don't want a clerk starting rumors."

"I understand."

"And the field operative who brings it shouldn't know what he's carrying."

"I'll keep him in the dark. But, Alex . . . if you have found her, it's very big news, isn't it?"

"Very big," Alex agreed. "Call me back when you've got things arranged and let me know when I can expect our messenger."

"Will do."

Alex put down the receiver and went to one of the drawing room windows. He stood watching the bicyclists and motorists in the crowded streets below. Every one of them seemed to comprehend the value of time; all of them were hurrying to get somewhere. As he watched, one cyclist made an error in judgment, tried to pass between two cars when there wasn't sufficient space for him. A white Toyota accidentally bumped the cyclist; man and machine went down in a violent, skidding, rolling, bouncing tangle of legs and twisted bicycle wheels, arms, and handlebars. Brakes squealed, traffic halted, and people rushed toward the stricken man. Alex, who was not superstitious, had the uncharacteristic and decidedly eerie feeling that he had just been sent an omen.

· 7 ·

At noon Alex met Joanna at Mizutani for lunch. When he saw her again, he realized the picture of her that he carried in his mind was only as fair to her as a snapshot of Niagara Falls is representative of the true beauty of wildly tumbling water. She was far more

golden, more alive, slimmer, saucier, her eyes a deeper
blue than he remembered, even though just a single
night had passed since he'd last seen her. She was wearing a soft tan pantsuit that one moment draped her
modestly, the next clung provocatively. A bright red
scarf was tied at her throat, and a red ceramic bracelet
decorated her left wrist. He took her hand and kissed
it, not because he was accustomed to European manners but because it provided him with an excuse to
touch his lips to her skin.

Mizutani was an *o-zashiki* restaurant, which meant
that it was divided by rice-paper partitions into many
private dining rooms where meals were served strictly
Japanese-style. The ceiling was not high, less than
eighteen inches above Alex's head, and the floor was
of brilliantly polished pine that seemed transparent
and as deep as a sea. In the vestibule, Alex and Joanna
exchanged their street shoes for soft slippers, then
followed a petite young hostess to a room where they
sat on the floor, side by side on thin but comfortable
cushions that were arranged in front of a low table.
They faced a six-foot-square window beyond which
lay a walled garden. This late in the year, there were
no flowers to brighten the view; but there were several
varieties of well-tended evergreens and a carpet of
moss that had not yet turned brown for the winter. In
the center of the garden, water fountained from a
seven-foot-high pyramid of rocks, spilled down the
individual stones in rivulets to a shallow, trembling
pool. Alex had never seen a restaurant so perfectly
suited for lovers as this one; it was the ideal setting
in which to erect the first few fragile building blocks
of a new romance.

Alex squirmed on his cushion, trying to find the
position that would allow his long legs the most room
under the table, and twice he unintentionally poked her
legs with his knees. Embarrassed by his awkwardness,
he smiled and said, "Japan is charming, but I'm so out
of place here. I was six foot two when I left Chicago,
but I swear I grew two feet on the airplane. Every-

thing's so delicate here. I feel like a clumsy, lumbering, hairy barbarian."

"On the contrary," Joanna said, "for your size you're quite graceful even by Japanese standards."

"I thank you for saying it, but I know it's not true."

"Are you calling me a liar?"

"What?"

"A liar." She pretended to be hurt.

"Of course not."

"Then what are you calling me?"

"You're just polite."

"Are you saying a person must lie to be polite?"

"I'm saying that I'm an ox, a hippo, and I know it."

"I wouldn't have told you that you're graceful unless I meant it. I never say things I don't mean."

"Everyone does," he said.

"Oh? Do you?"

"All the time."

"Well, you'd better never to me."

"I'll remember that."

"I mean it," she said. There was conviction in her voice; her clear blue eyes met his directly. "I like people who speak their minds, even when they tell me things I don't want to hear. That's the way I treat everyone, and I expect everyone to be the same to me and to hell with social diplomacy among friends. Stick around long enough and you'll see I'm telling the truth."

"Is that an invitation?" Alex asked.

"To what?"

"Is that an invitation to stick around?"

"Do you need one?" she asked.

"I suppose I don't." He saw even more character in her face now than he had initially; for the first time he was aware of the considerable strength and spunky self-assurance that lay beneath her soft, feminine surface. "If you didn't want me to stick around," he said, "you'd tell me pretty bluntly, wouldn't you?"

"Yes. Do you see some of the advantages of being honest with people? For one thing, it saves so much time and pain for everybody. Now, you great big clumsy ox, if you've finally settled down, let's order lunch."

He blinked in surprise, she grinned at him, he smiled, and they both began to laugh.

They ate *mizutaki,* the white meat of the chicken stewed in an earthenware pot and flavored with scallions, icicle radish, and many herbs. When the chicken was gone, they drank the excellent broth. This was accompanied by several tiny cups of steaming sake, which is delicious when piping hot, but which tastes like a spoiled sauterne when cool.

Throughout lunch they talked. He found conversation with her to be pleasant, unstrained; and in fact they were so at ease with each other that it appeared they'd been the best of friends for years. They discussed music, Japanese customs and art, films, books, personal histories. Alex wanted to mention the magic name, Lisa Chelgrin, to see what, if anything, would happen. At times he had the almost psychic ability to read guilt or innocence in the reactions of the suspect, in the fleeting facial expressions at the instant the accusations were made, in the anomalies of the voice affected by many different kinds of stress, and in the far more subtle changes that occurred deep within the eyes. However, Alex had no desire to discuss the Chelgrin disappearance with Joanna until he heard her story: where she was born and raised, where she learned to sing, why she came to Japan, how she ended up at the Moonglow Lounge in Kyoto. The biography of Joanna Rand might have enough detail, substance, and verisimilitude to convince him that she actually was who she said, and that her resemblance to the long-missing Chelgrin woman was only coincidence, in which case he would not need to bring up the matter at all. Therefore, it was essential that she spend a large part of the lunch hour talking unselfconsciously about herself. The trouble was that she resisted, not for a sinister motive but merely out of modesty. Ordinarily, Alex was as reluctant as she was to talk about himself, even with close friends; but oddly, in her company his inhibitions disintegrated. It's almost like talking to myself, he thought at one point. In the end, while trying unsuccessfully to probe into Joanna's past, he told her almost everything about his own.

"Are you really a private detective?" she asked.

"Yes."

"It's hard to believe."

"Why? What do I look like—a brain surgeon?"

"I mean, where's your trench coat?"

"At the cleaners. They're trying to remove all those ugly bloodstains."

"You aren't wearing a shoulder holster."

"It chafes my shoulder."

"Aren't you carrying a gun at all?"

"There's a miniature derringer in my left nostril."

"Come on. I'm serious."

"The Japanese government frowns on pistol-packing American tourists. Anyway, I don't intend to indulge in any duels while I'm here."

Even her laugh pleased him: a hearty, musical sound, not a girlish giggle. She said, "I'd expect a private detective to be . . . well, slightly seedy—"

"Oh, thank you so very much!"

"—and furtive, always looking over his shoulder, kind of squint-eyed, armed to the teeth, a sentimental and at the same time a really cold, cynical, everybody-can-go-to-hell sort of character."

"Sam Spade as played by Humphrey Bogart."

"Exactly."

"The business isn't like that any more," Alex said. "In fact I doubt that it ever was. We do mostly ordinary, mundane work, seldom anything dangerous, a hell of a lot fewer murders to solve than the mystery writers would have you believe. Our time's pretty much taken up with divorce investigations, skip-tracing, gathering evidence for defense attorneys in criminal trials. . . . We'll occasionally go searching for a missing person, and we're always playing bodyguards to the rich and the famous and the just plain nervous. By far the largest part of the company's yearly gross is derived from providing electronic security systems and uniformed security guards to department stores and office buildings. Not half as romantic or glamorous as Bogart, I'm afraid."

"Well . . . maybe so," Joanna said. "But it's still a whole lot more romantic than being an accountant." She took a minute to chew and savor a tender piece of chicken. She ate as daintily as the Japanese did, but with a healthy, undisguised, and decidedly erotic appetite.

Alex watched her surreptitiously as she swallowed the chicken and as she sipped her sake. The clenching of her jaw muscles, the sinuous movement of her throat muscles, and the exquisite line of her lips as she sucked the hot drink elicited a low-key sexual response from him.

She put down the sake cup and said, "How'd you get into such an unusual line of work?"

"Early on I decided not to live my life on the edge of poverty like my parents, and I thought that every last lawyer on earth was as rich as a Middle Eastern potentate. So with the help of a few scholarships and a long string of night jobs, I managed to get through college and law school."

"Summa cum laude?" she asked

Startled, he said, "How'd you know that?"

She smiled. "Just an educated guess."

"You should be the private detective."

"Samantha Spade. What happened after graduation?"

"I spent one year with a major Chicago firm that specialized in corporate law. But that kind of life turned out not to suit me very well."

"You gave up a promising career as an attorney to be a private eye?" Joanna asked, incredulous.

"It wasn't particularly promising. For one thing I found out that not all lawyers are rich. In fact the average salary these days is only twenty-five thousand dollars a year—and back then it was much less, especially for someone just starting. It seemed like a lot of money to me when I was young, but I quickly saw that the government would take a big bite in taxes. What I had left over would never put me behind the wheel of a Rolls Royce."

"And is that what you wanted, a Rolls Royce life-style?"

"Why not? I had the opposite as a child. I knew that poverty wasn't ennobling. I wanted everything I could get my hands on. But after a couple of months of writing briefs and doing legal research, I realized that the really enormous money was there only for senior partners of the big firms. By the time I could have worked my way to the top, I would have been too old to fully enjoy the rewards."

When he was twenty-five years old, Alex Hunter decided that the private security field was going to be a growth industry for the next few decades, and he left the law firm to work for the fifty-man Bonner Agency, where he intended to learn the business from the inside. He was paid a salary that was even smaller than that of a young attorney, but he also received relatively substantial commissions for every investigation that he settled satisfactorily. Because he was ambitious, intelligent, and clever, he did better than any of his associates. He invested his earnings wisely, and when he was just thirty years old, he was able to arrange a bank loan to buy the agency from Martin Bonner. Under Alex's guidance the company grew rapidly in size, reputation, and profitability. It moved aggressively into all areas of the industry, including sales, installation, and maintenance of electronic security systems. Today, with more than two thousand employees and with offices in eight cities, it was one of the largest corporations of its kind in the world.

"Are you really a millionaire?" Joanna asked.

"At least on paper."

"I'd expect a millionaire to travel with an entourage."

"Only the insecure travel with an entourage."

"I suppose you have your Rolls Royce?"

"Two of them."

"I've never had lunch with a millionaire before."

"Does the food taste different?" he asked, amused.

"I feel awkward."

"For heaven's sake, why?"

"All that money," she said. "It's . . . well, I don't know why exactly, but I feel awkward."

"Joanna, no one holds the dollar in higher regard than I do. But I also understand that money is neither dirty nor noble; it's a neutral substance; it's merely an inevitable part of any civilization, just as day and night are the natural consequence of the rotation of the earth. Of the two of us, you are the one to be admired. You're a gifted and obviously disciplined singer; besides which, you're truly a marvelous restaurateur, and that's as much an art as it is a business. *I* should feel awkward in the presence of so much talent."

For a long moment she regarded him in silence, and he could tell that she was judging him. She put down her chopsticks and patted her mouth with a napkin. "By God, I think you actually meant every word of that."

"Of course I did," Alex said. "Would I dare be insincere? Don't you remember your speech about our being completely honest with each other?"

Joanna shook her head as if she were amazed at him, and her thick golden hair shimmered softly. "Now I'm more than ever in awe of you. Most men who started out with nothing and piled up a large fortune by the age of forty would be insufferable egomaniacs."

Alex disagreed. "Not at all. There's nothing special about me. I know a good many rich men, and most of them have every bit as much humility as an office clerk or as some three-hundred-dollar-a-week guy working a Detroit assembly line. We laugh and cry and bleed, you know. And since the subject of humility has come up, I guess I should finally show some. We've talked way too much about me. What's Joanna Rand's story? How did you get to Japan? To the Moonglow Lounge? I want to hear all about you."

"There's not a lot to hear," she said.

"Nonsense."

"No, I'm serious. My life seems pretty boring compared to yours."

He grimaced. "Humility is a charming character trait. But *excessive* humility is not flattering. I told you about myself. Now it's your turn. Fair is fair. I guarantee you'll have an attentive audience."

"Let's order dessert first," Joanna said.

She was either secretive about her past or she was genuinely intimidated by him. He could not decide which it was. "Okay," he said, not yet prepared to press her or to make accusations. "What would you like?"

"Something light."

Their waitress, a pleasant round-faced woman dressed in a white *yukata* and short maroon jacket, suggested they have fruit of some kind, and they agreed, leaving the choice to her. They were served peeled mandarin orange slices coated with finely shredded almonds and coconut.

Alex ate two pieces of the orange before he said, "Where do you come from in the States?"

"I was born in New York City," she said.

"One of my favorite places in spite of the dirt and crime. Did you like it?"

"I don't remember it all that well. My father was an executive with one of those hydra-headed American conglomerates. When I was ten, he was promoted to a top-level management position with one of the company's British subsidiaries. I grew up in London and attended university there."

"What did you study?"

"Music for a while . . . then oriental languages. I became interested in the Orient because of a temporary but intense infatuation with a Japanese exchange student. He and I shared an apartment for a year. Our affair blossomed and died, but my interest in the Orient remained."

"When did you come to Japan?" Alex asked, trying

to be casual, trying not to sound like a private detective seeking information about an important case.

"Almost ten years ago," she said.

Coincidental with the disappearance of Lisa Chelgrin, he thought. But he said nothing.

She picked up another slice of orange with her chopsticks, ate it with visible delight. A paper-thin curl of coconut clung to the corner of her mouth, and she licked it in with a slow movement of her tongue. Watching her, Alex thought she resembled a tawny cat, sleek-muscled, full of kinetic energy. As if she heard the thought, she turned her head with feline fluidity and looked at him out of eyes that had that catlike quality of harmoniously blended opposites: sleepiness combined with total awareness, watchfulness mixed with cool indifference, a proud isolation yet a longing for affection.

She said, "My parents were killed in an auto accident during a short vacation to Brighton. I had no relatives in the States, no great desire to return there. And Britain seemed terribly dreary all of a sudden, full of bad memories. When my dad's life insurance was paid and the estate was settled, I took the money and came to Japan."

"Looking for that exchange student?"

"Oh, no. The affair was over by then. Besides, he was still going to school in London. I came because I thought I'd like it here. And I did. I spent a few months playing the tourist, then I put together an act, although I must admit not a good one, and eventually I landed a job singing Japanese and American pop music in a Yokohama nightclub. I've always had a fairly good voice, but I've not always had a stage presence. I was dreadful at the start, a clumsy grinning amateur, but I learned."

"I'll bet at least one out of every two Americans who passed through called you the—"

"Yokohama Mama," she said. "God, yes!" She smiled sourly. "They all thought they were hilariously clever. 'Yokohama Mama' never was one of my favorite songs—and especially not after I heard that tired old joke two or three thousand times."

"How'd you get to Kyoto?"

"There was a stopover in Tokyo," Joanna said, "a better job than the one in Yokohama. It was a big club called Ongaku, Ongaku."

"Music, Music," Alex translated. "I know the place. I was there only five days ago!"

"The club had a reasonably good house band back then. The musicians were as weary of working with all that sound-alike pop music as I was. They were willing to take chances. Risk is better than boredom; that's a motto of mine. Some of those musicians were familiar with jazz, and I taught everyone what I knew. The management was skeptical at first, but the customers loved it. A Japanese audience is usually more reserved than a Western audience, but the people at Ongaku let down their hair when they heard us." That first triumph was, Alex saw, a sweet recollection for Joanna; smiling faintly, she stared at the garden without comprehending it, eyes glazed, as if she were looking clearly back along the curve of time. "It was a crazy place for a while, wild and exciting; it really jumped. Swing music was new to them . . . or maybe it wasn't new, maybe it was only something they rediscovered, which is pretty much the same thing. Anyway, to my surprise I was the longest-running act in the history of that club. I was their main attraction for more than two years. If I'd wanted to stay, I'd probably still be there. But eventually I realized that I'd be better off if I worked for myself in a club of my own."

"Ongaku, Ongaku isn't the same as you describe it," Alex said. "Not any more. It lost too much when you left. It doesn't jump these days. It doesn't even twitch. It's nothing but a noisy plastic tourist trap. Americans who don't know a damned thing about swing go there for a sort of subtle racist pleasure, for the novelty of seeing a group of yellow men perform white men's music; and I suppose the Japanese go because they're nostalgic, because they remember what Ongaku used to be. The band is mediocre now, and the vocalist shouldn't be permitted to sing jazz anywhere, not anywhere, not even in her own bath!"

Joanna laughed and tossed her head to get a long wave of hair out of her face. That gesture, Alex thought, made her look like a schoolgirl—fresh, tender, innocent—and not one day older than seventeen. However, although he saw this special, fleeting burst of even greater beauty, he wasn't able to enjoy it; for in that brief moment she looked even more like Lisa Chelgrin than she had originally seemed to him. In those few transcendent seconds she was not merely a Chelgrin look-alike; she was a dead ringer for the missing woman.

Alex cleared his throat and said, "When did you come to Kyoto?"

"I came for a vacation in July, more than six years ago. It was during the annual Gion Matsuri."

"Matsuri . . . a festival."

"Yes. It's the city's most elaborate celebration. There were parties, exhibits, art shows, more gaiety and spontaneous friendliness than a Westerner like me could absorb. The old houses, especially on Muromachi, were open to the public with displays of family treasures and heirlooms. There was a parade of the most enormous, ornate floats you can imagine, all of them gorgeous, some of them carrying orchestras of flutes, gongs, and drums. . . . It was enchanting. I stayed an extra week, and I fell in love with Kyoto even when it wasn't in the midst of a festival. During the time I'd worked in Tokyo, I'd learned about the management of a nightclub, so I decided to use a big part of my savings to buy the building that's now the Moonglow. I hired the best people I could find, and we've been successful ever since we opened. Of course I'm nowhere near being a millionaire. And so there you have it, just as you insisted, the somewhat less than electrifying story of Joanna Rand, a girl entrepreneur. I warned you it would be dull compared to yours. Not a single murder mystery or Rolls Royce in the entire tale."

"I didn't yawn once," Alex said.

"Only because you're too polite."

"Only because I'm too fascinated."

"Remember our vow of honesty."

"I'm being straight with you. I *am* fascinated."

"Then you aren't as bright as I thought," she said.

"I want to hear more."

"There isn't any more," she said.

"Nonsense. No one's life can be retold adequately in five minutes, and especially not yours."

"Oh, yeah," she said, "especially mine. In every way I can, I try to make the Moonglow Lounge like Rick's place, the Café Américain, in *Casablanca*. But I'm sorry to report that the kind of wild, dangerous, romantic stuff that happened to Bogart in the movie simply doesn't happen to me and never will. I'm a lightning rod for the *ordinary* forces of life. The last major crisis I can remember was when the dishwasher broke down and for two days everything had to be done by hand. That's not the sort of material that makes for sparkling anecdotal conversation over lunch, and so I'm not going to talk about myself. Perhaps it doesn't bore you, but it bores the hell out of me."

Alex wasn't certain that everything Joanna Rand had told him was the truth, but he was favorably impressed. Her capsule biography was generally convincing, as much for the manner in which it was delivered as for its detail. Although she'd been reluctant to talk much about herself, there'd been no hesitation in her voice once she'd begun, not the slightest hint of a liar's discomfort. Her history as a nightclub singer in Yokohama and Tokyo was undoubtedly true. If she needed to invent a story to cover those years, she wouldn't create one that was so easy to investigate and disprove, especially not when she was trying to convince a man who'd parlayed a law degree and a private investigator's license into a multimillion-dollar fortune. The part about Britain and the parents who'd been killed while on a holiday to Brighton . . . well, he wasn't sure what to make of that. As a device for totally sealing off all of her life prior to Japan, it was effective but far too pat. Furthermore, there were a couple of minor points at which her biography touched that of Lisa Chelgrin, which seemed to Alex to be too much coincidence piled atop coincidence.

Joanna turned on her cushion and faced him directly. Her knee pressed against his leg, sending a pleasant shiver through him at the moment of contact. "Do you have any plans for the rest of the afternoon?" she asked.

"I've been away from the office little more than a week, and already I'm a shameless sloth. About the only thing I had planned for this afternoon was to digest lunch."

"If you'd like to do some sightseeing, I'll be your guide for a few hours."

Her knee was still against his leg, and the effect on him had not subsided. She reached him on a primal, sexual level as no woman had in years.

He cleared his throat softly and said, "It's nice of you to offer to take the time with me. But I know, when you own your own business, there's a thousand things to do every day. I don't want to interfere with—"

She interrupted him with a wave of her hand. "Mariko can handle things at the club until it opens. I don't have to put in an appearance until five thirty, maybe six o'clock."

"Mariko?" he asked.

"Mariko Inamura. She's my best friend and the assistant manager of the Moonglow. You'll like her. She's the best thing that's happened to me since I came to Japan. She's smart and trustworthy, and she works like a demon."

Alex repeated the name several times to himself until he knew he would remember it. He wanted to have a long and probing conversation with the assistant manager of the Moonglow. Mariko surely knew more about Joanna Rand's past than Joanna was willing to reveal to him. He would be a stranger to this Inamura woman, and she would be no more inclined to satisfy his curiosity than Joanna was. Nonetheless, if he were sufficiently charming and gracious, sufficiently casual, sufficiently indirect in broaching the subject (what he called a "soft interrogation"), Mariko might provide him with new bits and pieces of Joanna Rand's past.

Joanna touched his hand, jolting him from his reverie. "What do you say?"

"About what?" he asked.

"About my being your guide, of course?"

With mock gallantry, but also somewhat seriously, Alex said, "Dear lady, I would follow you anywhere."

She grinned. "Even to the jaws of death?"

"Dear lady, not just to the jaws of death but into them as well—if you insisted."

Her rich laughter filled the small *o-zashiki* room. "I'm afraid there's nothing *that* exciting in Kyoto. But you do a fine imitation of Douglas Fairbanks."

He inclined his head toward her in a gentle bow. "*Arigato,* Joanna-san."

She returned his bow.

Alex had expected to make up his mind about her during lunch, but now they had finished the meal before he'd reached any conclusions.

Her uncommonly dark blue eyes seemed to grow darker still. He stared into them, entranced.

Joanna Rand or Lisa Chelgrin?

He couldn't decide which.

8

At Joanna's request the hostess at Mizutani telephoned the Sogo Taxi Company, and the cab arrived in less than five minutes, an all-black car with red lettering. Joanna was delighted with the driver. No one could have been better suited than he was for the little tour she had in mind. He was a wrinkled, white-haired old man with an appealing smile that lacked one tooth. He sensed romance between her and Alex Hunter, and because of it he interrupted their conversation only to make certain they didn't miss some special bit of scenery, using his rearview mirror to glance furtively at them, always with bright-eyed approval.

For more than an hour, at the driver's discretion, they cruised randomly through the ancient city. Joanna drew Alex's attention to the most interesting houses, temples, and hotels, keeping up a stream of spritely and entertaining patter about Japanese history and architecture. At least she thought he was entertained. He smiled, laughed a lot, and asked questions about what he was seeing. He looked at her as much as he looked at the city, and again she felt the incredible force of his personality as it was revealed through his eyes.

They were stopped at a traffic light near the National Museum when he surprised her with a line of conversation that seemed inane for him. "Your accent intrigues me," he said.

She blinked. "What accent?"

"It isn't New York, is it?"

"I wasn't aware I had an accent."

"No, it's not New York. Boston?"

"I've never been to Boston."

35

"It's not Boston anyway. It's very difficult to pin down. Maybe there's a slight trace of British English in it. Maybe that's it."

"I hope not," Joanna said. "I've always disliked Americans who assume a British accent after living a few years there. It strikes me as phony."

"It's not British," he said. He studied her while he pondered the problem, and as the cab started up again he said, "I know what it sounds like! Chicago!"

"You're from Chicago," Joanna said, "and I don't sound like you."

"Oh, but I think you do," Alex said. "Just a little bit."

"Not at all. Besides, you can add Chicago to the list of places I've never been."

"You must have lived somewhere in Illinois," he insisted.

For an instant his smile struck her as being painted on and maintained only with considerable effort.

"No," she said, "I've never been to Illinois."

He shrugged, dismissing the subject as suddenly as he had begun to pursue it. "Well, then I'm wrong." He pointed to a building ahead of them, on the left. "That's an odd-looking place. What is it?"

She resumed her role as guide, but with the uneasy feeling that the questions about her accent had not been asked casually. The conversation had a purpose that eluded her.

A shiver passed through her, like an echo of the chills that she endured every night.

9

At Nijo Castle they paid the cab fare and continued their sightseeing on foot. They turned away from the small red-and-black Sogo taxi as it roared off into traffic, and they followed three other tourists toward the palace's huge iron-plated East Gate. Joanna glanced at Alex and saw that he was impressed.

"Now *this* is my idea of a castle!" But then he shook his head as if to clear his thoughts, and he said, "Except it looks too garish for Japan."

Joanna sighed. "I'm so glad you said that."

"You are?"

"If you liked Nijo Castle *too* much, then how could I ever like you? I admire a man with good taste."

"You mean I'm supposed to find it garish?" he asked.

"Most sensitive people do, if they understand Japanese style."

"I thought it was a landmark."

"It is, historically. But it's an attraction with more appeal for tourists than for the Japanese."

They entered through the main gate, then passed a second gate, the Kara-mon, which was richly ornamented with metalwork and elaborate wood carvings. Ahead of them lay a wide courtyard and then the palace itself.

As they crossed the court Joanna said, "Most Westerners expect ancient palaces to be massive, lavish. They're usually disappointed to find so few vast and imposing monuments here—but they nearly always like Nijo Castle. Its rococo grandeur is something they can relate to. Unfortunately, Nijo doesn't accurately represent the fundamental qualities of Japanese life and philosophy."

She realized she was beginning to babble nervously, but she could not help it. Over lunch, and especially later, in the confines of the stuffy taxi, she had been aware of a powerful sexual tension building between them, an aching erotic hunger. She welcomed it and anticipated the act that would satisfy it . . . yet at the same time she was frightened of the commitment she might be forced to make. For six months she'd had no lover, although for most of that time she'd lived with a longing for someone very like this handsome man. She wanted Alex Hunter in her bed, wanted the pleasure, giving and taking, sharing, that special tenderness, animal closeness, but she didn't know if she could fully enjoy all of that and then endure another painful separation. She was generally a solid, stable person, not easily shaken; but with Alex Hunter she felt she was walking the edge of a precipice, foolishly testing her balance. Her last affair had ended badly, as had every one before it—and as this one surely would. She harbored a strong, inexplicable, destructive urge, a need to demolish everything good that developed between her and any man, a need to blast it apart at that precise moment when it ceased to be merely a sex game and became love. All her life she'd wanted a permanent relationship, had sought it with quiet desperation. She didn't have the temperament for a life passed alone; however, in spite of that, she rebelled against marriage when it was offered, even if she cared deeply about the man who proposed. She fled from the desired intimacy when it was within her reach, and always for reasons she could not fathom. Each time that she was on the brink of accepting a proposal, she worried that her would-be fiancé might have more curiosity about her when he was her husband than he'd shown when he was merely her lover; she worried that he would probe too deeply into her past and learn the truth. *The truth*. The worry swelled into fear, and the fear swiftly became debilitating, unbearable, all-

consuming. But why? Dammit, *why?* She had nothing
to hide. She was certain of that. She hadn't been lying
when she'd told Alex that her life history was singularly lacking in momentous events and dark secrets.
Nevertheless, she knew that if she had an affair with
him, and if he wanted more than a casual romp with
her, she would reject and alienate him with a sudden-
ness and viciousness that would leave him stunned. And
when he was gone, when she was alone, she would be
crushed by the loss and would learn to hate herself as
she had never done before. The fear was irrational,
but it was not something she could conquer. For this
reason, walking beside him across the courtyard of
Nijo Castle, she talked incessantly, stalled, filled the
silence with trivial chatter that left no room for anything of a personal nature.

"Westerners," Joanna told him pedantically, "seek
action and excitement from the instant they wake until
they go to bed. They complain endlessly about the
awful pressures that twist their lives, but in fact they
thrive on tension. They're born hustlers, movers, shak-
ers. Life here is quite the opposite: calm and sane.
The key words of the Japanese experience, at least for
most of its philosophical history, are *serenity* and *sim-
plicity.*"

Alex grinned winningly and said, "No offense meant
. . . but judging from the hyperactive state you've been
in since we left the restaurant, you're still more a child
of the West than of Japan."

Embarrassed, Joanna said, "Sorry. It's just that I
love Kyoto and Japan so much that I tend to run on
as if I'm an idiot when I take someone sightseeing.
I'm so anxious for you to like it too."

They stopped at the main entrance to the largest of
the palace's five connected buildings, and Alex said,
"Joanna, are you worried about something?"

"Me? No. Nothing." She was unsettled by his perception. Again, she had the feeling that she could hide
nothing from this man; he had some extraordinary

power with which he could discern her innermost thoughts.

"Are you certain you can spend the day with me?" Alex asked solicitously. "As I said before, if business calls, we can get together another time."

"No, no," Joanna said. She wasn't able to look directly into his penetrating dark eyes. "I'm just trying my best to be a good guide."

He stared at her. With two pinched fingers, he tugged at one point of his neatly trimmed mustache. Already she knew that was something he did unconsciously when he was lost in thought.

"Come along," she said brightly, trying to cover her uneasiness. "There's so much to see here."

As she and Alex followed a group of tourists through the ornate chambers, Joanna shared the long and colorful history of the palace with him. Nijo Castle did indeed house and embody an enormous quantity of worthwhile art, even if a substantial measure of it tended to gaudiness. The first buildings in the compound had been erected in 1603, at which time they served as the Kyoto residence of the first shogun of the honorable Tokugawa family. Later it was enlarged considerably with sections of Hideyoshi's dismantled Fushimi Castle. Clearly, in spite of its moat and turrets and truly magnificent iron gate, Nijo had been constructed by a man who had no doubts about his safety; for with its low walls and broad gardens, it never could have withstood a determined enemy. Although the palace was not representative of the core of Japanese history and style, it was nonetheless quite successful as the meant-to-be-impressive home of a very rich and powerful military dictator who commanded absolute obedience and could afford to live as well as the emperor himself.

In the middle of the tour, when the other visitors had drifted far ahead, as Joanna was explaining the meaning and the value of a particularly beautiful and complex mural, Alex said, "Sorry to interrupt. But you know what?"

"What?"

"Nijo Castle is wonderful. But I'm even more impressed with you than I am with the palace."

Confused, she said, "With me? Whatever for?"

"Well, if you came to Chicago," Alex said, "I wouldn't be able to do anything like this."

"Not to worry. I don't expect I'll be coming to Chicago very soon."

The other tourists were out of sight now. Joanna and Alex were alone. Their voices echoed ever so slightly, wrapping them in familiar whispers.

As softly as he might have spoken in a house of worship, Alex said, "I mean, I don't know a damned thing about the history of my own hometown. I couldn't even tell you the year that the great fire burned it all to the ground. There aren't many people around who've bothered to keep in touch with their own roots. Yet here you are, an American in a strange country and a strange city, and you know everything!"

She nodded agreement. "It amazes me, too, sometimes," she said quietly. "I know Kyoto better than most of the people who were born here. Japanese history has been a hobby of mine ever since I moved from England. More than a hobby, I guess. Almost an avocation. In fact . . . at times I've thought it's an obsession with me."

His eyes narrowed slightly; to her they seemed to shine with professional curiosity. "Obsession," Alex said. "That's rather an odd way of putting it, don't you think?" He tugged at his mustache.

She felt once more that his conversation had ceased to be entirely casual, that he was leading her, that he was probing gently but insistently, motivated by more than friendly interest. What did this man want from her? Sometimes he made her feel as if she were concealing a dreadful crime. She wished that she could change the subject before another word was said, but she could see no polite way to do so.

"I buy and read more than a hundred books on Japanese history each year," Joanna said. "I attend lectures in history, and I spend most of my holidays poking around in ancient shrines and museums. It's almost as if I—"

"As if you what?" Alex prompted her.

God, I must be schizophrenic, Joanna thought. *One minute I'm contemplating an affair with him; and the very next minute I'm suspicious, afraid of him. It's his profession that disturbs me. Private detective. Bad vibrations. Most people are probably tense and a little bit paranoid around him until they get to know him well.*

"Joanna?"

She looked at the mural again. "I guess it's as if . . . I'm obsessed wiht Japanese history because I have no real roots of my own. Born in the United States, raised in England, my parents dead for ten years now, Yokohama to Tokyo to Kyoto, no living relatives—"

Alex interrupted her. "Is that true?"

"Is what true?"

"That you have no relatives?"

"None living."

"Not any grandparents or—"

"Like I said."

"Not even an aunt or uncle?"

"Not a one." She turned to him. Which was his handsome face lined with—sympathy or calculation? Concern for her or suspicion? *There I go again,* she thought sourly. *What's wrong with me? Why am I always so tense with a new man, so worried that he'll be too nosy?* "So you see, when I came to Japan it was because there was nowhere else for me to go, no one I could turn to."

He frowned. "That's unusual. Almost anyone your age can claim at least one relative kicking around somewhere . . . maybe not someone you know well or care much about, but a bona fide relative nonetheless."

Joanna shrugged and said, "Well, if I do have any folks out there, I don't know about them."

His response was quick. "I could help you search for them. After all, investigations are my trade."

"I probably can't afford your rates."

"Oh, I'm very reasonable."

"You *do* buy Rolls Royces with your fees."

"I'll do this for the cost of a bicycle."

"A very large bicycle, I'll bet."

"I'll do it for a smile."

Joanna smiled. "That's generous of you. In fact it's too generous. I couldn't possibly accept."

"I'd charge it to overhead. It would save the company tax dollars, so in a sense the United States government would pay for the work."

Although she couldn't imagine his reasons, he was eager to dig into her past. She wasn't just paranoid. He *was* pressuring her. Still, she wanted to talk to him because she felt that he would understand her more than anyone had for a long time. There was good chemistry between them. "No," she said. "Forget it. Even if I've got folks someplace, they're strangers to me. I mean nothing to them. That's why it's important to me to get a solid grip on the history of Kyoto and Japan. This is my hometown now. It's my past and present and future. They've accepted me here. I don't have roots like other people do; mine have been dug up and burned. So maybe I can *create* those deep cultural ties for myself, generate brand new roots, grow them right here; and maybe they'll be as good and strong and meaningful as the roots that were destroyed. In fact it's something I've *got* to do. I don't really have any choice in the matter. I need to feel that I belong, not just as a successful immigrant but as an integral part of this lovely country. Belonging . . . being securely and deeply connected to it all, like a fiber in the cloth . . . that's what counts. I need desperately to be a thread in the fabric, to lose myself in . . . combine myself with Japan. A lot of days . . . well, there's a terrible emptiness in me. Not all the time. Just now and then. But when it comes, it's almost too much for me. And I believe . . . I *know* that if I melt completely into this society, then I won't have to suffer that emptiness any longer."

Joanna amazed herself, for with Alex she was allowing, even encouraging, an unusual intimacy, talking now as if they were lifelong lovers resting in bed together. She was telling him things she had never told anyone before. The palace walls seemed to have grown distant, cloudy, less real than a fuzzy projection on a film screen. It was easy to imagine that she was encapsulated, that she and Alex were drifting in a milky bubble outside of the ordinary flow of time. In spite of her usually strong desire for privacy, in spite of her slightly paranoid response to him as a private detective, she enjoyed being near him, alone with him. She had the urge to put her arms around Alex, but she knew it was too soon for that.

Alex spoke so quietly that she could barely hear what he said. "Emptiness? That's another odd word choice."

"I guess it is."

"What do you mean by it?"

Joanna groped for words that could convey the hollowness, the unpleasant sensation of being different from all other people, the cancerous alienation that crept over her and ate at her once or twice every month, always when she least expected it. Periodically she fell victim to a brutal, disabling loneliness that bordered on despair. Bleak, unremitting loneliness, yet more than that, worse than that. *Aloneness*. That was a better term for it. Without apparent reasons, she sometimes felt certain that she was separate, hideously unique, living in a dimension of her own beyond the normal currents of human existence. *Aloneness*. The depressions that accompanied these inexplicable moods were black pits out of which she clawed her way only with fierce determination.

Haltingly, she said, "The emptiness is . . . well, it's like I'm nobody."

"You mean you're bothered that you have no one."

"That's not it. I feel I *am* no one."

"I still don't understand."

"It's like I'm not Joanna Rand . . . not anybody at

all . . . just a shell . . . a cipher . . . hollow . . . not the same as other people . . . not even human. And when I'm like that I wonder why I'm alive . . . what purpose I have. My connections seem tenuous . . ."

"Are you telling me that you've considered suicide?" Alex asked worriedly.

"No, no. Never. I couldn't."

"I'm relieved to hear it."

She shook her head. "I'm too damned tough and stubborn ever to take the easy way out of anything. I was merely trying to express the depth of these moods, the blackness of them, so you could see why I need to establish roots and some sort of lasting connections here in Kyoto."

Alex's face was lined with compassion. "How can you live with this attitude, this emptiness, and still be outgoing and cheerful?"

"Oh," Joanna said quickly, "I don't feel this way all the time. The mood comes over me only once in a while, once every couple of weeks, and never for longer than a day at a time. I fight it off."

He touched her cheek with his fingertips. They were blunt and cool.

Abruptly Joanna was aware of how intently he was staring, and she saw a trace of pity mixed with the compassion in his eyes. The reality of Nijo Castle and the actuality of the limited relationship they shared now flooded back to her; and she was surprised, even shocked, by how much she had said and how far she had opened herself to him. Why had she cast aside the armor of her privacy in front of this man rather than at the feet of someone before him? Why was she willing to reveal herself to Alex Hunter in a way and to a degree that she had never allowed Mariko Inamura to know her? She began to see that her hunger for companionship and love was much greater than she had realized until this moment.

She blushed and said, "Enough of this soul-baring. You aren't a psychoanalyst, are you?"

"Well, every private detective has to be a bit of a psychiatrist . . . just like any popular bartender."

"Besides, I'm not a patient. I don't know what in the world got me started on that craziness."

"I don't mind listening."

"You're sweet."

"I mean it."

"Maybe you don't mind listening, but I mind talking about it," she said.

"Why?"

"It's private . . . and silly."

"It's probably good for you to talk."

"Probably," she admitted. "But it's not like me to babble about myself to a perfect stranger."

"Hey, I'm not a perfect stranger!"

"Well, almost."

"Oh, I see," he said. "I get it. You mean I'm perfect but not a stranger."

Joanna smiled. She wanted to touch him; she didn't. "Anyway," she said, "we're here to show you the palace, not to have long, boring Freudian discussions. There are a thousand things to see, and every one of them is more interesting than my psyche."

"You underestimate yourself," Alex said.

Another group of chattering tourists rounded the corner and approached from behind Joanna. She turned to look at them, using them as an excuse to avoid Alex's dissecting eyes for the few seconds she needed to regain her composure; but what she saw made her gasp.

A man with no right hand.

Twenty feet away.

Walking toward her.

He was at the front of the oncoming group: a smiling, grandfatherly Korean gentleman with a softly creased face and iron-gray hair. He was wearing sharply pressed slacks, a white shirt, blue tie, and light-blue sweater with the right sleeve rolled up a few inches. His arm was deformed at the wrist: There was nothing but a smooth, knobby, pinkish stub where the hand should have been.

"Are you all right?" Alex asked, apparently sensing the sudden tension in her.

She wasn't able to speak.

The one-handed man came closer.

Fifteen feet away now.

She could smell antiseptics. Alcohol. Lysol. A strong lye soap.

That's ridiculous, she told herself. *You can't smell antiseptics. There's no such odor here. Imagination. There is nothing to fear at Nijo Castle.*

Lysol.

Alcohol.

Nothing to fear! This one-handed Korean is a stranger, a kindly little old ojii-san *who couldn't possibly hurt anybody. Get hold of yourself. For God's sake, will you take a look at the poor man?*

"Joanna? What's happening? What's wrong?" Alex asked, touching her shoulder.

The Korean seemed to advance with the sludgy, slow-motion single-mindedness of a creature in a nightmare; and Joanna felt herself trapped in the same unearthly, oppressive gravity, in the same syrupy flow of time.

Her tongue was thick, and there was a bad taste in her mouth, the coppery flavor of blood, which was no doubt as imaginary as the stench of antiseptics, although it was as sickening as if it had been real. Her throat was constricted. She might start gagging uncontrollably at any moment. She heard herself straining for air; her breathing was stentorian.

Lysol.

Alcohol.

She blinked, and the flutter of her eyelids magically altered reality even further, so that the Korean's pinkish stump now ended in a mechanical hand. Incredibly, she could hear the compact servomechanism purring with power, and the oiled push-pull rods sliding in their tracks, and the gears clicking as the fingers opened from a tight fist.

No. That was imagination too.

When the Korean was less than three yards from her, he raised his twisted limb and pointed with the hand that wasn't there. Intellectually, Joanna knew that he was interested only in the mural she and Alex had been studying, but on a more primitive and affecting emotional level she reacted with the certainty that he was pointing at *her,* reaching for *her* with unmistakably malevolent purpose.

From the deepest ranges of her own mind came a frightening sound: a gravelly, jagged, icy voice filled with hatred and bitterness. The voice was familiar; it was synonymous with pain and terror. She wanted to scream. Although the man in her nightmare, the faceless man with the steel fingers, had never spoken in her sleep, she knew this was his voice. Furthermore, she realized with a jolt that while she had never heard him speak in the nightmare, she *had* heard him when she was awake. Somehow . . . someplace . . . sometime . . . The words that came to her now were not imagined or dredged up from her worst dreams; they were recollected, summoned from memories of a long-forgotten time and place that was as much a part of her past as yesterday. A cold voice was saying: *"Once more the needle, my lovely little lady. Once more the needle."* It grew in volume, reverberating with monstrous impact. She alone could hear it; the rest of the world was deaf to this voice. The words exploded inside her—*"Once more the needle, once more the needle, once more the needle"*—boomed with firecracker repetitiveness, until she thought her head would come off.

The Korean stopped two feet from her.

Lysol.

Alcohol.

"Once more the needle, my lovely little lady."

Joanna ran. She cried out like a wounded animal and turned away from the startled Korean, pushed at Alex Hunter without fully realizing who he was, and darted past him, her heels tapping noisily on the hardwood floor, hurried into the next chamber, wanting to scream but unable to find her voice, ran without looking back, certain that the Korean was pursuing her, ran past the dazzling seventeenth-century artworks of the master Kano Tan'yu and his students, fled between strikingly beautiful wood sculptures that were famous for their fine detail, and all the while she struggled for breath, the air like thick dust that clogged her lungs, ran past richly carved transoms, past intricate scenes painted on sliding doors, her footsteps echoing off the gilded and coffered ceilings, ran past a surprised guard who called to her, then went through an exit into the cool November air, started across the courtyard, heard a familiar voice calling her name, finally stopped, stunned, in the center of the Nijo garden, shaking, shaking.

• 10 •

Alex led her to a garden bench and sat beside her in the brisk autumn breeze. Her eyes were unnaturally wide, and her face was as pale and delicate as bridal lace. He held one of her slender hands. Her fingers were cold and such a chalky white that it seemed there was no blood or life in them at all. But she was not slack and stuporous. She squeezed his hand so hard that her manicured nails bit into his skin; however, he didn't complain for fear she would withdraw from him. Whatever her problem, she needed human contact now, and he wanted to be the one to comfort her.

"Should I get you to a doctor?"

"No. It's over. I'll be all right."

"Tell me what you want."

"Just to sit here awhile."

He watched her closely for a moment and decided

she was telling the truth; she would be all right. She looked ill, but a trace of color was slowly returning to her cheeks. "What happened, Joanna?"

Her lower lip quivered like a suspended bead of water about to surrender to the insistent downward pull of gravity. Bright tears glistened in the corners of her eyes.

"Hey. Hey now," he said softly.

"Alex, I'm so sorry."

"About what?"

"I'm sorry I made a fool of myself in front of you."

"Hush."

"It was so important to me . . . important that you think well of me. But now—"

"Don't be absurd. You're not a fool. No such thing. I know what you are. You're a beautiful, talented, and very intelligent woman, the most intriguing woman I've met in God knows how many years. If I thought of you in any way but that, then *I'd* be a fool."

Joanna regarded him with evident hope and doubt, making no effort to daub her watery eyes. He wanted to kiss her red, swollen eyelids. She said, "You mean it, what you said you think of me?"

With his finger he flicked a solitary tear from her face. "Must I keep reminding you that we're pledged to be strictly honest with each other? After all, that was your idea." He sighed, pretending exasperation. "Of course I meant it, every word."

"But the way I ran out of there—"

"I'm sure you had good reason."

She grimaced. "I'm not as certain of that as you are, but I'm glad you don't think I'm a fool." She sniffled, used her free hand to wipe her eyes.

Alex was touched by the childlike fragility that lay just beneath the surface image of toughness and un- qualified self-confidence that she had maintained from the first moment he'd seen her.

She relaxed her grip on his hand, but only enough to stop her nails from drawing blood. "I'm sorry for the embarrassment I caused you. I acted like a mad-woman."

"Not true," Alex said patiently. "You acted like you'd had the scare of your life."

She was surprised. "How did you know?"

"I'm a detective."

"That's exactly what it was. I was so afraid."

"Of what?" he asked.

"The Korean."

"I don't understand."

"The man with one hand."

"Was he Korean?"

"I think so."

"Did you know him?"

"Never saw him before."

"Then what? Did he say something?"

"No," Joanna said. "What happened was . . . he reminded me of something awful . . . and I panicked." Her hand tightened on his again.

"Can you share it with me?"

She told him about the nightmare.

"You have it *every* night?" he asked.

"For as far back as I can remember."

"When you were a child?"

"I guess . . . no . . . not then."

"Exactly how far back?"

"Seven . . . maybe eight or ten years."

"The odd thing about it," Alex said, "is the fre-quency. *Every night.* That would be unbearable. It must drain you. Actually, the dream itself isn't particu-larly strange. I've had worse."

"I know," Joanna said. "Everybody has had worse. When I try to describe the nightmare, it doesn't sound all that terrifying or threatening. But at night . . . I feel as if I'm dying. There aren't any words to tell the horror of it, what I go through, what it does to me." Alex felt her stiffen as if she were steeling herself against the recollected impact of the nightly ordeal. She bit her lip and for a while said nothing, merely stared at the funereal gray-black clouds that scudded from east to west across the city. When at last she looked at Alex again, her eyes were haunted. "Years ago I used to wake up from the nightmare and be so damned scared I'd vomit. I was physically ill with fear, hysterical. Since then I've known that people really can be frightened to death. I was close to that, closer than I like to think. These days I seldom react so strongly . . . although more often than not I'm unable to go back to sleep after the dream. At least not right away. The mechanical hand, the needle . . . it all makes me feel so . . . slimy . . . sick in my soul."

Alex held her hand in both of his hands now, cupping her frigid fingers in his warmth. "Have you ever talked to anyone about the dream?"

"Just with Mariko . . . and now with you."

"I was thinking of a doctor."

"Psychiatrist?"

"It might help, you know."

"He'd try to free me of the dream by discovering the cause of it," she said tensely.

"What's wrong with that?"

"I don't want to know the cause."

"If it will help cure—"

"I don't want to know."

"All right. But why not?"

"Knowing would destroy me."

"How?" he asked.

"I can't explain . . . but I feel it."

"That's irrational, Joanna."

She didn't respond.

"Okay," Alex said. "Forget the psychiatrist. What do *you* suppose is the cause of the nightmare?"

"I haven't the slightest."

"You must have given it a lot of thought over the years," he said.

"Thousands of hours," Joanna said bleakly.

"And? Not even one idea?"

"Alex, I'm tired. And still embarrassed. Can we not talk about it any more?"

"All right."

She cocked her head. "You'll really drop it that easily?"

"What right have I to pry?"

She smiled thinly. It was her first smile since they'd sat down, and it looked unnatural, forced. "Shouldn't a private detective be pushy at a time like this, inquisitive, absolutely relentless?"

Although her question was meant to sound humorous, Alex detected a genuine fear that he would probe too far. He said, "I'm not a private detective here. I'm not investigating you. All I am is a friend who's offering a shoulder if you feel like crying on one." As he spoke he felt a pang of guilt, for he actually was investigating her. He had called Chicago and ordered the Chelgrin file.

"Can we walk out to the street and find a taxi?" Joanna asked. "I'm not up to any more sightseeing today."

"Sure."

He stood, helped her up. She clung to his arm as they crossed the palace garden toward the Kara-mon, the ornate inner gate.

Overhead, a pair of large birds wheeled against the somber sky, keening shrilly as they dived and soared. With a dry flutter of wings, they settled into the exquisitely sculptured branches of a bonsai pine.

Alex, wanting to pursue the conversation but resigned to her silence, was surprised when she suddenly began to talk about the nightmare again. Evidently, a part of her wanted him to be an aggressive inquisitor so that she would have an excuse to tell him more.

"For a very long time," Joanna said as they walked, "I thought it was a symbolic dream in the best Freudian tradition. I thought the mechanical hand and the hypodermic syringe were not what they seemed, that they represented other things. I figured the nightmare was symbolic of a real-life event so traumatic that I couldn't approach it in real terms even when I was asleep. But . . ." She faltered. Her voice grew shaky on the last few words, faded altogether.

"Go on," he said carefully.

"A few minutes ago in the palace, when I saw that one-handed man . . . well, what scared me so much was that for the first time I realized the dream *isn't* the least bit symbolic. It's a memory that comes to me in sleep, an accurate, totally realistic scrap of memory."

They passed the Kara-mon. There were no other tourists in sight. He stopped Joanna in the space between the inner and outer gates of the castle. Even the cool breeze had not restored the color to her cheeks. She was as white-faced as a powdered geisha.

"So what you're saying is that somewhere in your past there actually was a man with a mechanical hand."

She nodded.

"And for reasons you don't understand, he used a hypodermic syringe on you."

"Yes. I'm positive of it." She swallowed hard. "When I saw that Korean, something snapped in me. I remembered the voice of the man in the dream. He was saying, 'Once more the needle, once more the needle,' over and over again."

An iciness uncoiled snakelike in Alex's chest. "But you don't know who he was?"

"Or where or when or why," she said miserably. "I'm suffering from amnesia. But I swear to God it happened. I'm not crazy. It happened. And it . . . something was done to me against my will . . . something I don't . . . can't remember."

"Try."

She spoke in a whisper, as if she were afraid that the beast in her nightmare might hear her. "That man hurt me . . . did something to me that was . . . this sounds melodramatic, but I feel it . . . something as bad as death, maybe worse than death in some ways."

Her voice electrified Alex; each whispered sibilant was like the hissing of a current as it leaped in a bright blue arc across the tiny gap between two wires. In her face, still pretty but drawn, he saw the effects of a terror that he could never fully comprehend.

Joanna trembled.

So did Alex.

With enchanting timidity, she took a step toward him. Instinctively, he opened his arms, and she moved against him. He held her.

"It sounds bizarre," she said. "I know it sounds quite impossible. A man with a mechanical hand, like a villain out of a comic book. But I swear, Alex—"

"I believe you," he said.

Still in his embrace, Joanna looked up. "You do?"

He studied her closely as he said, "I really do—Miss Chelgrin."

"Who?"

"Lisa Chelgrin."

Puzzled, she stepped back.

He waited, watched.

"Alex, I don't understand."

He said nothing.

"Who is Lisa Chelgrin?"

"I think you honestly don't know."

"Are you going to tell me?"

"*You* are Lisa Chelgrin," Alex said.

He was intent upon perceiving that fleeting expression that would betray her, that glimpse of hidden knowledge, that look of the hunted in her eyes, or perhaps guilt expressed in briefly visible lines of tension at the corners of her lovely mouth. But even as he searched for those signs, he lost his conviction that he would find them. She was genuinely perplexed. If Joanna Rand were the long-lost Lisa Chelgrin—and Alex was certain now that she could be no one else—then all memory of her true identity had been scrubbed from her either by accident or by intent.

"Lisa Chelgrin," she said, dazed. "Me?"

"You," Alex said, but without an accusatory tone this time.

She shook her head slowly. "I don't get it."

"Neither do I," he said.

"What's the joke?"

"It isn't a joke, Joanna. But it is a long story. Too long for me to tell it standing here in the cold."

· 11 ·

During the return trip to the Moonglow Lounge, Joanna huddled in one corner of the taxi's rear seat while Alex told her who he thought she was. Her face remained blank; her dark eyes were guarded. He could not determine how his words were affecting her.

The driver shared the front seat with a transistor radio that occupied his attention. He hummed along with the current Japanese hit songs that played just loud enough to be heard but not so loud as to annoy his passengers. He could speak no English, a fact Alex ascertained before launching into the story he had to tell Joanna.

"I'm not sure where to start," Alex said. "Background, I guess. Our lead in this strange little tale is Thomas Morely Chelgrin. He's been a United States senator from Illinois for almost fourteen years. Before that he served two . . . no, *one* term in the House of Representatives. He's a moderate, neither conservative nor liberal, although he tends to be more liberal on social issues, to the right on defense and foreign policy. About four years ago he was cosponsor of the Kennedy-Chelgrin Resolution that led to sweeping rules changes in the Senate. I gather he's generally well liked in Washington, primarily because he's earned a reputation as a dependable legislative team player. Although I've never been to one of his parties, I gather he throws some of the best shindigs in the capital; and that keeps his stock high too. They're a bunch of partying fools in Washington. They appreciate a man who knows how to set a table and pour whiskey. Apparently, Tom Chelgrin satisfies his constituents too; there must be some reason they keep returning him to office with

56

ever-larger vote margins. I've sure as hell never seen a more clever politician in my life—and I sincerely hope I never do! He knows how to stroke the voters, how to herd them as if they're animals—blacks and whites and browns, Catholics and Protestants and Jews and atheists, young and old, right and left—no one escapes him. Out of five times at bat, he's lost only one election, and that was his first. He's a very imposing man: tall, lean, with the trained voice of an actor. His hair turned a distinguished shade of silver when he was in his early thirties, and virtually all of his opponents have attributed his success to the fact that he *looks* like a senator. That's awfully damned cynical, and it's a simplification, but I guess there's also some truth in it." He stopped and waited for Joanna to respond.

The only thing she said was: "Go on."

"Can't you place him yet?"

"I never met him."

"I think you know him as well or better than anyone."

"Then you're wrong."

The cab driver tried to get through a changing traffic signal, then decided not to risk it and tramped on the brakes. When the car stopped rocking, he glanced at Alex, grinned disarmingly and apologized. *"Gomennasai, jokyaku-san."*

Alex bowed. *"Yoroshii desu. Karedomo . . . untenshu-san yukkuri."*

The driver nodded vigorously in agreement. *"Hai."* Henceforth, he would go slowly, as requested.

Alex turned back to Joanna. "Perhaps I haven't given you enough details to refresh your memory. Let me tell you more about Thomas Chelgrin."

"Go right ahead. I want to know what you're leading up to," she said. "But I tell you there's no memory to refresh."

"When Chelgrin was twelve or thirteen years old, his father died. The family hadn't been much more than lower middle class to begin with, but after that

there were years of outright poverty. Tom Chelgrin
worked his way through college and earned a degree in
business management. Soon after graduation, when he
was in his early twenties, he was drafted into the army
and wound up with the first wave of United Nations
troops in Korea. That was August of 1950. I believe
it was sometime in September, after the invasion of
Inchon, when he was captured by the Communists.
Do you know much about the Korean War?"

"Only that it happened."

"One of the most curious and disturbing aspects of
that so-called police action was the way American
prisoners of war conducted themselves. During both
the World Wars, nearly all of our soldiers had
been stubborn in captivity, difficult to contain. They
conspired against their keepers, resisted, engineered
elaborate escapes. It wasn't the same in Korea. Somehow, with brutal physical torture and maybe with highly
sophisticated brainwashing techniques, with the application of continuous psychological stress, the Communists broke their spirit. Not many attempted to
escape, and those who actually got away can just
about be counted on my fingers. Chelgrin was one of
the few who refused to be passive and cooperative.
Seven or eight months after he was imprisoned, he
found a way out of the concentration camp and eventually reached the United Nations' lines. *The Saturday
Evening Post* even devoted a cover story to him, and
he wrote a moderately successful book about his ad-
ventures. Anyway, the whole experience provided him
with a lot of political hay when he ran for office several
years later. He was a war hero in a time when that
still counted for something, and he milked his service
record for every vote it was worth."

"I've never heard of him," Joanna insisted.

As the taxi moved through the heavy traffic on
Horikawa Street, Alex said, "Be patient. The story gets
considerably more interesting—and more pertinent.
When Chelgrin got out of the army, he met a girl, got
married, and fathered a child. His mother had died

while he was in that prison camp; and young Tom had a modest inheritance from an insurance policy waiting for him when he was discharged from the army, something like twenty-five or thirty thousand dollars after taxes, which was maybe more than modest in those days. We should all be so lucky. He put that money together with his book earnings and whatever he could borrow—his war hero status helped with bankers, too—and he purchased a Volkswagen dealership, built an auto showroom and a huge garage. In a couple of years it seemed like half the people in the country were driving VWs. Tom branched out, began to sell Renaults and MGs and Triumphs and Jaguars, then got into other businesses as well, and by the late fifties he was a rich man. He did charity work, earned a reputation as a humanitarian in his community, and finally campaigned for a congressional seat in 1958. Like I said, he lost that first time, but he came back in sixty and won. He was reelected in sixty-two and ran for the Senate in sixty-four, and he's been there ever since."

Joanna interrupted him. "What about the name you used, what you called me?"

"Lisa Chelgrin."

"Yes. How's she fit in?"

"She was Thomas Chelgrin's only child."

Joanna's eyes opened wide. She stared at him as if she expected him to start laughing, and when he didn't even smile she shifted uneasily on the vinyl car seat. Again, Alex was unable to detect any deception in her response. She was surprised. "You think I'm this man's *daughter?*"

"Yeah. Or at least I believe there's a better than even chance that you are."

"Impossible."

"Not when you know—"

"I *know* whose daughter I am."

"Or you think you know."

"Robert and Elizabeth Rand were my parents."

"And they died in an accident near Brighton."

"Yes. A long time ago."

"And you've no living relatives."

"Do you think I'm a liar?"

The driver had sensed the antagonism in her voice. He glanced at them in the rearview mirror, then looked straight ahead, hummed a bit louder with the radio, too polite to eavesdrop even when he didn't know their language.

"Joanna, you're overreacting."

"How am I overreacting?"

"There's no reason for you to be angry with me."

"I'm not," she said curtly.

"You certainly sound as if you are."

She didn't reply.

"And you're afraid of what I'm leading up to," Alex said.

"That's ridiculous. And you haven't answered my question. Are you calling me a liar?"

"I didn't accuse you of that. I only—"

"Then what are you accusing me of?"

"Nothing. Joanna, if you—"

"I feel like you *are* accusing me."

"I'm sorry. I didn't mean to give you that impression. But you react as if I've said you're guilty of something criminal. I don't believe that at all. In fact, I think it's other people who are guilty of doing things to you. I think you're the victim."

"Victim of what?"

"I don't know."

"Of whom?"

"I don't know."

"Well, for Christ's sake!" Joanna was shrill, not at all like herself, and finally she appeared to realize how strangely she was behaving. She looked out the side window at the cars and cyclists on Shijo Street, and when she turned again to Alex, she had control of herself. "It's just not possible. Nevertheless, you've got me curious. I have to know how you came up with such a bizarre idea."

Alex continued as if her outburst had never occurred.

"One night in July, 1972, the summer after Lisa Chelgrin's junior year at Georgetown University, she disappeared from her father's vacation villa in Jamaica. Someone got into her bedroom through an unlocked window. Although there were signs of a struggle, smears of her blood on the bedclothes and windowsill, no one in the house heard her scream. It was clear she'd been kidnapped, but no ransom demand was ever received. The police were positive she'd been abducted and murdered. A sex maniac, they said. On the other hand, they weren't able to find her body, so they couldn't just assume that she was dead. At least not right away, not before they went through the motions of an exhaustive search. Even the Jamaican authorities have some sense of decorum when they're dealing with a U.S. senator. After three weeks, Chelgrin lost all confidence in the island police—which he should have done the second day he dealt with them. Because he was from the Chicago area, and because a friend of his had used my company and recommended us, Chelgrin asked me to fly to Jamaica to look for Lisa. My people worked on the case for ten months before Chelgrin gave up. We used eight or nine of our best men full time and hired as many Jamaicans to do a lot of the footwork. It was an expensive deal for the senator, but he didn't care. I'll give him that much. He did seem to care about his daughter. But it wouldn't have mattered if we'd had ten thousand men to use. I mean, this case was cold, absolutely airtight, the perfect crime. It's one of only two major investigations that we've failed to settle satisfactorily since I took over the business."

The taxi swung around another corner. The Moonglow Lounge lay half a block ahead.

"But why do you think I'm Lisa Chelgrin?"

"I've got two dozen reasons at least. For one thing, you're the same age she'd be if she were still alive. Most important of all, you're a dead ringer for her, just ten years older."

Frowning, Joanna said, "Do you have a photograph?"

"Not on me. But I'll get one."

The taxi slowed, pulled to the curb and stopped in front of the Moonglow Lounge. The driver switched off the meter, opened his door and began to climb out.

"When you have a photograph," Joanna said, "I'd like to see it." She extended her hand in an almost regal gesture, meaning for Alex to take it. When he touched her, she said, "Thanks for a wonderful lunch. The conversation was the best I've had in ages. I hope you enjoyed it as much as I did, and I'm sorry I spoiled the sightseeing."

He realized she was dismissing him, and he said, "Can't we have a drink and—?"

"Not right now, Alex." Suddenly she had grown distant, as if willing and able to give him no more than a small fraction of her attention. "I don't feel well."

The driver opened her door, and she started to slide out of the car.

Alex held on to her hand until she stopped and looked back at him. "Joanna, we have a great deal to talk about."

"Can't we discuss it later?"

"Aren't you still curious?"

"I'm not nearly as curious as I am ill. Queasy stomach, headache . . . It must be something I ate. Or maybe all the excitement."

"Do you want a doctor?"

"No, no. I just need to lie down awhile."

"When *can* we talk?" He sensed a gulf between them that had not been there a minute ago; and it was getting wider and deeper by the second. "Tonight? Between shows?"

"Yes," she said distractedly. "We'll chat then."

"Promise?"

"Promise," she said. "Now really, Alex, the poor driver will catch his death of pneumonia if he stands there holding the door for me any longer. It's gotten fifteen degrees colder since lunch."

Reluctantly, he let go of her.

As she got out of the taxi, a blast of frigid air rushed past her and struck Alex in the face.

• 12 •

Joanna felt threatened.

She had the unshakable notion that her every move was being watched and recorded.

She locked the apartment door, went into the bedroom and latched that door as well.

For a minute she stood in the center of the room, listening. Then she poured herself a double brandy from a crystal decanter, drank it quickly, poured another shot and put her snifter on the nightstand.

The room was too warm.

Stifling. Tropical.

She was sweating.

Each breath seemed to scorch her lungs.

She opened the window two inches and let in a cold draft, took off her clothes and dropped them on the floor, stretched out nude atop the silk bedspread; but still she felt as if she were smothering. Her pulse raced. She was dizzy, and she experienced a series of mild hallucinations too, nothing new to her, images that had been a part of other days and other moods exactly like this one. The ceiling appeared to descend between the walls as if it were the ceiling of a torture chamber in one of those corny old Tarzan movie serials. And the mattress, which she had chosen for its firmness, now softened to her touch, not in reality but in her mind, became marshmallowy, gradually closed around her as if it were a living amoeboid creature. No. Imagination. Nothing to fear. She gritted her teeth and tried to suppress all sensations that she knew were false; but they were beyond her control.

She shut her eyes—opened them immediately, suffocated and frightened by the brief self-imposed darkness.

She was familiar with this peculiar state of mind, these emotions, this unfocused dread. She suffered the same terrors every time she allowed a friendship to develop into more than a casual relationship, every time she traveled beyond mere desire and approached the special intimacy of love. She lusted after Alex Hunter, but she didn't love him. Not yet. She hadn't known him long enough to feel more than a strong affection. But the signs were there to be read; it was certain to happen. And now events, people, inanimate objects, the very air itself, acquired an evil sentience, became supercharged with a malevolent life force that had her as its sole target and would pressure her until she destroyed whatever love might spring up; a monstrous energy was at work here, a raging fear that lay dormant within her most of the time, but that had now been translated into physical power that squeezed all hope from her. She knew how it would end. The way it always ended. She would break off the relationship that sparked this irrational, emotional claustrophobia; for that was the only way that she could get relief from the terrible closed-in, listened-to, watched-over feeling.

She would never see Alex Hunter again.

He'd come to the Moonglow, of course. Tonight. Maybe other nights. He'd sit through both shows. Until he left Kyoto, however, she would not mingle with the audience between performances.

He'd telephone, and she'd hang up.

If he came around to visit in the afternoon, she'd be unavailable.

If he wrote to her, she'd throw his letters away without reading them.

Joanna could be cruel. She'd had plenty of practice with other men.

The decision to freeze Alex Hunter out of her life had a markedly beneficial effect on her. Imperceptibly at first, then with rapidly increasing relief, she felt the immobilizing fear evaporate. The bedroom grew steadily cooler. The humid air became less oppressive, more breathable. The ceiling rose to its proper height, and the mattress beneath her was firm once again.

• 13 •

The Kyoto Hotel, the largest first-class hotel in the city, was Western-style in most details; the telephones in Alex's suite even had message indicators, those insistently flashing reminders of the hyperactive American way of life. When he returned from his afternoon with Joanna Rand, Alex saw that the red light on the drawing room phone was blinking. He snatched up the receiver, dialed for the message, certain that she had called him during the time he'd taken to get from the Moonglow to the hotel.

But it wasn't Joanna. The front desk was holding a transpacific cablegram for him. At his request, a bellhop brought it upstairs.

Alex exchanged polite greetings and bows with the man, accepted the cable, tipped him, went through the bowing again. When he was alone, he sat at the drawing room desk and tore open the flimsy envelope.

COURIER ARRIVES YOUR HOTEL NOON FRIDAY YOUR TIME STOP—BLAKENSHIP

By twelve o'clock tomorrow, he would have the complete Chelgrin file, which had been closed for nine years or longer but which was now definitely reopened. In addition to hundreds of field agent reports and meticulously transcribed interviews, the file contained several excellent photographs of Lisa taken just a few days before she disappeared. Perhaps those pictures would shock Joanna out of her eerie detachment.

Alex thought of her as she'd been when she'd gotten out of the taxi a short while ago, and he wondered why she had so suddenly turned cold toward him. She might be Lisa Chelgrin; but if so, she didn't know it. He was as sure of that as he was of his own name. Yet she acted like a woman with dangerous secrets and a sordid past to hide.

He looked at his digital watch—4:30.

At 6:30, he would take his nightly stroll through the bustling Gion district to the Moonglow Lounge for drinks and dinner—and for that important conversation with Joanna. He had time now for a hot leisurely soak in the tub; and he looked forward to balancing the steamy heat with sips of cold beer.

He went to the suite's narrow pantry, fetched an icy bottle of Asahi beer from the small rattling refrigerator, and was halfway across the bedroom, only three or four steps from the bathroom door, when he stopped dead, aware that something was wrong. He looked around, tense and baffled. The chambermaid had straightened the pile of paperback books, magazines and newspapers on the dresser, and she'd remade the bed while he was gone. The drapes were open; he preferred to keep them drawn. He had left the television set at the foot of the bed; she had wheeled it into the corner. What else? He couldn't see anything out of the ordinary—and certainly nothing sinister. The warning that continued to echo within him was strictly intuitive. Call it a hunch, a sixth sense, or even a nose for trouble. He'd experienced it before, and usually he'd found it worth heeding.

Alex put the Asahi on the vanity bench and approached the bath with caution. He put his left hand against the heavy swinging door, listened, heard nothing, hesitated, then threw the door inward and stepped quickly into the room. The lambent late-afternoon sun pierced a frosted window high up in one wall; the bathroom glowed with soft golden light. He was alone.

This time his sixth sense had misled him. False alarm. He felt slightly foolish.

He was jumpy. And no wonder. Although his lunch with Joanna had been immensely enjoyable, the rest of the day had been a grinding emory wheel that put a sharp, ragged edge on his nerves: her mad flight from the Korean at Nijo Castle; her description of the oft-repeated nightmare; the syringe-wielding, mechanical-handed man who played a major role in her forgotten past; the unsettling discovery that this very beautiful, gifted woman had emotional problems that were perhaps more severe than she understood; and finally, but not least of all, there was his growing belief that the unexplained disappearance of Lisa Jean Chelgrin had been an event with powerful causes and effects, with countless layers of complex and mysterious meaning that went far deeper than anything he'd uncovered or even imagined at the time. He had a right to be jumpy.

Alex stripped off his shirt and put it in the laundry bag. He brought a magazine and the bottle of beer from the other room, put them on a low utility table that he had moved next to the bath. He bent down at the tub, adjusted the faucets until the water flowed at precisely the desired temperature.

In the bedroom again, he went to the walk-in closet to choose his suit for the evening. The door was ajar. As Alex pulled it open, a man leapt at him from the dark closet. Dorobo, Alex thought. *Dorobo: a burglar.* He was a short man. Stocky. Muscular. Japanese. And very quick. As he came he swung a fistful of wire coat hangers, struck Alex in the face.

In a flash of panic, Alex thought: *My eyes!*

But the hangers, terrifying as they were, spared his sight, merely slashed one cheek, and rained about him in a burst of dissonant music.

Counting on the surprise and confusion that the coat

hangers would cause, the stranger tried to push past him to the bedroom door. Alex plucked handfuls of the man's jacket and whirled him around. Unbalanced, they fell against the side of the bed, then to the floor, with Alex on the bottom.

The first punch landed in Alex's ribs, then another at the same spot, then a third on the point of his chin. He wasn't in a good position to use his own fists, and at last he was able to pitch the man off.

The stranger rolled into the vanity bench, knocked it over. Cursing continuously in Japanese, he scrambled to his feet.

Dazed only for an instant, still on the floor, Alex turned in time to seize the stocky man's ankle. He jerked hard, and the stranger toppled, struck the floor with a loud *boom!* He kicked and was lucky enough to strike Alex's left arm squarely on the funny bone. Alex howled. Sharp pain flowed from elbow to wrist, from elbow to shoulder, and brought stinging tears to his eyes.

A second later the Japanese was up and moving through the open doorway, into the drawing room, toward the suite's small entrance foyer.

Alex went after him; his training as a detective and his combative nature made it impossible for him to let well enough alone. In the drawing room, when he saw he couldn't stop the intruder from getting to the corridor and all the escape routes beyond, Alex grabbed a large vase from a decorative pedestal and tossed it with anger and accuracy. The glass exploded against the back of the *dorobo*'s skull. He stumbled and dropped to his knees, and Alex dashed past him to block the only exit.

Both of them were breathing like long-distance runners. For half a minute their gasping seemed to fill the room with rhythmic thunder.

Shaking his head, flicking shards of glass from his broad shoulders, the *dorobo* got up. He glared at Alex and motioned for him to get away from the door.

"Don't try to be a hero," he said in heavily accented but understandable English.

"What are you doing here?" Alex asked.

"Get out of my way."

"I asked you what you're doing in my room."

The man didn't answer.

"A *dorobo*?" Alex asked. "No. I don't really think so. I think you're more than just a cheap burglar."

"And I don't care what you think." He was losing his patience. There was an animallike growl in his voice now. "Get out of my way."

"It's the Chelgrin case, isn't it?"

"Move, damn you!"

"Who's your boss?"

The stranger balled his chunky hands into formidable fists and advanced a single threatening step.

Alex refused to stand aside.

The *dorobo* stopped, considered him for a moment, then withdrew a bone-handled switchblade from a jacket pocket. He touched a button on the haft; faster than the eye could follow, a thin eight-inch blade popped into sight. "Now are you going to move?"

Alex licked his lips. His mouth was dry and filled with a bitter taste. While he considered his alternatives, none of which was attractive, he divided his attention between the man's hard little eyes and the point of the blade.

Sensing fear and imminent surrender, the stranger waved the knife and chuckled.

"No," Alex said. "I don't give up that easily."

The smile faded. A scowl replaced it. "I was ordered—"

"By whom?"

The burglar ignored the question. "You better understand that you're no danger to me. An irritation. Nothing more."

"We'll see about that."

"I can break you if I must."

"Like a doll, I suppose."

"Yes. A doll."

"I'm a student of martial arts."

"So?"

Alex smiled, but the smile was a sham. At first glance this square-faced man left an impression of buttery softness. On closer inspection, however, Alex saw that he was iron-hard beneath the masking layer of fat. A sumo wrestler had that same look in the early days of his training, before he attained his final, gross physique.

"I wasn't given authority to terminate you," the burglar said, as if he had learned English from a prissy instructor who taught euphemisms for such nasty words as *kill* and *murder*. "In fact I was warned not to hurt you if you interrupted me in my work. Do you understand?"

"Yes. However you got your job, it obviously wasn't through the *Times*."

The stranger blinked stupidly. "What?"

"It was a poor joke."

"This is no joking matter, Mr. Hunter."

"My apologies."

"You are safe if you step aside."

"But then how could I face myself in the morning?"

"I don't want to annoy my superiors by terminating you without permission."

"That would be dreadful, wouldn't it?" Alex said, trying not to appear intimidated.

"However, if you're adamant, if it becomes necessary for me to cut you to pieces—"

"I know you said you're not interested in what I think, but I think there's a damned good chance I can take that thing away from you," Alex said, pointing to the knife.

The stranger came at him faster than any man ever had, fluid as a dancer in spite of his stockiness. Alex clutched the thick wrist of the hand that held the knife; but with the amazing dexterity of a stage magician, the *dorobo* tossed the weapon from one hand to the other and struck. The cold blade sliced smoothly, lightly along the underside of Alex's left arm, which still tingled unpleasantly from the kick it had sustained.

The man retreated as abruptly as he had attacked. "Just a scratch, Mr. Hunter."

The knife had skipped across the flesh; there were two wounds, one three inches long, and the other five inches. Alex stared at them as if they had opened completely without cause, like miraculous stigmata. The blood oozed copiously from the shallow cuts, trickled into his hand and dripped from his fingertips, but it didn't spurt; no major artery or vein was severed; the flow was stanchable. What left him so badly shaken was the lightning-swift movement of the knife; it had happened so fast that he still had not begun to feel any pain.

"It won't require stitches," the stranger said, "but if you force me to cut again . . . I can make no promises about the next time."

"There won't be a next time," Alex said. He found it difficult to admit defeat, but he wasn't a fool. "You're a superb knife fighter. I'll move out of your way."

"Wise," the man said, smiling like an ugly Buddha. "Cross the room and sit on the couch."

Alex did as he was told, cradling his bloodied arm and thinking furiously, hoping to conjure up some wonderful trick that might win this for him even now. But there seemed to be nothing he could do.

The burglar remained in the foyer until Alex was seated, then left, slamming the door behind him.

The instant he was alone, Alex jumped up from the couch and sprinted to the telephone on the desk. He pulled a plastic card out of the base of the receiver; it was a list of important service numbers. He dialed hotel security. While the number rang, however, he had a change of heart, and he hung up just as someone answered.

As was his habit, Alex analyzed the situation aloud, in a conversation with himself. "Hotel security will call in the city police. Is that what you want?"

He went to the door, latched it. He braced it with a straight-backed chair.

"He wasn't a burglar. That's for damned sure."

Alex hugged himself with his injured arm so that the blood would soak into his undershirt instead of dripping on the carpet.

"He works for someone who knows Joanna is Lisa. Someone who's worried I'll find out."

He went into the bathroom and shut off the taps just as the water was about to overflow onto the floor. He opened the tub drain.

"So what was he doing here? Searching my rooms? For what? Maybe . . . yeah . . . a letter or a diary . . . maybe a notebook . . . anything in which I might have committed my suspicions to print. Has to be it."

The knife wounds were beginning to burn and throb. He hugged himself harder, attempting to stop or slow the bleeding by applying direct pressure to the cuts. The entire front of his undershirt was crimson.

He sat on the edge of the tub.

Perspiration seeped into the corners of his eyes, making him blink. He wiped his forehead with a washcloth. He was thirsty. He picked up the bottle of Asahi beer and chugged a third of it.

"So who's the knife man's boss? He's got damned good connections, international connections. He might even have a man planted in the Chicago office. How about that? Huh? How else did he manage to put someone on my ass so soon after I talked to Blakenship?"

Alex glanced at the tub and saw it was half empty. He turned on the cold water.

"Of course," he told himself, "it's more likely that my phones here are tapped. And I've probably been followed since I reached Kyoto."

Gingerly he moved his arm and held it away from his chest. Although the wounds continued to bleed freely, he didn't think they were serious enough to require a doctor's attention. He hadn't any desire to explain the injury to anyone—except to Joanna. The

burning sensation had grown worse, like two dozen
wasp stings now. He plunged his arm under the cold
water that foamed out of the faucet. Relief was in-
stantaneous. He sat like that for a minute or two,
thinking.

The first time he'd seen Joanna Rand at the Moonglow, when first he'd suspected that she was Lisa Chelgrin, he had thought that she must have engineered
her own kidnapping in Jamaica, more than a decade
earlier. He couldn't imagine *why* she'd wanted to do
that; but his years as a private detective had taught
him that people often committed strange, drastic acts
for the thinnest reasons; they hurtled off the rails in
quest of freedom or self-destruction, although they
were most frequently motivated by a desperate need
for change and didn't care much whether it was for
better or worse. After talking to Joanna for a few
minutes, he knew she wasn't one of those people; it was
ludicrous to suppose she could have planned her own
abduction and confused all of Alex's best investigators,
especially when she had been, at that time, an inexperienced college girl.

He considered amnesia, too, but that explanation
was even less satisfying than the other. As an amnesiac
she might have forgotten every detail of a large portion
of her life; but she would not have created and come
to believe a completely false set of memories in order
to fill the gap. And Joanna had done precisely that.

"Okay," Alex said aloud. "So Joanna's not consciously deceiving anyone. And she's not an amnesiac,
at least not in the classic sense. So what possibilities
are left?"

He withdrew his arm from the cold water and saw
that the flow of blood had been reduced by about one-
third. He wrapped the arm tightly in a damp towel.
Eventually blood would seep through; but as a temporary bandage the towel was adequate.

He went into the drawing room and telephoned
the bell captain's station in the hotel lobby. He asked
for a bottle of rubbing alcohol, a bottle of Mercuro-

chrome, a box of gauze pads, a roll of gauze, and a roll of adhesive tape. "If the man who brings it is fast, there'll be an especially generous tip for him," Alex said.

The bell captain said, "If there's been an accident we have a doctor who—"

"Only a minor accident. I don't need a doctor, thank you. Just those things I requested."

While he waited for the bandages and antiseptics, Alex made himself presentable. In the bathroom he stripped out of his blood-drenched undershirt. He scrubbed his chest vigorously with a washcloth and combed his hair.

Although the wounds continued to burn, the worst of the stinging pain had subsided into a pounding but tolerable ache. The arm was stiff, too, as if it were undergoing a medusan metamorphosis: flesh into stone.

In the drawing room Alex picked up the largest pieces of the shattered vase and threw them in a wastebasket. He took the straight-backed chair away from the door and put it where it belonged.

Blood was beginning to work its way up through the layers of the towel that was wrapped around his arm.

He sat down at the desk to wait for the bellhop, and the room seemed to move slowly around him.

"Well," he said, resuming the dialogue with himself, "if we can rule out fraud and traditional amnesia, that leaves only one thing, doesn't it? Brainwashing. Crazy as it sounds."

The third explanation was simple—and also quite incredible; yet Alex believed it. The people who kidnapped Lisa Jean Chelgrin had used modern brainwashing techniques on her—drugs, hypnosis, subliminal reeducation, and a dozen other methods of psychological conditioning. They had wiped her mind clean. Absolutely spotless. Actually, he wasn't certain if that was possible; but he thought it was a good bet. In the past ten years there had been truly amazing ad-

vances made in those areas of research—psychophar-
macology, biochemistry, psychosurgery, psychology—
that directly and indirectly contributed to the less
reputable, but nonetheless hotly pursued, science of
mind control.

He hoped that something less severe had been done
to Lisa. If complete eradication of a life-set of memories was as yet still just a gleam in some would-be
Hitler's eye, then the girl's kidnappers might have been
able only to repress the original personality that had
inhabited her lovely body. In other words, Lisa might
be buried deep beneath the Joanna cover, missing but
not gone. If that were true, Lisa could be reached,
resurrected, and made to remember the circumstances
of her premature burial.

In either case the kidnappers had stuffed her full
of fake memories. They had provided her with phony
identification, and then they had turned her loose in
Japan, with a substantial bankroll, which supposedly
came from a settlement of her make-believe father's
estate.

"But for God's sake, why?" Alex asked the empty
room.

Motes of dust floated in the shafts of wan light that
lanced through the nearby window.

Alex stood, walked nervously back and forth on
legs that felt more rubbery with every step.

"And who could have done it to her?" he asked.
"And why are they still interested? What are the stakes
in this game? How important is it to them that Joanna
Rand's true identity be kept a secret? Will they kill me
if I get proof of who she is? Will they kill her if she's
convinced by what I tell her?"

He didn't have answers to those questions, but he
knew that he would have them eventually. He wouldn't
be able to stop probing this affair until he knew everything about it. His rooms had been searched; he had
been cut with a knife. He owed them more than a little
humiliation and pain.

• 14 •

West of Kyoto the last light of the day gradually faded out, like a bank of dying embers; the city smouldered into evening under a shale-colored sky.

The streets of the Gion district were crowded. In the bars, clubs, restaurants, and geisha houses, another night of escape from reality had begun.

On his way to the Moonglow Lounge, immaculately dressed in a charcoal-gray suit, matching vest, pale-gray shirt, and green tie, with a gray topcoat thrown capelike across his shoulders, and with his left arm cradled in a sling that was fashioned from a silk scarf, Alex walked at a tourist's pace. Although he appeared to be engrossed by the passing scene, he actually paid scant attention to the whirl of color and activity on all sides. His mind was occupied with the kind of cloak-and-dagger business that usually seemed childish to him, but which was now a commonsense reaction to the developments of the past two hours; he was trying to learn if the opposition had put a tail on him. In the busy throng that hurried this way and that over the freshly washed stone pavement, Alex had difficulty detecting any one person who might be following him. Every time he turned a corner or stopped at a crosswalk, he glanced casually behind, as if taking a second look at some landmark of the Gion; and without appearing to do so, he studied the people in his wake. Eventually he grew suspicious of three men, each of them walking alone, each of them caught watching him at some point, each of them staying behind him, block after block. The first was a fat man with deeply set little eyes, enormous jowls, and a wispy chin beard. However, his size made him the least likely of the three candidates; for he was highly visible, and people in that line of work were nearly always nondescript. The second suspect was a slender man in his forties; his face was narrow and the bones starkly prominent in it. The third was a young man, no older than twenty-five, dressed in jeans and a yellow nylon windbreaker; as he walked he puffed nervously on a cigarette. By the time Alex reached the Moonglow Lounge, he still had not dceided which, if any, of the three men was tailing him; but he had committed every detail of their faces to memory, had filed them away for future reference.

Just inside the front door of the Moonglow, there was an easel supporting a yard-square posterboard sign. The red-and-black announcement was neatly hand-printed, first in Japanese characters and then in English.

DUE TO ILLNESS
JOANNA
RAND
WILL NOT PERFORM TONIGHT

THE MOONGLOW ORCHESTRA
WILL PROVIDE MUSIC FOR DANCING

Alex left his topcoat with the hatcheck girl and went for a drink. The restaurant was doing good business, but the lounge had only six customers. He sat alone at the curved end of the bar and ordered Old Suntory. When the bartender brought the whisky, Alex said, "I hope Miss Rand's illness isn't serious."

"Not serious," the bartender said in heavily accented English. "Only sore throat."

"Would you please call upstairs and tell her that Alex Hunter is here?"

"Too sick see anyone," the man said, nodding and smiling reflexively.

"I'm a friend."

"Much too sick."

"She'll talk to me," Alex insisted.

"Sore throat."

"I heard. But—"

"Can't talk much."

"We have an appointment."

"So sorry."

They went around and around like that for a while, until the bartender finally gave in, walked to the cash register, and picked up the phone beside it. As he spoke with Joanna, he glanced repeatedly and somewhat furtively at Alex. When he hung up, he came back slowly, avoiding Alex's eyes. "Sorry."

"What do you mean?"

"She say can't see you."

"You must be mistaken."

"No."

"Call her again."

The bartender was embarrassed for him. "She say she don't know anyone name Alex Hunter."

"That's ridiculous!"

The bartender said nothing.

"Joanna and I had lunch together."

The man shrugged.

"It was just this afternoon!" Alex said.

A pained smile. And: "So very sorry."

A customer called for service down at the far end of the counter, and the bartender scurried away from Alex with obvious relief.

For a minute or two Alex stared at his own reflection in the bluish bar mirror; then he spoke to it. "What the hell's going on here?"

• 15 •

When Alex asked for Mariko Inamura, the bartender put him through even more trouble than when he'd wanted to see Joanna; but at last the man relented and made the call.

A minute later she came through a door marked
PRIVATE, behind and to the left of Alex. She was
Joanna's age and very pretty. Her thick black hair
was held up with ivory pins.

He stood up and bowed to her.

She returned the bow; they introduced themselves;
and she sat on the stool next to his.

As he sat down again he said, "Mariko-san, I've
heard many good things about you."

"I could return that compliment in exactly those
words." Her English was flawless. She didn't have the
slightest difficulty pronouncing the "l" sound, which
had no equivalent in her native tongue, and which was
usually the greatest obstacle a Japanese student of
English had to overcome. "What happened to your
arm?" she asked, indicating the silk sling.

"Oh, nothing serious," he said. "A cut. Some broken
glass. How's Joanna?"

"She has a sore throat."

He sipped his whiskey. He said, "Excuse me if I
start acting like the stereotypical American; I don't
mean to be blunt and boorish, but I wonder if that's
really the truth—that story about a sore throat."

"What an odd thing to say."

"That's not an answer."

"Do you think I'm a liar?"

"No. I don't mean to offend, Mariko-san."

"And no offense is taken, Alex-san."

"I'm only trying to understand the situation."

"I'll help if I can."

"You see, I asked the bartender to call Joanna and
tell her I'd arrived. She and I have something important
to discuss this evening. But she told the bartender she
didn't know anyone named Alex Hunter."

Mariko sighed. "She spoke so well of you. She was
like a young girl. I began to hope it would be different
this time."

"What's wrong with her?"

Mariko's eyes clouded. She looked away from him,
stared at the polished counter in front of her. The

Japanese have a highly developed sense of propriety, a complex system of social graces, and a very rigid set of standards concerning the conduct of personal relationships. She was reluctant to talk about her friend, for in doing so she would not be performing entirely according to those standards.

Hoping to convince her that he was not a total stranger, and that he was not the sort of person from whom she needed to protect Joanna, Alex said, "I already know about the bad dream she has every night."

Mariko was surprised. "Joanna's never told anyone about that—except me."

"And now me."

She glanced at Alex, and there was greater warmth in her coal-colored eyes than there had been a minute ago. Nevertheless, he could see that she was still wrestling with her code of honor and manners. To stall for a bit more thinking time, she signaled the bartender and ordered Old Suntory over ice.

Alex sensed that in many ways Mariko was a conservative, old-fashioned girl. He understood that she could not easily overcome the traditional Japanese respect for other people's privacy; and he was actually rather pleased that, unlike many of her contemporaries, she had not been corrupted by Western mores and the computer age. He was patient with her.

When her drink came she sipped it slowly, rattled the ice in the glass, and at last said, "If Joanna's told you about her nightmare, then she's probably told you as much about herself as she ever tells anyone."

"She's secretive?"

"Not that, exactly. She just doesn't talk about herself much."

"Modest?"

"That's part of it, but only part. It's also like . . . like she's afraid to talk about herself too much."

He watched Mariko closely. "Afraid? What do you mean?"

"I can't explain it. But if I know something about her that you don't, it's probably only what I've ob-

served during the six or seven years I've worked for
her. There's nothing terribly revealing or secret."

He waited, aware that she had capitulated. She
needed a moment to decide where to begin.

After another sip of whiskey, Mariko said, "What
Joanna did to you tonight . . . pretending not to know
you . . . well, this isn't the first time she's behaved
that way."

"It doesn't seem to be her style."

"Every time she does it, I'm shocked," Mariko said.
"It's out of character. She's basically the sweetest,
kindest person you'd ever meet. Yet, whenever she
starts feeling very close to a man, whenever she begins
to fall in love with him—or he with her—she kills
the romance. And she's never nice or gentle about it.
She's always mean. Like she's an entirely different
woman. She hurts feelings, Mr. Hunter. She breaks
hearts . . . including her own."

"I don't see how that applies to me. After all, I
saw her for the first time just a few days ago. We've
only had one date, an innocent lunch together."

Mariko nodded solemnly. "She's fallen for you faster
and, I think, much harder than she has for any other
man."

"No. You're wrong about that."

"Just before you came on the scene, Joanna was
horribly depressed, almost suicidal."

"She didn't seem that way to me."

"That's what I mean. You had an instant effect on
her. She's always in bad shape for a few weeks or even
a few months after she drops someone she cares for,
but recently she's reached new lows. You cheered her
up overnight."

"If she really hates to live alone, then why does she
keep destroying these relationships?" Alex asked.

"She never wants to. She seems compelled."

"Compelled? By whom?"

"It's as if she's . . . possessed. It's as if there's a
second Joanna hiding deep within her, an inner demon
that forces her to live alone and be unhappy."

"Has she tried psychotherapy?"

Mariko frowned and shook her head. "My uncle is a very fine psychologist. I've urged her to see him about this and about the nightmare, but she refuses. I worry about her all the time. I've seldom any peace of mind. As her depression gets deeper and blacker it also begins to be contagious. If she didn't need me, and if I didn't care for her like my own sister, I'd have left long ago. She needs to share her life with friends and with a partner, a lover. But she pushes everyone away—even me to some extent. The last couple of months she's been more depressed and more depressing than usual. In fact she's been so bad that I'd just about decided to get out no matter what—and then you came along. She wouldn't admit it, not even to herself, but she fell for you so suddenly and completely that it seemed there was a chance she would overcome that inner voice and build something permanent this time."

Alex shifted on the bar stool. This turn in the conversation made him uneasy. "Mariko-san, I'm afraid that you are seeing more in this relationship than there really is."

"Joanna is not a loner. She needs someone."

"I imagine that's true. But she doesn't love me. Love doesn't happen that fast."

"Don't you believe in love at first sight?"

"That's a poet's conceit," he said.

"I think it can happen."

"Oh? Have you experienced it?"

"No. But I hope I will eventually."

"Good luck. I don't think I believe in love at all, much less in love at first sight."

His statement clearly amazed her. "If you don't believe in love," Mariko said, "then what do you call it when a man and a woman—"

"I call it lust—"

"Not just that."

"—and affection, mutual dependence, and sometimes even temporary insanity."

"That's all you've ever felt?"

"That's all," he said.

"I don't believe it."

He shrugged. "It's true."

"Love is the only thing we can depend on in this world," she said. "To deny it exists—"

"Love is the last thing we can depend on. People say they're in love, but it never lasts. The only constants are death and taxes."

"Some men don't work," Mariko said. "Therefore, they pay no taxes. And there are many wise men who believe in life everlasting."

He opened his mouth to argue, grinned instead. "I have a hunch you're a natural-born debator. I better stop while I'm only slightly behind."

"What about Joanna?" she asked.

"What about her?"

"Don't you care for her at all?"

"Well, of course I do."

"But you don't believe in love."

"I *like* Joanna enormously. But as for love—"

Mariko waved one hand to silence him. "Wait. I'm sorry. This is rude. I'm extremely impolite. You don't have to reveal so much of yourself to me. I'm being presumptuous. Please forgive me."

"If I didn't want to talk, you couldn't pry a single word from me," Alex said.

"I just wanted you to know that regardless of what you may feel for her, Joanna loves you. That's why she rejected you so bluntly tonight—because she's afraid of that sort of commitment." Mariko drank the last of her whisky and got up to leave.

"Wait," Alex said. "I've got to see her."

Mariko smiled knowingly.

He didn't want to explain about Lisa Chelgrin, so he let Mariko think whatever she wished. "It's important," he said.

"Come back tomorrow night," she said. "Joanna can't take off work forever."

"Won't you just go upstairs right now and persuade her to see me?"

"You seem surprisingly anxious about her—for a man who says he doesn't care."

"Mariko-san, will you talk to her?"

"It wouldn't help. She's at her worst just after she's broken off with someone. When she's in this mood, she won't listen to me or anyone. For the next day or two, until the depression sets in again, she'll hate the whole world."

"I'll be back tomorrow."

"She'll be nasty with you."

"I'll charm her." He smiled weakly.

"You don't know how mean she can be."

"She won't drive me away," he said.

"Other good men have given up."

"I won't."

Mariko lay one hand on his arm. "I hope you *do* keep trying," she said. "If those other men hadn't given up so easily, one of them might have gotten through to her sooner or later. I still think you have a better chance with her than any of the others ever did. You and Joanna are alike in many ways. Both of you have accepted loneliness as a way of life. For a long time you've desperately wanted to love someone, but neither of you has ever been able to come to grips with that. Pursue her, Alex-san. You need her every bit as much as she needs you."

Mariko walked away from him, vanished through the door marked PRIVATE.

For a while after she left, Alex stared at himself in the blue mirror.

Alex was surprised and disturbed by his own reaction
to Joanna's behavior. He had great difficulty main-
taining his characteristic equanimity; and in fact he
did maintain it only outwardly. Inside he was afire.
He wanted to punch someone. Quite irrationally, he
had the urge to pitch his whisky glass at the blue bar
mirror. He restrained himself, but only because he
was aware that such an act would be an admission
of the effect this woman had on him. It was an effect,
a degree of control from which he'd thought he'd
always be free. Now he was uneasy about his response
to her—and as yet unwilling to think seriously about it.

He ate a light dinner at the Moonglow and left before the orchestra had finished its first set of the
evening. The brassy, bouncy music—"A String of
Pearls"—followed him into the street.

The sun had abandoned Kyoto. The city gave forth
its own cold, electric illumination. With the arrival of
darkness, the temperature had plummeted. It was just
below freezing now. Fat snowflakes circled lazily
through the light that issued from windows, open doors,
neon signs, and passing automobiles; but they melted
upon contact with the pavement, where the lights were
reflected in a skin of icy water.

For a moment Alex stood outside the Moonglow,
looked around as if deciding where to go next, and
spotted one of the three men who had appeared to be
following him earlier in the evening. The gaunt, mid-
dle-aged Japanese with the narrow face and prominent
cheekbones waited only thirty yards away, in front of
a neon-emblazoned nightclub called The Serene Dragon. His coat collar was turned up and his shoulders

were hunched against the wintry wind. Although he tried to blend with the pleasure-seekers who were streaming through the Gion, he had a sly, furtive, and somewhat sleazy manner that made him conspicuous. Alex dubbed him "Shifty"; and no matter what the man's real name might be, this new one surely fit him better.

Smiling, pretending not to have the slightest interest in Shifty, Alex considered the possibilities. There were basically two. He could take an uneventful stroll to the Kyoto Hotel, return to his suite, and go to bed for the night—still buzzing with energy, still tied in knots by frustration, and none the wiser about the people behind the Lisa Chelgrin kidnapping. *Or* he could have some fun, lead Shifty on a twisting chase, and perhaps play turnabout.

In his current, agitated state of mind, the choice was easily made. The chase.

Whistling happily, Alex walked deeper into the glittering Gion district. After five minutes, having changed streets twice, he glanced behind and saw that Shifty was following at a discreet distance.

In spite of the rising wind and snow flurries, nearly as many people were out now as had been at sunset. Sometimes the nightlife in Kyoto seemed too frantic for Japan—perhaps because it was squeezed into fewer hours than in Tokyo and most Western cities. The nightclubs opened in late afternoon and usually closed by eleven thirty; the one and a half million citizens of Kyoto had the provincial habit of going to bed before midnight. Already, by their schedule, half the night was gone; and those who had not yet made the happiness connection were rushing about in search of it.

Alex was fascinated by the Gion. It was a complex maze of streets, alleys, winding passages, and covered footpaths, all crowded with nightclubs, bars, craft shops, short-time hotels, sedate inns, restaurants, public baths, temples, movie theaters, shrines, snack shops, geisha houses, and much more. The larger streets were noisy, exciting, garish, ablaze with rainbow neon that was reflected and refracted in acres of glass, chrome, and plastic; here, the wholesale adoption of the very worst elements of Western style made it clear that there *were* exceptions to the supposedly universal artistic sensitivity of the Japanese people. In many of the alleyways and cobbled lanes, however, a more appealing Gion flourished. One step back from the major thoroughfares, pockets of traditional architecture survived; there were houses that still served as homes, as well as old-style houses whose interiors had been transformed into expensive spas, restaurants, bars, and intimate cabarets, all of which shared the time-honored construction of satiny, weather-smooth woods and polished stones, and, occasionally, heavy bronze or ironwork.

Alex walked these back streets, thinking furiously, searching for an opportunity to play turnabout with Shifty.

For his part Shifty also assumed the role of a tourist. He did his phony window-shopping half a block behind Alex and, amusingly, in perfect harmony with him.

Finally, seeking respite from the wind, Alex went into a bar and ordered sake. Just when he was beginning to feel warm again, he had a thought that sent a shiver through him: Shifty might have been given the permission to kill that had been withheld from the burglar. Perhaps I'm leading him on, looking for a way to set him up . . . while he's waiting for the right moment to blow my head off.

However, even if it meant his life, he could not walk away from Joanna now. If the men behind the Chelgrin-Rand hoax felt that he knew too much already, his only hope was to learn everything about them and then use that knowledge either to break them or to bargain with them. Besides, he owed the bastards for what the burglar had done to him; and he had not built a great fortune by being a forgiving soul.

He drank another cup of hot sake.

When Alex came out of the bar, Shifty was waiting, a shadow among shadows, twenty yards away.

There were fewer people on the street than when he had gone into the bar, but there were still too many for Shifty to risk murder—if that was his intent. The Japanese were generally not as apathetic about crime as were most Americans. They respected tradition, stability, order, and the law. Most of them would attempt to apprehend a man who committed murder in public.

Alex walked to a beverage shop and purchased a bottle of Awamori, an Okinawa sweet-potato brandy —smooth and delicious to the Japanese palate but coarse and acrid by Western standards. He was not concerned about the quality of the liquor; after all, he didn't intend to drink it.

When Alex came out of the shop, Shifty was fifty or sixty feet to the north, standing at a jewelry store window. He didn't look up, but as Alex walked south, so did he.

Hoping to find a place where he could be alone with the man behind him, Alex turned at the first crossroads, ventured into a lane that was only open to pedestrians. The beauty of the old buildings was just slightly spoiled by neon; fewer than a dozen signs shone in the night, and all of them were much smaller than the monstrous, flashing signs elsewhere in the Gion. Snowflakes spiraled around decades-old globe-type streetlamps. Alex passed a shrine, flanked by bars and bathed in dim yellow light, where amateurs practiced ancient Central Asian temple dances to the accompaniment of finger bells and eerie string music. People were walking in this block, considerably fewer than in the lane he had just left, but still enough to discourage murder.

With Shifty tagging along, Alex tried other branches of the maze. He progressed from commercial blocks to areas that were at least fifty percent residential. Shifty became increasingly conspicuous in the thinning crowd and fell back farther than thirty yards. Eventually, Alex came into a lane upon which fronted single-family

homes and apartments. It was deserted and quiet. The
only lights were those that hung above the front doors
of the houses: accordionlike paper lanterns suspended
on electric cords. The lanterns swung in the wind, and
macabre shadows capered demonically across the
snow-wet cobblestones. Alex hurried to the next alleyway, peered into it, and grinned. He had found precisely what he needed.

It was a six-foot-wide, brick-paved service alley. On
both sides the backs of houses faced the narrow passage. The first block had three lights, one at each end
and one in the middle; and the spaces between were
very dark. He could see groups of trash barrels and
a few bicycles that were chained to iron racks. Otherwise, the alley was lined with amorphous shapes that
could be anything or nothing. He was fairly sure that
none of these mysterious lumps was a man—which
meant that he would be alone here with Shifty.

Good.

Alex turned the corner and pulled off the topcoat
that was thrown capelike across his shoulders. Holding
the coat with his right arm, still gripping the bottle of
Awamori with his right hand, he broke into a run. In
order for the setup to work and the turnabout to be
successful, he first had to cover three-quarters of the
block without Shifty seeing him. His shoes slipped on
the damp bricks, but he didn't fall. He ran out of the
light, into a long patch of darkness, his heart pounding,
ran under the midpoint lamp, breath exploding from
him in sharp bursts of steam, plunged into the dark
again, his injured arm bumping against his chest as
the sling jerked in sympathy with each footfall. When
he reached the lambent circle of pavement beneath
the third and final streetlight, he stopped and turned
and looked back.

Shifty was not yet in sight.

Alex dropped his topcoat in the center of the
puddle of light.

No sign of Shifty.

Alex hurried back the way he had come, but only

for ten or fifteen feet, until he was out of the light once more and had become just one of the many formless objects that lined the passageway.

He was still alone.

He stepped quickly behind a row of five enormous trash barrels and hunkered down. The space between the first barrel and the wall provided him with an unobstructed view of the intersection where the gaunt man would soon appear.

Footsteps.

Sound carried well in the cold air.

Alex tried to quiet his own ragged breathing.

Shifty entered the far end of the alleyway and stopped abruptly, surprised by the disappearance of his prey.

In spite of the tension and apprehension that had pulled him taut as the membrane on a drum, Alex smiled.

For nearly a minute Shifty stood without moving, without making a sound.

Come on, you bastard.

He walked slowly toward Alex. Less certain of himself than he had been, he stepped lightly as a cat now; there was almost no noise to betray him.

Alex slipped his left arm out of the sling. He hoped he wouldn't need to use that hand; he was worried about breaking open the wound. He did not intend to struggle with the other man, but he wanted both hands free just in case something went wrong with the setup.

As Shifty approached he looked behind the trash cans on both sides of the passage.

Alex hadn't expected him to do that. If he remained that cautious for the length of the alley, he would spring the trap and escape it. Alex had only one advantage—surprise—and he watched with increasing trepidation as it was stolen from him.

The gaunt man moved in a half crouch. He jammed his right hand into his coat pocket and kept it there.

Holding a gun? Alex wondered.

The man walked out of the first pool of light and into darkness.

Although the night was cold and Alex was without a coat, he began to perspire.

Shifty reached the midpoint light. He continued methodically to inspect every object and shadow behind which or in which a man might hide.

The garbage in the cans beside Alex exuded the nauseous odor of spoiled fish and rancid cooking oil. He'd been aware of the stench from the moment he'd hidden behind the barrels; but second by second, the odor seemed to grow riper, ever more disgusting. He imagined that he could taste as well as smell the fish. He wanted to gag, cough, clear his throat, and spit out the offending substance. He wanted to stand up and walk away from here and get a breath of fresh air.

And then what? he asked himself. As likely as not —a bullet in the brain.

Shifty was almost out of the light at the halfway point, ready to step into the second patch of darkness, when again he stopped and stood as if quick-frozen.

He's seen the topcoat, Alex thought. *He knows that I was wearing it like a cape. So what's he going to think? That I tumbled to him, that I began to worry about him following me, that I ran to get away from him, that the coat fell off my shoulders, that I was a bit panicky and didn't want to waste the time it would have taken to stop and retrieve it. Please, God, that's what he's got to be thinking.*

Shifty moved again—not slowly, as before, and not with caution either. He strode purposefully toward the third streetlight, toward the discarded topcoat, the echoes of his footsteps bouncing back and forth between the houses that bracketed him; and he didn't look closely at any more of the trash barrels.

Alex held his breath.

The man was twenty feet away.

Ten feet.

Five.

As soon as he passed by, literally close enough to touch, Alex rose in the shadows.

Shifty didn't see him. He had his back toward Alex now. Besides, his attention was fixed on the topcoat.

Alex slipped into the passageway and went after him. He walked fast, closing the distance between them; and he stayed mostly on his toes, trying to be silent. What little noise he made was masked by his adversary's footsteps. At the perimeter of the light he had a bad moment when he thought he would reveal himself by his shadow; but the shadows fell behind them.

Shifty stopped in the center of the circle of light, bent down, and picked up the coat. Then, with some sixth sense that was akin to the intuition Alex had experienced earlier in his hotel suite, Shifty knew that he was not alone. He gasped and began to turn.

Alex swung the bottle of Awamori with all of his might. It struck the other man on the side of the head, squarely along the temple. The bottle exploded; glass flew everywhere; and the night was filled with the peculiar stench of sweet-potato brandy.

Shifty staggered, dropped the coat, put one hand to his head, reached for Alex with the other hand, and fell as if his flesh had been transformed into lead by some perverse alchemy.

Alex jumped back a step. He didn't want to be grabbed by the ankle and brought down.

But there wasn't any danger. Shifty was unconscious. Blood glistened on his hair, forehead, cheeks, and chin.

Alex looked up and down the passageway. He expected people to come out of the houses and start shooting at him. The *pop* of the bottle as it broke and the atonal rattle of glass on the bricks had sounded thunderous to him. He stood with the neck of the bottle clamped in his right hand, ready to flee at the first sign of response, but after a while he realized that he had not been heard.

· 17 ·

The snow flurries had grown into a squall. Dense sheets of fat white flakes swirled through the passageway.

The man he called Shifty was unconscious but not seriously hurt. His heartbeat was strong; his breathing was shallow but steady. An ugly bruise marked the spot where the bottle had struck him, but the superficial cuts on his face had already begun to clot.

Alex searched the man's pockets. He found coins, a wad of paper money, a book of matches that bore no advertising, a green plastic toothpick, a packet of facial tissues, a roll of breath mints, and a comb. He did not find a wallet or credit cards or a driver's license or any other identification. And there was a gun, of course—a Japanese-made 7 mm. automatic with a skillfully crafted silencer. It was in the man's right overcoat pocket, which was much deeper than the left pocket; which meant that he usually carried the pistol and probably used it regularly. He also had a spare magazine of ammunition, twenty bullets altogether.

Alex propped him against the wall on one side of the alley. Shifty sat where he was placed—his hands at his sides, palms turned up and fingers somewhat curled, his chin resting on his chest.

Alex retrieved the soiled topcoat and draped it over his shoulder, then eased his left arm into the silk sling, relieved that the healing wound had not been disturbed.

By now a thin, icy lace of snow covered Shifty's hair. In his battered condition, the snowflake mantilla made him look like a pathetic yet determinedly jaunty drunk who was trying to get laughs by wearing a doily on his head.

Alex stooped beside him and gently but repeatedly slapped his face.

After a while Shifty stirred, opened his eyes, blinked stupidly, looked around and then at Alex. Comprehension came gradually.

Alex pointed the pistol in the general direction of the other man's heart. When he was sure that Shifty was no longer disoriented, he said, "I have quite a few questions to ask you."

"You'll suffer for this," the man said in Japanese. "That much I promise you."

Alex spoke the same language. "Why have you been following me?"

"I wasn't following you."

"Do you think I'm a fool?"

"Yes."

He grunted in pain as Alex poked him twice in the stomach with the gun barrel.

"All right," Shifty said. "I wanted to rob you."

"That's not the reason."

"You looked like a rich American."

"Someone ordered you to watch me."

"You're wrong."

"Who's your boss?"

"I'm my own boss."

"Don't lie to me."

Shifty didn't respond.

Although Alex was incapable of using physical abuse to extract information, he was not squeamish about engaging in some light psychological torture. He put the cold muzzle of the pistol against the man's left eye.

"The eyeball's like jelly," Alex said. "And the brain isn't much more solid than that. They'll find you splashed all over the wall."

Shifty stared unwaveringly with his free right eye; he didn't appear to be intimidated.

"Do you want to sleep forever?" Alex asked.

"You won't kill me."

"Don't be too sure."

"You aren't a murderer."

"I've killed two men."

"Yes," Shifty said. "And both times you killed in self-defense."

"Is that what they told you?"

"It's true."

"Perhaps it is," Alex said. "But I think this could be considered self-defense, too."

"That would be true only if I tried to take the gun away from you."

"Why don't you do that?" Alex asked.

"I'm content." Shifty smiled humorlessly. "You may keep the pistol, Mr. Hunter."

Alex continued to press the muzzle against Shifty's eye.

For a while neither of them spoke.

The wind fluted through the clusters of garbage barrels as if they were organ pipes, producing a hollow, ululating, unearthly music that made the night seem twice as cold as it actually was.

Finally Alex sighed and stood up. Staring down at the other man, still training the gun on him, Alex said, "Although you didn't answer any of my questions, I've found out a couple of things about you."

Shifty didn't move. "You obviously want me to ask, and so long as you have the gun I should be cooperative. What have you found out about me?" he asked derisively.

"First of all, I've learned what you aren't. You aren't an ordinary hired gun. You aren't a common hoodlum. You don't perspire."

"Oh?" he asked, obviously amused. "Does a common hoodlum perspire a lot?"

"He does when someone pokes a gun in his eye and threatens to blow his brains out. Usually he doesn't just sweat—he breaks down altogether. You see, the average gunman has no respect for human life, and he assumes that you're as ruthless as he is. He believes you'll carry out your threat, as he would, and so he sweats. I know it for a fact. I've dealt with that type more than a few times."

Shifty nodded. "Interesting."

"There are only two kinds of people who have the very strong, unshakable self-confidence that you've shown me," Alex said.

"The right and the just?"

Alex ignored that. "The first are homicidal maniacs, psychopaths who can't grasp the fundamental relationship between cause and effect, killers who can't comprehend that punishment often follows crime."

"Is that what I am—a psychopath?"

"No. You're the other kind—a fanatic."

"A true believer," Shifty said.

"Yes."

"And what am I fanatical about?"

"It always comes down to one of two things," Alex said.

"Does it?"

"Either religion or politics."

The snow squall subsided as they talked. The force of the wind declined; and now the music emanating from the barrels was a soft, ghostly lullaby.

Frowning, Shifty said, "You're a clever man. But I fail to see the point of this conversation."

Alex waved the pistol at him. "I want your people to understand that they cannot play with me as if I were some inexperienced country boy. Every time the bastards harass me, no matter how indirectly they do it, I'll learn something more about them. It's inevitable. They may think they're being circumspect, even invisible, but without realizing it, they'll reveal things about themselves every damned time. I am observant. I'm astute. After all, at least financially I'm the most successful private investigator in the world. If they know anything about me, they know I started out at the bottom of the heap, knee-deep in crap. And if they have any grasp of human nature, they know that guys like me, guys who live with a memory of hunger . . .

we're terriers; we bite into the rat and shake it, shake it, shake it; we never let go of the rat until he's dead, no matter how many times he bites us on the nose. Sooner or later I'll put together all of the pieces they give me; I'll know who they are and what they're doing with Joanna Rand and why."

"If you live long enough."

"Oh, I'll live," Alex said. "As you know, when it comes to self-defense I have no compunctions about killing. So I think you should take this message to them. Tell them that if they force me to squeeze out the story drop by drop, then I'll shout it to the world when I've got it all. I'll put a very public end to the Chelgrin case. On the other hand, if they save me the time and trouble, if they come to me and explain themselves, there's a slim chance that I'll find it advisable and acceptable to keep my mouth shut. It's up to them. One way or the other, I'll have the secret."

"You're insane if you think they'll sit down and talk to you," Shifty said, almost sneering. "You haven't the faintest idea what's at stake."

"Neither have you," Alex said. "Don't try to make yourself sound important. They haven't told you much. You're an errand boy. So just deliver the message. I'll expect a call from them at the hotel before noon tomorrow. And tell them I'm tired of this game already. I don't like having my room searched, getting cut up, being followed, and messing in dirty little alley fights. They'd better put a stop to this. And if they don't want to stop it, then they'd better understand that I can be a vindictive son of a bitch."

"So can I," Shifty said.

"I'm faster and smarter than you, my friend. You better pray to God for the strength to overcome your vindictiveness this time."

Still aiming the gun at him, Alex backed off. When they were separated by approximately twenty yards of pavement, Alex turned and walked away. At the end of the alley, before Alex rounded the corner, he glanced back at Shifty.

The man was still sitting against the wall. He hadn't moved an inch. He wasn't going to give Alex the slightest excuse for shooting him.

Alex switched the safeties on the pistol. He tucked the gun under his belt, against his belly, and buttoned his suit jacket over it.

Shifty didn't get up.

Alex turned the corner and walked swiftly through the maze toward the major thoroughfares of the Gion.

It was dark.

It was cold.

He wished he didn't have to sleep alone tonight.

• 18 •

In the lightless room, on the bed, staring at the shadowy ceiling, Joanna startled herself by saying aloud: "Alex." She spoke unexpectedly, involuntarily—a soft cry for help. It was almost as if the single word had come from someone else; but there was no one with her —which, in fact, was the reason she had cried out.

The name seemed to reverberate in the air for a couple of minutes while Joanna contemplated all of the meanings it had for her.

She felt miserable. She was being forced, as she had been so many times in the past, to choose between a man and her obsessive need for an extraordinary degree of privacy. This time, however, she knew that either choice would destroy her. She was on the edge. Her strength had been drained by years of unquestioning obedience to the devil within her that demanded this unnatural solitude. She felt weak. Helpless. If she pursued Alex Hunter, the world would close like a vise around her; the ceiling, walls, and floor, the earth and the sky would squeeze her in a claustrophobic nightmare, crushing the juice of sanity from her, leaving only the dry fibers of madness. But if she did not pursue him, she would have to face and accept with finality the most important truth about herself: *She would always be alone.* Such resignation and the dreary future that it ensured also encompassed the prospect of madness. Either way, she would soon have no more endurance for pain of any sort.

However, it was now two o'clock in the morning, and she couldn't tolerate thinking about her predicament any longer. Her head ached; her eyes burned; her body felt as if it was made of lead. She had to get to sleep. In sleep there would be a few hours free of stress and anxiety—at least until she was awakened once again by the nightmare.

She raised herself from the sheets, sat on the edge of the bed. Without switching on the light, she opened the nightstand drawer and located the small bottle of sleeping tablets, a prescription drug upon which she had to depend more nights than not. She had taken one sedative an hour ago, but she wasn't even drowsy; one more couldn't possibly do any damage.

But then she thought: *Why just one more? Why not take every damned pill I've got?*

Her exhaustion, her terror of being alone forever, and her depression were so grave that she did not reject the idea immediately, as she would have done only yesterday.

In the darkness, like a penitent reverently fingering rosary beads, Joanna counted tablets.

Twenty.

Surely enough for a long sleep.

Oh, no. No, no. Don't call it a long sleep, she told herself sourly. *Don't use euphemisms. Hold on to that much self-respect. Be honest with yourself, if nothing else. Call it what it is. Suicide. Does that word scare you? Suicide. Suicide.*

She was not frightened, offended, or embarrassed by the word; and she knew that her weary acceptance represented a terrible loss of will. Until now she had

not realized that there had been a gradual eating away
of the steel resolve and personal ambition in which
she had always taken pride. She was caught in a
maelstrom of evil, that special evil of weakness and
easy surrender to fate that grew from insidious self-
hatred. Seeing such ugliness in herself, she should have
gotten angry; she should have fought back; she should
have cheered herself with a recitation of all her fine
qualities and many good deeds, with an optimistic
prediction of all the wonderful things that she could
do and be and have if only she went on living. Even
if the stalking enemy was herself in the form of a
suicidal compulsion, she should have waged a desperate, relentless battle for survival. But she did not. She
had absolutely no resources left. She merely sat on the
edge of the bed and recounted the sleeping tablets.

Suicide.

The word, once taboo, now seemed musical, filled
with promise. No more loneliness. No more wanting
love with all her mind and body but fleeing from it.
No more feeling that she didn't belong, that she was
inadequate, that she was very different from all other
people. No more doubts. No more pain of any sort.
No more nightmares, visions of syringes and grasping
mechanical hands. No more.

At least for the moment, Joanna did not have to
choose between Alex Hunter and her sick compulsion
to smash love when and where it arose. Now the
choice was simpler yet far more profound. She had to
decide whether to take one more pill—or all twenty.

She held them in her cupped hands.

They were smooth and cool like tiny pebbles from
a creek bed.

• 19 •

Alex was accustomed to wasting as little time in sleep as possible; but this night he was not going to have even the few hours of rest he required. His mind raced; he couldn't downshift it.

Finally he got up, fetched a bottle of beer from the pantry, and sat in an armchair in the drawing room. The only light was that which came through the tall windows—the pale, ghostly luminescence of predawn Kyoto.

Alex analyzed his situation, walked around it in his mind as if it were a piece of sculpture. He wondered what Shifty's bosses would do next. Perhaps they would actually telephone and tell him enough about the Chelgrin case to buy him off, as he had suggested to their errand boy. On the other hand, there was not much chance of them changing their style merely because he told them they should. They would figure that he couldn't be bought with either information or money, and they would be correct in that assumption. Nevertheless, the phone might ring; the possibility could not be ruled out altogether. More likely than not, they would opt for an escalation of violence. Beat him up. Put him out of action. Teach him a lesson. Maybe even murder him. He was not particularly impressed by the danger. Other people had tried to kill him and had lived—briefly, in two cases —to regret it. He had come to private investigation with a talent for staying alive (one of the few advantages of growing up in poverty and domestic chaos, under the quick, heavy hands of alcoholic parents who regarded child abuse as an acceptable release of tension), and over the years he had explored, developed, and honed that talent.

In fact, it was not worry or fear that kept Alex awake. When he was honest with himself, he had to admit that the single cause of his insomnia was Joanna Rand. A torrent of images cascaded through his mind: Joanna in the tan pantsuit that she had worn to lunch at Mizutani; Joanna on the stage of the Moonglow Lounge, moving sinuously in a clinging, red silk dress; Joanna laughing; Joanna tossing her head and tucking her hair behind her ears with a swift flutter of her hands . . . He wanted to massage her supple body, caress her, comb her golden hair with his fingers, learn the shape and texture of her breasts and belly and hips and buttocks; he wanted to make love to her and feel her respond. When he lay in bed, seeking sleep, he could think of nothing but the way she would be against, above, and beneath him. He had an erection that felt as stout and large as a post. His unremitting state of heat amused and embarrassed him. *Like an adolescent with no self-control,* he thought. It had been many years since any woman had generated such intense fantasies for him.

What he found most interesting and disturbing, however, was the fact that lust was neither the only nor the most powerful emotion that she stirred in him. He felt a tenderness toward Joanna that was more than affection; he had a liking for her that was stronger than friendship.

Not love.

He didn't believe in love.

His parents had proved to him that love was a word that had no meaning; it was a sham, an emotional drug with which people deluded themselves, a tissue-paper wall behind which they concealed their true feelings and hid from themselves all knowledge of the primitive jungle reality of life. Occasionally and always with apparent sincerity, his mother and father had told him that they loved Little Alex. (His father was Big Alex;

and often it seemed to him that his mother hurt him most severely when she was angriest with the old man, and that Big Alex, too, was nastiest with Little Alex when transported by fits of self-loathing.) Sometimes, when the mood seized them—usually after the morning's hangover had been conquered but before the new day's intake of whisky had awakened the dragons in them—they hugged Little Alex and wept and loudly despised themselves for what they had done, for the latest black eye or bruise or cut or burn that they had administered. When they felt especially guilty they bought lots of inexpensive gifts for Little Alex —comic books, cheap toys, candy, ice cream—as if a war had ended and reparations were required. But this thing they called love had never lasted. It faded in a few hours and vanished altogether within a day or two. Eventually Alex had come to dread his parents' slobbering, boozy displays of "love"; for when love waned, as it always did, the anger and hostility and brutality seemed worse by comparison with the brief interlude of peace. At its best, love was just a seasoning, like pepper or salt, which was used to enhance the bitter flavor of loneliness, hatred, and pain.

Therefore, he had not, would not, and simply could not fall in love with Joanna Rand. He did feel something for her, something rather strong, but he didn't know what to call it. More than lust and affection. Something new. And strange. Although he was not falling in love, he knew he was sailing in uncharted waters and needed caution for a guide.

He drank two bottles of beer and returned to bed. He couldn't get comfortable. He lay on his back, right side, stomach, in every position permitted by his injured left arm. The injury wasn't the problem; Joanna was. Finally he tried to banish the vivid images of her by picturing the hypnotic motion of the sea, the gracefully rolling masses of water, the endless chains of waves that surged through the night and broke on the beach, the spume that was cast like lace shawls into the air; and he did grow sleepy after a time, but he did not manage to bar her from his mind, for she appeared as a mermaid riding the crests of the waves, a series of mermaids, a hundred million Joannas with sleek fishy tails and fins, all hundred million parading toward the beach, rolling and surging and breaking, rolling, surging. . . .

An alarm sounded.

Alex sat up in bed as if thrust forward by a spring. He groped in the dark for the pistol he had taken from Shifty and found it on the nightstand, where he had left it. He got out of bed and stood swaying as if he were in a strong wind.

Then he realized that the ringing was the telephone. He put the gun back where he had gotten it and sat down on the edge of the mattress.

According to the luminous dial on the travel clock, it was four-thirty in the morning. He had been asleep less than an hour.

He picked up the receiver, expecting to hear the voice of one of Shifty's bosses. "Yes?"

"Is that you, Alex-san?"

"Mariko-san?" Alex asked, surprised.

"I'm sorry to wake you," she said.

He was confused. Mariko? At this hour?

"It's all right," he said.

"Joanna asked me to call you."

"I'm listening."

"Can you come here right away?"

His heart began to pound.

"Where? The Moonglow?"

"Yes."

"What's wrong?"

"A very bad thing has happened, Alex-san."

"A very bad thing . . . to Joanna?"

"Yes."

He shuddered. He was suddenly nauseated.

Mariko sounded as if she were going to cry. "Alex-san, she tried . . ." Her voice trailed away.

"Mariko! For God's sake, tell me!"

Mariko got hold of herself, drew a deep breath. The words came out in a rush, as if they were one word: "Joanna-tried-to-kill-herself."

· 20 ·

The taxi dropped Alex at the Moonglow Lounge.

The sky was still spitting snow, but the accumulation on the streets was less than a quarter of an inch.

Mariko was waiting for him at the front door.

"Where's Joanna?" he asked as he stepped inside.

"Upstairs, Alex-san."

"How is she?"

"She'll be all right."

"You're sure?"

"The doctor's with her."

"And he said she'd be okay?"

"Yes."

"Is he a good doctor?"

"He's treated her for years."

"A specialist might—"

"No need. And what kind of doctor specializes in ... this sort of thing?"

"I mean, I can afford the best."

Mariko smiled. "That's very kind. But Joanna is not poor, you know. And I assure you, Alex-san, that our Doctor Mifuni is capable of handling it."

He followed Mariko past the bar with the blue mirror, into an elegantly decorated office, up a set of stairs to Joanna's apartment.

The living room was furnished with cane, rattan, wicker, many potted plants, and half a dozen excellent Japanese watercolors painted on scrolls.

"She's in the bedroom with the doctor," Mariko said. "We'll wait here."

They sat on the couch.

"Was it a gun?" Alex asked.

"A gun?"

"What did she use?"

"Oh. Sleeping tablets."

"Who found her?"

"She found me. I have a three-room apartment on this floor. I had gone to bed at one o'clock. I was asleep and I heard . . . I heard her . . . I . . ." Mariko's voice broke. She trembled uncontrollably.

Alex put one hand on her shoulder. "It's all right now, isn't it?" he asked. "You said she'd pull through."

Mariko bit her lip and nodded. "She came into my room and woke me. She said, 'Mariko-san, I'm afraid I'm making a goddamned silly fool of myself, as usual.' "

"Jesus."

"There were twenty pills in the bottle," Mariko said. "Joanna took fourteen before she realized suicide wasn't the answer. She asked me to call an ambulance."

"Why isn't she in the hospital?"

"The paramedics came with emergency equipment," Mariko said. "They made her swallow a tube. . . . They pumped out her stomach right here." She closed her eyes and grimaced.

"I've seen it done," Alex said. "It isn't pleasant."

"I couldn't watch, but I held her hand. By the time they were finished, Doctor Mifuni arrived. He talked to her and examined her. He didn't think a hospital was necessary."

Alex looked at the bedroom door. What was going on in there? Had complications set in?

He looked at Mariko again and said, "Is this the first time she tried to kill herself?"

"Of course!"

"Some people make a habit of it."

"Are you serious?"

"Yes."

"Well, not Joanna."

"Do you think she actually intended to kill herself?" Alex asked.

"To begin with, yes."

"What changed her mind?"

"She realized it was wrong."

"Some people only pretend suicide."

"What are you saying?"

"They want sympathy and—"

She interrupted him. Her voice was like the cold steam rising from dry ice. "If you think Joanna would stoop to such a thing, then you don't know her at all." Mariko's body was stiff with anger. Her small hands were fisted on her lap. She glared at Alex.

He thought about it and said, "You're right. Joanna just isn't that petty or selfish."

Mariko watched him closely for a moment, until she saw that he meant what he said; then some of the stiffness went out of her.

"But I wouldn't think she's the type to seriously consider suicide either," Alex said.

"She was terribly depresssed before she met you. Then after she . . . rejected you . . . it got worse. For at least one minute there, she was so far down that she was capable of suicide. But she's strong. Even stronger than my mama-san, who is an iron lady. Joanna was able to beat the depression at the last minute."

The bedroom door opened, and Doctor Mifuni walked into the living room.

Mariko and Alex got up.

Mifuni was a short man with a round face and thick black hair. When meeting someone new, the Japanese were quick to smile. Mifuni was somber.

Has something gone wrong? Alex wondered. His mouth was suddenly dry as talcum.

Even under these less than ideal circumstances, Mariko took the time to formally introduce the two men, with a good word said about the qualities of each. And now there were smiles all around.

Alex wanted to yell at them to shut up; he wanted to grab the doctor by the lapels and shake him until he told them about Joanna. At the same time he wondered why he was so deeply, frantically, concerned about a woman he had known for such a short time.

He controlled his violent impulse and bowed to the doctor. "Isha-san, *dozo yoroshiku.*"

Mifuni bowed, too. "I am honored to make your acquaintance, Mr. Hunter."

"Is Joanna feeling better?" Mariko asked.

"I've given her something to calm her and help her sleep," Mifuni said. "However, there will be time for Mr. Hunter to talk with her before the sedative takes effect." He smiled at Alex. "She insists on seeing you."

Frightened by the emotional turmoil that gripped him, Alex walked slowly across the living room, stepped into the bedroom, and closed the door behind him.

• 21 •

Alex expected her to be drawn, haggard, marked by her ordeal; but she was beautiful. She was sitting up in bed, propped up with pillows. She wore blue silk pajamas that outlined her full breasts; he could see the tantalizing suggestion of nipples against the thin material. Although her hair was somewhat damp and lank, it was still soft enough and rich enough and golden enough to make him think again of combing it with his fingers. Of course she was terribly pale; there was a blue tracery of veins at her temples; she seemed translucent. Vague rings of weariness outlined her eyes; but those could have passed for smudges of mascara. It was only in her amethyst-blue eyes that the suffering showed; and the pain he saw there made him weak.

Joanna patted the edge of the bed, and he sat down beside her.

"What happened to your arm?" she asked.

"A cut. It's nothing serious."

"Have you seen a doctor?"

"It didn't even need stitches."

They were silent for a while.

At last she said, "What must you think of me?"

"I think you look lovely."

"I'm a mess."

"Well, if you can bottle something to make other women look as good as you do when you're a mess, then you'll make millions of dollars in the cosmetics business."

"My God," Joanna said, "I thought only Cary Grant could be that charming. No wonder women swoon over you."

"Do they?"

"Don't they?"

"Swoon? Really?"

"Don't be so modest."

"Have you swooned over me?"

With surprising shyness, she said, "You're going to make me blush, and I haven't blushed in years."

"I'd like to see some color in your face."

"Listen," she said, "the doctor gave me a sedative. But before I fall asleep, I've got something important to say to you."

"I'm listening."

"Do you still think I don't know who I am?"

"If you're asking me whether I still believe you're Lisa Chelgrin—yes."

"How can you be so positive?"

"There have been developments since we had lunch."

"What developments?" she asked.

"I'm being followed everywhere I go."

"By whom?"

"I need time to explain."

"I'm not going anywhere."

"Your eyes are beginning to droop."

She blinked hard. "I reached the breaking point tonight. I almost did a stupid thing."

"Hush. It's over."

"I knew I either had to die—or find out why I behave the way I do."

He held her hand.

"There's something wrong with me," she said. "I've always felt so hollow, empty—detached. Something happened to me a long time ago, something to make me the way I am. I'm not just making excuses for myself, Alex."

"I realize that," he said. "God knows what they did to you."

"I have to find out what it was."

"You will," he said.

"I've got to know his name."

"Whose name?"

"The man with the mechanical hand."

"We'll find him."

"He's dangerous."

"So am I."

Joanna slid down on the bed until she was flat on her back. "Dammit, I don't want to go to sleep yet."

He took one of the two pillows from beneath her head and drew up the covers.

Her voice was getting thick. "There was a room . . . a room that stank of antiseptics . . . maybe a hospital somewhere."

"We'll find it."

"I want to hire you to help me."

"I've already been hired. Senator Chelgrin paid me a small fortune to find his daughter. It's about time I gave him something for his money."

"You'll come back tomorrow?"

"Yes."

"What time?" she asked.

"Whenever you want."

"One o'clock."

"I'll be here then."

"What if I'm not awake by then?"

"I'll wait."

She was silent so long that he thought she had fallen asleep. Then she said, "I was so scared."

"It's all right now."

"I'm still scared . . . but not as bad as I was."

"Everything will be fine."

"I'm glad you're here, Alex."

"So am I."

She turned onto her side.

She slept.

The only sound was the faint hum of the electric clock.

Neither of us used the word "love," Alex thought.

After a while he kissed her forehead and left the room.

· 22 ·

Mariko was sitting on the couch. Mifuni had gone.

"The sedative worked," Alex said.

"The doctor told me she'd sleep for five or six hours. He'll be back this afternoon."

"You'll stay here with her?"

"Of course." She got up. She straightened the collar of the heavy, shapeless, brown robe that she wore. "Would you like some tea?"

"That would be nice."

While they sat at the small kitchen table, sipping tea and nibbling almond wafers, Alex told Mariko Inamura all about the Chelgrin case, about the burglar he had found in his hotel suite, and about the man he had met in the Gion alleyway a few hours ago.

"Incredible," Mariko said. "But *why?* Why would

they change the girl's name, identity . . . *change her
complete set of memories* . . . and bring her to Kyoto?"

"I haven't any idea," Alex said. "But I'll find out.
Look, Mariko, I've told you this so you'll understand
that there are dangerous people manipulating Joanna.
They've gotten nasty with me, and when they learn that
she's asked for my help, they'll get even nastier.
Tonight, when you opened the door for me downstairs,
you didn't ask who was there. From now on you've
got to be more careful."

"But I was expecting you," she said.

"That doesn't matter. From now on, when someone
rings the bell, don't open the door until you know who
it is. Do you have a gun?"

"Surely they wouldn't harm Joanna."

"The worst thing we can do is underestimate them."

"We can't possibly protect her every minute. What
about when she appears on stage? She's a perfect
target then."

"If I have anything to say about it, she won't perform again until this is settled."

"But in spite of all the horrible things they've done
to her, they haven't hurt her physically."

"If they know she's investigating her past, and if
they think she might learn enough to expose them,
they could get very rough. You've got to keep in mind
that we don't know who they are or what's at stake
for them."

She thought for a moment. Then: "I can't imagine
anyone wanting to hurt Joanna. But I suppose you
know all kinds of people that I don't."

"Exactly. They're the kind you never want to meet."

"All right. I'll do as you say. I'll be careful."

"Good."

He finished his cup of tea while she telephoned the
Sogo Taxi Company for him.

At the downstairs door, as he stepped into the street,
Mariko said, "Alex-san, you won't be sorry that you
helped her."

"I didn't expect to be."

"You'll find what you've been looking for in life."

He raised his eyebrows. "I thought I'd found it already."

"No. You need Joanna as much as she needs you."

"You've told me that before," Alex said.

"Have I?"

"You know you have."

She smiled, bowed to him, and assumed an air of oriental wisdom that was partly a joke and partly serious. "Honorable detective should know that repetition of a truth does not make it any less true, and resistance to the truth can never be more than a temporary folly."

She closed the door, and Alex stood by it until he heard the lock slide into place.

The taxi was waiting for him.

A red Toyota followed his cab all the way to the hotel.

· 23 ·

Exhaustion overcame insomnia. Alex slept four hours and got out of bed at ten minutes past eleven, Friday morning.

He shaved and showered quickly; decided that he shouldn't take time to change the bandage on his arm. He wanted to be ready to meet the courier from Chicago in case the man arrived a few minutes early.

He went into the walk-in closet to choose a suit, and the telephone rang. He picked it up in the bedroom. "Hello?"

"Mr. Hunter?"

"Yes."

"We met last night."

"Dr. Mifuni?"

"Who?"

"Who is this?" Alex asked.

"You have my pistol."

Shifty.

"Go on," Alex said.

"My superiors have instructed me to tell you that they'll be sending a message within the hour."

"You mean they're willing to cooperate?"

Shifty hung up.

Alex put down the receiver. "What was the purpose of that?" he wondered aloud. "Was he making a promise or a threat?" He considered the brief conversation for a minute, replayed it in his mind, and finally said, "Threat."

He dressed hurriedly. He slipped the 7 mm. automatic inside his shirt, buttoned up. If he left the suite he would also button his suit coat. The weapon was too cumbersome to ride under his belt all day; and although it was not easily contained inside his shirt, at least now he could sit down without being poked in the groin.

He didn't know of any country in the world where it was legal to carry a concealed silencer-equipped handgun without a permit. He had made the choice between being a live criminal and a good but dead citizen.

He waited in the drawing room.

At eight minutes past noon, there was a sharp knocking on the door.

Alex went into the foyer. He withdrew the pistol from his shirt and said, "Who's there?"

"Bellhop, Mr. Hunter."

Under the circumstances, those three words were too much of a cliché to be anything but the truth.

Alex opened the door but left the security chain in place. The chain was pretty much useless; it wouldn't hold if someone hit the door hard. But perhaps it would give him the edge, that extra second or two he would need to stay alive.

The man in the corridor was one of the two bell-hops who had brought Alex's luggage upstairs when he'd checked into the hotel. He was clearly distressed. He fidgeted. "I'm sorry I have to disturb you, Mr. Hunter. But I must ask—do you know a man named Kennedy?"

The unexpected question stumped Alex for a moment. Then he blinked and said, "Yes, of course. He works for me."

"There's been an accident."

"When?"

"Fifteen minutes ago. Not much longer than that," the bellhop said nervously. "A car. Right in front of the hotel."

Blakenship hadn't mentioned the courier's name in the cablegram; Kennedy was the man.

The bellhop said, "The ambulance crew wants to take Mr. Kennedy to the hospital, but every time they get close to him he kicks and punches and bites them."

Alex thought he had misunderstood. They were speaking Japanese, and the bellhop was talking very fast. "Did you say he kicks and punches them?"

"Yes, sir. And bites. He refuses to let anyone touch him or take him away until he talks to you. The police don't want to handle him because they're afraid of aggravating his injuries."

"I'll be with you in a second."

Alex had been holding the pistol out of the bellhop's line of vision. Now he closed the door, stuffed the gun inside his shirt, buttoned both his shirt and suit coat, released the safety chain, and opened the door again.

They ran to the elevator alcove. Another bellhop was holding one of the lifts for them.

On the way down, Alex said, "Did you see it happen?"

"Yes," said the first bellhop. "Mr. Kennedy got out of the taxi, and a red Toyota angled through traffic, jumped the curb and hit him."

"Do they have the driver?"

"He got away."

"He didn't stop?"

"No, sir."

"What's Mr. Kennedy's condition?"

"It's his leg," said the first bellhop. He studiously avoided Alex's eyes.

"Broken?" Alex asked.

The first bellhop didn't want to talk about it.

"There's a lot of blood," said the second bellhop.

The hotel lobby was nearly deserted. Everyone except the desk clerks was at the scene of the accident in the street, just outside.

Alex pushed through the crowd until he saw Wayne Kennedy. The man was sitting on the sidewalk with his back against the building. There was an open space on three sides of Wayne, as if he were a wild animal that no one dared approach. He was flanked by two suitcases, both of them blood-smeared and badly battered; and he kept a hand on one of them. He was shouting furiously at a white-uniformed ambulance attendant who had dared to venture within five feet of him but who was reluctant to go closer than that.

Kennedy was an impressive sight. He was a handsome black man, about thirty years old, with a modified afro haircut and a penchant for clothes that were as stylish and nearly as expensive as those that Alex wore. But it was not Kennedy's good looks nor the color of his skin nor the high quality of his wardrobe that kept the paramedics at bay. They were intimidated by Wayne's size and ferocity, as any prudent man should have been. Kennedy was six foot five and weighed at least two hundred and forty pounds, all bone and muscle. Wild-eyed, cursing at the top of his voice, shaking one huge fist at the medics—he seemed to be constructed of big chunks of stone, two-by-fours, railroad ties, and railroad bolts; not like mortal men; Gargantua.

When Alex glimpsed Kennedy's injuries, he was stunned and doubly impressed by the man's screaming, fist-swinging bravado. The leg wasn't just broken; it was crushed. A splinter of bone had pierced the flesh and trousers. The pants were soaked with blood.

Alex pushed past the innermost ring of onlookers and started toward Kennedy.

The black man caught the movement from the corner of his eye, turned his head, shouting, then saw who it was. "Thank God you're here," he said.

Alex knelt beside him.

Kennedy slumped back as if someone had cut strings that were supporting him. He seemed also to grow smaller; and the wildness, the maniacal power that had charged him, vanished. He was dripping sweat and shaking with fever chills. His face was contorted, a graphic illustration of pain. His eyes bulged. He was on the verge of shock; and it was amazing that he had summoned sufficient adrenalin to hold everyone off for a quarter of an hour.

"Have you really punched the medics, like they say?"

"None of the bastards speaks English!" Kennedy said, as if Chicagoans, in a reverse of the situation, would have held forth in fluent Japanese. "You don't know . . . what I had to go through . . . to find someone who spoke English. I couldn't . . . let them cart me off . . . until I'd delivered the file to you." He indicated the suitcase at his side.

"Good God, man, the file isn't *that* important!"

"It must be," Kennedy said. "Someone tried . . . to kill me for it. This wasn't . . . an accident."

"How do you know that?"

"I saw the son of a bitch coming," Kennedy said. He was wincing with pain. "A red Toyota. I stepped . . . out of his way . . . but he turned straight toward me."

Alex signaled the medics, and they rushed in with a stretcher.

"Two men . . . in the Toyota," Kennedy said.

"Save your strength," Alex said. "You can tell me all about it later."

"I'd rather . . . talk now. Keeps my mind off . . . the pain. The Toyota hit me . . . knocked me into the wall . . . ass over tea kettle . . . pinned me there . . . then backed off. The guy on the passenger side . . . got

out and made a grab for the suitcase. We played . . .
tug of war with it . . . for a while. Then I bit his hand
. . . pretty nearly chewed off the bastard's thumb. He
gave up."

Alex knew that the message from Shifty's bosses had
been delivered.

With considerable effort the paramedics lifted Kennedy onto the wheeled stretcher.

The black man howled as he was moved. Tears burst
from him and streamed down his face.

The wheeled legs of the stretcher folded under as it
was shoved into the van-type ambulance.

Alex picked up the suitcase that contained the
Chelgrin file and followed Kennedy. No one tried to
stop him. In the van he sat on a built-in stool at the
patient's feet.

Someone slammed the rear doors.

One of the paramedics stayed with Kennedy. He
began to prepare an intravenous plasma transfusion.

The ambulance began to move. The siren wailed.

Without raising his head from the stretcher, Kennedy said, "You still there?"

"Right here," Alex said.

Kennedy's voice was twisted with pain, but he
wouldn't be quiet. "You think I'm a fool?"

"What do you mean?"

"Waiting for you like I did."

Alex was staring at the hideously crumpled leg that
was still shrouded by the trousers. "Wayne, for Christ's
sake, you were sitting there bleeding to death!"

"If you'd been . . . in my shoes . . . you'd have done
the same."

"Never in a million years, my friend."

"Oh, yeah. You would have. I know you," Kennedy
insisted. "You hate to lose."

The paramedic cut away the coat and shirt on Kennedy's left arm. He swabbed the ebony skin with an
alcohol-damp sterile pad, then quickly placed the needle in the vein.

Kennedy's bad leg twitched. He groaned and cleared

his throat. He said, "I've got something to say . . . Mr. Hunter . . . but maybe I shouldn't."

"Say it before you choke on it," Alex told him. "Then shut the hell up if you don't want to talk yourself to death."

The ambulance turned the corner so sharply that Alex had to grab a safety rail to keep from sliding off the stool.

"You and me . . . we're alike in a lot of ways. I mean . . . like you started out with nothing . . . so did I. You were determined to make it . . . to the top . . . and you did. *I'm* determined to . . . make it . . . and I will. We're both smooth . . . on the surface . . . and street fighters underneath."

Alex was beginning to think the man was delirious, but he answered anyway. "I know all that, Wayne. Why do you think I hired you? I knew you'd be the same kind of field man that I was when I started."

Grinding the words out between clenched teeth, Kennedy said, "So I'd like to suggest . . . when you get back . . . to the States . . . and you've got to make a decision . . . about filling Bob Feldman's job . . . don't forget me."

Bob Feldman was in charge of the company's entire force of field operatives, and he was retiring in two months.

"I get things done," Kennedy said. "I'm right . . . for the job . . . Mr. Hunter."

Alex laughed and shook his head. "I can almost believe you traveled halfway around the world and *arranged* to be hit by that goddamned car just so you could trap me in here for that sales pitch."

"I'm a hustler," Kennedy said. "I don't believe . . . in wasting an opportunity."

"I know," Alex said. "And I like that."

"You'll keep me in mind?"

"I'll do better than that. I'll give you the job."

Kennedy raised his head. "You mean that?"

"I said it, didn't I?"

"Every cloud," Kennedy said, "has a silver lining."

After Wayne Kennedy was taken into surgery, Alex used a hospital phone to call Joanna.

Mariko answered. "She's still asleep, Alex-san."

He told her what had happened. "So I'm going to stay here until Wayne comes out of surgery and the doctors can tell me whether the leg stays or goes. I won't be able to get to your place by one o'clock, like I promised Joanna."

"Of course not," Mariko said. "You belong there with your friend. I'll explain to her."

"I don't want her to think I'm backing out."

"She'll understand."

"Does Joanna have a spare bedroom?" he asked.

"For your Mr. Kennedy?"

"No," Alex said. "He'll be staying here for quite a while. The room would be for me. These people we're up against only know one way to play the game. They're crude. They're going to resort to more and more violence. I don't think either you or Joanna ought to be alone until this is finished. Besides, it's better strategy to work out of one place. It saves time. I'd like to check out of the hotel and move in with you—if it won't ruin anyone's reputation."

"I'll prepare the spare room, Alex-san."

"You're sure it'll be all right?"

"Don't give it another thought."

"I'll be there as soon as I can."

"I'll keep the doors locked."

"These people are scum, Mariko."

"Worse," she said.

"They aren't going to scare me off."

"Good," Mariko said.

"We aren't quitting until we know what was done to Joanna and why."

"Good," Mariko said.

"We'll nail the bastards to the barn wall."

"Excellent," Mariko said.

His anger, level of energy, and determination were greater now than at any time in the past five years. Until this moment he hadn't realized that success had dampened the fire in him. His fortune, his eighteen-room house, and his Rolls Royces had mellowed him. But now, once again, he was a driven man.

PART TWO

CLUES

The hanging bridge;
Creeping vines
Entwine our life.

—Bashô, 1644–1694

• 25 •

At six o'clock the chief surgeon, Doctor Ito, came to the hospital lounge where Alex was waiting. The doctor was a thin, elegant man in his fifties. He had been working on Wayne Kennedy for five hours. He looked tired, but he smiled because he brought good news. Amputation would not be necessary. Kennedy wasn't entirely out of danger. There was the chance of phlebitis after such extensive tissue damage; and in the future there might be a need for further surgery. More likely than not, Kennedy would limp for the rest of his life, but at least he would walk on his own two legs.

Doctor Ito was leaving the lounge when Mariko arrived in the company of an armed plainclothes guard. Alex had hired a private security firm to mount a twenty-four-hour-a-day watch over Kennedy. It probably was not necessary; Shifty's bosses had already made their point; but he owed Kennedy the best protection available. Mariko was there to take over the vigil from Alex and free him so that he could move his things from his hotel to the Moonglow. When Kennedy came out of anesthesia, he would need to see a friendly face other than those of the nurses and the guard, and he would want someone close by who spoke fluent English.

Joanna had not been left alone at the apartment above the Moonglow. Doctor Mifuni was with her.

The bodyguard stood at the door of the lounge, watchful.

Alex led Mariko to the far end of the room. They sat on a yellow leatherette couch and spoke in whispers. "The police will want to talk to Wayne," Alex told her.

"Tonight? The way he is?"

"Probably not until tomorrow when he's got his wits about him. So when he wakes up and you're certain he understands what you're saying, tell him that I want him to cooperate with the cops—"

"Of course."

"—but only up to a point."

Mariko frowned.

"He should give them a description of the car and the men in it," Alex said. "But he mustn't tell them about the file he was carrying from Chicago. He'll have to pretend he's just an ordinary tourist. He hasn't any idea why they were trying to steal his suitcase. There was nothing in it but underwear and shirts. Got that?"

Mariko nodded. "But wouldn't it be better to tell the police everything and have them working for us?"

"No. We want to put pressure on the men we're after —but not too much pressure. Just enough to keep them nervous. Just enough to put them on edge and keep them there until they make a mistake. They tend to react violently even when they've got the upper hand. If they found out we'd spilled the entire story to the cops, if they felt cornered, they'd be even more vicious. Later on it may be necessary to go to the police—or to threaten to go to them in order to get what we want from these people. But not yet."

Mariko's traditional Japanese upbringing had instilled in her a respect for authority that was as much a part of her as grain is a part of wood. "But the police have the facilities and the manpower to—"

Alex interrupted. "There's something else to consider. Another possibility. The Chelgrin-Rand transformation might not be quite so tightly held a secret as it seems. Are Joanna's forged passport and phony identification really so convincing that no one's ever doubted them? Hasn't anyone wondered about her— not even for a minute?"

"What do you mean?"

"The cops, at least a few of them, might be in on it. They might know more of the story than we do. And if they know—then they aren't friends of ours and never will be."

Mariko was amazed. "That's . . . paranoid."

"Yes," he said. "But it still could be true."

"In Japan the police—"

"Shall we take chances with Joanna's life?"

"No," Mariko said worriedly. "Of course not."

"Trust me."

"I do."

Alex stood and stretched. With the news that Wayne would not be an amputee, a reservoir of tension had begun to drain out of Alex. For more than five hours he had felt ready to burst. Now he was relaxed, even logy.

"I've arranged a private room for Wayne," he told Mariko. "You'd better go up there now. They'll be transferring him from the recovery room in a few minutes."

"Is it safe for you to leave here alone?" Mariko asked.

He picked up the suitcase that contained the Chelgrin file. "No problem," he said. "They think they've scared me off. For a while they'll be laying low, just watching."

He left her with the bodyguard.

Outside, the night was cold, but there was no snow falling. Fast-moving trains of clouds were back-lighted by the moon.

Alex took a taxicab to the hotel, packed his bags, and checked out of his suite. From the hospital to the hotel, then from the hotel to the Moonglow Lounge, he was followed by two men in a white Subaru.

By seven thirty he had deposited his things in the spare room at Joanna's place. It was a small but cozy room with a low, slanted ceiling and a pair of dormer windows.

Shortly before Doctor Mifuni left, Joanna darted into the kitchen to check on the dinner that she was preparing, and the physician took advantage of the moment to draw Alex aside and speak with him. "Once or twice a night, you should look in on her to be certain she is only sleeping."

"You don't think she'd try it again?"

"No, no," Mifuni said. "There's virtually no chance of that. It was strictly an impulsive thing she did, and she is not really impulsive by nature. Nevertheless . . ."

"I'll watch over her," Alex said softly.

"Good," Mifuni said. "I have known her since she first came to Kyoto. A singer who performs nearly every night is bound to have throat problems once in a while. I have treated her for that, and I have come to like her enormously. She's more than a patient; she's a friend, too." He sighed and shook his head. "She's an amazingly resilient woman, isn't she? Last night's experience appears to have left only minor psychological scars. And physically, she doesn't seem marked at all. She looks untouched."

Joanna returned from the kitchen to say good-bye to the doctor, and indeed she did look perfect. Even in faded jeans and a midnight-blue sweater with sleeves worn shiny at the elbows and tattered at the cuffs, she was a vision. To Alex she looked as elegant as if she had been wearing an expensive gown. Her eyes were quick and bright and penetrating; the dark rings that framed them last night were gone now. She was fresh, vibrant, no longer pale and drawn. She was the golden girl once more: beautiful, self-assured, glowing with health.

"*Arigato,* Isha-san."

"*Do itashimashita.*"

"*Konbanwa.*"

"*Konbanwa,* Joanna-san."

Suddenly, as he watched Joanna and Mifuni bowing to each other at the apartment door, Alex was caught up by a wave of desire so powerful, so poignant, that it transported him to a strange state of mind. As if the desire for her were a crystal lens with magical properties, he was able to see himself as he never had before. He felt that he had stepped out of himself to look back and down upon not only his body but his mind as well. As a dispassionate observer, he saw the familiar Alex Hunter, the carefully crafted persona that was on view to all the world—the quiet, self-assured, self-contained, determined, no-nonsense businessman—but he was also aware of an aspect of himself, his anima, which had never been visible to him until now. He saw that within the cool, analytical Alex Hunter there was an insecure, lonely, seeking, hungry creature driven by emotional needs and wants; it was as valid and real as the more externalized Alex. And as he stared down at this newly revealed self, he understood that he could see it now only because of Joanna. For the first time in his life, he was nearly overwhelmed by a desire that could not be satisfied through hard work and the application of his intellect; he was filled with a longing for something more abstract and spiritual than the comparatively impersonal goals such as success, money, and status. Joanna. He wanted Joanna. He wanted to touch her. He wanted to hold her. He wanted to make love to her. But he required much more than physical contact. He sought from her a number of things that he could only partially understand: a kind of peace that he could not describe; satisfactions he had never known; feelings he was unable to explain; a depth of commitment that he felt but could not probe with words; there were no words adequate to the task. In short, after a lifetime shaped by his unwavering denial of love's existence, he wanted love from Joanna Rand. Old convictions and reliable psychic crutches were not easily cast aside; he could not yet accept the reality of love—but a part of him desperately *wanted* to believe.

It scared him.

· 26 ·

Joanna wanted the dinner to be perfect. She viewed it as a crucial test; she had to pass it in order to convince him that she was still the capable and controlled woman he had first seen on the Moonglow stage, and that she was not the pathetic victim she had permitted him to glimpse last night. She needed to regain his complete confidence. She placed a great deal of importance on his trust. By planning, cooking, and serving a splendid meal, and by being the engaging conversationalist that she had been at lunch with him on Wednesday, she felt that she would be proving that last night's melodramatic act had been out of character, that it had been a momentary lapse that ought to be forgotten, an ugly aberration that couldn't happen again.

She served dinner at the low table in her Japanese-style dining room. She used royal-blue placemats, several shades of gray dinnerware, and dark red napkins. Six fresh white carnations were spread in a fan on one end of the table; and she sprinkled a few dozen loose petals around the stems.

The food was hearty but not heavy. *Igaguri:* thorny shrimp balls filled with sweet chestnuts. *Sumashi wan:* clear soup with soybean curd and shrimp. *Tatsuta age:* sliced beef garnished with red peppers and radish. *Yuan zuke:* grilled fish in soy-and-sake marinade. *Umani:* chicken and vegetables simmered in a richly seasoned broth. And of course they also had steamed rice—the most common staple of the Japanese menu—and they washed everything down with cups of hot tea.

The dinner was a success, and throughout it she felt

130

better than she had in many months. In a curious way,
the suicide attempt had been a beneficial experience,
for it had purged her of certain attitudes and fears that
had restricted her choices in life. Having reached the
bottom, having sunk deep into the ultimate despair,
having experienced at least a few minutes during which
she had no reason to live, Joanna knew that now she
could face anything that might come. The worst was
behind her. It was a cliché, but it was also true: there
was nowhere to go but up. For the first time she felt
that she could triumph over the paranoia and the
strange symptoms of claustrophobia that had destroyed
so many opportunities for happiness in the past.

Immediately after they had eaten, Joanna had a
chance to test her newfound strength. She and Alex
moved into the living room, sat on the sofa, and began
to look through the Chelgrin file, which filled both
halves of a large suitcase—and which, according to
Alex, held the true story of her first two decades of life.
It contained thick stacks of field investigators' reports in
the gray-and-green folders of the Bonner Security
Corporation, Alex's company; hundreds of transcrip-
tions of interviews with potential witnesses, as well as
with friends and relatives of Lisa Chelgrin; plus copies
of the Jamaican police records and other official documents. There were five or six thousand pages in all—
many of them onionskin, some of them Xeroxes, and
some of them in the form of handwritten memos in
pocket notebooks. The sight of all that evidence and the
realization of what it might mean had a negative effect
on Joanna; for the first time that day, she felt threatened. The familiar strains of paranoia played like
distant, ominous music in her mind and gradually grew
louder.

More than anything else in the suitcase, the photographs disturbed Joanna. Here was Lisa Chelgrin in
jeans and a T-shirt, standing in front of a Cadillac
convertible, smiling and waving at the camera. Here
was Lisa Chelgrin in a bikini, posed at the foot of an
enormous palm tree. Here was Lisa Chelgrin in close-

up, just her face, grinning. A dozen photos in all. Snapshots and eight-by-ten glossies. The settings in which Lisa posed and the people with whom she was occasionally photographed meant nothing whatsoever to Joanna; however, the young girl herself—blonde, with a full but lithe figure—was as familiar as the image in a mirror. For a long while Joanna stared in disbelief at the face of the missing woman. She shivered as if a cold breath had been expelled against the back of her neck, and finally she got up and retrieved a half-dozen photographs of her own from a box in the bedroom closet. These had been taken the first year she was in Japan, when she had been working in Yokohama. She laid them out on the coffee table with the photos from the Chelgrin file. As she studied the resemblance, a dynamic but formless fear stirred in her.

"It's a remarkable likeness, isn't it?" Alex asked.

"Identical," she said weakly.

"You see why I was so certain the moment I saw you?"

Symptoms of claustrophobia streamed up from the well of her psyche. Suddenly the air was almost too thick to breathe. The room was warm. Hot. Blazing. The walls seemed to move in and out like living membranes, and the ceiling was coming down, relentlessly down, slowly down upon her. Although she knew it was her imagination, she was nonetheless terrified of being crushed to death.

"Joanna? Is something wrong?"

She was trembling violently.

Speaking for only part of her but speaking with tremendous force, a voice inside of her said: *Tell the bastard to pack up his stinking pictures and his goddamned reports! Tell him to get the hell out of here! Tell him. Do it. Now! He must not learn the truth. Nobody can be permitted to know about you. Get rid of him. Quickly!*

"Joanna?"

"The walls are closing in again," she said in a whisper filled with fear.

"Walls?" Alex looked around, perplexed.

To her, the room appeared to be only one-third its former size.

The air was so hot and dry that it scorched her lungs, parched her lips.

"And the ceiling," she said. "Coming lower."

She was sweating. Dissolving in the heat. Melting. As if she were made of wax.

"Is that really what you see?" Alex asked.

"Yes."

She stared at the walls, willed them to return to their true dimensions. She was determined not to let fear get the best of her this time.

"You're hallucinating," Alex said.

"I know." Briefly she told him about the extreme claustrophobia and paranoia that gripped her whenever someone became too interested in her past and whenever she enjoyed more than a casual affair with a man.

"Mariko warned me that you can be abrupt, even cruel. But she didn't explain why. She didn't say you suffer from this—"

"She doesn't know about the attacks of claustrophobia," Joanna said. "I've never told anyone. And I've never told anyone about the bouts of paranoia either. There are times when I think the whole damned world's against me, out to get me, all of it a clever cardboard backdrop, a conspiracy, a grand deception. When I start thinking like that, I want to run off and hide, escape into the wilderness where no one can see me or find me or hurt me." She was talking fast, partly because she was afraid she'd lose the courage she needed to tell him this, and partly because she hoped conversation would distract her from the advancing walls and ceiling. "I guess I've never told anyone about it because . . . well, because I've always been afraid that people would think I was crazy. But I'm not mad. If I were truly out of my mind, I wouldn't realize that I'm occasionally paranoid. If I were crazy, I'd accept paranoia as a perfectly normal state of mind. Wouldn't I? But I don't."

The hallucination did not abate; indeed, it grew worse. Although she was sitting down, the ceiling appeared to be no more than ten or twelve inches above her head. The walls were a yard away on every side, and they were rolling slowly closer on well-oiled tracks. The atmosphere was being compressed within this space, molecules jamming against molecules, until the air ceased to be a gas and became a liquid, first as dense as water, then syrupy. When she breathed, her throat and lungs seemed to fill with fluid. She was whimpering; she could hear it, but she could not control it.

Alex leaned toward her, took hold of her hand. "Joanna, remember that the things you're seeing aren't real. They're hallucinations. You can stop them. You can turn them off if you try."

The air was so thick that she choked on it. She bent forward, coughed, and gagged.

Alex tried to explain what was happening to her, hoping thereby to guide her through it, out of it, and into relative tranquillity. She listened because that was what she wanted, too; but it was difficult to divide her attention between him and the menacing walls. "You've been brainwashed," Alex said. "All memories of your past have been eradicated and replaced with totally false recollections." She understood, but she didn't see how this understanding could stop the ceiling from pressing her flat against the floor. "After they did that to you," Alex said, "they implanted a couple of posthypnotic suggestions that have twisted your life ever since. One of those suggestions is affecting you right this minute. Yeah. That has to be the explanation. Every time you meet someone who's interested in your past and who might uncover the entire deception, you suffer from claustrophobia and paranoia *because the people who brainwashed you told you that would happen.*" To her ear at least, his voice boomed and echoed within the shrinking room. "And each time you reject the person with whom you've become close, the claustrophobia goes away—again, *because they told you it would.* That's a very effective method for keeping inquisitive people out of your life. You're programmed to be a loner, Joanna. *Programmed.* Do you understand?"

She stared at him and knew that he was not a friend. He was one of Them. He was one of the people who had been trying to kill her, part of the conspiracy. He could not be trusted. He was despicable, rotten—

No, she thought. *That's paranoia. Alex Hunter is on my side.*

She jerked reflexively as the ceiling shuddered and moved closer to her. She slid down on the couch.

The air had been compressed to such an extent that she could feel it against her skin. Insistent. Heavy. Metallic. All around her. Like a suit of armor. A suit of armor that was constantly growing tighter, smaller. Inside it, she was drenched with perspiration. Her flesh was bruised.

"Fight it," Alex said.

"The walls!" Joanna cried, as the room began to close more quickly on all sides. It had never been this bad before. She was gasping. Her lungs were clogged. Her throat had been seared. She realized that the room was shrinking to the size of a coffin, and she foresaw the conditions of the grave—cold and damp and tight and lightless. "Oh, my *God!*"

"Close your eyes," Alex said urgently.

"No!" That would be unbearable. If she closed her eyes, the darkness would surely aggravate the claustrophobia. She had to see what was happening, even if the sight of the advancing walls drove her mad.

"Close your eyes," Alex insisted.

"Will you quit bothering me? Will you just let me the hell alone?"

"Trust me," he said.

"I don't dare."

"Why not?"

"Because of what you are."

"I'm your best hope."

She found the strength to draw herself up into a

sitting position from which she could confront him. For the moment she was able to bear up under the terror of moving walls. The most important thing was to get rid of him. "Get the hell out of here," she said sharply.

"No."

"This is my place."

"It's Joanna's place. But right at this moment you aren't Joanna. You don't act like her at all."

She knew what he said was true. She was behaving like a woman possessed. She didn't want to argue with him or drive him away, but she could not stop herself. "Bastard. Stinking, lousy bastard. I know who you are."

"Oh? Who am I?"

"One of Them."

"Stop this, Joanna."

"I'll call for help if you don't leave."

"You don't really want me to go."

She slapped him hard across the face.

He didn't move.

She slapped him again.

He winced, but he continued to hold her hand.

She tried to wrench her hand away from him.

He would not let go.

She could see the red imprint of her fingers on his face where she had slapped him, and she began to feel embarrassed.

"I'm going to stay here until you close your eyes and cooperate with me," he said. "Or until the walls and the ceiling crush you. Which will it be?"

She slumped again. The claustrophobia was stronger than the paranoia. Alex's trick had worked. She lost interest in getting rid of him; once more, she became acutely aware of the shrinking room, and that was her primary concern. She began to choke on the air, which she imagined to be thicker than motor oil; and she wept.

"Close your eyes," he said gently.

Joanna watched the walls with great trepidation, glanced at the lowering ceiling, looked at her hand in his, looked into his eyes, bit her lip, closed her eyes, and immediately knew that she was in a coffin, and the lid was snugly in place, and now someone was hammering nails into the lid, and then she heard shovelfuls of dirt cascading onto the coffin, and it was such a narrow space and shallow and dark, so very dark, without even one breath of air between its rough wooden walls, but she kept her eyes closed and listened to Alex, and his voice was a beacon that marked the way to freedom.

"You don't have to look for yourself," Alex said. "I'll tell you what's happening."

"All right."

"The walls are slowly coming to a halt. They aren't closing as rapidly as they were. And the ceiling has stopped descending altogether. And now the walls have stopped, too. Do you hear me, Joanna?"

"Yes."

"No, don't open your eyes yet. Squeeze them tight shut. Just visualize what I'm telling you. Everything's stopped. Everything's still. Do you see that?"

"Yes," she said softly.

The air was not normal, but it was thinner than it had been during the past several minutes—breathable, sweet.

"And now look what's happening," Alex said. "The ceiling is starting to move up, away from you, back where it belongs. The walls are sliding into their proper places. Slowly. Very slowly. But they are moving away. See? The room is getting bigger. Do you feel the room getting gradually larger? Do you see it?"

He talked to her like that for a long time, and Joanna listened to each word and visualized each statement. Eventually, after the air pressure returned to normal, when she was no longer suffocating, she opened her eyes and saw that the living room was as it should be.

Joanna sighed and said, "It's all gone. You chased it away."

He smiled and shook his head. "Not just me. We

did it together. And from now on you'll be able to do it alone."

"Oh, no. Never by myself."

"Yes, you will," Alex said. "Because this phobia isn't truly an integral part of your psychological make-up."

"You think it's the result of a posthypnotic suggestion."

"That's right. So you don't need lengthy psychoanalysis to break its hold on you—as you would if it was caused by some real trauma in your past. Whenever you feel an attack beginning, you'll simply shut your eyes and picture everything opening up and moving away from you. It'll work every time."

"Why didn't it ever work before?"

He tugged at one end of his mustache. "The first time you went through it," he said, "you needed someone to hold your hand. Besides, until tonight, you regarded it as an interior problem, an embarrassing mental illness. Now you can see it as pretty much an exterior problem—like a curse someone's hung on you."

She looked at the ceiling, as if daring it to descend.

Alex said, "Subsequent attacks will be less and less fierce—until they stop altogether. You'll be cured of claustrophobia in a few weeks. And the same goes for those moments of paranoia. I'll bet on it. Because neither of these problems has any genuine roots in you. They were both grafted on to you by the bastards who transformed you from Lisa into Joanna. You've been programmed. And by God, now you can reprogram yourself to be like other people."

To be like other people . . .

In her mind those words pealed like the joyous music of a Liberty Bell.

For the first time in more than ten years, Joanna was in full control of her life—at least to the extent that anyone can ever be. At last she could deal with the malignant forces that had made a loner of her. From this day forth, if she wanted an intimate relation-

ship with Alex or with anyone else, there would be no
limits to it; there would be nothing within her to stop
her from having whatever she wished. The only obstacles remaining were external ones. That thought was
wildly exhilarating. Like a rejuvenation drug. Water
from the fountain of youth. The years dropped from
her. Time ran backward. She was a girl again. It felt
that way. She would never hereafter cringe in fear as
the ceiling fell and the walls advanced. She would
never again experience the devastating terror and loneliness of uncontrollable paranoia; there would never be
another of those spells when she needed to hide in a
locked room, and when she could not eat because she
was convinced that her food and drink were poisoned;
and there would be no more of that irrational suspicion
that kept her from the succor and sanctuary of her
friends.

To be like other people ...
"Hey," Alex said, "what's wrong?"
"Everything's perfect."
"But you're crying."
"Because I'm happier than I've ever been," she said.

· 27 ·

The photographs no longer disturbed Joanna. She
studied them with the sort of awe that people must
have known when looking into the first mirrors centuries
ago, with a superstitious fascination, but not with fear.
Alex sat beside her on the sofa, sipping brandy and
reading aloud from some of the reports in the massive
Chelgrin file. They discussed each minim of information, trying to see it from every angle, searching for a
perspective that might have been overlooked when the
investigation was fresh.

As the evening wore on, Joanna made a list of ways in which she and Lisa Chelgrin were alike. Intellectually, she was more than half convinced that Alex was right, that she was the missing daughter of the senator. But emotionally, she lacked conviction. Could it really be possible that the mother and father she remembered so well—Elizabeth and Robert Rand—were merely phantoms, a couple of cardboard people who had never existed except in her mind? And the apartment in London—was it conceivable that she had never actually lived there? Before she could seriously consider that idea, she needed to see the proof in black and white, a list of reasons why she should believe the unbelievable.

LISA	ME
1) She looks like me.	1) Ergo, I look like her.
2) She is five foot six inches tall.	2) The same.
3) She weighs approximately 115 pounds.	3) So do I.
4) She studied music.	4) Likewise.
5) She had a sweet singing voice.	5) So do I.
6) Her mother died when she was ten.	6) My mother is dead, too.
7) Wherever she is, she's separated from her father.	7) My father is dead.
8) She had surgery for appendicitis when she was nine.	8) I have a small appendix scar.
9) She has a brown birthmark as big as a dime on her right hip.	9) So do I!

As Joanna was reading the list for the tenth or eleventh time, Alex pulled another report from the file, glanced at it, and said, "Hey, here's something damned curious. I'd forgotten all about it."

"What?"

He showed her a folder that contained approximately a dozen onionskin pages. "It's an interview with Mr. and Mrs. Morimoto."

"Who are they?"

"Lovely people," Alex said. "Servants. They've been employed by Tom Chelgrin since Lisa was five years old."

"You mean the senator brought a couple from Japan to work in his home?"

"No, no," Alex said. "They were both second generation Japanese-Americans. Raised in San Francisco, I think."

"Still, like you said, it's damned curious. Now there's a Japanese link between me and Lisa."

"You haven't heard half of it."

Joanna frowned. "Do you think maybe the Morimotos had something to do with my . . . with Lisa's disappearance?"

"Not at all. They were good people. Charming and very proper. Not a drop of larceny in their blood."

"You can be so sure?"

"I'd have sensed something like that," Alex said. "I'd have smelled it. Don't laugh. I'm not kidding."

She couldn't suppress a grin. "You're a detective, not a bloodhound."

"Yes, but bloodhound or not, when you've been in my line of work a long time, you develop a nose for that sort of thing. Naturally I don't mean I literally smell them. It's an aura . . . a subliminal radiation they put out. Calling it an odor is just the simplest way to describe it. A lot of people have a paper-thin veneer of civilization. Beneath the pretty sugar coating they're full of larcenous and psychotic urges. Savages in tuxedos. They have their own special stink. But the

Morimotos aren't like that. Not anymore than you are. And besides, they weren't in Jamaica when Lisa vanished. They were at the senator's house in Virginia, near Washington."

"So what is it exactly that you find so curious about them?" Joanna asked.

He put down the transcript of the Morimoto interview and picked up his brandy. "Well, you see, the Morimotos were around the house all day, every day while Lisa was growing up. Fumi was the cook. She did a little bit of light housework, too. Her husband, Koji, performed some of the services of a butler, but he was primarily a handyman. He could fix anything. And of course both Fumi and Koji did a great deal of baby-sitting with Lisa. She adored them. She picked up a lot of Japanese words from them, and the senator approved of that. He thought it was a good idea to teach languages to children when they were very young and hadn't many mental blocks against learning. He sent Lisa to a private elementary school where she was taught French beginning in the first grade—"

"I speak French."

"—and where she was taught German starting in the third grade," he finished.

"I speak German, too," Joanna said.

She added those items to her list of similarities. The pen trembled slightly in her fingers.

"So what I'm leading up to is that Tom Chelgrin used the Morimotos to tutor Lisa in Japanese," Alex said. "She spoke it fluently. Better than she spoke either French or German."

Joanna looked up from the list. She felt dizzy. Everything was happening fast, too fast. "My God."

"Yeah," Alex said. "To my way of thinking, it's just too incredible to be coincidence."

"But I learned Japanese in England," she said.

"Did you?"

"At the university—and from my boyfriend."

"Did you?"

They stared at each other.

For Joanna, for the first time, the impossible suddenly seemed probable.

• 28 •

Joanna found the letters in the bedroom closet, at the bottom of the same box in which she kept her snapshots. They were in one thin bundle, tied together with faded yellow ribbon. She brought them back to the living room and gave them to Alex. "I don't really know why I've held on to them all these years," she said.

"No doubt you've kept them because you were told to keep them," Alex said.

"Told—by whom?"

"By the people who kidnapped Lisa. By the people who tinkered with your mind. Letters of this sort are superficial proof of your Joanna Rand identity."

"Only superficial?"

"We'll soon find out," he said.

The packet contained five letters. Three of these were from J. Compton Woolrich, a London solicitor and the executor of the Robert and Elizabeth Rand estate. The final letter from Woolrich mentioned the enclosure of an after-tax estate settlement check that amounted to more than ninety thousand dollars, American.

Joanna had expected Alex to be surprised. She wondered how he could explain this. So far as she was able to see, that money from Woolrich blasted an enormous hole in the Chelgrin-Rand conspiracy theory.

"You actually received such a check?" he asked.

"Yes."

"And it cleared?"

"Yes."

"You got the money?"

"Every dime."

Alex read the letter again. As he studied the few formal lines that J. Compton Woolrich had written, he absentmindedly groomed his mustache with the thumb and forefinger of his right hand.

"If there was such a large Rand estate," Joanna said, "then my father and mother—Robert and Elizabeth— must have been real people. They existed."

"Perhaps," Alex said doubtfully. He shifted uneasily on the couch. "But even if they did exist, that doesn't mean you were their daughter."

"How else could I inherit from them?"

He didn't answer that. He read the last two of the five letters, both of which were from the claims office of the United British-Continental Insurance Association, Limited. Upon its receipt of the medical examiner's official certification of the death of Robert and Elizabeth (née Henderson) Rand, British-Continental had honored Robert's life insurance policy and had paid the full death benefits to the sole surviving heir—Joanna. The sum received—which was in addition to the more than ninety thousand dollars that had been acquired from the liquidation of the estate—was forty thousand pounds minus the applicable taxes.

"And you received this, too?" Alex asked.

"Yes."

"Quite a lot of money."

"It was," Joanna agreed. "But I needed virtually all of it to purchase this building and renovate it. The place needed a lot of work. Then I had to use most of what was left to operate the Moonglow until it became profitable—which, thank God, wasn't all that long."

Alex shuffled the letters, stopped when he found the last one from the London solicitor, and said, "This Woolrich guy . . . Did you do all of your business with him by mail and on the phone?"

"Of course not."

"You met him face to face?"

"Sure. Lots of times."

"When? Where?"

"He was my father's . . . he was Robert Rand's personal attorney; and they were also friends. He was a dinner guest at our apartment at least two or three times a year."

"What was he like?"

"Very kind and gentle," Joanna said. "After my parents were killed in the accident near Brighton—well, if they *were* my parents—Mr. Woolrich came to see me a number of times. And not just when he needed my approval or signature to proceed with the settlement of the estate. He visited almost every day for at least a month. He worried about keeping my spirits up. I was horribly depressed. He always had a few new jokes to tell. Very funny jokes, too. I don't know how I'd have gotten through it without him. He was extraordinarily considerate. He never made me go to his office on business. Not once. He always came to me. Never put me out in the least. He was warm and considerate. I liked him."

Alex studied her with narrowed eyes. He looked very much like a detective again, and she was bothered by that, although not as much as she had been on Wednesday.

"Did you listen to yourself just now?" Alex asked.

"What do you mean?"

"The way you sounded."

"How did I sound?"

Rather than answer, he stood, indecisive for a moment. Then he began to pace. "Tell me one of his jokes."

"Jokes?"

"You said that Woolrich humored you, tried to cheer you up with lots of jokes. So tell me one of his jokes."

"Are you serious?"

"Entirely."

"But surely you don't think I could remember after all these years."

"He cheered you up. His jokes were funny. You stressed that," Alex said. "So it seems reasonable to assume you might remember one of them."

She was puzzled by his interest. "Well, I don't."

"Just one," he insisted.

"Why is it important?"

He stopped pacing and stared down at her.

Those eyes. Once again she was aware of their power. They opened her with a glance and left her defenseless. She had thought she was armored against their effect. But she wasn't. She felt a surge of paranoia, the stark terror of having no secrets and no place to hide; but she fought the brief madness successfully and retained her composure.

"If you could recall one of his jokes," Alex said, "you'd provide some much needed detail for your recollections of him. You'd be adding verisimilitude."

"You've used that word before."

"It's important to a detective."

"I'm not trying to hide anything," Joanna said. "I'm giving you all the details I can."

"I know. That's what bothers me."

"I don't understand."

Alex sat beside her again. "Didn't you notice anything odd about the way you summed up Woolrich a minute ago?"

"Odd? In what way?"

"Your voice changed," Alex said. "In fact, your whole manner changed. Subtly. But I noticed it. As soon as you started talking about this Woolrich character, you spoke in a kind of monotone—as if you were reciting something you'd memorized."

"You make me sound like a zombie. You're imagining it," she said.

"My business is observation, not imagination," Alex said. "Tell me more about Woolrich."

"Such as?"

"What does he look like?"

"Does it really matter?"

Alex was quick to press the point. "Don't you remember that either?"

"Of course I do."

"Tell me."

"He was in his early forties when my parents were killed. A slender man. Five foot ten. Maybe a hundred and forty or a hundred and fifty pounds. Very nervous. Talked kind of fast. Energetic. He had a pinched face. Rather pale. Thin lips. Brown eyes. Brown and somewhat thinning hair. He wore heavy-looking tortoiseshell glasses, and he—"

Joanna stopped because suddenly she could hear what Alex had heard a moment ago—the slight change in her voice. She sounded as if she were standing at attention in front of a class of school children, reciting an assigned poem. It was eerie. She shivered.

"Do you correspond with Woolrich?" Alex asked.

"Write him letters? Why should I?"

"He was your father's friend."

"They were casual friends, not best buddies."

"But he was your friend, too."

"Yes, in a way he was."

"And after all he did for you when you were feeling low—"

"Maybe I should have kept in touch with him."

"That would have been like you."

"But I didn't."

"Why?" Alex asked.

"You know how it is. Friends drift apart."

"Not always."

"Well, they do when they put ten or twelve thousand miles between each other." She grimaced. "You're making me feel guilty as hell."

Alex shook his head. "You're missing my point. I'm not trying to make you feel guilty. Quite the opposite."

"Well, you're doing a damned good job anyway."

"I meant to imply that your memories of Woolrich are either inaccurate or entirely false."

"But I—"

"Give me a chance," he said. "Look, if Woolrich was

really a friend of your father's, and if he actually was extraordinarily helpful to you after the accident, you would have maintained some sort of contact with him, at least for a couple of years. That would be like you. From what I know of you, I'd say it's entirely out of character for you to forget a friend so quickly and so easily."

Joanna smiled ruefully and said, "I think maybe you have an idealized image of me."

"No. Absolutely not. I'm aware of your faults. But ingratitude isn't one of them. I believe this J. Compton Woolrich never existed. And so far as I can see, your failure to keep in touch with him is strong circumstantial evidence that supports my theory."

"But I remember him!" Joanna said.

"I've explained that. You've been made to remember a lot of things that never happened."

"Programmed."

"That's right. But you're still finding it hard to believe, aren't you?"

"If you were in my shoes, you'd have doubts, too."

"I'm sure I would," he said gently. "But it's true, Joanna. You are Lisa."

Without realizing it until this moment, she had grown extremely tense. She was leaning forward, shoulders drawn up, hunched as if in anticipation of a blow to the back of her neck. She was surprised to find that she was biting her fingernails. She stopped that, leaned back, and tried to relax.

"I guess you're right," she said, "I heard that change in my voice when I was telling you what Woolrich looked like. Just the way you described it—a monotone. It's spooky. And when I try to expand on those few memories of him, I don't get anything new. Not anything more at all. There's no color or detail. It seems flat. Like a photograph or painting. And yet . . . I *did* receive those three letters from him."

Alex said, "That's another thing that bothers me. You said that after the accident Woolrich came to visit you nearly every day."

"He did."

"So why would he need to write to you at all?"

"Well, of course he had to be careful not to . . ." Joanna frowned. "I'll be damned. I don't know. I hadn't thought about that."

Alex shook the thin packet of correspondence as if he hoped a secret would drop out of it. "There isn't anything in these three letters that requires a written notice to you. He could have conducted all of this business in person. He didn't even have to deliver the settlement check by mail." Alex tossed the letters onto the coffee table. "The only reason those were sent to you is so you'd have superficial proof of your phony background."

Joanna still could not discern a pattern that made as much sense as the one that he had convinced her to disregard. She said, "If Mr. Woolrich never existed . . . and if Robert and Elizabeth Rand never existed . . . then who in the hell sent me that ninety thousand dollars?"

"Maybe it came from the people who kidnapped you when you were Lisa."

She couldn't believe he had said that. "I must be hearing things."

"Maybe for some reason they wanted to set you up well in your new identity."

"But that's crazy!" Joanna said. "You've got it all backwards, don't you? Kidnappers are out to get money, not to give it away."

"These weren't ordinary kidnappers," Alex said. "They never sent a ransom demand to the senator. Their motives were unique."

"So who were they?"

"I've got a glimmer of an idea, but I'd rather not talk about it yet."

"Why not?"

Alex shrugged. "That's the way I work best. When I get a hunch, I like to let it stew for a while before I ask anyone else to consider it. If I keep it to myself until I've found all the holes in it and patched them, then I don't risk being turned off a possibly valid theory by someone's skepticism." He smiled broadly. "Besides, if I *can't* patch all the holes in a theory, then I don't ever have to tell anyone about it—and I don't wind up making a fool of myself."

"That's fine for you," she said. "But what am I supposed to do while you're playing Sherlock Holmes?"

Alex pointed to the telephone that stood on a rattan desk in one corner of the room. "You're going to make a couple of important calls."

"To whom?"

He smiled again, and she could see that he was enjoying the challenge provided by her case. "To a London solicitor named Woolrich—"

"Who probably doesn't exist."

"Right."

"Then why—"

"There's a telephone number on his stationery," Alex said. "We're obligated to try it. Any good detective would. It's a lead of sorts."

"Who else do I call?"

"The London office of the United British-Continental Insurance Association."

"Limited."

"Yes."

"Why?"

He said, "For the same reason that a curious little boy might poke a sharp stick into a hornets' nest: to see what will happen."

29

The Japanese operator needed more than an hour to place the calls to England.

Joanna sat at the rattan desk, and Alex pulled up a chair beside it. While they waited he read aloud from a few more reports that were in the Chelgrin file.

When the first call went through, it was midnight in Kyoto; but in London it was two o'clock in the afternoon.

The insurance company's switchboard operator had a sweet girlish voice. She sounded too young to be working. "May I help you?"

"Is this British-Continental Insurance?"

A pause. Then: "Yes."

Joanna said, "I need to speak to someone in your claims department."

Another pause, longer than the first. Then: "Do you know the name of the claims officer you want?"

"No," Joanna said. "Anyone will do."

"What sort of policy does the claim concern?"

"It's life insurance," Joanna said.

"One moment, please."

For a while the line carried nothing but background static: a steady hissing, intermittent sputtering, and the curious beeps and buzzes of computers talking to one another.

The man in the claims department finally came on the line. He clipped his words as if his voice were a pair of scissors. "Phillips speaking. Something I can help you with?"

As an excuse for soliciting information from Phillips, Joanna told him the story she and Alex had concocted while the call was being placed:

Her father had been insured by British-Continental, and the company had paid promptly upon his death. Shortly thereafter, she had moved to Japan to start a new life. Now, she explained, after all these years, she was having trouble with the Japanese tax authorities. They wanted to be certain that the money she had started with in Japan had not been earned there. Otherwise, they would seek back taxes from her. Unfortunately, she had thrown away the cover letter that had come with the insurance company's check—which would have furnished proof of the source of the money.

She was utterly convincing. Even Alex thought so; he kept nodding to let her know that she was doing a good job.

"Now I was wondering, Mr. Phillips, if you can possibly send me a copy of that letter, so that I can satisfy the tax people here."

Phillips said, "When did you receive our check?"

Joanna gave him the date.

"Oh," Phillips said, "then I can't help. Our records don't go back that far."

"What happened to them?"

"Threw them out. We're legally obligated to store them only seven years. In fact I'm surprised it's still a worry to you. Don't they have a statute of limitations in Japan?"

"Not in tax matters," Joanna said. She hadn't the slightest idea whether that was true. "With everything on microfilm these days, I would think nothing gets thrown out."

"Even microfilm takes up space," Phillips said.

She thought for a moment, then said, "Mr. Phillips, were you working for British-Continental when my claim was paid?"

"No. I've been with the company just eight years."

"What about other people in your department? Weren't some of them working there ten years ago?"

"Oh, yes. Quite a few."

"Do you think one of them might remember?"

"Remember back ten years to the payoff on an ordinary life policy?" Phillips asked, incredulous. "Highly unlikely."

"Just the same, would you ask around for me?"

"You mean now, while you hold long distance from Japan?"

"No," she said. "That would be a bit expensive. If you'd just make inquiries when you've got the time, I'd appreciate it. And if anyone does remember anything, please write me immediately."

"A memory isn't a legal record," Phillips said doubtfully. "I'm not sure what good someone's recollection would do you."

"It can't do any harm," she said.

"I suppose not."

"Will you?"

"All right."

Joanna gave Phillips her mailing address, thanked him, and hung up.

"Strike out?" Alex asked.

She told him what Phillips had said.

"Convenient," Alex said sourly.

"It doesn't prove anything."

"Exactly," he said. "It doesn't prove anything—one way or the other."

At twenty minutes past midnight, Kyoto time, the telephone rang again. The Japanese operator had put through the call to the London number that was on J. Compton Woolrich's beige vellum stationery.

The woman who answered the phone in London had never heard of a solicitor named Woolrich. She was the owner and manager of an antique shop on Jermyn Street, and the number had belonged to her for more than eight years. She didn't know to whom it might have been assigned prior to the opening of her shop.

Another blank wall.

30

The Moonglow Lounge had closed at eleven thirty, nearly an hour ago, and the staff had all gone home by the time Joanna concluded the second call to London. Music no longer drifted up through the floor, and without a background melody, the winter night seemed preternaturally quiet, impossibly dark at the windows, menacing.

Joanna switched on the stereo. Bach.

She sat beside Alex on the sofa. They continued to leaf through the gray-and-green Bonner Security Corporation file folders that were stacked on the coffee table.

Suddenly Alex said, "I'll be damned!" He took a pair of eight-by-ten-inch black-and-white glossies from one of the folders.

"What are they?" she asked.

He held them up so that she could get a better look at them. "Photographic enlargements of Lisa Chelgrin's thumbprints. We got one from her driver's license application, and we lifted the other from the clock radio in her bedroom. I'd forgotten they were here."

Joanna regarded the photographs with mixed emotions. They would either demolish or affirm Alex's theory that she was Lisa; and either way, there would be an extremely complicated mystery to solve, a long and perhaps dangerous ordeal ahead. "Hard proof," she said softly.

"We'll need an ink pad. And paper with a soft finish . . . but nothing *too* absorbent. We want a clear print, not a meaningless blot. And we've got to have a magnifying glass, too."

154

"The paper I have," Joanna said. "And the ink pad. But not the magnifying glass."

Alex stood, suddenly energized. "Where can we buy one?"

"At this hour? Nowhere. Not until morning. Then . . ." She hesitated. "Come to think of it, I *do* have a magnifying glass of sorts. Come on."

She led him out of the living room, down the narrow stairs, and into the first-floor office.

The magnifying glass was on her large work desk. It was a paperweight—a clear, inch-thick lens, four inches in diameter. It had no frame or handle, and it was not optically flawless; but when Alex held it above the ledger filled with Joanna's neat handwriting, the letters and figures were three to five times larger than they appeared to the unassisted eye.

"It'll do," he said.

Joanna got the ink pad and paper from the center drawer of the desk. After several tries she managed to make two nearly smudge-free thumbprints.

Alex placed them beside the photographs. While she scrubbed at her inky fingers with paper tissues and spit, he used the lens to compare the prints.

When Joanna had cleaned up as best she could without soap and hot water, Alex passed the magnifying glass to her. He made no comment about what she would see. She bent over, peered through the lens, moved it slowly back and forth between the photographs and the fresh prints. Finally she straightened up, looked at him, and said, "They're alike, aren't they?"

"Identical," he said.

· 31 ·

When the private security guards in Wayne Kennedy's room changed shifts, Toshio Adachi, the man who had been on the first watch, drove Mariko home. In Joanna's apartment above the Moonglow, Alex and Joanna were waiting for her in the kitchen. They had made hot tea and a stack of small sandwiches. She took off her coat and sat at the table, opposite them.

Mariko was tired. More than tired. Weary. Exhausted. Her face felt grimy, and her eyes burned as if sand had settled in the corners, under the lids. Her feet ached, and her legs were swollen and leaden like the legs of an old woman. She had slept less than three hours in the last thirty-six; and the day had been filled with more activity and a great deal more nervous strain than usual. When she first sat down at the table and began to nibble at a sandwich, she yawned repeatedly behind her hand, and she had trouble keeping her eyes open.

They wanted a full report on Wayne Kennedy's condition, but Mariko had little to tell them. Kennedy had first come out of anesthesia at 6:45, but he had not been coherent then. He dozed off and on, and he was somewhat more in command of himself each time he woke. He was fully awake by nine o'clock, at which time he complained of a dry mouth—"about as much spit as it takes to lick half a stamp"—and gnawing hunger. The nurses allowed him to suck on chips of ice, but made it clear that for tonight at least his dinner would be dripped into him from an IV bottle. He became terribly vocal about his desire for solid food—"at least some goddamned eggs and some goddamned bacon"—and considering his circumstances,

156

Mariko was amazed and impressed by his vitality. He was in some pain, but drugs masked most of it. Doctor Ito had visited Kennedy around nine thirty, and Wayne had been depressed to learn that he would be in the hospital for a month or longer and might need additional surgery. Mariko had done her best to cheer him after the doctor left; and by the time the nurse had come with his sedative shortly before midnight, Wayne had argued that he was feeling too good to go to sleep again so soon—"haven't slept this much since I went off breast-feeding." He told Mariko a dozen very funny stories about his job with Bonner Security in Chicago, and he wanted to tell her more. She persuaded him to do what the nurse asked, and half an hour later he was sound asleep. The police had not yet questioned him, but they had left word that they would be around early in the morning. Mariko didn't envy them if they hoped to get more out of Kennedy than Alex had asked him to give; for even from a sickbed, with one leg hoisted in traction, Wayne would be a match for the police.

When she finished telling them about Kennedy, Mariko dealt aggressively with the sandwiches, having suddenly discovered that she was ravenous. While she ate, Alex and Joanna told her what they had discovered in the Chelgrin file—the amazing similarities between Lisa and Joanna—told her about the two calls to London, and about the thumbprints.

As she listened to this series of revelations, Mariko became gradually less and less sleepy. Her eyes continued to burn, but she no longer found it difficult to keep them open. Physically, she was still exhausted; but mentally, she was alert. It was not entirely their fantastic story that brought her back to life so unexpectedly. Although she was shocked and fascinated to hear that Joanna was the daughter of a United States senator and the victim of a bizarre conspiracy, Mariko was equally interested in the way in which they were responding to each other. They were touching more than they had since she had first seen them together—innocent encounters of hands and elbows and knees, not full embraces, but subconsciously intentional. They were relaxed with each other now. Joanna's dark blue eyes had become sharper, clearer; and they regarded Alex with obvious affection, trust, and proprietary concern. For his part, Alex Hunter had loosened up considerably. Until she had walked in the door a few minutes ago, Mariko had never seen him in anything but a suit and tie; usually a vest, too. He had always looked very proper, sober. Now he was wearing neither a jacket nor a tie; his shirtsleeves were rolled up; and he kicked off his shoes even though Joanna did not maintain the traditional shoeless Japanese house. He was comfortable here because finally he was comfortable with Joanna. Mariko did not think they had been to bed together. Not yet. But soon. You could see it in their eyes, hear it in their voices—that special, sweet anticipation. And then, when he knew Joanna intimately and completely, would Alex be able to argue that love did not exist?

No.

He would be swept away.

He was half gone now.

Mariko smiled at that thought. She knew Alex and Joanna were right for each other, and she was pleased to see them drawing close in spite of themselves. For some reason, Mariko believed their wedding would have as profoundly beneficial an effect on her own life as it would on theirs. She did not know why she should think such a thing or what she meant by it. It was actually intuition more than reason. Nonetheless, that was exactly how she felt—that their marriage was a template for her own hopes, that without their happiness, her own would never come.

Mariko finished a sandwich, sipped the tea, and said, "Now that you've matched the thumbprints, what will you do? Call the senator and tell him?"

"I guess so," Joanna said, although the idea clearly disturbed her.

"No," Alex said. "We don't call him. Not yet."

"Why not?" Mariko asked.

Alex stirred his tea and stared into the cup as if he were reading the future there. After a long hesitation he said, "We aren't going to call him just yet because I have a hunch he's part of this whole thing."

"A part of it?" Joanna asked.

"In what way?" Mariko asked.

"I think he knows you're here in Kyoto," Alex said to Joanna. "I think he knows and always has known who kidnapped his daughter. It's even possible that it was the senator who arranged the kidnapping."

"But for God's sake, why?" Joanna asked.

"I don't know."

"Then how can you say—"

He interrupted Joanna by taking hold of her hand, and Mariko smiled. "I told you," Alex said, "it's just a hunch. But a damned strong hunch. And I've learned to listen to my hunches. Besides, it makes sense in some ways; it explains a few things."

"Like what?" Joanna asked.

"Like where you got more than a hundred and fifty thousand dollars," Alex said. "We know now that it didn't come from the Rand estate or from Robert Rand's life insurance."

Mariko put down her teacup and patted her lips with a napkin. "Excuse me, please," she said. "I'm very tired, and I'm having difficulty understanding all of this. You say the senator had his own daughter kidnapped from the vacation house in Jamaica, handed her over to people who brainwashed her, and arranged for her to be set up in a new life with an entirely new identity. Then he took more than a hundred and fifty thousand dollars of his own money and channeled it to her through a phony insurance payoff and a phony estate settlement. Is that what you're telling us?"

Alex nodded. "I don't pretend to know why, and I don't have any proof of it. But I'm pretty much convinced. It's the only explanation I can see at the moment. Where else could all that money come from?"

Perplexed, Mariko said, "But how could a father

send his daughter away like that? For what reason? How could he be happy if he could not see her? How could he enjoy the fullness of life without the chance to share the future with her?"

"Here in Japan," Alex said, "you have an awareness of the continuity of generations. You have an extremely strong sense of the value of the family. But it isn't always like that in other parts of the world. Where I come from, some parents have the instincts of the rogue male lion; in certain circumstances, they're capable of emotional cannibalism, and they devour their offspring. I see you doubt that, but I speak from experience. My parents were alcoholics. They nearly destroyed me. Both emotionally and physically. They hit me, cut me, and hurt me in a thousand ways. They were animals."

"We have a few like that."

"Far fewer than we do."

"Even one is too many. But this thing you say Joanna's father did . . . It is still beyond my comprehension," Mariko said, deeply saddened to think of it.

He smiled so beautifully that for an instant Mariko wished she had found him first, before Joanna ever saw him, before he saw Joanna.

He said, "It's beyond your comprehension because you are so exquisitely civilized, Mariko-san."

She blushed and acknowledged the compliment with a slow bow of her head.

"There's something you haven't accounted for," Joanna told Alex. "The senator hired you to find his daughter. He spent a small fortune on the search. Why would he do that if he knew all along where she was?"

As he poured more tea for himself, Alex said, "It was an excellent bit of misdirection; that's why. He was playing the bereaved father who would stop at nothing, spend anything to get his child back. Who could suspect him? And he can afford to play expensive games; he's got a lot more millions than I do."

Joanna was grim. "What he did to me—*if* he did it to me—wasn't a game."

"To you it wasn't," Alex agreed. "But perhaps to Tom Chelgrin it was."

"Then he's a monster," Mariko said firmly.

"You'll get no argument from me about that," Alex said.

As he had taken Joanna's hand a couple of minutes ago, now she reached spontaneously for his; and once again Mariko, with both hands folded around her tea-cup, was delighted. Joanna said, "Alex, since Wednesday afternoon, in the taxi, when you first mentioned that name, Thomas Chelgrin, you've made it clear you don't like him."

"Or trust him," Alex said.

"Why not?"

"He manipulates people."

"Don't all politicians?"

"I don't have to like them for it."

"But they'll always be with us."

"So will death, but it sometimes makes me feel good to rail against it. Chelgrin is smoother than most politicians. He's oily." Alex picked up his sandwich, hesitated, put it down again without taking a bite; he seemed to have lost his appetite. "I was around Chelgrin quite a lot, and I never saw a more carefully controlled, calculating man in my life. I finally figured he had just four facial expressions that he put on in public: a kind of somber, attentive look that he used when he made believe he was listening intently to the views of a constituent; a fatherly smile that crinkled up his whole face but went no more than a micrometer deep; a stern frown when he wanted to portray himself as a hardworking, no-nonsense guy; and grief, which he used when his wife died, when his daughter disappeared, and whenever he was called upon to say a few words about the death of anyone who contributed heavily to his campaign fund. I think he enjoys manipulating people even more than the average politician does; for him it's a form of masturbation."

"Whew!" Joanna said.

"I'm sorry if I come on a bit strong about him,"

Alex said. "But that's how I feel. And this is the first time I've had an opportunity to tell anyone. He was an important client, so I always hid my true feelings. But in spite of all the money he spent to find Lisa, and in spite of all his weeping about his lost little girl, I never believed he was as devastated by the kidnapping as he wanted everyone to think. He seems . . . hollow. When you look into his eyes, there's coldness, emptiness. He doesn't have a full measure of humanity in him."

"Then hadn't we better stop?" Joanna asked.

"Stop what?"

"The whole investigation we've undertaken."

"We can't. Not now."

Joanna frowned. "But if the senator is the kind of man you say . . . if he's capable of anything . . . well, we might all be better off if we forget him. Now I know a little bit about why I've made a loner of myself. I know why I've suffered. It's like you said—I was programmed. I don't really have to know anything more. I can live without knowing how it was done or who did it or for what reasons."

Mariko glanced at Alex.

His eyes met hers.

He doesn't like what Joanna said any more than I do, she thought.

Mariko spoke first. "Joanna, you can say that and believe it now. But later you'll change your mind. You'll be curious. It'll eat at you like acid. Everyone has to know who he is, what his role is meant to be. Everyone has to know why and how he got where he is. Otherwise, there is no basis for growth and change, no meaning to the rest of the journey through life."

"Besides," Alex said, taking a less philosophical approach, "it's too late for us to walk away from this. They won't let us. We've learned too much. When I moved in here with you, when I hired the guards for Wayne's hospital room, and when we made those calls to England, we pushed it too far. We made a declaration of war. At least that's how they'll see it. So now we're targets."

Joanna raised her eyebrows. "You think they might try to kill us?"

"Or worse," he said.

"What's worse?"

Alex pushed back his chair and got up. He went to the small window, stood with his back to them, and stared at the Gion and the dark city beyond. Finally he turned and said, "You want to know what's worse. Okay. Maybe one day we'll all wake up in other parts of the world with new names and new pasts and new sets of memories—and we won't know that we were ever Joanna Rand, Mariko Inamura, and Alex Hunter."

Joanna turned sickly white, as if a pale beam of moonlight had pierced the window and lit nothing in the room except her face.

"Would they really do it again?" Mariko asked.

Alex shrugged. "Why not? It's an effective means of silencing us. And that way they don't leave behind any dead bodies to excite the police."

"No . . . no," Joanna said softly, hauntingly. "Everything that's happened to me in Japan, everything I am and want to be, all of it wiped out of my mind . . ."

Mariko shuddered.

"But *why?*" Joanna demanded. In frustration she slammed one fist onto the table, rattling the teacups and saucers. "Why did all of this happen? It's insane! It makes no sense."

"Wrong," Alex said. "It makes perfect sense to the people who did it."

"It would make sense to us, too, if we knew what they know," Mariko said.

Alex nodded. "Right. And we won't be safe until we *do* know what they know. As soon as we understand what motivated the Lisa-Joanna switch, we can expose it. We'll make headlines. It'll be like the Lindbergh baby suddenly turning up alive after all these years. And when we've done that, when we've turned the spotlight on the kidnappers and made them vulnerable to prosecution, when they don't have any secrets left to hide, then they won't have any reason to grab us and play name-changing games."

"No reason except revenge," Joanna said.

"There's that," he admitted. "But maybe it won't matter to them once the game is over. And if it does matter, we can deal with that. We're only in really serious danger now, while we're searching for the next foothold, only so long as we don't have sufficient facts to go public with the story, while they still have a chance of stopping us."

"So what's next?" Joanna asked.

Alex came back to the table, looked down at Mariko. While he spoke, he tugged repeatedly at one end of his dark mustache. "Mariko-san, you have an uncle who's a psychiatrist."

"Yes."

"And he sometimes uses hypnotic regression to help his patients."

"That's right," Mariko said. For several years she had tried to persuade Joanna to see Uncle Omi, but always without success.

Alex turned to Joanna. "He can pry open your mind and help you remember things we need to know."

Joanna was skeptical. "Yeah? Like what?"

"Like the name of the man with the mechanical hand."

Joanna bit her lip, scowled. "Him. But what's it matter? He's just a man in a nightmare."

"Oh? Don't you recall what you told me about him on Wednesday?" Alex asked.

Joanna shifted uneasily, glanced at Mariko, looked down at the table, stared at her own slim hands, which were twisted together like trysting snakes.

"At Nijo Castle," Alex prompted.

"I was hysterical."

"You told me that you suddenly realized the man in your nightmare was someone you'd actually known, that he wasn't just a figment of a dream. Do you still believe that?"

Reluctantly she said, "Yeah."

"And if he's real, he must sure as hell be a part of what happened to you. He's one of the people behind it all."

"I believe it," she said. "But . . . I'm not sure . . . not sure at all that I want to find him."

Joanna's face turned even whiter than when Alex had mentioned she might possibly be subjected to another change of identity. She looked as if she had peered into an open grave and had seen therein a putrescent corpse reaching for her, a grin on its dissolving lips.

"Joanna, he's like a demon riding inside of you," Alex said. "You've got to exorcise him before you'll be able to sleep peacefully. Until you find him and learn what he did to you, you'll suffer that same bad dream every night."

"I've lived with it for ten years," she said. "I guess I can go on another ten."

Mariko disagreed. "You can't. I know what those dreams do to you. I hear your screams at night."

Joanna did not respond.

"When you meet this man with the mechanical hand," Mariko said, "when you confront him face to face, you'll discover he isn't half so frightening in reality as he is in the nightmare."

"I wish I could believe that," Joanna said.

"You should," Mariko said. "And you would if you thought about it just once without letting your emotions get in the way. The known is never as terrifying as the unknown. Dammit, Joanna, you *must* talk with Uncle Omi!"

Joanna was obviously surprised to hear Mariko swear. She looked at Alex—who nodded emphatically —then she looked down at her own hands again. Finally she sighed heavily and said, "Very well. I'll talk to him."

To Mariko, Alex said, "Can you arrange it?"

"I'll phone him in the morning."

"Can you get Joanna an appointment for tomorrow?"

"Probably. Or the day after at the latest."

"Alex, I want you to go to the doctor's with me," Joanna said. "I need someone to hold my hand."

"Well, I'm not sure a psychiatrist is going to want someone looking over his shoulder while—"

"You've got to be there," she insisted.

"If it's okay with the doctor—"

"If it isn't all right with him, then the deal's off. I won't go into this alone."

"I'm sure Uncle Omi won't mind," Mariko said. "After all, this is a very special case."

"You really think he'll let Alex come along?" Joanna asked anxiously.

"Once you've told him your story," Mariko said, "he'll be so intrigued he won't be able to say no."

Joanna was relieved. She leaned back in her chair.

Mariko fancied that she could see tension evaporate from the other woman.

Joanna gave Alex a radiant smile, which he returned.

Later, in her own apartment, in her own bed, Mariko remembered those dazzling smiles. Their faces had been full of love and trust. Before many more hours had passed, they would surrender to the persistent forces that were drawing them together. Romance, passion, and emotional commitment were ineluctable; Alex and Joanna might just as well attempt to hold back hurricane winds with their upraised hands as try to resist what they felt for each other. That thought made Mariko feel warm and safe.

Swinging rhythmically on the smooth edge of sleep, she realized why she regarded Joanna's fate as a template for her own. Mariko had not been fortunate enough to find a man she could love—or who would love her. Always too busy. And too shy. Might as well admit it. Shy. Awkward around men whenever the conversation became at all personal. Self-conscious. Always holding men at arm's length. She could talk to Alex about Joanna's love for him; but she could not express her own similar feelings to a man. Most thought she was cold. Frigid. They could not see the woman

within—very much alive, lively, eager, afire, with an
enormous capacity for love. She had never found a
man with an outgoing personality strong enough to
compensate for her reticence, or with sufficient perse-
verence to break through her shell. So she was alone
at thirty. Almost thirty-one. Still quite young, actually.
Except that she didn't like being alone, as some people
did, and dreaded the years ahead that might have to
be passed without the companionship she desired. She
didn't want to be a wallflower, but no matter how
hard she tried, she could not change. Therefore, she
hoped Joanna would connect with Alex, for she imagined that such a connection would be proof that she,
too, would find the right lover some day. Increasingly
over the years, she had come to think of Joanna as
the mirror of her own future. *And,* she thought, *that's
because we've both put up barriers against personal
relationships with men. But Joanna has erected so
many, many obstacles to her own happiness, far more
than I have; so if she can find someone to share her
life, then I can, too.*

Perhaps she was too confident. Perhaps none of
them would find happiness. Perhaps this Chelgrin
business was indeed very serious and would get them
all killed. But she refused to worry about that. In the
darkness, tucked snugly under the covers, Mariko
smiled.

• 32 •

Pump, pump, pump . . .

   He had no sense of time.

   He had no sense of place.

   He was just a machine—pumping.

   Ignacio Carreras was working on his arms. He

strained. He grunted. He groaned. He inhaled with
asthmatic gasps and exhaled explosively, breathing
violently but metronomically, as if he listened to
martial music that played only within him. The barbells with which he struggled weighed more than he
did. Judging from the sounds of agony that echoed
in the nine-hundred-square-foot private gymnasium,
the work seemed too difficult for him, but he continued
without pause. If the task had been any nearer possibility, it would not have been worthwhile. His strenu-
ous efforts distilled alcohol-clear droplets of sweat
from him; perspiration streamed down his slick flesh,
dripped off his earlobes, nose, chin, elbows, and fingertips. He wore nothing but a pair of royal-blue boxer
trunks, and his strikingly powerful body glistened like
every boy's dream of brute strength. You could almost
hear the tortured tissues being torn down, while new
and much stronger fibers grew in their place.

On Mondays, Wednesdays, and Fridays, without exception, Ignacio Carreras worked diligently on his
calves and thighs and buttocks and hips and waist and
lower back and stomach muscles. He had a prodigious
set of stomach muscles; his belly was hard and concave,
and it resembled a corrugated sheet of steel. Ignacio
yearned for the transmutation of his flesh, every
ounce, every cell. For relaxation he read science fiction,
and he longed to have the body of the perfect robot
that occasionally appeared in those books—flexible
yet invulnerable, precise and capable of grace yet
charged with crude power. On Tuesdays, Thursdays,
and Saturdays, he labored to improve his chest, upper
back, neck, shoulders, biceps, triceps, and all the
muscles of his forearms. On the seventh day he rested,
although inactivity made him nervous.

Carreras was only thirty-eight years old, but he
looked younger than that. His hair was coarse, thick,
and black; there was not a strand of gray in it. While
he exercised, he wore a bright yellow elastic ribbon
around his head to keep the hair out of his face.
His strong features, prominent nose, dark and deeply

set eyes, dusty complexion, and the headband combined to give him an American Indian look.

He did not claim to be an Indian, American or
otherwise. He said he was a Brazilian. He was neither.

Pump, pump, pump . . .

The gymnasium was on the first floor of the Carreras house, and at one time it had been a music
room. In the center of the Italian marble floor, there
was a circular dais upon which the piano had stood.
Now, the thirty-foot-square room was partially carpeted with scattered vinyl mats, and furnished with
exercise equipment of all kinds, including half a
dozen expensive Nautilus machines. The ceiling was
high and richly carved; the raised areas were painted
white; the sunken areas, powder blue; and all of it
was trimmed with narrow lines of gold.

Carreras stood on the dais, imitating a machine,
steadily working through a set of two-arm presses. His
behavior in the gym was indicative of his approach to
every aspect of life; he was relentless; he was not a
quitter; he would almost rather die than lose, even
when his only competition was himself. Wincing fiercely each time he exerted himself, Carreras began with
the huge barbells in start position, which was against
his shoulders, arms bent back to support the bar,
fingernails touching his chest, and then he raised the
weight straight up, in one smooth movement, exhaling
as he did so, raised it the length of his arms, until his
elbows locked, until the weight was directly overhead,
held it two beats, screaming in pain, but pleased because the pain meant that the effort was great enough
to build muscle, inhaling noisily as he brought the bar
slowly down to start position, held it there for a second
while his biceps and deltoids thumped with relief, then
pressed it up and up and up again, into the haze of
pain again, determined to complete the set of ten, just
as he had completed two sets of ten already this afternoon (but with somewhat lighter weights), and just as
he had endured thousands of sets and hundreds of
thousands of repetitions over the years.

Another bodybuilder, Antonio Paz, who was body-guard and exercise partner to Carreras, stood slightly behind and to one side of his boss. He counted aloud as each repetition was concluded. Paz was forty years old, but he, too, looked younger than his age. At six foot two, Paz was three inches taller than Carreras, and fifteen pounds heavier. He had none of the other man's good looks; his face was broad, flat, with a low brow. He also claimed to be Brazilian, but he was not.

Paz said, "Three," which meant that there were seven repetitions remaining in the set.

The telephone rang. Carreras could barely hear it above his own labored breathing. Through a veil of sweat and tears, he watched Paz cross the room to answer the call.

All the way up with the barbell. Hold it at any cost. Four. Bring it down. Rest. Take it up. Hold. Five. Lungs burning. Bring it down. Machinelike.

Paz was talking rapidly into the phone, but Carreras could not hear what the man was saying. The only sound was that of pain and blood rushing, rushing.

Up again. Hold. Arms quivering. Back spasming. Neck bulging. The pain! *Glorious!* Bring it down.

Paz left the receiver off the hook and returned to the dais. He took up his former position and waited.

Carreras did four more presses. When he dropped the barbell at the end of the set, he felt as if quarts of adrenaline were pumping through him. He was soaring, lighter than air. He was never tired after pumping iron. That feeling of freedom, that wonderful effervescence was one of the advantages that weight-lifting had over all other forms of exercise; and in fact the only other act that provided a similar sensation was killing.

Ignacio Carreras enjoyed killing. Men. Women. Children. It didn't matter which. He didn't get the chance often, of course. Certainly not as often as he lifted weights or as often as he would have liked.

Paz picked up a damp washcloth and a towel from

a chair at the edge of the dais. He handed these to
Carreras and said, "Marlowe is on the wire from
London."

"What does he want?"

"He wouldn't say. Except that it's urgent."

Both men spoke English as if they had learned
the language at an upper-class British university, but
neither of them had been to school in England.

Carreras stepped off the platform and went to deal
with Marlowe. Paz walked with heavy, purposeful
steps, but Carreras moved so lightly and gracefully
that he appeared to be on the verge of learning the
secret of levitation.

The telephone was on a table by one of the big
mullioned windows. The velvet drapes were drawn
back, but most of the light in the room came from the
huge chandelier that hung above the dais; its hundreds
of crystal beads and finely cut pendants gleamed with
rainbow beauty. Now, in late afternoon, the winter
sunlight was thin, tinted gray by curdled masses of
snow clouds; it semed barely able to force its way
through the many panes of the window. Beyond the
leaded glass lay one of the most interesting cities in
Europe. Zurich, Switzerland: the clear blue lake, the
crystalline Limmat River, the massive churches, banks,
solidly built houses, glass office buildings, the ancient
guildhalls, the twelfth-century Grossmünster cathedral,
the smokeless factories; altogether a curious and fascinating mixture of oppressive Gothic somberness and
alpine gaiety, modern and medieval. The city shelved
down the rolling hills and spread along the shores of
the lake; and the Carreras house stood above most of
it. The view was spectacular. The telephone table
seemed to be perched on top of the world.

Carreras sat down and picked up the receiver. He
was somewhat breathless from the last set of presses.
"Marlowe?"

"Here."

"What's wrong?"

He could be direct with Marlowe, for both his phone

and the one in London were equipped with the most sophisticated state-of-the-art scrambler devices, which made it nearly impossible for anyone to tap the line and obtain a sensible conversation.

"I've been trying to reach you for more than two hours," Marlowe said.

"I've been here all day."

"Not your fault. The goddamned bloody telephone. One foul-up after another. These operators—"

"You've reached me now," Carreras said impatiently.

"Joanna Rand called British-Continental to inquire about the payoff on her father's life insurance."

"You spoke to her?"

"And I told her we hadn't any files that old. I used the Phillips name, of course. Now what do we do?"

"Nothing yet," Carreras said.

"I should think time is of the essence."

"Think what you will."

"Obviously the whole charade is crumbling."

"Perhaps."

"You're damned cool about it."

"So should you be."

"And what am I to do if she comes calling?"

"She won't."

"After all, if she's beginning to question her entire past, what's to keep her from popping up here in London for a closer inspection?"

"For one thing," Carreras said, "she carries a post-hypnotic suggestion that makes it difficult if not impossible for her to leave Japan. That moment she attempts to board an airplane—or a ship, for that matter—she'll be overcome with fear. She'll become so dizzy and violently ill that she'll need a doctor, and she'll miss her flight."

"Oh." Marlowe thought about that for a moment. The open line hissed between them. "But maybe a posthypnotic suggestion won't have much force after all these years. What if she finds a way around it?"

"She might," Carreras admitted. "But I'm on top of the situation. I'm getting daily reports from Kyoto.

If she gets out of Japan, I'll know within an hour. You'll be warned."

"Nevertheless, I simply can't have her nosing around here. There's far too much at stake."

"If she gets to England," Carreras said, "she won't stay very long."

"How can you be sure? Besides, she can cause irreparable damage in a day or two."

"When and if she reaches London, she'll be looking for an unraveled thread of the conspiracy. We'll provide several that she can't overlook, and all of them will lead to Zurich. She'll quickly decide that this is where the mystery can best be solved, and she'll come here at once. When she gets here, I can deal with her."

"What threads, for instance?" Marlowe asked.

"We'll work that out if it becomes necessary."

"Look here," Marlowe said, "if she *does* slip past your people in Kyoto and out of the country, if she *does* show up in London by surprise, I'll have to make my own decision about her. And I'll have to move fast."

"That would not be wise," Carreras said ominously.

"I'm not just part of your game, you know. In fact, it's little more than a sideline to me. I've got quite a few irons in the fire. Interests to protect. Responsibilities. I won't jeopardize the whole pot of stew for this one ingredient. If the woman comes knocking at my door without warning, and if I feel she's endangering my entire operation, then I'll have her terminated, weighted with chains, and dropped from a boat in the middle of the Channel. I'll have no choice. Is that clear?"

"She won't arrive without notice," Carreras said.

"Let us hope not."

"But you should realize that if you harm her without my permission, there are others who will see that you take a short sea voyage of your own."

Marlowe was cold. "Are you threatening me?"

"I'm merely explaining the consequences."

"I don't like to be threatened."

"Will you be sensible, Marlowe? I haven't the power

to carry out such a threat. You know that. And you know me well enough to understand that I don't ever make empty threats. I'm just telling you what others will surely decide to do with you."

"Yeah? Who would pull the trigger on me?" Marlowe asked skeptically.

Carreras sighed and gave him the name of a singularly powerful and ruthless man.

It had the desired effect. Marlowe hesitated, then said, "Him? Are you serious?"

"Perfectly."

"No. You must be bluffing."

"To prove I'm not," Carreras said, "I'll arrange for you to receive a message from him."

"When?"

"Within twenty-four hours."

Finally Marlowe believed. "But for God's sake, Ignacio, why would a man of his position be so intently interested in a minor matter like this?"

"If you would do more thinking and less talking, you'd know the answer."

"Because it *isn't* a minor matter?"

"Such perception. In fact, my dear Marlowe, it's very likely the most important thing that either you or I will ever be involved in."

"But what makes this woman different from the others?"

"I can't tell you that."

"You can, but you won't."

"Yes."

Carreras stood up with the receiver in his hand, anxious to end the conversation and return to his exercises.

"I've never seen her," Marlowe said. "She's liable to show up on my doorstep at any time, and I wouldn't even recognize her. What's she like?"

"You don't need to know yet. If the need arises, you'll be shown a photograph."

A moment ago Marlowe had felt superior to Carreras and to everything with which Carreras was involved. Now he was worried about being relegated to a secondary role in a major job. To a man like Marlowe, who felt that he was born to the executive office and special privileges, advancement was all-important, the only alternative to failure; for he knew that if he lost his momentum, if he once slipped down a rung on the ladder, it would be a thousand times more difficult to continue the climb, and he would never be satisfied with just holding his place. Carreras could hear the burgeoning anxiety and self-concern in the other man's voice, and it amused him.

Marlowe said, "Surely a description of this woman can't hurt anything. I believe you're exaggerating the need for security. After all, I'm on your side."

"No description yet," Carreras said simply.

"What's her name?"

"Joanna Rand."

"I mean her real name."

"You know you shouldn't even ask," Carreras said, and he hung up.

A strong gust of wind pressed suddenly and insistently against the window. Carreras thought he saw a few specks of powdery snow. A storm was on its way.

• 33 •

Help!

Shortly after six o'clock in the morning, having slept only four hours, Alex woke. At first he thought he had wakened naturally; he seldom slept longer than four or five hours. Then he heard Joanna in the room next to his, and he realized that her cries had stirred him.

"Help me!"

Alex threw back the covers, got out of bed.

"Oh, God, God, help me!"

He grabbed the gun that was on the nightstand. It was the silencer-equipped 7 mm. automatic that he had taken from the man in the alley two nights ago.

When he burst into Joanna's room and switched on the lights, she sat up in bed. She was breathing hard, blinking, dazed.

Alex went to the half-open closet door, pushed it back, and looked inside. No one.

He started toward the windows to see if anyone had gone out that way.

"It was only the nightmare," Joanna said.

Alex stopped and turned to her. "The man with the mechanical hand?"

"Yeah."

He went to her, sat on the edge of the bed. "Want to tell me about it?"

"I already have," she said. "It's always the same."

Her face was pale; her mouth was soft and slack from sleep; her golden hair was slightly damp with perspiration; but she was beautiful.

She wore yellow silk pajamas that draped her breasts with promise, so that he could see nipples outlined against the fabric, which made his mouth go dry. He was suddenly aware that he was wearing only his pajama bottoms, and she touched his broad chest with one hand, just her fingertips, then both hands, and he didn't know quite how it happened but the next minute he had put down the gun and they were holding each other, not just holding but demanding, and her fingers were tracing patterns on his bare back, and her mouth was on his, her tongue between his lips. Licking. Sweet. Quick. Hot. Then their mouths seemed to melt together, and his hands moved down her sleek back and then around to her breasts, which were full and heavy and wonderfully upswept, and he located the buttons and in spite of his trembling opened them and touched her and moaned softly at the same instant she did, cupped her breasts and gently thumbed the

stiffening nipples and felt more than need, more than
lust, more than affection, felt all of that plus something
new as well, and abruptly he realized what he was
thinking—love, love, I love her—and he remembered
his parents (their protestations of love followed swiftly
and invariably by anger, shouting, cursing, fists, pain),
and he must have become tense with the memory because the quality of their kiss changed, and the mood
changed, and Joanna felt it too, so they pulled apart.

"Alex?"

"I'm confused."

"Don't you want me?"

"Oh, yes."

"So what's to be confused about?"

"About what we can have together."

"Didn't I just make that clear?"

"I mean in the long run."

"This isn't a one-night stand."

"I know. That's what I mean."

She put her hand to his face.

"Let the future take care of itself."

"I can't, Joanna. I've got to know."

"What then?"

"What you expect."

"Of you?"

"I mean . . . what you think we can have."

"Everything. If we want it."

"I don't want to disappoint you."

"You won't, darling."

"I will."

"No, no."

"I will."

She smiled.

"You mean you're determined to disappoint me?"

"I'm serious about this, Joanna."

"Yes, you are. But why?"

"You don't know me."

"I know enough."

"I'm an emotional cripple."

He was amazed that he had said it. Admitted it.

Had he believed it all along? Was Mariko right?

"You seem whole to me," she said.

"I've never said, 'I love you.'"

"But I've known it."

"I mean, I've never said it to *anyone.*"

"Good. Then I'll be the first."

"That's just it."

"What's just it?"

"I'm not sure I can say it to you."

"Oh."

"And mean it."

"I see," she said.

"No. You don't see. Joanna, I feel more for you than I've ever felt for anyone, and yet . . ."

He told her about his parents. He revealed more to her than he had thought he could reveal to anyone. He talked steadily for nearly an hour, dredging up the familiar as well as long-forgotten details of his nightmarish childhood. He recalled the many ways his mother and father had hurt him. The bruises. Split lips. Blackened eyes. Chipped teeth. Broken bones. Cuts. All the cursing, shouting. All the insults, the vicious teasing. Scalded once with a pan of hot water, the scar still there between his shoulderblades. The times they locked him in a tiny closet for a day, two days, three. In the beginning his voice was supercharged with hatred, but gradually that was replaced by grief; and although he was a man who never cried, he wept that night, beside Joanna. The ugly stuff welled in him, memory sludge—cancerous muck gushing from him in much the same way that guilt flowed mercifully from a devout Catholic in a confessional. When at last he stopped, out of words, he felt cleaner and freer than ever in his life.

She kissed his eyes.

"Sorry," he said.

"What for?"

"I never cry."

"That's part of your problem."

"I didn't want them to have the satisfaction of seeing me cry, so I learned to keep it inside."

She kissed his forehead, his nose, his cheeks.

"This is the man you're relying on to help you discover the truth about yourself," he said shakily. "Do you still have any confidence in him?"

"All the confidence in the world. He seems human now."

"You're really something."

"What, for instance?"

"Wonderful."

"Tell me more."

"Beautiful."

"I love you, Alex."

He tried to answer. He could not.

She kissed the corners of his mouth.

"Make love to me," she said.

"But if I—"

"I'm not asking for a commitment."

"Neither of us wants it without one."

"It'll be better when you've made peace with yourself—"

"Much better," he agreed.

"—but it'll still be good now. And we need it."

"We need it, but we won't take it," he said, although the temptation was almost more than he could bear. "With you it's got to start right. It has to be special. With you I want to wait until I *can* say those three little words and mean them. For the rest of my life I'll carry with me every detail of our first time, and from now on I don't intend to lug around anything but good memories."

"Then I'll wait until you say."

"Soon."

"But lay down with me now."

Alex switched off the lights.

They lay together on the bed in the womblike penumbral light. The morning sun shone behind the drawn drapes, but little of it penetrated the room. As the day grew slowly older, they passed the minutes nuzzling, cuddling, and kissing almost chastely. The experience was odd and pleasant, Alex thought, but not particularly sexual. They were not yet lovers; they were like animals in a burrow, pressing against each other for reassurance, warmth, and protection from the mysterious forces of a hostile universe. At first they petted in silence, but after ten minutes they began to talk, not about the Chelgrin case or about themselves but about books and music and art. Alex had never been happier.

An hour later, reluctantly, he gave Joanna a last kiss and returned to his room.

He chose a shirt, suit, and shoes for the day. But he made his choices automatically; his mind was not on the task.

While he was selecting a tie, he said aloud, "If love is a myth, what's this feeling you've got for Joanna? It's new to you, isn't it? So perhaps you're wrong."

In the bathroom, as he watched water spilling into the tub, he said, "And God knows, if there *is* such a thing as love, if there *is* a possibility of lasting happiness with Joanna, you'd better grab it."

He undressed, soaped, rinsed himself in a corner shower, then returned to the tub for the relaxing soak that was a Japanese ritual. "Right now," he told himself, "you're rudderless, adrift. You've made a life of your business so far, but the business has been a bore for the last couple of years. That's why you travel so much. That's why you spend so much time learning languages instead of working in the office. You're searching for a new center for your life, something that can give it meaning, some chance of happiness. So take this chance. Before it's too late."

Then after a while, when he got out of the tub and began to towel himself, he said, "But what if you take the chance and it turns sour? What if it doesn't work out? Will you be able to swallow the pain, or will you choke on it? Hell, you don't need this. You don't need it, man. You're perfectly fine on your own. You aren't lonely."

And then: "Oh, yeah? If I'm not lonely, then why do I spend so goddamned much time talking to myself like this?"

He sighed. An interior debate, regardless of how long or intense or well argued it was, would not settle the matter now. He needed more time.

He removed the damp, soiled gauze and adhesive tape that bound his left arm. The shallow knife wound was healing rapidly. He swabbed it with iodine and made the new bandage simple; he no longer required a sling.

By the time he dressed and got to the kitchen, Joanna was preparing a light breakfast. They each had a single bowl of *shiro dashi,* white *miso*-flavored soup. Floating on the soup was a neat tie of *kanpyo*—paper-thin gourd shavings—topped by a dab of hot mustard. The soup was properly served in a red dish with a gold rim, in keeping with the Japanese belief that a man "eats with his eyes as well as his mouth."

In this instance, however, Alex had little regard for Japanese wisdom. He did not look at the food because he could not keep his eyes from Joanna. She was even more appealing than usual; her freshly washed hair was thick and shiny.

After breakfast Alex called Ted Blakenship's home number in Chicago. He wanted Blakenship to use the Bonner Corporation's contacts in England, respected colleagues in the private security trade, to dig up all available information on the United British-Continental Insurance Association and on the phantom solicitor, J. Compton Woolrich.

They passed the remainder of the morning with the Chelgrin file, looking for new clues. They didn't find any.

Mariko ate lunch with Alex and Joanna at a restaurant two blocks from the Moonglow, and then all three of them went to the hospital to see Wayne Kennedy. The police had already been there; Kennedy had told them only what Alex wanted him to tell, and they had seemed satisfied—or at least not suspicious. Wayne

was just as Mariko had described him last night—
full of energy in spite of his condition, joking with
everyone and demanding to know when he would be
permitted to walk, "because if I lay here much longer
my legs are going to atrophy." One of the nurses spoke
English, and Wayne tried to convince her that he had
come all the way to Japan to enter a tap-dancing
contest and was determined to participate on crutches
if necessary. The nurse was amused, but Kennedy's
best audience was Mariko. She was obviously intrigued
and delighted by him, and it seemed to Alex that Wayne
played increasingly to her. Alex had never seen Mariko
quite so animated and cheerful as she was in that
small, clean, and decidedly dreary hospital room.

At three o'clock he and Joanna had to leave to keep
an appointment with Dr. Omi Inamura.

Mariko intended to remain at the hospital with
Kennedy until the guards changed shifts at six o'clock;
however, she accompanied Alex and Joanna as far as
the elevators. She was smiling and humming a pleasant
tune, and her mind seemed to be drifting miles away.
While they waited for the lift to arrive, she glanced
from Joanna to Alex to Joanna again; and her pre-
dominant expression, with which she had favored them
all day, was one of unconcealed, dreamy self-satisfac-
tion. Mariko had noticed something new and revealing
in the way he and Joanna reacted to each other; evidently, she had spotted telltale traces of their timid,
tentative romance. She appeared to be saying, *You
see? I told you so, didn't I? I was right all along. The
two of you have fallen in love.*

Mariko was so excessively smug that Alex almost
teased her about it, but the elevator came before he
could decide what to say. He and Joanna stepped into
the cab. Mariko wished them good luck with her Uncle
Omi, and in the second before the doors slid shut she
winked at Joanna. As the lift descended, Alex looked at
Joanna. She smiled. He grinned. She chuckled, and
he laughed.

As they left the elevator on the ground floor and

crossed the busy lobby, Joanna said, "Ever since you showed up, Mariko's been playing matchmaker. It surprises me."

"She's never done it before?"

"No. I didn't think she was the type."

"She's got a talent for it."

"She's persistent, at least."

The day was cold and clear. They walked north along the street toward Joanna's car, heads tucked down, hands deep in their pockets.

"Wayne's next," Alex said.

"Next what?"

"Next target for Mariko's matchmaking."

"You mean she's got him lined up with someone already?"

"Yeah. Herself."

Joanna stopped. "Mariko and Wayne?"

"She doesn't realize it yet," Alex said, "but that's what she's going to do."

"But she hardly knows him."

"Love at first sight."

"I thought you didn't believe in love."

"I'm not sure whether I do or not. But Mariko does. And she believes in love at first sight, too."

"Are you serious about this?"

"Do you think I'd spread baseless gossip?"

They walked. A stiff wind flapped their coattails. Their breath rushed from them in visible plumes of mist.

"Did she say something to you?" Joanna asked.

"No. As I said, she doesn't realize it yet."

"So how do you know? A crystal ball?"

"Didn't you see the way she was looking at Wayne?"

"What way was that?" Joanna asked.

"The same way she's been looking at us."

"Oh, no. Poor Wayne hasn't got a chance of staying free."

"I don't think he'll want to."

"You're turning into a regular clairvoyant."

"No. I'm just observant. That's my—"

"—business," she finished for him. "Observation, not imagination."

"Right. And Wayne's looking lovesick at her, too."

"I *thought* he was losing track of you and me—as if we were fading into the walls."

Joanna got in the driver's side of the car. She didn't pull into traffic immediately. She let the engine run awhile, until the heater started.

"Will he be good for her?" she asked Alex.

"He's one of my best men. I just promoted him. He's honest, reliable, intelligent. Will she be good for him?"

"She's a wonderful woman," Joanna said. "I love her. I don't want to see her hurt."

Alex laughed and said, "We're sitting here talking like a couple of matchmaking Marikos."

At the start of the drive across town, Joanna was happy. She made jokes about American men who were so desperate that they had to travel halfway around the world to find women who would have them. As they drew nearer to Dr. Inamura's office, however, her mood changed. She grew silent. Somber. Grim. By the time she parked the car half a block from the doctor's building, Joanna looked as if she were listening to a host of prophetic spirits that whispered nothing but bad news about the future.

Alex held her hand. It was moist and cool.

"I'm scared," she said.

"I'll be with you."

"What if the doctor *can* help me remember the face and name of the man with the mechanical hand?"

"Let's hope he does."

"But if we have a name, then we'll go looking for him, won't we?"

"We'll have to."

"And when we find him—"

"It's like Mariko said last night. When you finally find him, he won't be half so scary as he is in your nightmare."

"And like I said—I wish I could believe that."
"The doctor's waiting. We don't want to be late."
"I'm ready," she said.
She shuddered.

• 34 •

When they entered Dr. Inamura's reception room, Alex felt as uneasy as Joanna looked. He had a strong urge to turn and walk out.

Alex Hunter did not like doctors. Internists, general practitioners, ophthalmologists, urologists, pediatricians, surgeons, every other kind of specialist, even dentists—he disliked them all equally. In his childhood he had been to a great many doctors. Frequently his parents were so rough with him that the injuries they inflicted could not be ignored. While bruises could be left to heal themselves and abrasions could be trusted to scab over without attention, broken bones and very deep cuts and damaged teeth required the hands of a physician. His mother would not take him to the same doctor more than twice, for she was worried that someone would become suspicious about the endless series of "accidents" that befell Little Alex. And she always had at least marginally believable lies to tell the doctors—"Little Alex tripped and fell down the stairs; Little Alex fell off the swings at the playground; Little Alex pulled a pan of boiling water off the stove when I turned my back, and I'll never forgive myself for being so careless when I *knew* he was in the kitchen; Little Alex was playing with a knife when I wasn't looking, although I've told him a thousand times to leave sharp things alone, scissors and knives and needles and so forth, but of course it never does any good for a mother to talk because children these days think they know everything"—and Little Alex supported her stories because he was afraid the doctors would not believe him if he dared to tell the truth, and then he would have to go home and take an even worse beating than the one that had brought him to a physician in the first place. Most doctors listened to his mother's lies without a flicker of suspicion, perhaps because they wanted to believe; *not* believing meant involvement and commitment, which none of them desired. A few did seem to see through the gossamer veil of deception, but not one of them had the courage to act. Little Alex had not been able to understand their lack of concern, but as he grew older he realized they had been troubled by the possibility that Big Alex might sue them. He knew that he was being irrational when he judged everyone in the medical profession by the examples he had encountered. Nevertheless, he did not like them and generally felt uncomfortable when he was in their company.

Dr. Omi Inamura appeared to be an exception. He was in his fifties, slender, an inch shorter than Joanna, with slightly crinkled, papery skin and warm brown eyes. His smile was quick and genuine. He used every instrument—his eyes, his voice, gestures, the way he inclined his head when he was listening to either of them, and a score of calculated mannerisms—to convince them that he cared deeply about the people who came to see him; and after five minutes Alex believed him.

The inner office, where the doctor treated his patients, was reassuringly cozy. The desk was small and set in a corner. One wall held shelves from floor to ceiling, and these were crammed full of books. Another wall was covered by a tapestry that depicted a wooded mountainside, a waterfall, and a river where accordion-sail boats were running with the wind toward a small village just below the falls. The carpet was brown and thick. Alex was surprised to find there was not a traditional analyst's couch. The furnishings consisted primarily of a low coffee table around which were arranged four armchairs. The chairs were beige, maroon, and comfortable. The pine-slat blinds were shut at both large rectangular windows, and the electric lighting was indirect, soft, relaxing. The air was threaded with a sweet, elusive fragrance that Alex kept trying to identify—perhaps lemon incense.

Alex and Joanna sat in the beige chairs, and Inamura sat in one of the maroon; and they told him about the Chelgrin case and why they thought Joanna was Lisa. The doctor was fascinated and sympathetic. He understood why they did not want to go public with their discovery—why they did not *dare* go public —until they knew more about the people responsible for her miraculous transformation, and he was cautiously optimistic about conducting a successful program of hypnotic regression therapy.

"However," Dr. Inamura said, "there is apparently one problem. Ordinarily I would not employ hypnosis until I had done extensive groundwork with you. I find that it's always wise to begin with certain standard tests, a series of casual conversations, another series of investigative dialogues, the familiar questions and probes of a psychiatrist. I progress slowly, and I thoroughly explore the patient's problems, both those that are real and those that are imagined, until trust has been established. *Then* I use hypnosis—if it is indicated. Before I can expect to do my best for you, Miss Rand, I must know you well—your likes and dislikes, joys, fears, anxieties, what depresses you, what lifts you up, a thousand and one other things as well. If I don't have all that background, I won't know precisely how best to use hypnosis on you; I won't know the exact points in your past to which you ought to be regressed. This takes time, you see. Weeks. Even months. But I gather you wish to start with hypnosis immediately."

"I realize you usually proceed slowly," Joanna said, "and I understand why. I appreciate your concern for the patient. But we don't have weeks and months."

Alex said, "What these people did to Wayne Kennedy was meant as a warning. They'll give us a day or two to learn from it. When they see we haven't been scared off, they'll try something more violent with Joanna or me. Maybe even with Mariko."

The doctor frowned.

Joanna said, "Isha-san, I am no psychiatrist, and perhaps it's not my place to say this, but it seems to me that my case is unique. Each and every one of your other patients suffers from a condition that developed subtly and unconsciously over a period of many years, neuroses that are primarily the result of environmental factors. But everything that I suffer from was *implanted* in me ten years ago or so, in that room that stinks of antiseptics and disinfectants, wherever it might be . . . and by the man with the mechanical hand. With your other patients you do a great deal of what you call groundwork in order to discover the sources of their illnesses. But in my case we know the source, and it is outside of me. We just don't know *why* or *who*. Considering all that, couldn't your customary method of treatment be set aside just this once?"

Alex was impressed by the vigor with which Joanna made her argument. He knew she would have preferred to be anywhere but here. She dreaded being regressed to the time she had spent in the room that smelled of antiseptics; yet she understood the necessity of it. In addition to beauty and intelligence, she had more than her share of courage.

Omi Inamura was careful and conscientious. For a quarter of an hour they discussed the situation with him, studied it from every conceivable point of view, before he finally agreed to begin with hypnotic regression therapy.

"But you must realize that we very likely will not finish today," Inamura said. "Indeed, it would be amazing if we did. Unless you respond much better than I expect you will, this is going to take time."

"How much time?" Joanna asked.

The doctor shook his head. "I can't say. The therapy creates its own pace. It's different with each patient.

But I understand how urgent this is, and I'll see you for at least an hour or two every day until we've learned everything you need to know."

Joanna said, "That's kind of you, Isha-san, but I don't want to interfere with your regularly scheduled appointments. I don't want you to go to a lot of trouble just because I'm a friend of Mariko's."

Dr. Inamura insisted that Joanna was not causing him any trouble. "In Japan a psychiatrist is in somewhat the same position as that proverbial American salesman who tries to sell refrigerators to Eskimos. Because they live in a society that respects tradition, meditation, and kindness, most of my people are at peace with themselves. Furthermore, in this country the public baths do the work of psychiatrists. A long, leisurely soak once a day in pleasant surroundings and in good company—well, it relieves tensions that might otherwise grow into serious psychological problems." With typical Japanese modesty, Inamura said, "While some of my colleagues might be so kind as to say I am moderately successful in my profession, I nevertheless have one or two hours of open appointments most every day. Believe me, Miss Rand, you are not an inconvenience. Quite the opposite. It will be an honor to provide treatment for you."

She inclined her head toward Inamura. "It is a privilege to be your patient, Isha-san."

"You regard me too highly, Joanna-san."

"As you do me."

"Shall we begin now?"

"Yes, please," Joanna said.

She tried to appear calm and relaxed, but a quaver in her voice betrayed her. She was frightened.

"It has to be done," Alex said.

"I know," she said.

"It won't be so terrible."

"And you'll be here," she said.

"Every minute."

The doctor got up and came around the table, soundless on the thick carpet. He stood beside Joanna's chair. "Lean back, please. Relax. Put your hands in your lap with the palms up. Very good. Look straight ahead. Do you see the tapestry on the wall, Joanna?"

"Yes," she said.

"Do you see the river in the tapestry?"

"Yes."

"Do you see the small boats?"

"I see them."

"Concentrate on those boats, Joanna. Look closely at the little boats. Imagine yourself on one of them. You are standing on the deck of one of them. Water is lapping at the hull. Lapping gently. The water makes a soothing, rhythmic sound. And the boat sways in the current. Not violently. Gently. Gently. The boat sways gently in the water. Can you feel it swaying?"

"Yes," Joanna said.

Alex looked away from the tapestry and blinked rapidly. Inamura's voice was so mellow and convincing that Alex had felt himself on the deck of the small boat.

Joanna continued to stare straight ahead.

"The boat is like a baby's cradle." Inamura's voice was softer and more intimate than it had been at the start. "It rocks gently, gently like a cradle. Putting the baby to sleep. If you feel your eyes getting heavy, you may close them."

Joanna closed her eyes.

"Now I'm going to tilt your chair back a little," Inamura said. "To help you relax." He touched a button on the side of the armchair, and it hummed and changed positions until it was halfway between a chair and a couch. "Now I want you to think of your forehead, Joanna. You are frowning. There are lines in your forehead. You will relax those lines. I will touch you, and when I do, those lines will vanish." He placed his fingertips on her forehead, then on her eyelids. "You are clenching your teeth, Joanna. I want you to relax all the muscles in your face." He touched her jaw, her lips. When Inamura withdrew his hand, Alex saw that she virtually radiated serenity—like a painting of the Madonna. "And now your neck," Inamura

said, "relax your neck muscles . . . and now your left
shoulder . . . very relaxed . . . and your right shoulder
. . . and both arms . . . left and right arms . . . limp
and relaxed . . . You're deeply, pleasantly relaxed . . .
deeper . . . deeper . . . your abdomen and your hips
. . . limp . . . no tension in them . . . relaxed . . . and
now your legs . . ." He mentioned every part of her
legs, including a count of her toes. Then: "And now
you feel as if you're floating on a vast body of water
. . . floating on blue water under a blue sky . . .
drowsy . . . very drowsy . . . drowsier . . . you are in
a deep and natural sleep." Her breathing had become
slow and regular, but Inamura continued. "I am
taking hold of your right hand, Joanna. I am lifting
your right arm. And now you find that your arm is
becoming stiff . . . rigid . . . cannot be moved . . .
cannot be lowered. It is impossible for you to lower
your arm. It is rigid and will stay where I have put it.
I am going to count down from three, and when I
say 'one' you will be unable to put your arm down.
Three . . . and you are sleeping deeply . . . two . . .
deeper and deeper into sleep . . . a relaxed and
natural sleep . . . one . . . your arm is rigid now . . .
Put your arm down, Joanna." She tried to put it down.
The arm shook as she forced it, but she could not
lower it. "You may now lower your arm, Joanna. I am
now allowing you to lower it. Indeed, your arm is
now so limp you cannot possibly hold it up." Her arm
dropped into her lap. "And now you are in a deep,
deep, very relaxed sleep, and you will answer several
questions for me. You will enjoy answering them. Do
you understand?"

"Yes," she murmured.

"Speak more clearly, please."

"Yes."

Inamura returned to his chair.

Joanna was limp, but now Alex was tense. He slid
to the edge of the chair and turned to his right, so
that he faced her.

To Alex, Inamura said, "She's an excellent subject

for hypnosis. Usually there's at least a little resistance, but not with her."

Alex said, "Perhaps she's had practice."

"Quite a lot of it, I think," said Inamura.

Joanna waited.

Inamura thought for a moment, then said, "Joanna, what is your full name?"

"Joanna Louise Rand," she said.

"Is that truly your name?"

"Yes."

"Recently you learned that Joanna Rand is a fake name and that you were born with another. Is that true?"

"No," she said.

"You don't remember making the discovery?"

"My name is Joanna Louise Rand."

"Have you heard the name Lisa Chelgrin?"

"No."

"Think about it before answering."

Silence. Then: "I never heard the name."

"Do you know a man named Alex Hunter?"

"Of course. He's here."

"Did he mention Lisa Chelgrin to you?"

She did not answer.

"Did Alex mention Lisa Chelgrin?"

"I've never heard that name."

"Joanna, you can't lie to me. Understand?"

"Yes."

"You must always tell me the truth."

"Always."

"It is utterly impossible for you to lie to me."

"I understand."

"Have you heard the name Lisa Chelgrin?"

"No."

Alex glanced at the doctor. "What's happening?"

"She's not responding naturally," Inamura said.

"I see that. But why?"

"She's following a program," Inamura said.

"You mean someone anticipated this question?"

"This question and probably many others."

"How do we get around the program?"

"Patience."

"I haven't much of that at the moment."

Inamura said, "Joanna, we will now do something amazing. Something you might think is impossible. But it is not at all impossible or even difficult. It is easy. Simple. We are going to make time run backwards. You are going to get younger. It is beginning to happen already. You can't resist it. You don't want to resist it. The hands of the clock are turning backwards . . . and you feel yourself floating in time . . . getting younger . . . steadily and rapidly younger . . . younger . . . and you are now twenty-nine years old . . . but getting younger . . . and now you are twenty-eight years old . . . floating back through time . . ." He continued that line of patter until he had regressed Joanna to her twentieth year, where he stopped her. "You are in London," he said. "The apartment in London. You are sitting at the kitchen table. Your mother is cooking something. It smells good. What is your mother cooking, Joanna?"

Silence.

"What is your mother cooking?"

"Nothing," Joanna said.

"What is she doing?"

"Nothing."

"Are you in the kitchen?"

"Yes."

"What's happening?"

"Nothing."

"What is your mother's name?"

"Elizabeth Rand."

"What does she look like?"

"She has blonde hair like mine."

"What color are her eyes?"

"Blue like mine."

"Is she pretty?"

"Yes."

"Heavy or thin?"

"Slender."

"How tall is she, Joanna?"

Silence.

"How tall is your mother?"

"I don't know."

"Does your mother like to cook?"

"I don't know."

"What is her favorite food?"

Silence.

"What is your mother's favorite food?"

"I don't know."

"What kind of meals does she cook?"

"Regular meals."

"Beef? Does she favor beef dishes?"

"I don't remember."

"Yes, you do. You're in the kitchen now."

Silence.

"Joanna, does your mother like to go to the movies?"

Joanna shifted uneasily but kept her eyes shut.

"Does your mother like the theater?"

"I guess she does."

"Does she like the movies, too?"

"I guess she does."

"Don't you know for sure?"

No response.

"Does your mother like to read?"

Silence.

"Does your mother enjoy books?"

"I . . . I don't know."

"Does it seem strange to you that you know so little about your mother?"

Joanna squirmed in the chair.

Inamura said, "What's your mother's name?"

"Elizabeth Rand."

"Tell me everything you know about her."

"She has blonde hair and blue eyes like mine."

"Tell me more."

"She's pretty and slender."

"And?"

Silence.

"Surely you know more, Joanna."

"I can't remember, dammit! Leave me alone!"

Her face was contorted.

"Relax," Inamura said.

Her hands were no longer in her lap. She was gripping the arms of the chair. Her knuckles were white.

Alex wanted to touch and comfort her, but he was afraid that he would break the spell the doctor had created.

"Relax and be calm," Inamura told her. "You are very relaxed and calm. That's much better. Relaxed . . . calm . . . in a deep, natural sleep. Joanna, you can't remember those things because you never knew them. And you never knew them because Elizabeth Rand never existed."

"My mother is Elizabeth Rand," Joanna said woodenly.

"And Robert Rand never existed either."

"Robert Rand is my father."

"No. They do not exist, Joanna. Neither does the kitchen or the apartment in London. I want you to float freely in time. I want you to drift. You are drifting in time. You are looking for a special place, a unique and important place in your life. You are searching for a place that smells strongly of antiseptics . . . and of disinfectants . . . a time when you were in that place . . . and now you have found it . . . you are drifting toward it . . . drifting toward that special time and place . . . settling into it . . . and now you are there, in that room."

"Yes," she said.

"Are you sitting or standing?"

"Lying down. I'm naked."

"Are you on a bed?"

"I'm naked on a bed."

"How do you feel?"

"S-scared."

"Of what?"

"I'm . . . s-strapped down."

"Restrained?"

"Oh, God. My ankles and wrists."

"Who did this to you?"

"The straps are so tight. They hurt."

"Who did this to you?"

"I smell ammonia. Strong. Makes me sick."

"Look around the room, Joanna."

She lifted her head from the chair in which she reclined and looked obediently from left to right. She did not see Alex or the office; she existed now in another day; in her haunted eyes a transparent veil of weeks and months and years seemed to shimmer like a sheet of tears.

"What do you see?" Inamura asked.

She lowered her head. Closed her eyes.

"What do you see in that room?"

She made a strange, guttural sound.

Inamura repeated the question.

Joanna made the peculiar noise again, then louder, an ugly asthmatic wheezing, and suddenly her eyes popped open and rolled up until only the whites were visible, and she tried to lift her hands from the arms of the chair, but clearly they seemed to her to be strapped down, and she struggled, and the wheezing got worse, much worse.

Alex jumped up. "She can't breathe!"

Joanna began to jerk and twitch violently, as if great jolts of electricity were slamming through her.

"She's choking to death!"

• 35 •

Crying out as if he felt her pain and fear, Alex reached for Joanna.

"Don't touch her," Inamura said.

The quiet authority and self-assurance in the doctor's voice stopped him. Alex stood over Joanna, looking down at her, trembling. He had never been so helpless as he was at that moment.

Inamura appeared silently on the other side of her chair. He watched her painful contortions with interest but with no apparent concern.

Joanna's blank eyes l ged. Her face was red, turning purple. Foamy flecks of spittle glistened on her lips. She was still wheezing, choking, writhing under the lash of her own involuntary muscle spasms.

"For God's sake, help her!" Alex said.

Inamura said, "Joanna, you will be calm and relaxed. Let your throat muscles relax. The tension is draining out of you. You are having no trouble breathing. No trouble at all. Breathe slowly . . . deeply . . . deeply . . . evenly . . . very relaxed. You are in a deep, natural sleep . . . peaceful sleep."

The magic worked. She grew quiet. Her eyes rolled down; she closed them. She was breathing normally again.

"What in the hell was that all about?" Alex asked.

The doctor touched Joanna's forehead. "Do you hear me?"

"Yes," she said.

"I'm going to tell you why you had that respiratory problem, Joanna. And when you understand, you will not allow such a thing to happen ever again."

"I can't control it," she said.

"Yes, you can," Dr. Inamura said confidently. "You had difficulty breathing only because *they* told you that would happen if you were ever questioned thoroughly while under the influence of a drug or hypnosis. They implanted a posthypnotic suggestion that caused you to choke when I probed too deeply."

Joanna scowled. "That's the same thing that caused my claustrophobia."

"Exactly," Inamura said. "And now that you are aware of it, you won't allow it to happen, will you?"

"Those bastards," she said.

"Will you allow it to happen again, Joanna?"

"No."

"Good," Inamura said. He returned to his chair.

Alex continued to stand beside her. She looked so pale. He was worried. To Inamura, he said, "Maybe we shouldn't continue with this."

"It's perfectly safe," the doctor said.

"I'm not so sure."

"I'm all right, Alex," she said in that same slightly hollow voice with which she answered the doctor's questions.

Alex hesitated but finally sat down on the edge of his chair.

Inamura began again. "Joanna, you are still in the room that stinks of antiseptics and disinfectants."

"Ammonia . . . Lysol . . . alcohol. It's sickening. It's so strong I can smell it *and* taste it."

"You are unclothed—"

"—naked—"

"—and strapped to the bed."

"The straps are too tight. I can't move. I can't get up. I've got to get up and out of here. I can't get out of here!"

"Relax," Inamura said.

Alex watched her anxiously.

"Be calm," Inamura said. "You will remember all of it, but you will do so quietly. You will be calm and relaxed, and you will not be afraid."

"At least the room's warm," she said.

"That's the spirit. I want you to look around and tell me what you see."

"Not much," she said.

"Is it a large place?"

"No. Small."

"Any furniture other than the bed?"

"I don't know if you'd call it furniture."

"What is it?"

"It's beside my bed. It's a . . . I guess it's one of those . . . cardiac monitoring machines . . . you know . . . like they use with intensive-care patients in hospitals."

"Are you hooked up to it now?"

"Sometimes. Not now. When it's operating, it makes a beeping sound."

"Any other furniture?"

"A chair. And a glass cabinet."

"What's in the cabinet?"

"Lots of small bottles . . . vials . . . ampules."

"Drugs?"

"Yes. And hypodermic syringes wrapped in plastic."

"Are those drugs used on you?"

"Yes. I . . . I hate the needle."

"What else do you see?"

"Nothing."

"Does the room have a window?"

"Yes. One."

"Does it have a blind or drapes?"

"A blind."

"Is the blind open or shut?"

"Open."

"What do you see through the window, Joanna?"

She was silent.

"What do you see through the window?"

Her voice had changed. It was flat, hard, cold. "Tension, apprehension, and dissension have begun."

Inamura was persistent. "Joanna, what do you see beyond the window?"

She chanted woodenly, mindlessly: "Tension, apprehension, and dissension have begun."

"You are relaxed and calm. You are not tense or apprehensive. You are in a deep, natural, relaxing sleep."

"Tension, apprehension, and dissension have begun."

Perplexed, Inamura leaned forward. "What do you mean by that, Joanna?"

She was rigid, tense, hands fisted. "Tension, apprehension, and dissension have begun."

A chill scurried like a centipede along Alex's spine. Reflexively, he put a hand to the back of his neck.

"Very well," Inamura said. "Forget about the window for the time being. Let's talk about the people

who came to see you when you were in that little room.
Were there many of them?"

"Tension, apprehension, and dissension have begun."

"Now what?" Alex asked.

The doctor sighed and settled back in his chair. "The
posthypnotic suggestion that gave her breathing difficulties was their first line of defense. This is their
second. And I suspect this one is going to be harder
to crack."

• 36 •

"Tension, apprehension, and dissension have begun."

"Do you hear me, Joanna?" the doctor asked.

"Tension, apprehension, and dissension have begun."

Alex closed his eyes and listened intently to her
chant. It was vaguely familiar.

Inamura said, "At the moment, Joanna, I'm not
trying to steal any of your secrets. I just want to know
if you are listening."

"Yes," she said.

"That phrase you keep repeating is a memory block.
It was implanted posthypnotically by the same people
who caused you to have breathing difficulties a short
while ago. It's the work of the same people who programmed your claustrophobia. You will not use that
sentence—'Tension, apprehension, and dissension have
begun'—when you talk with me. You neither need nor
want to avoid my questions. You came here to learn
the truth, and learn it you will. Relax. Be calm. You
are in a deep, natural sleep, and you will answer all
of my questions. I want you to *see* that memory block.
It's lying in your mind. Visualize it. It's a large brick.
A heavy cement block. You see it . . . you put your

hands around it . . . straining . . . lifting it . . . lifting it up . . . casting it aside . . . out of the way. It is gone. Now you will remember. You will co-operate. Is that clear?"

"Yes."

"Good. Very good. Now, Joanna, you are still in that room. You smell the alcohol . . . the ammonia . . . taste it even. You are still strapped to the bed . . . and the straps are biting into you . . . and the blind is open. What do you see beyond the window?"

"Tension, apprehension, and dissension have begun."

"As I expected," Inamura said.

Alex opened his eyes. "I've heard that chant before."

Inamura blinked. "You have? Where? When?"

"I can't recall. But it's familiar."

"You must remember," Inamura said. "It's important. I've got several tools with which I might be able to reach her, but I wouldn't be surprised if none of them worked. She's been programmed by incredibly clever and capable people, and more likely than not they've anticipated most methods of treatment. I suspect there are only two ways I can break through the memory block. And under the circumstances, with time so short, the first method—years and years of intensive therapy—isn't acceptable."

"What's the second way?" Alex asked.

"An answering sentence."

"Answering sentence?"

Inamura nodded. "She might be requesting a password, you see. It's unlikely. It's rather too colorful, even melodramatic. But it is possible. Once she gives me the first line—'Tension, apprehension, and dissension have begun'—she might be waiting for me to respond with the appropriate second line. A sort of code. If that's the case, then she won't answer my questions until I've supplied the second part of the password."

Alex gaped at him. He was impressed by Inamura's insight and imagination. "A puzzle consisting of two pieces. She has one piece, and we've got to find the other one before we can proceed."

"Yes. Perhaps."

"I'll be damned!"

"If we knew the source of the line she uses," the doctor said, "we might be able to discover the answering sentence."

"I believe it's from a book."

"It sounds like part of a poem."

"I'll try my damnedest to think of it," Alex said. He slid back in his chair and unconsciously began to groom one end of his mustache.

"While you think," Inamura said, "I'll see what I can do with her."

For thirty minutes the doctor tried to break down the memory block. He cajoled and argued and reasoned with her; he used humor and discipline and logic; he demanded and asked and pleaded; he pried, probed, thrust, and picked at her resistance.

Nothing worked.

She continued to answer with the same six words. "Tension, apprehension, and dissension have begun."

"I've got it!" Alex said suddenly, jubilantly. "It's from a science fiction novel. I read it years and years ago."

Dr. Inamura picked up a notebook and pencil. "What's the title?"

"The Demolished Man."

"You're certain?"

"Absolutely," Alex said. "It's a classic of the genre. When I was young I read a lot of science fiction. It was a perfect escape from . . . well, from everything."

"Who's the author of this book?"

"Alfred Bester."

The doctor made a note of the name. "And the line Joanna keeps repeating—what's the significance of it?"

Alex got up, walked to the shuttered windows, trying to recall the details of the story. He turned and said, "The novel is set a few hundred years in the future, during a time when the police use telepathy to enforce the law. They're mind readers. It's impossible for anyone to commit murder and get away with it in the society that Bester creates, but there's one character who's determined to do it. He finds a way to conceal his incriminating innermost thoughts. In order to prevent the telepathic detectives from reading his guilt in his own mind, he learns to mentally recite a cleverly constructed, infectious jingle, while retaining the ability to concentrate on other things at the same time. The monotonous repetition of the jingle acts like a shield to deflect the snooping telepaths."

Inamura put down the notebook and pencil. "And I gather that one of the lines he recites is 'Tension, apprehension, and dissension have begun.' "

"Yeah."

"Then if there *is* an answer sentence that will dispose of her memory block, it is almost certainly another line of that jingle."

"Yeah. Probably."

"Do you remember the rest of it?"

"No," Alex said. "We'll have to get the book. I'll call my office in Chicago and have someone buy a copy. We—"

"That might not be necessary," Dr. Inamura said. "If the novel is a classic in its field, there's a good chance it will have been translated into Japanese. I'll be able to obtain it from a bookstore here, or from a man I know who deals in rare and out-of-print books."

That put an end to their first session. There was no use continuing the therapy until Inamura had a copy of *The Demolished Man.* Once more the doctor turned his attention to Joanna. He told her that when she woke she would remember everything that had transpired between them. Also, he said, she would be more easily hypnotized tomorrow than she had been today. In fact, in the future she would slip into a deep trance upon hearing Inamura speak just two words—"Dancing butterflies." With that firmly established, he brought her slowly back from the past to the present, and at last he woke her.

Outside, the cold winter day had grown colder.

The wind was a living presence.

A large black-and-yellow cat scurried along the gutter. It jumped the curb to the sidewalk in front of Alex and Joanna, glanced warily at them, then dashed down a set of shadowed basement-level steps. Alex was glad for the touch of amber in its coat.

"Dancing butterflies," Joanna said as they walked toward the car.

"You find that curious?" Alex asked.

"I find it very Japanese. Dancing butterflies. It's such a lovely, delicate image to be associated with a grim business like this."

"He's nice."

"Uncle Omi?"

"Yeah," Alex said.

"He's got Mariko's eyes."

"I like him."

"So do I," she said. "But I'm not going to like the things he'll make me remember."

As evening approached, the high clear sky was like a translucent sheet of dark blue ice.

• **37** •

Twenty-four hours later.

Sunday afternoon.

In Dr. Omi Inamura's office, the pine-slat blinds were now open. Outside, Kyoto lay under a low, gunmetal-gray sky. Hard, dry, wind-driven snowflakes showered upon the city and brushed over the windows with a soft hissing sound.

Alex thought the room was a bit darker than it had

been the previous day. Evidently the lights operated on a rheostat.

"Dancing butterflies."

Joanna's eyes fluttered and closed when the doctor spoke those words. Her breathing changed. She went limp in the big reclining chair.

With great skill, Inamura took her back over the years, until she was once again settled securely in the past, in the room that stank of antiseptics and disinfectants.

"There is a window in that room, isn't there, Joanna?" Inamura asked.

"Yes. One."

"Is the blind open?"

"Yes."

The doctor hesitated, then said, "What do you see beyond that window?"

"Tension, apprehension, and dissension have begun."

Inamura opened his copy of the Japanese edition of *The Demolished Man*, one page of which he had marked with a ribbon. Joanna had recited the last line of the jingle that was such an integral part of Bester's story. Inamura read aloud the next to last line, hoping it was the answer sentence—if there was such a thing. " 'Tenser, said the Tensor.' "

Although the doctor had not asked a question, Joanna responded. "Tension, apprehension, and dissension have begun."

"Tenser, said the Tensor."

Joanna was silent.

Inamura leaned forward in his maroon chair. "You are in the room that stinks of alcohol . . . ammonia . . . detergents . . . and you are strapped to the bed . . . and there is a window . . . an open window. What do you see beyond the window, Joanna?"

"The roof of a house," she said without hesitation. "It's a mansard roof. Black slate. No windows in it. I can see two brick chimneys."

Inamura looked at Alex.

"It worked," Alex said.

"So it appears. I got the Bester novel last night and read it in a single sitting. It is engrossing science fiction. Do you remember what happens to the killer at the end of the novel?"

"He's caught by the telepathic police," Alex said.

"Yes. Caught in spite of all his cleverness. And after they apprehend him, rather than imprison or execute him, they 'demolish' the man. They tear down his psyche, wipe out his memory. They remove every twist and quirk that made it possible for him to commit murder. Then they reconstruct him as a model citizen. *They make an entirely new person out of him.*"

"So in some ways it's similar to Joanna's experience," Alex said. "Except she's an innocent victim."

"Some things that were science fiction thirty years ago are fact today. For better or worse."

"I've never doubted that modern brainwashing techniques could produce a total identity change," Alex said. "I just want to know why it was done to Joanna."

"Perhaps we'll find the answer today," the doctor said. He faced Joanna again. "What else do you see beyond the window?"

"Just the sky."

"Do you know what city you're in?"

"No."

"What country?"

"No."

"Let's talk about the people who visit you in that room. Are there many of them?"

"A nurse. Heavyset. Gray hair. I don't like her. She has an ugly smile."

"Do you know her name?"

"I can't remember."

"Take your time."

She did. Then: "No. It's gone."

"Who else visits you?"

"A woman with brown hair and brown eyes. Sharp features. She's very cold, very businesslike. She's a doctor."

"How do you know that?"

"I . . . I guess she told me. And she does things . . . doctor things."

"Such as?"

"She takes my blood pressure and gives me injections and runs all kinds of tests on me."

"What's her name?"

"I haven't any idea."

"Is there anyone else who comes to see you there?"

Joanna shivered but did not answer.

"Who else comes to see you?"

She whispered: "Oh, God, no, no."

She chewed on her lower lip.

Her hands were fisted.

"Relax. Be calm," Inamura said.

Alex fidgeted. He wanted to hold her.

"Who else comes to see you, Joanna?"

"The Hand," she said thinly.

"You mean the man with the mechanical hand?"

"Him."

"Is he a doctor, too?"

"Yes."

"How do you know that?"

"The woman doctor and the nurse call him 'Herr Doktor.' "

"Did you say *Herr*, the German form of address?"

"Yes."

"Are the women German?"

"I don't know."

"Is the man German?"

"The . . . The Hand? I don't know."

"Do they speak German?"

"Not to me. Only English to me."

"What language do they speak among themselves?"

"The same, I think. English."

"Do you *ever* hear them speak German?"

"Just the word *Herr*."

"Do they speak with German accents?"

"I . . . I'm not sure. Accents . . . but not all German."

"Do you think this room is in Germany?"

"No. Maybe. Well . . . I don't know where it is."

"The doctor, the man—"

"Do we have to talk about him?"

"Yes, Joanna. What does he look like?"

"Light brown hair. He's going bald."

"What color eyes?"

"Light brown. Pale. Almost yellow."

"Tall or short? Thin or fat?"

"Tall and thin."

"What does he do to you in that room?"

Joanna whimpered.

"What does he do to you?"

"T-t-treatments," she said.

"What sort of treatments?"

Joanna wept quietly.

Alex reached for her.

"No!" the doctor said.

"But she needs—"

"Trust me, Mr. Hunter."

Anguished, Alex drew back from her.

"What sort of treatments?" Inamura asked.

"Awful," she said shakily. "Horrible."

"Describe one of them."

She could not speak.

"All right," Inamura said gently. "Relax. You are calm . . . relaxed . . . sleeping deeply . . . in the room that stinks of antiseptics and disinfectants. You are alone . . . on the bed. Are you strapped down?"

"Yes."

"Are you naked?"

"Yes. Under a sheet."

"You have not yet had your daily treatment. Herr Doktor will be here in a moment. You will describe what is happening. You will describe it calmly. Begin."

She swallowed hard. "The woman doctor . . . comes into the room and pulls the sheet down to my waist. She makes me feel . . . so helpless, utterly defenseless. She hooks me up to the machine."

"The cardiac monitor?"

"Yes. She tapes electrodes to me. They're cold. And that goddamned machine keeps beeping, beeping, beeping! It drives me crazy. She slips a board under my arm, tapes it in place, and hooks me up to the glucose bottle, too."

"You mean you're being fed intravenously?"

"That's always how the treatment starts." Gradually Joanna's speech becomes slower and thicker than normal. "And she covers my breasts with the sheet . . . watches me . . . watches . . . takes my blood pressure . . . and after a while . . . I start to float . . . feel so light . . . but aware of everything . . . too aware, in fact . . . sharply, terribly aware . . . but all the time . . . just floating . . ."

"Joanna, why are you talking like that?"

"Floating . . . numb . . . drifting . . ."

"Does the IV bottle contain a drug in addition to glucose?"

"Don't know. Maybe. Light . . . feathery . . ."

"It must be a drug," Alex said.

Inamura nodded. "Now, Joanna, I don't want you to talk in that thick, sluggish way. Speak normally. The drug is still dripping into you, but it won't affect your speech. You will continue to experience this treatment, and you will tell me about it in your usual, unaffected voice."

"All right."

"Good. Continue."

"The woman leaves, and I'm alone again. I'm still floating. But I don't feel high or happy. I'm scared. Then the door opens and . . ."

"Has someone entered the room?" Inamura asked.

"The Hand."

"Herr Doktor?"

"Him, him."

"What's he doing?"

"I want out of here."

"What is the doctor doing?"

"Please, please, let me out."

"What is the doctor doing, Joanna?"

She continued grudgingly: "Pushing the cart."

"What cart is that?"

"It's covered with medical instruments."

"What does he do next?"

"Comes to the bed. His hand . . ."

"What about his hand, Joanna?"

"He . . . he . . . he holds his hand in front of my face."

"Keep going."

"Opens and closes his metal fingers."

"Does he say anything?"

"No. Just the s-s-sound of his fingers—clicking."

"How long does this go on?"

"Until I'm crying."

"Is that what he wants—to see you cry?"

She was shivering.

The room seemed cold to Alex, too.

"He wants to scare me," she said. "He enjoys it."

"How do you know he enjoys it?" Inamura asked.

"I know him. The Hand. I hate him. He grins."

"After you've begun to cry, what's he do?"

"No, no, no," she said miserably.

"Relax, Joanna."

"I can't go through this again."

"Be calm. You're all right."

"I can't! Don't you see? Don't you see it?"

"See what, Joanna?"

She tries to sit up in the reclining chair.

"God help me. Is there a God? *Is there?*"

"Lay back," Inamura said. "Sleep. Be calm."

Alex was suffering with her. He trembled.

"What do you see?" Inamura asked.

"The n-needle!"

"The IV needle?"

"Yes. No, no. I mean another IV. I'll die."

"You won't die. You won't be hurt."

"The needle will kill me!"

"Rest easy. What's so special about this needle?"

"It's so big. Huge. It's filled with fire."

"You're afraid it'll sting?"

"Burn. Burn like acid. It'll squirt fire into me."

"Not this time," Inamura assured her. "No pain this time."

The storm thumped the windows, howled.

The glass vibrated.

It seemed to Alex that the man with the mechanical hand was in Inamura's office, had just walked through the door. He could feel an evil presence, a sudden and chilling change in the air.

"Let's continue," Inamura said. "The doctor uses the needle and then—"

"No. My neck. Not my neck. Oh, Jesus, no!"

"What's wrong with your neck, Joanna?"

"The needle!"

"He puts the needle in your neck?" Inamura asked.

Alex felt sick. He touched his own neck.

Mentally, emotionally, spiritually, Joanna was not in Omi Inamura's office. She was back in the past, living through hell once more, convulsed by the memory of pain as if it were happening at this very moment. She talked breathlessly, running the words together, voice rising and falling as if carried on the waves of recollected pain that crashed through her.

"It hurts, everything hurts, my veins are on fire, blood's boiling, bubbling, evaporating, it's eating me up, eating me up, God, it's eating me like acid, like lye, turning me black inside. What is it? What's he putting into me? What's the stuff in that goddamned bottle? God, it hurts, God, God, exploding in me, it's chewing me, searing. It hurts! My heart, my heart's pumping faster, faster, so hot, burning up, just dissolving and melting. God, let me out, out, let me out of here, dammit!"

She was a definition of terror. Her lips were drawn back from her teeth. Her eyes were squeezed tightly shut, as if she could not bear what she would see if she opened them. The veins throbbed at her temples. The muscles in her slender neck were taut. She writhed and cried out and gagged. She clawed at the arms of the chair.

Dr. Inamura spoke comfortingly to her. He tried to talk her down from the ledge of hysteria on which she appeared to be precariously balanced.

Joanna responded to him, but not as quickly as she had done previously. She relaxed, although not completely. Still in a trance, she rested for a few minutes. Now and then her hands fluttered up from the arms of her chair and described meaningless patterns in the air before settling down like two drifting autumn leaves. Occasionally she murmured worriedly to herself.

Dr. Inamura and Alex waited silently for her to be ready.

Alex glanced at the windows and saw nothing but a dense swirl of snowflakes like a monochromatic kaleidoscope scene in which all of the glass chips were white.

At last the doctor stirred. "Joanna, you are in the room that stinks of antiseptics and disinfectants. The odor is so heavy that you can taste it. You are strapped to the bed. You are connected to both IV bottles." Inamura went on like that for a while, reestablishing her inner place and mood. Then he said, "So the treatment has begun. Now I want you to tell me what it's like. What happens?"

"I'm floating, very high, and I still feel like I'm being eaten by acid."

"What does Herr Doktor do?"

"I'm not sure."

"What do you see?"

"Brilliant colors. Whirling, pulsing colors."

"What else do you see?"

"Nothing else. Just the colors."

"What do you hear?"

"The Hand. He's talking. Very distant."

"What's he saying?"

"Too distant. I can't make out the words."

"Is he talking to you?"

"Yes. And sometimes I answer him."

"What do you say to him?"

"My voice is as distant as his."

"You mean you don't know what you're saying?"

"I can't make out my words—"

"That's not true—"

"—because I'm floating a thousand miles above myself—"

"—Joanna. He must be talking to your subconscious—"

"—high, high above myself—"

"—and it's only your conscious mind that's floating up there. Perhaps your conscious mind cannot hear him, but your subconscious hears clearly. I want you to let your subconscious speak. What is Herr Doktor saying?"

Joanna was silent.

"What does he say to you?"

"I don't know, but I'm scared."

"What are you scared of?"

"Losing things."

"What things?"

"Everything."

"Please be more specific."

"Pieces of myself."

"You're afraid of losing pieces of yourself?"

"Pieces are falling away. I'm like a leper."

"Pieces of memory?" Inamura asked.

"I'm crumbling."

"Is it memory you're losing?"

"I don't know. I don't know. But I feel it going."

"What does he say to you to make you forget?"

"I don't know. I can't quite hear."

"Think. Strain for it. You can remember."

"No. He took that away from me, too."

Inamura followed that line of questioning until he was convinced that he would learn nothing more from it. "You've done very well, Joanna. Very well, indeed. And now the treatment is finished. The needle has been removed from your neck. The other needle has been removed from your arm. You are gradually settling down."

"No. I'm still floating. I keep floating for a long time afterwards. For an hour, anyway."

"All right. You're floating, but the needles are out of you. What happens now?"

She covered her face with her hands.

The therapy was not going to move any more smoothly than it had heretofore, Alex thought. She was going to force the doctor to squeeze the story from her.

"Joanna, what is happening to you?"

"I'm ashamed," she said miserably.

"There's no need to be ashamed."

"You don't know. You can't."

"No need at all. You haven't done anything wrong."

"I'm going to die. I want to die. For Christ's sake, let me out of here or let me die!"

"You are perfectly well and safe."

"Sick. Sick inside. In my soul."

"What's happening to you?"

She was furious. "Damn you, can't you hear? Are you totally deaf?"

Inamura was patient, unruffled. "Hear what?"

"The clicking! Click, click, click! The gears. They're as loud as gunshots. The gears in his fingers!"

"Where is Herr Doktor now?"

Her fury became fear again. "B-beside the bed. He strokes my f-face . . . with . . . with those steel f-f-fingers."

"Go on."

Her hands moved down to her neck.

"He massages my throat. I try to pry his hand away. I really do try. But I can't. It's steel. So powerful. So hard and cold. He grins. Filthy bastard. I'm floating very high, but I can see his grin. What a grin. Like on a pirate flag or on a bottle of poison. Danger: high voltage. Danger: radiation. That kind of grin. I'm way up high, but I can feel what he's doing. Oh, yeah. Yeah. I know what he's going to do. I know. Oh, God, I know, I know."

"Don't bottle it up," Inamura said. "Don't make a secret of it. Tell me. Free yourself of it."

Joanna quickly lowered her hands from her throat to her breasts.

She was quaking.

"The clicking," she said. "It's so loud I can't hear anything else. It fills the room. It's deafening. The gears in his hand—clicking, clicking . . ."

"What does he do?"

"He pulls the sheet away. He draws it all the way down to the bottom of the bed. Uncovers me. And I'm naked."

"Go on."

"He stands there. Grinning. Then he takes the electrodes off me, tosses them aside. He touches me. Make him get away. Don't let him touch me. Not there. Don't let him touch me there. *Please!*"

"Where is he touching you?"

"My breasts. Squeezing, stroking with those awful steel f-f-fingers. The Hand. He's hurting me. He knows it. Then he touches me with the other hand, the real one. It's clammy. He's rough with that hand, too." Suddenly she lost control; the terror, anger, shame, hatred, and frustration overwhelmed her. She began to keen eerily, like a madwoman: *"Ahhhhhh, ahhh, ahhh, ahhh, ahhh, ahhh . . ."* She went on and on like that.

In the realm of emotions, her primal wails struck Alex with the force of thunderbolts. In the past few days he had learned to feel things he had never felt before. Within himself, he had discovered many human possibilities of which he had been ignorant all his life. Joanna had sensitized him. However, everything he had experienced since meeting her was only as powerful as a spring breeze compared to the emotional storm that shook him now. He could not bear to see her like this. The horror of her past affected him more severely than it would have done if it had been his own agony; for if it were only a gash in him, he could grit his teeth and stitch it up with the stoicism he had long cultured, but because it was her wound he could do little to influence the healing of it. He was shattered by the full and unwelcome knowledge of his help-lessness. He felt that he was being torn apart. As he watched Joanna, his chest and throat swelled and grew tight with grief. He began to weep silently with her, for her.

For two or three minutes Dr. Inamura patiently recited a litany of reassurances, until Joanna finally regained her composure. When she was quiet he urged her to pick up her story where she had left it. "What is Herr Doktor doing now, Joanna?"

Alex interrupted. "Surely, Isha-san, you don't have to pursue this thing any further."

"But I must."

"I think we know all too well what he did to her."

"Yes, of course we know. And I understand how you feel," the doctor said sympathetically. "But it's essential that she say it. She's got to reveal everything, not for your benefit or mine but for her own. If I allow her to stop now, the ugly details will remain in her forever, festering like filthy splinters."

"But it's so hard on her."

"Finding the truth is never easy."

"She's suffering—"

"She'll suffer even more if I let her stop now."

"Perhaps we could give her a rest and pick up here tomorrow."

"Tomorrow we have other tasks. I need only a few minutes to finish this line of questioning."

Without enthusiasm Alex admitted the superiority of Inamura's argument.

The doctor said, "Joanna, where are Herr Doktor's hands right now?"

"On me."

"On what part of you?"

"My breasts."

"What does he do next?"

"The s-steel hand moves . . . down my body."

"Go on."

"Down to . . . my thighs."

"And then?"

"No. I can't."

"You can. You will."

"He touches me . . . there."

"Where does he touch you?"

"B-b-between my legs."

"And then?"

"Please."

"You must say it."

"He's grinning."

"And then?"

"The finger gears are clicking . . ."

"Go on."

". . . clicking so loud . . . like explosions."

"And then?"

"He . . . opens me."

"And then?"

"Puts one of those . . . fingers . . ."

"Go on. Puts it where?"

". . . puts it into me."

"Be more specific."

"Isn't that enough—what I've said?"

"No. You mustn't be afraid to say it clearly."

"Into me."

"You've got to be free of this. Where does he put it?"

"Into . . . my vagina."

"You're doing well."

"I feel terrible. Used."

"You were used. And not prettily. But in order to forget, you must first remember. Go on."

Her hands were still placed protectively at her breasts. "He puts the finger . . . in me . . . down there. The clicking noise fills me. It's inside, down there, inside me, cold, clicking."

"And then?"

"I'm afraid he'll hurt me."

"Does he hurt you?"

"He threatens me."

"What does he threaten to do?"

"He says he'll . . . tear me apart."

"And then?"

She shook. "He grins."

"And then?"

And then? And then? And then? Go on. Go on. And then? And then? Go on.

Alex wanted to put his hands over his ears. He forced himself to listen. If he wanted to share the best with her, he must be prepared also to share the worst.

Inamura probed at Joanna's psyche as if he were a dentist meticulously drilling away every trace of rotten matter and bacteria in a tooth, prior to refilling the hole that he had made.

The brutal revelations of repeated rape and perverse sex—in addition to the chilling story of the "treatment," which she had told earlier—left Alex drained, weak. Deep within him, there flourished the blackest hatred for the people who had stolen her past and who had dealt with her as if she was just meat. He nourished an ever growing determination to find and destroy the man with the mechanical hand and every one of the monster's associates. But revenge would have to come later. At the moment, shell-shocked by the hideous events that Joanna was recalling for Dr. Inamura, Alex didn't have even enough strength to speak.

The remainder of the interrogation lasted only five or six minutes; however, under the circumstances, minutes seemed to stretch magically into dreary hours. When Joanna finally answered the last question, she was exhausted, devastated, and soul weary. She turned on her side and slumped against one arm of the reclining chair. She drew her legs up as far as she was able, seeking the security of the fetal position. She mumbled to herself and wept steadily. The expression on her face was that of a lost and frightened child.

Unconcerned about what the doctor might say, Alex went to her. The sight of her in such desperate need of consolation tapped new wells of energy in Alex. He scooped her up as if she weighed no more than fifteen or twenty pounds, took her to his chair, and sat down with her. He cradled her; and although she was still anchored in a past peopled by enemies, she sensed his compassion and clung to him.

"Enough," he told Inamura. "That's enough for today. Bring her back, Isha-san. Bring her back to me."

• 38 •

At six o'clock Monday morning, Joanna was awakened by thirst. Her lips were chapped, her throat dry. She felt dehydrated. Last night they had eaten a large dinner—thick steaks, Kobe beef, the finest meat in the world, from cattle that had been hand-massaged daily and fed nothing but rice, beans, and plenty of beer. With the steaks, they had drunk two bottles of fine French wine, a rare and expensive luxury in Japan. Now the alcohol had leeched moisture from her. She pursed her lips as if to pinch off the powdery, sour taste of her own mouth.

She got up, went into the bathroom and greedily drank two glasses of tap water. It tasted almost as good as wine.

Returning to bed, she realized that for the first time in longer than ten years, her sleep had not been interrupted by the familiar nightmare. She had not dreamed about the man with the mechanical hand.

She was free at last.

She stood very still for a moment, stunned.

Then she laughed aloud.

Free!

In bed, wrapped in a newfound sense of security as well as in wool blankets and linen sheets, Joanna sought sleep again. She found it only a minute after her head touched the pillow.

She woke naturally, three hours later, at nine o'clock.

Although her sleep had been dreamless, she was less enthusiastic about her new freedom than she had been in the middle of the night. At first she was not certain why her attitude changed; but whatever the reasons, the mood of innocent optimism was definitely gone. She was wary, cautious, operating primarily on intuition now, bracing herself for trouble yet to come.

Curious about the weather, she went to the nearest window and drew back the drapes. The storm had passed in the night. The sky was clear. Kyoto lay under six or seven inches of fresh, dry snow. The streets held little traffic.

Joanna saw all of that the instant she opened the drapes, but she also saw something more important. Across the street, on the second floor of a popular geisha house, a man stood at a window; he was watching her apartment through a pair of binoculars. He saw her at the same time that she saw him. He lowered the glasses and stepped back, out of sight.

That was why her mood had changed. Subconsciously, she had expected something like this; subconsciously, she had been looking for a man with binoculars when she pulled back the drapes. They were out there. How many of them? Waiting. Watching. Until she knew who they were and why they had brainwashed her, she was neither safe nor free. In spite of the fact that the nightmare no longer had the power to disrupt her sleep, the sense of security she had enjoyed during the night was false, illusory. Although she had lived through several kinds of hell, the worst of them all might be ahead of her.

The wind pressed against the frost-streaked glass.

That morning, at eleven o'clock Kyoto time, Ted Blakenship called from Chicago. He had received Telex reports from the company's British associates, in answer to the questions that Alex had asked two days ago.

Who was J. Compton Woolrich, the man who allegedly acted as executor of the Rand estate? According to the investigators in London, he wasn't anyone. There was no record of his ever having existed. No passport in that name. No driver's license. No vehicle registration. No work or identity card of any sort. No insurance policy covering him or naming him as beneficiary. Nothing. No one named J. Compton Woolrich had been licensed to practice law at any time in this century. Nor had anyone with that name possessed a telephone number in Greater London since 1946. As Joanna had discovered on Friday, Woolrich's telephone was actually that of an antique shop on Jermyn Street. Likewise, the solicitor's return address was borrowed; it was actually that of a library that had been established prior to the Second World War.

"What about British-Continental Insurance?" Alex asked.

"Another phony," Blakenship said. "There's no such firm registered or paying taxes in Britain."

"And although by some fluke they might have escaped registration, no one there escapes taxes."

"Exactly."

"But we talked to someone at British-Continental just last Friday."

"Whoever it was deceived you."

"Yes, I suppose so. What about the address on their stationery?"

"Oh, that's real enough," Blakenship said. "But it sure as hell isn't the headquarters for a major corporation. Our British friends say it's just a grimy, three-story office building in Soho.'"

"And there's not even a branch office of an insurance company in the place?"

"No. There are about a dozen other businesses, though, cubbyhole operations, nothing particularly successful, at least not on the surface of it. Importers. Exporters. A mail-forwarding service. A couple of talent bookers who service the cheapest clubs in the neighborhood. But no British-Continental."

"What about the telephone number?"

"It's listed to one of the importers at that address. Fielding Athison, Limited. They deal in furniture, clothes, dinnerware, crafts, jewelry, and a lot of other stuff that's made in South Korea, Taiwan, Indonesia, Hong Kong, Singapore, and Thailand."

"Last Friday we talked to a Mr. Phillips at that number," Alex said.

"They don't have a Mr. Phillips."

"Is that what they say?"

"Yes."

"They're playing games."

"I wish you'd tell me what kind of games," Blakenship said. "And how does this tie in with the Chelgrin case? I'm dying of curiosity."

"I'd prefer to let you go on dying for a while," Alex said. "It's not a good idea for me to talk too much about my plans—at least not on this phone."

"Tapped?"

"It's been transformed into a regular party line, I suspect."

"Then should we be talking at all?" Blakenship asked worriedly.

"It doesn't matter if they hear what you're going to tell me," Alex assured him. "None of it's news to them. What else have you got on this Fielding Athison company?"

"Well . . . it's a profitable business, but only by a hair. In fact they're so overstaffed it's a miracle they manage to stay afloat."

"What does that mean to you?"

"You can guess. Other import companies their size make do with ten or twelve employees. Fielding Athison has twenty-seven, the majority of them in sales. There just doesn't appear to be enough work to keep them all busy."

"So the importing business is a front," Alex said.

"In the words of our British friends, 'The distinct possibility exists that the employees of Fielding Athison engage in some sort of unpublicized work in addition to the importation of Asian goods.' "

"A front for what? For whom?"

"If you want to find out," Blakenship said, "it's going to cost us dearly. And it's not the sort of thing that can be dug up quickly—if at all. I'd bet a thousand for one that the people using Fielding Athison are breaking a serious law or two. And being very industrious about it. And I'll bet two thousand for one that they'll try to smash anyone who interferes. They're obviously damned good at keeping secrets; they've been in business for fourteen years, and no one's tumbled to them yet. Do you want me to Telex London and order deeper work on this?"

"No," Alex said. "Not right now. "I'll see what develops here in the next couple of days. If it's necessary to put the Englishmen on the job again, I'll call you back."

"How's Wayne?" Blakenship asked.

"Better. Much better."

"The leg?"

"He'll keep it."

"Thank God."

"Yeah."

"Look, do you want me to send help?"

"I'm all right," Alex said.

"I've got two good men free at the moment."

"If they came they'd only be targets. Like Wayne."

"Aren't you a target?"

"Yeah. But the fewer the better."

"A little protection—"

"I don't need protection."

"Wayne needed protection."

"He *was* the protection."

"I guess you know best."

"What I need," Alex said sourly, "is divine guidance."

"If a voice comes to me from a burning bush anytime soon, I'll let you know right away what it says."

"I'd appreciate that," Alex said.

"Count on it."

"Seriously, though, I want to keep a lid on this. I don't want to attack the problem with an army. I'd like to find the answers I'm after without, in the process, filling up the Japanese hospitals with my employees."

• 40 •

Five o'clock Monday afternoon. Dr. Inamura's office. Alex in a beige chair. Joanna in the matching chair beside him. The doctor sitting primly in one of the maroon chairs opposite them. The beginnings of night on the far side of the windows. Soft lights inside. Lemon incense.

It seems almost like a religious ritual, Alex thought.

"Dancing butterflies."

In the final session with Omi Inamura, Joanna recalled the exact wording of three posthypnotic suggestions that had been deeply implanted by the man with the mechanical hand. The first involved the memory block—"Tension, apprehension, and dissension have begun"—with which they already had dealt. The second concerned the devastating attacks of claustrophobia and paranoia that she suffered when anyone became more than casually interested in her. Inamura finished administering the cure that Alex had begun several days ago, patiently convincing Joanna that the words of Herr Doktor no longer had any power over her, and that her fears were not valid. They never had been valid. Not surprisingly, the third of Herr Doktor's directives was that she would never leave Japan; and if she *did* attempt to get out of the country, if she *did* try to go aboard a ship or an aircraft that was bound for any port beyond Japan's borders, she would become dizzy, sick to her stomach, disoriented. Any attempt to escape from the prison to which she was assigned would end in terror and hysteria. Her faceless masters had boxed her up every way they could: emotionally, intellectually, psychologically, chronologically, and now even geographically. Inamura relieved her of that last restriction.

Alex was impressed by the cleverness with which Herr Doktor had programmed Joanna. Whoever and whatever else he might be, the man was a genius, an evil genius, as mesmerizing as a cobra's dance of death in front of its prey, as demanding of attention as a wild dog with a human infant in its jaws—hideous but fascinating.

When Inamura was positive Joanna could not remember any more about what Herr Doktor had done to her, he turned to another line of questioning. He urged her to move further into the past.

She squirmed. "But there's nowhere for me to go."

"Of course there is. You weren't born in that room."

"Nowhere."

"Listen," Inamura said. "You're strapped to the bed. There's one window. Outside there's a mansard roof."

"Yeah. Big black birds are sitting on the chimneys," she said. "A dozen big black birds."

"You're approximately twenty years old," Inamura said. "But now you're growing younger. Minute by minute you're growing younger. You have not been in the room long. In fact you haven't met the man with the mechanical hand. You haven't yet undergone a treatment. You have just come awake in that room for the first time. And now time is running backwards. You are drifting further back in time . . . back beyond the room . . . and the hours are slipping away, faster and faster, the hours and now the days . . . and you are floating in time . . . time like a great river . . . carrying you always back, back, back . . . Where are you now?"

Joanna didn't answer.

Inamura repeated the question.

"Nowhere," she said hollowly.

"Look around you."

"Nothing."

"What is your name?"

She didn't reply.

"Are you Joanna Rand?"

"Who?" she asked.

"Are you Lisa Chelgrin?"

"Who's she? Do I know her?"

"What's your name?"

"I . . . I don't have a name."

"Concentrate."

"I'm so cold. Freezing."

"Where are you?"

"Nowhere."

"What do you see?"

"Nothing."

"What do you feel?"

"Dead."

Alex said, *"Jesus."*

Inamura stared thoughtfully at her. After a while he said, "I will tell you where you are."

"Okay," Joanna said, a nervous tremor in her voice.

"You are standing in front of a door. An iron door. Do you see it?"

"No."

"Try to visualize it," Inamura said. "Look closely. You really cannot miss it. The door is huge, absolutely massive. Solid iron. If you could see through to the far side of it, you would find four large hinges, each as thick as your wrist. The iron is pitted and spotted with rust, but the door is impregnable. It's five feet wide, nine feet high, rounded at the top, set in an arch in the middle of a great stone wall."

What the devil's he doing? Alex wondered.

"You see the door now, I'm sure," Inamura said.

"Yes," Joanna said.

"Touch it."

She lifted one hand, felt the empty air.

"What does it feel like?" Inamura asked.

"Cold and rough," she said.

"Rap your knuckles on it."

She rapped silently on nothing.

"What do you hear?"

"A dull, ringing sound. It's a very thick door."

"Yes, it is," Inamura said. "And it's locked."

Resting in the reclining chair but simultaneously existing in another time and place, Joanna tried the door that was not there. "Yeah," she said. "It's locked."

"But you have got to open it," Inamura said.

"Why?"

"Because beyond it there's twenty years of your life. The first twenty years. That's why you can't remember any of it. They have put it behind that door. They've locked it away from you."

"Oh. I see."

"Luckily, I've found the key that will unlock that door," Inamura said. "I have it right here."

Alex grinned, pleased by the doctor's creative approach to the problem.

"It's a large iron key," Inamura said. "A large iron key attached to an iron ring. I'll shake it. There. Do you hear it rattling?"

"I hear it," she said.

Inamura was so skilled that Alex almost heard it, too.

"I'm putting the key in your hand," Inamura told her, even though he didn't move from his chair. "There. You have it now."

"I've got it," Joanna said, closing her hand around the imaginary key.

"Now put the key in the door and give it a full turn. That's right. Just like that. Fine. You've unlocked it."

"What happens next?" Joanna said. She was noticeably apprehensive.

"Push the door open," the doctor said.

"It's so heavy."

"Yes, but it's coming open just the same. Hear the hinges creaking? It's been closed a long, long time. But it's coming open . . . open . . . open all the way. There. You've done it. Now step across the threshold."

"All right."

"Are you across?"

"Yes."

"What do you see?"

"No stars."

"What do you mean?"

She was silent.

"Take another step," Inamura said.

"Whatever you say."

"And another. Five steps in all."

"Three . . . four . . . five."

"Now stop and look around."

"I'm looking."

"Where are you?"

"I don't know."

"What do you see?"

"Midnight."

"Be more specific."

"Just midnight."

"Explain, please."

Joanna took a deep breath. "Well . . . I see midnight. The most perfect midnight imaginable. Silky. Almost liquid. A fluid midnight sky runs all the way to the earth on all sides, sealing everything up tight, melting like chocolate over the whole world. Inky. No stars at all. Flawless blackness. Not a speck of light. And not a sound either. No wind. No odors. Blackness is the only thing, and it just goes on and on forever."

"No," Inamura said. "That's not true. Twenty years

of your life will begin to unfold in front of you. It's
starting now. Don't you see it? Don't you see the world
coming to life around you?"

"Nothing."

"Look closer. It may not be easy to see at first,
but it's all there. I've given you the key to your past."

"You've only given me the key to midnight," Joanna
said. Despair echoed in her voice.

"The key to the past," he insisted.

"To midnight," she said miserably. "A key to darkness and hopelessness. I don't know who I am. I don't
know where I am. I'm alone. All alone. I don't like
it here."

• 41 •

By the time they left Omi Inamura's office, night had
claimed Kyoto. The north had stored up a great wind
that it was paying out at a generous rate, with occa-
sional gusts that drove the cold winter air through
clothes and skin and flesh, all the way to the bone. The
streetlamps cast pale light and created stark shadows
on the wet pavement, on the dirty slush in the gutters,
and on the piled-up snow that had fallen yesterday.

Saying nothing, going nowhere, Alex and Joanna
sat in her car for several minutes, shivering, steaming
up the windshield with their breath. The engine was
running. The chilled exhaust vapor plumed up from
the tailpipe, rushed forward, writhed against the side
windows as if it were a sentient fog, then was scattered
by another burst of wind. Alex and Joanna were waiting for the heater to take the painfully sharp edge off
the frigid air inside the car. And they were thinking.

Dr. Inamura could do nothing more for Joanna. He
had brought to the surface every scrap of memory

involving the man with the mechanical hand, but he
had not been able to help her recall enough to provide
Alex with new leads; there simply was nothing more
in her. The fine details of the horrors that had transpired in the strange hospital room had been expertly
clouded, for the most part scattered like the ashes of
a long-extinguished fire; and the two-thirds of her life
that she had spent as Lisa Jean Chelgrin had been
thoroughly, painstakingly eradicated. The final answers
would not come from within her, as Alex had hoped,
but from without. And out there, in a world that could
spawn this weird scheme, out there was where the
greatest danger waited.

The fans in the dashboard clicked on and began to
push warm air out of the vents, and the patches of
condensation on the windshield shrank steadily.

Finally Joanna sighed and said, "I don't really mind
that I've forgotten all about Lisa. I don't mind that
they stole my other life from me. I like being Joanna.
I'm well off . . . and perhaps far better off than if I'd
never exchanged one identity for the other. Joanna
Rand is a damned good person to be."

"And to be with," he said.

"I can accept the loss. I can live as Joanna Rand
without feeling like a fraud or like a cardboard woman.
I can live without a past. I'm strong enough."

"I've no doubt of that."

She faced him. She was terribly drawn. But still so
beautiful. "But I can't just pick up and go on without
knowing *why!*" she said angrily.

"We'll find out why."

"How? There's no more in me for Inamura to pry
out."

Alex nodded. "And I don't believe there's anything
more to be discovered here in Kyoto. Not anything
important."

"The man who followed you into the alley," she
suggested.

"Shifty."

"The one you had to bash over the head."

"That's Shifty."

"Can we find out who he is?"

"Not worth the trouble. Small fish."

"Or the one you caught in your hotel room."

"Small fish."

"Or one of these others who follow us everywhere."

"Minnows."

"Where are the big fish? In Jamaica—where Lisa Jean disappeared?"

"No. More likely Chicago. That's Senator Tom's stomping grounds."

"You're not thinking Chicago. I can tell."

"You've become a mind reader, have you?"

"Call it a woman's intuition."

"Well, you're right. I'm thinking London."

"But you proved I never lived there. The entire background's a fake."

"Yeah. But Fielding Athison Limited—"

"—which sometimes calls itself United British-Continental Insurance—"

"—*is* in London," he said. "And I'm pretty damned sure they're not small fish."

"Will you put your British contacts on it again?"

"No. At least not by long-distance. So far as possible, I'd prefer to deal with these Fielding Athison people myself."

"You mean go to London?"

"That's right."

"When?"

"As soon as possible. Tomorrow or the day after. I'll take the train to Tokyo and fly from there."

"We'll fly from there."

He glanced at her and frowned.

"Both of us," she insisted.

"You have the Moonglow to worry about."

"Mariko can handle it."

"Sure. But the customers expect to hear you sing."

"They get good food and a first-rate dance band," Joanna said. "They can do without me for a while longer."

"I'm going to look into the Fielding Athison business. I'm going to ask questions and poke into corners. I'm going to push and push and push until they react. That's the surest way to get them to reveal what they want to keep secret. If I get them angry enough, they might even make a mistake. But it's dangerous work."

"What am I—a china doll?"

"Hardly," he admitted.

"I'd be in just as much danger here, alone."

"You'll have Mariko. And I'll arrange for twenty-four-hour protection while I'm away."

"You're the only protection I can trust," Joanna said. "I'm going to London with you."

• 42 •

Senator Thomas Chelgrin stood at one of the windows in his second-floor study. He was watching the sparse traffic in front of his house and waiting for the phone to ring.

Tuesday night, December first, Washington and its suburbs lay under a heavy blanket of cool, humid air. Occasionally, people hurried from houses to parked cars or from parked cars to welcoming doorways, their breath white before them, their shoulders drawn up and heads tucked down and hands jammed in pockets; but it was not quite cold enough for snow. According to the television weathermen, an icy rain would lash the city before morning.

Chelgrin was in a warm room, but he felt as cold as the solitary night walker who was now strolling along the street, beneath the window.

Guilt, he told himself. The same guilt and remorse that always overtakes me on the first day of every month.

During most of the year, when the upper house of
the United States Congress was in session, or when
there was other government business to be done (both
above and under the table), the senator made his
home in a huge twenty-five-room house on a tree-lined
street in Georgetown. He lived in Illinois less than
one month out of every year. Although he had not
remarried after the death of his wife, and although
his only child had been kidnapped more than a decade
ago and had never been found, the enormous house
was not too large for him. Tom Chelgrin wanted the
best of everything, and he had the money to buy it
all; his extensive collections, which ranged from rare
coins to the finest antique Chippendale furniture, required a great deal of space. He was not driven merely
by an investor's or a collector's passion; his need to
acquire valuable and beautiful things was no less than
obsessive. He had more than five thousand first editions
of American novels, short-story collections, and books
of poetry—Walt Whitman, Herman Melville, Edgar
Allan Poe, Nathaniel Hawthorne, James Fenimore
Cooper, Stephen Vincent Benet, Thoreau, Emerson,
Dreiser, Henry James, Robert Frost, and hundreds of
others. Two large rooms contained his Steuben art
glass, more than two hundred pieces, including all of
the most expensive works that had been created during
the past fifteen years. His rare stamps were worth
almost half a million dollars. The walls of his house
were hung with one hundred and nine original paintings and limited-edition signed prints, but that was
only a tenth of the fine art that he owned; most of
his holdings were in storage or in the Chicago house.
His Salvador Dali portfolio alone consisted of eighteen
prints and nine originals. He collected crystal paper-
weights, Lalique crystal of many kinds, oriental tapes-
tries and screens, exquisite porcelain, bronze sculpture
by the foremost contemporary artists working in that
medium, real handmade Persian carpets, historical
letters and autographs, Navajo blankets (one of his
best investments, having appreciated an astounding

two thousand percent in just ten years), wine, railroad memorabilia from the eighteenth and nineteenth centuries, precious stones, antique Chinese and Japanese silk and rice-paper fans, and more. Much more. The Georgetown house was overflowing with such stuff; he carried ten million dollars of insurance on the contents. Every room had a smoke detector. Nearly invisible but reliable heat-activated sprinkler systems were embedded in the ceilings. The burglar alarm was a marvel; it could detect intruders by means of pressure mats under the carpets, hidden electronic eyes, and infrared scanners.

Chelgrin did not share the house only with inanimate objects. A butler and cook (who were married to each other), a chauffeur, and a maid all lived in. Weekdays, Mrs. Finch, the senator's girl Friday, flitted in and out on errands; and Berton Talbot, his financial advisor and sometimes business partner, visited more days than not. On weekends Chelgrin usually entertained guests. He did not like to be alone, for when he was alone he had too much time to think; and in moments of solitude, some of the things he had to think about, if dwelt upon for long, were terrible enough to drive him out of his mind.

The telephone rang.

Chelgrin rushed to his desk and picked up the receiver. "Hello."

"Senator?"

It was Peterson.

"Go ahead," Chelgrin said.

"How are you?"

"I'm fine."

"Nice night for it."

"Miserable."

"It's going to rain. I like rain."

Chelgrin said nothing.

"Enough?" Peterson asked.

Chelgrin hesitated.

"How's it look?" Peterson asked.

Chelgrin was studying an electronic device—a Tap

Alert B409 sold over the counter by Communications Control Systems—that stood on the desk beside the phone. "Okay. It's okay. Nobody's listening to us," he said at last.

"Good. We've got the report."

Chelgrin could hear his own heartbeat. "Where should I meet you?"

"We haven't used the Safeway Market for a while. Let's try that."

"When?"

"In thirty minutes."

"I'll be there."

"Of course you will, dear Tom," Peterson said smugly. "Of course you will."

"What do you mean by that?"

"Why," Peterson said, feigning bewilderment at the senator's sharp tone, "I just mean that I *know* you wouldn't miss it for the world."

"You think you've got me on a tight line," Chelgrin said. "You think I'm a dog on a leash, and you enjoy jerking me around."

"Dear Tom, you're too sensitive. I never said such a thing. I never would."

"Just remember that you'll be there tonight for one reason—because they've told you to bring the report to me. That's why you're there the first day of every month," the senator said angrily. "It's not your free choice. You're on a leash, too."

"Easy, boy. Easy."

"Don't patronize me."

"I worry about your heart, dear Tom."

"You're no more in charge of your life than I'm in charge of mine," Chelgrin said. "In fact, less so."

"Dear, dear Tom," Peterson said with mock sympathy. He chuckled and hung up.

The senator's hands were shaking. He listened to the dead line for a moment, still watching the Tap Alert to be certain they had not been monitored, then finally put down the phone. The black plastic receiver glistened with sweat from his palm.

He went to the bar cabinet and poured two ounces of Scotch. He drank it in two swallows, without benefit of ice or water.

"God help me," he said softly.

• 43 •

When Chelgrin left the house to keep his appointment at the supermarket, he took his dark gray Cadillac Seville. He drove himself. He had given the chauffeur and the other three servants the day off. He could have driven something else—either a Mercedes 450-SEL, or a Citroën-Maserati S/M, or a white Rolls Royce. He chose the Cadillac because it was less conspicuous than any of the others.

The senator arrived at the rendezvous five minutes early. The supermarket was the cornerstone of the small shopping center, and even at eight o'clock on a blustery winter night, the place was busy. He parked the Cadillac at the end of a row of cars, fifty yards from the market entrance. He waited a minute or two, then got out, locked the doors, and stood self-consciously by the rear bumper.

He turned up his coat collar, pulled his hat down a bit, and kept his distinctive face away from the light; he was trying to look casual, but he was certain he looked just like someone playing at spies. However, if he didn't take precautions, he would surely be recognized. He was not merely a United States senator from Illinois; he was also a man who aspired to the White House, to the office of the Presidency, and he spent countless hours in front of television cameras and in the poor company of obnoxious but powerful newspapermen, gradually laying the foundationn for a campaign that would commence either three or seven years from now, depending on the fate of the new man who had won the highest post only a year ago. (Considering the sanctimonious and self-righteous lecturing, the many episodes of undisguised political duplicity, and the incredible bungling that marked the new fellow's first ten months at the helm, Tom Chelgrin was growing increasingly confident about his chances in three rather than seven years. He knew how to thoroughly conceal his own duplicity. By spring he would have to make up his mind whether to establish a preliminary campaign advisory group.) At any rate, his face was very well known, and he did not want to be found in the supermarket parking lot, for if someone spotted him, the meeting with Anson Peterson would have to be canceled and rescheduled for another night; one could not be too careful.

Two rows away the lights of a dirty yellow Chevrolet snapped on, and the car pulled out of its parking slip. It came down one aisle, around another, and stopped directly behind the senator's Cadillac.

Chelgrin opened the passenger-side door and bent down. He knew the driver from other nights like this —a short, stout man with a prim mouth and thick glasses—but he did not know his name. He had never asked. He got in and buckled his seatbelt.

"Anybody on your tail?" the stout man asked.

"If anyone were, I wouldn't be here."

"We'll play it safe just the same."

"No need."

"Just the same."

For ten minutes the stout man drove through a maze of residential streets and alleyways. He had an eye for the rearview mirror as much as for the road ahead.

Eventually he said, "We're clean."

"As I told you," Chelgrin said impatiently.

"Just doing my job."

"But not very well."

"What's eating you?"

"I can't abide incompetence."

"And you think I'm incompetent?"

"You like playing this game. You like to zip around, pretending you're losing a tail. It's childish. You don't act like a professional."

"Can't figure it out," the stout man said.

They stopped at a traffic light.

"Can't figure what out?" Chelgrin asked.

"How you ever got elected. You're such a disagreeable son of a bitch."

"Oh, but not in public," Chelgrin said. "I can be very charming with constituents, newsmen, and campaign contributors. But what do I have to gain by being charming to you?"

Chelgrin was not ready to drop the matter. Peterson had gotten on his nerves, and he wanted revenge for that. He could not strike out effectively at Anson because the man was his equal in most ways and his superior in a few respects. By humiliating the driver, by grinding him down and breaking him, Chelgrin was acquiring the self-confidence he needed for the approaching session with Peterson.

"You are thoroughly outclassed in this exchange," the senator said. "You don't have the wit to embarrass me or the strength to harm me physically. And worst of all, you're at least a dozen rungs below me on this particular ladder. You would do anything I want because you know that I have the authority to see that you're sent home. Sent home, my friend. Think about that. You don't want to go home, do you?"

The driver did not respond.

"Do you want to go home?"

The driver bit his lip.

"Answer me, damn you! Do you want to go home? Home this very week? Home forever?"

The driver was shaking. "No. No."

Chelgrin laughed. "Of course you don't. None of us

wants to go home. What a dreadful thought. Now be a good boy. Just keep your mouth shut and drive."

They went straightaway to a roadhouse discotheque, seven miles from the supermarket. The place was called Smooth Joe's, and it boasted a pair of ten-foot-tall neon dancers doing a stiff, flickering jitterbug on the roof. Business was good for a Tuesday night; more than a hundred cars surrounded the building. One of these was a chocolate-brown Mercedes with Maryland plates, and the stout man pulled in beside it.

Without another word to the driver, Chelgrin got out of the Chevrolet, took a deep breath of the cold night air that was vibrating with thunderous disco rock, and then climbed quickly into the rear seat of the Mercedes, where Anson Peterson was waiting.

The instant the senator slammed the door, Peterson spoke to his own driver: "Let's roll, Harry."

The man in the front seat was big, broad-shouldered, and totally bald. He held the steering wheel almost at arm's length, and he drove well. They headed away from the suburbs, into the Virginia countryside.

The interior of the car smelled of butter-rum–flavored Lifesavers. They were an addiction of Peterson's.

"You're looking very well, dear Tom."

"And you."

In fact Peterson did not look at all well. Although he was only five foot ten, he weighed well in excess of three hundred pounds. His suit pants strained to encompass his enomous thighs, so that when he was sitting down it appeared he was wearing leotards. The buttons on his shirt met but not without strain, and he never attempted to close his suit jacket. Anson Peterson always wore a hand-knotted bow tie—tonight it was white polkadots on a field of deep blue, to match his blue suit—which emphasized the extraordinary circumference of his neck and the pendulous state of his chins. His face was a great, round pudding paler than vanilla—but within it shone two fiercely intelligent tar-black eyes.

Offering the roll of candy, Peterson said, "Do you care for one?"

"No, thank you."

Peterson took a circlet of butter-rum for himself and, with girlish daintiness, popped it into his mouth. He carefully folded shut the end of the roll, as if it must be done just so to please a stern nanny, and put it in one of his jacket pockets. From another pocket he took a clean white handkerchief, shook it out, and scrubbed vigorously at his fingers.

In spite of his size, or perhaps because of it, he was compulsively neat. His clothes were always clean; never a spot on shirt or tie. They were also neatly pressed when he put them on, although he rendered them creaseless and shapeless the moment he sat down. His hands were pink, and the nails were manicured and highly polished. He always looked as if he had just come from the barber, and not one hair was ever out of place on his round head. Tom Chelgrin once had eaten dinner with the fat man, and Peterson had finished his double servings without leaving a solitary crumb or drop of sauce on his end of the tablecloth. The senator, hardly a sloppy man, had left the modest but expected detritus from a meal consisting of red wine, crunchy hard rolls, and spaghetti, and he had felt like a pig when he compared his place with Peterson's absolutely virginal expanse of linen.

They cruised along wide streets with half-acre estates and large houses on both sides, heading out toward the hunt country. Their monthly meetings were always conducted in this fashion. An automobile could be checked for electronic listening devices and stripped of them more easily than could a room in any building; furthermore, a moving car with a well-trained and observant chauffeur was almost proof against a directional microphone—even one that was aimed from a sophisticated mobile unit.

Of course it was not likely that Anson Peterson would ever be a target of any kind of electronic surveillance. His cover as a successful real estate entrepreneur was well established, faultless. He was a methodical man, circumspect in all things, and highly security conscious. His other work, that which was done in addition to the real estate dealing, that which he did not talk about at parties, that which was patently illegal, was carried out in utmost secrecy.

As they sped toward the countryside, the fat man talked around his candy. "If I didn't know better, I'd think you engineered the election of this man in the White House. What a fool he is. Such a fumbler. He seems to be determined to set himself up precisely so you'll have no trouble knocking him down three years from now."

"I'm not here to talk politics," Chelgrin said shortly. "May I see the report?"

"Dear Tom, since we must work together, we should try our very best to be friendly."

"The report?"

"It really takes so little time and effort to be at least minimally sociable."

"The report."

The fat man sighed. "As you wish."

Chelgrin held out one hand for the file folder, but Peterson made no move to give him anything.

Instead, the fat man said, "There's nothing in writing this month."

The senator stared at him in disbelief. "What? What did you say?"

"It's a verbal report this month."

"Ridiculous. Impossible!"

Peterson crunched what remained of his Lifesaver and swallowed. When he spoke he expelled fumes of butter-rum. "No, dear Tom. It's true. You see—"

"Dammit, these reports concern my daughter!" Chelgrin said sharply. "*My* daughter. Not yours. Not anyone else's." He struggled with his temper, determined not to lose it; for if he lost it, the fat man would have the advantage. And that was unthinkable. "These reports are private, Anson," the senator said in a carefully measured voice. "Extremely private."

Peterson smiled. "Dear Tom, you know perfectly well that they're read by at least a dozen other people. More likely two dozen, even though they are labeled top secret. I read them before you do. I've read them every month for all these years."

"Yes, but then I always get to read them, too. I get to read them to myself. That's important. You don't know how important that is. To have you give *verbal* reports on what she's been doing . . . Well, suddenly you become an interpreter. Worse. An interloper. It's not as personal. It's not as private or meaningful."

The senator's voice rose steadily through that speech, and he began to breathe fast and noisily, and Peterson said, "Easy, boy. Easy, dear Tom."

Chelgrin realized that he sounded irrational, but this was something he felt deeply. He had little contact with Lisa—now Joanna—and all of it was third hand, a one-way communications bridge constructed of flimsy sheets of paper. In more than a decade not one spoken word had passed between him and his daughter; therefore, he jealously guarded these few minutes of reading, the first of every month.

"That day in Jamaica, when we made these arrangements," said Chelgrin, "you promised you'd provide me with reports of her progress. I wasn't prepared to be totally cut off from her. I wanted to know what she was doing. We agreed that the reports would be written. They're *always* written. Four pages, five, sometimes six or seven. *Always written.* You hand it to me, and I read it by a goddamned flashlight in this goddamned moving car, then I give it back to you, and you destroy it. That's how it works, Peterson. That's how it always works. That's what we agreed to. I have *not* sanctioned any changes. I simply won't permit this!"

"Calm down, dear Tom."

"Don't call me that!"

"No need to shout."

"Do you at least have pictures?"

"Oh, yes. Several pictures. Very interesting pictures."

"Let me see them."

"They need some explanation."

"What explanation? They're pictures of my daughter. I know who she is. I—" He stopped suddenly. The words were choked off by a terrible fear. He closed his eyes. His mouth was dry. "Is she . . . hurt . . . dead?"

"Oh, no," Peterson said. "No, no. Nothing like that, dear Tom."

"Do you mean it?"

"Of course. If it was that, I wouldn't break the news like this, for God's sake!"

Relief brought anger back with it. He opened his eyes and said harshly, "Then what's this all about?"

"I'll give you time to calm down first," Peterson said.

"I don't need to calm down!"

"If you could hear yourself, dear Tom, you wouldn't say that."

The driver slowed the Mercedes, turned left onto a narrow lane, and accelerated again. He didn't seem to be aware of or at all interested in anything that transpired in the rear seat.

At last Peterson picked up his attaché case, which had been wedged between him and the car door, and put it on his lap. He opened it and withdrew a file folder of the sort that usually contained photographs of Lisa.

Chelgrin reached for it.

But Peterson was not ready to relinquish the folder. He said, "The report's verbal this time only because it's too complex and important to be committed to paper. I haven't changed the routine without your permission, dear Tom. I have to do it this way, this one time, just this one time, because this is a special case. We have a crisis of sorts."

Exasperated, Chelgrin said, "Really? Just this once? Well, why didn't you say so straight off?"

Peterson smiled. He briefly placed one chubby hand on Chelgrin's shoulder. "Dear Tom, you didn't give me a chance."

Peterson opened the file folder. It contained several eight-by-ten-inch photographs. He passed the one on top to Chelgrin.

A flashlight lay on the seat between them. The senator picked it up and switched it on.

In the photograph, Lisa and a rather handsome man were sitting on a bench, in some sort of outdoor plaza.

"Who's she with?" Chelgrin asked.

"Oh, you know him."

The senator held the flashlight at an angle, in order not to cast a glare on the glossy picture. He leaned closer and stared at the black-and-white face. "The mustache . . . something familiar about him . . ."

"You'll have to go back in time a bit," Peterson said. "You haven't seen him for seven or eight years, perhaps even longer than that."

Chelgrin suddenly felt as if some invisible, godlike beast had seized his heart in sharp talons. "Ah. Ah, no. It can't be him."

"It is, dear Tom."

"That detective."

"Hunter."

"Alex Hunter. My God."

"He's become bored with his business and with Chicago," Peterson said. "So he's been taking a couple of month-long vacations every year. Last spring he went to Brazil. Two weeks ago he went to Japan. And to Kyoto."

"And to the Moonglow Lounge," Chelgrin said. He could not take his eyes from the photograph, for it had ceased to be merely a picture and had become an omen of disaster, had become danger incarnate, danger crystallized in his two hands. "But Hunter turning up in

that place of all places—the odds must be a million to
one against it!"

"I certainly wish I'd had a few hundred bet in favor
of it," Peterson agreed.

The fat man chewed the shrinking skeleton of his
Lifesaver, and he sounded as if he was grinding the
bones of a small animal, perhaps a bird.

"But we're safe," the senator said anxiously. "Aren't
we safe? I mean, even if Hunter perceives some resemblance between Joanna Rand and the girl he was
looking for all those years ago—"

"He seems to have recognized her at first sight," said
Peterson.

"Oh? Well, then. Well. That's a problem all right.
But he can't prove—"

"He can prove quite a lot, actually," Peterson said,
with an ominous note in his voice that reverberated in
the senator's mind—and in his flesh, too, it seemed—
in the same way that the bass tolling of a giant bell
shivers for some time afterward in the air around the
vibratile clapper. "Hunter has shattered the Rand illusion already. He's taken Joanna's fingerprints and
compared them to Lisa's. He's encouraged her to place
a telephone call to United British-Continental Insurance of London—which upset everyone there, let me
tell you. He's also taken her to a psychiatrist who's
used hypnotic regression therapy. A man named Omi
Inamura, her friend Mariko's uncle. We bugged Inamura's office, and I can tell you we didn't like what we
heard. We didn't like it one bit, dear Tom. Inamura's
managed to find out a lot more than we thought possible. In fact they know virtually everything except our
names and why we did it."

"But why hasn't Hunter contacted me? I was his
client. I paid him a hell of a lot of money to find
her. You'd think when he finally came across—"

"He hasn't contacted you because he suspects you're
part of the conspiracy that put her in Japan with a new
name," Peterson said. "Hunter thinks you hired him
in the first place just to make yourself look good, just

so you could play the concerned, grieving father—all for political purposes. Which is true, of course."

Lightning stepped down the dark sky, jagged heels gouging the thick cloud cover. The flash illuminated the countryside for a second, outlining leafless black trees.

An instant later rain fell. Fat droplets snapped against the windshield.

The driver slowed the car and turned on the wipers.

"What's Hunter going to do?" the senator asked. "Will he go to the newspapers?"

"Not yet," Peterson said. "He figures if we wanted to remove the girl permanently, we could have killed her a long time ago; and he realizes that after we've gone to all the trouble of creating this deception, we intend to keep her alive at nearly any cost. So he supposes she's safe in pushing this thing—at least up to a point. He wants to go as far as possible before he risks bringing in the press. He knows that we're most likely to turn nasty and try to kill them only when they go public with what they've found, and he wants to be certain he's got most of the story before he dares that."

The senator frowned. "I don't like all this talk about killing."

"Dear Tom, I didn't mean Lisa! Not your daughter. Of course not! What do you think I am? I'm no monster. I feel close to her, too. Almost as if she were my own child. My very own child. A darling girl. But Hunter's another matter altogether. He'll have to be taken out at the proper time—which should be soon."

Chelgrin was searching frantically for some way in which to put the fat man at a disadvantage. "What's happened is all your fault. You ought to have had him killed when you learned he was going to Kyoto."

Peterson was not disturbed by the accusation. "We didn't know he was going until he was there. We weren't keeping tabs on him. No reason to. It's been a long, long time since he investigated Lisa's disappearance. We weren't sure he'd even recognize her. And we counted on her keeping him at arm's length—as she was programmed to do."

"So after Hunter's been eliminated, what will we do with her?" the senator asked.

Peterson shifted his great bulk, seeking the comfortable posture that his thick thighs, huge ass, and expansive gut would always deny him. The springs in the car seat protested shrilly. "She can't live as Joanna Rand any longer, of course. She's finished with that life. We think the best thing we can do for her is send her home."

Those last three words pulled the starter on a motor of fear that lay within Tom Chelgrin. *Send her home, send her home, send her home, send her home:* In his mind that phrase repeated like the rhythmic, noisy laboring of a machine. It was the same threat he had used to dominate the driver of the yellow Chevrolet, and now he was made weak and dizzy by this totally unexpected, awful turnabout.

He pretended to misunderstand the fat man. "Send her back to Illinois?"

Peterson stared hard at him. "Dear Tom, you know that's not what I mean."

"But that's home to her," Chelgrin said. "Illinois or maybe Washington." He looked away from the fat man, looked down at the photograph and then out at the rain-swept night. "Where you want to send her . . . that's your home and mine, but it's not hers."

"Neither was Japan."

The senator said nothing.

"We'll send her home," Peterson said.

"No."

"It's really for the best."

"No."

"She'll be well taken care of."

The senator glared at him.

"She'll have the best of everything at home, dear Tom."

"Bullshit."

"She'll be happy there."

"No, no, no!" Chelgrin felt blood rushing to his face; his ears were blazing. He dropped the photograph; his right hand held the flashlight in a viselike grip, and his left hand curled into a fist. "This is the same god-damned argument we had in Jamaica, years ago. We settled it then—forever. I won't let you send her home. Forget it. Period. End of discussion."

"Why are you so set against it?" Peterson asked. He was amused.

"It would give you too great a hold on me."

"Dear Tom, we have the same hold on you regard-less of where we put her. You know that. Japan, Thai-land, Greece, Brazil, Russia. Wherever she is, we can break her, smash her, or use her as we wish; therefore, we control you."

"If you send her home, I won't do a damned thing for you, not ever again. You understand?"

"Dear Tom, why is it that we need to hold your daughter hostage in order to ensure your cooperation?"

"That's ridiculous," Chelgrin said without conviction. "You don't have to do any such thing."

"Ah, but we do. We really do. That's very clear to us. And why? Aren't you and I on the same side? Aren't we working toward the same goal?"

Chelgrin switched off the flashlight and looked out the side window at the dark land rushing past. He was uneasy. He wished it were even blacker in the car, so that the fat man could not see even the slightest detail of his face.

"Aren't we on the same side?" Peterson asked again.

Even in the poor light, the senator could see that the fat man was smiling. More a grin than a smile. Fine white teeth. They looked like extremely sharp teeth. It was a hungry grin.

Chelgrin cleared his throat. "It's just that . . . send-ing her home . . . Well, that's an entirely alien way of life to her. She was born and raised in America. She's used to certain . . . freedoms."

"She'd have freedom at home," Peterson said. "She'd

move in the very highest circles, with all sorts of special privileges."

"None of which equals what she could have here."

"Things have improved at home."

"Oh? When were you there last?"

"I hear things. From reliable people."

"No," Chelgrin said. He was adamant. "She wouldn't be able to adapt. We'll have to put her somewhere else. That's final."

For some reason Peterson was delighted with Chelgrin's bravado—perhaps because he knew that it was hollow, that it was simply a shell of pretended strength, that it was nothing more than the tremulous defiance of a child crossing a graveyard at night—and he giggled girlishly. The giggle swiftly became a full-fledged laugh. He reached for Chelgrin, gripped the senator's leg just above the knee, and squeezed affectionately. But Chelgrin was edgy, and he misinterpreted the action. He saw hostility where there was none, and he stiffened under the heavy hand; he tried to jerk away. The overreaction tickled the fat man. Seeing that the senator was as tense as a cat on a fence with barking dogs leaping up on both sides, Peterson laughed and chortled and cackled and brayed, spraying spittle and expelling clouds of butter-rum breath, until at last he had to gasp hoarsely to keep from choking to death. As Peterson gulped air and continued to spit out weak, wet chains of giggles, Chelgrin could sense the man's big moon face turning red with exertion.

"I wish I knew what was so funny," Chelgrin said.

At last Peterson got control of himself. He mopped his face with his handkerchief.

While the senator waited anxiously for the fat man's next words, the thumping of the windshield wipers seemed to grow louder by the minute. The sound jarred his bones.

"Dear Tom, why don't you admit it?"

"Admit what?"

"We both know the truth."

"What truth is that?"

"The awful, wonderful truth. You don't want Lisa to go home to Mother Russia because you don't believe in what we stand for any more. In fact you've come to despise our philosophy."

"Nonsense."

"You're no longer the good Russian you once were. And you're no longer a Communist at all. You've gone over to the other side—gone over in spirit, though not entirely in practice. You still do your work for us because you have no choice, but you hate yourself for it. The good life here has diverted you, dear Tom. Diverted, subverted, and thoroughly converted you. If you were able, you'd make a clean break with us, turn on us, and cast us out of your life after all we've done for you. But of course you can't. You can't do that because we've acted like smart capitalists in the way we've handled you. We repossessed your daughter. We have a mortgage on your career. Your fortune is built upon credit we've extended to you. And we have a very substantial—I say, *enormous*—lien against your soul."

The senator was still wary. "I don't know where you get these ideas about me. I'm committed to the proletarian revolution and the people's state every bit as much as I was thirty years ago."

That statement elicited another spate of giggling from the fat man. "Dear Tom, be frank with me. I'm being frank with you. We've known about you for fifteen years! More like twenty years. In fact, I think we knew about the changes in you well before you were aware of them yourself. We realized that the capitalist façade was not just a façade any longer. But it doesn't matter to us. It truly doesn't matter. We aren't going to give you the ax merely because you've had a change of heart. There'll be no garroting, no bullets in the night, no poison in the wine, dear Tom. You're still very valuable property. You still answer to us and only to us. You still pass us a splendid lot of information—

although for much different reasons now than when we all started on this little adventure. It was idealism and Russian patriotism that drove you back then. Now it's pragmatism. The difference is nothing that worries us."

The senator felt as if lumps of ice filled his bowels. "Very well, then, we'll be honest. You're right. I've been converted. Every day of my life, I pray to God that whatever help I give you will never be enough. I don't want you to win this battle. I've got to do what you want because, as you so cleverly put it, you've got a lien against my soul, but I pray there's nothing important in all these secret papers I've passed you. Nothing critically important. I pray there's nothing worthwhile, nothing vital, nothing in the technical papers that will advance Soviet weapons research or missile development or your space program. I hope it's garbage that I'm giving you, stuff you already know. I hope those State Department and White House policy briefs have never given you even a slight edge at the bargaining table. I pray, I honestly do pray, I swear I do, I'm not sure I'm even an atheist anymore, so I pray that nothing I ever give you will make it possible for you to smash this big, bustling, freewheeling, wonderful goddamned country." He paused for breath. "Is that what you wanted to hear from me?"

"Ah," Peterson said with conscious dramatic flair, "at last we can strip off the masks we've been wearing for such a long time. It's refreshing, isn't it?"

"Yeah," Chelgrin said, although he thought he might come, in time, to prefer the old illusions.

Peterson said, "That is, it's refreshing, so long as you continue to pass along what we need, in spite of your change of heart."

"Do I have a choice?"

"Not really."

The senator was suspicious of this new honesty. In his youth he had been a risk-taker; but as he had grown older, after he had made his fortune, he had become a creature of carefully chosen habits and strict routine. This sudden turn of events disquieted him. He wondered about other surprises the fat man might have in store.

Rain drummed on the car roof. The spinning tires sang sibilantly on the wet macadam roadway.

"Would you like to see the other photographs?" Peterson asked.

Chelgrin switched on the flashlight and took the stack of eight-by-ten glossies from the fat man.

After a while the senator said, "What'll happen to Lisa?"

"We didn't expect you to be enthusiastic about sending her home," Peterson said. "So we've worked out something else. We'll turn her over to Dr. Rotenhausen, and—"

"The one-armed wonder."

"—he'll treat her at the clinic again."

"He gives me the creeps."

"Rotenhausen will erase all of her Joanna Rand memories, and he'll give her a new identity. When he's finished with her, we'll provide forged papers and set her up in a new life in West Germany."

"Why West Germany?"

"Why not? We knew you'd insist on a capitalist country with the so-called 'freedoms' you cherish."

"I thought . . . well, perhaps she could come back."

"Back here?" Peterson asked incredulously.

"Yes."

"Impossible."

"I don't mean Illinois or Washington."

"There's not a safe place in the States."

"But surely, after all these years, if we gave her a new identity and stuck her someplace like Utah or Colorado or maybe Wyoming—"

"Too chancey," said Peterson.

"You won't even consider it?"

"That's right. I won't. This trouble with Alex Hunter should make it clear to you why I *can't* consider it, dear Tom. But I can't resist reminding you that she could have been here in the States all along, instead of way out there in Japan. She could have returned after the Joanna Rand personna was firmly established—if only you'd agreed to plastic surgery."

Chelgrin spoke through gritted teeth. "I don't want to talk about that."

Your ego overruled your common sense," the fat man said. "You saw her as something you'd created, and that made her sacrosanct. Her face had a few elements of your own face in it, so you couldn't bear to see it altered."

"I said I won't talk about it. It's settled. I haven't changed my mind, and I never will. I won't let a surgeon touch her face. She won't be changed that way."

"Stupid, dear Tom. Very stupid. If the surgery had been done immediately after the screw-up in Jamaica, Alex Hunter wouldn't have recognized her last week. We wouldn't be in trouble now."

"My daughter's one of the two or three most beautiful women I've ever seen," Chelgrin said. "She's exquisite. I won't allow changes."

"My dear Tom, the point of the surgery wouldn't be to make her ugly! She'd still be beautiful. It would just be a different beauty."

"Any difference would make her less than what she is now," the senator insisted. "She's perfect. So just forget it. I won't have her carved into someone else."

Outside, the storm was growing more violent by the minute. Rain fell in dense sheets. The driver was forced to slow the Mercedes to a crawl.

Uninterested in the weather, Peterson smiled and shook his head wonderingly. "You amaze me, dear Tom. I find it so strange that you'd fight to the death to preserve her face——in which you can so readily see yourself—yet you don't feel any remorse for letting us change her *mind*."

"There's nothing strange about it," Chelgrin said defensively.

"Well, after all, the true person is in the mind, not

in the features of the face and body. You adamantly rejected the comparatively simple process of altering her face, but you approved, without the slightest twinge, a far more fundamental tampering."

The senator didn't respond.

"I suspect," said the fat man, "you didn't care about the brainwashing because she wasn't intellectually her father's disciple. Her political beliefs, social expectations, goals, attitudes, her way of thinking, her hopes, her dreams, and her basic personality were all different from yours. Therefore, it didn't matter to you if we erased all of that. Preservation of the physical Lisa— the color of her hair, the shape of her nose and jaw and lips, the proportions of her body—was damned important to your ego; but the preservation of the actual *person* called Lisa—those very special, individual patterns of the mind; that unique creature of wants and needs and intentions so different from your own desires— was none of your concern."

"So you're calling me an egotistical bastard," Chelgrin said. "So what? What am I supposed to do? Try to change your opinion of me? Beg forgiveness? Promise to be a better person? What the hell do you want from me?"

"Dear Tom, let me put it this way———"

"Put it any way you like."

"I don't think it was any loss to our side when you were won over spiritually to their philosophy," the fat man said. "And I'd wager that the average capitalist wouldn't look at you as much of a prize either."

"If this is meant to wear me down somehow, and make me agree to plastic surgery for her, you're just wasting your time. Let's drop it."

Peterson laughed softly. "You've got inch-thick armor, dear Tom. It's impossible to insult you."

Chelgrin hated him.

For a minute or two they rode in silence.

They were in a long pocket of woodlands and open fields between suburbs, and there were only scattered lights on the gentle hills that bracketed the lane.

Thin patches of fog drifted across the road ahead, stirring ghostily. Each time that lightning sparked the sky, the ground mist glowed briefly, as if it was a strange incandescent gas.

Finally the fat man said, "There's some danger involved if we try to tamper with the girl's memory a second time, and you ought to know about it."

"Danger?"

"The good Dr. Rotenhausen has never worked his magic twice on the same patient. He has doubts."

"What sort of doubts?"

"This time the treatment might not take. In fact it might end badly."

"What do you mean? What could happen?"

"Madness, perhaps."

"Be serious."

"I am serious, dear Tom. Absolutely, perfectly serious. She might be turned into a raving lunatic. Or she might wind up in a catatonic state. You know—just sitting, staring into space, a vegetable, unable to talk, unable to feed herself. It could even end in death."

Chelgrin stared at the fat man for a long time, and at last he said, "No. I don't believe it. You're making this up."

"I assure you it's true."

"You're making it up so that I'll be afraid to send her to Rotenhausen. Then my only choice will be to let you take her home, which is what you most want to do."

"I'm being honest with you, dear Tom. Rotenhausen says her chances of coming through the treatment a second time are not good. Less than fifty-fifty."

"You're lying," Chelgrin said. "But even if you weren't lying, I'd take the chance with Rotenhausen. I refuse to have her taken to Russia. I'd rather see her dead."

"You might," Peterson said. "You might see her dead—or worse."

Rain was falling with such force and in such tremendous quantity that Harry, the fat man's driver, had to pull off the road. The headlights could pierce no more than fifteen or twenty feet of the wet night. They parked in a roadside rest area, near trash barrels and picnic tables. Harry said he was certain the downpour would slack off in a minute or two, and then they could get moving once more.

The fat man slipped another butter-rum circlet between his pursed lips, scrubbed his fingers with his handkerchief, and snuffled with delight as the candy began to melt on his tongue.

The air inside the Mercedes was close, moist, stifling. The windows were beginning to cloud.

The roar of the rain was so loud that the senator had to raise his voice to be heard. "Moving her secretly from Jamaica to Switzerland was a nightmare."

"I remember it all too well," said Peterson.

"How do you propose to get her out of Japan and all the way to Dr. Rotenhausen?"

"She's making it easy for us. She and Hunter are going to England to look into the British-Continental Insurance Association."

"When?"

"The day after tomorrow. We've got something planned for them. We'll drop clues they can't miss, steer them away from London and straight to Switzerland. We'll put them on to Rotenhausen, and when they go after him, we'll let the trap fall shut."

"You sound so confident."

"Oh, I am, dear Tom! They won't make any more trouble for us. They're just two little mice, already nibbling at the bait cheese. By Saturday or Sunday, Hunter will be dead . . . and your lovely, lovely daughter will be in Rotenhausen's clinic."

· 44 ·

Wednesday afternoon, when the time came for Joanna to leave the Moonglow with Alex and take a taxi to the train depot, she did not want to go. Each step out of the second-floor apartment and down the stairs and across the lounge was difficult; she felt as if she were walking through deep water, through mud up to her hips. The very carpet and walls and furnishings seemed to be trying to hold her back. She stopped several times, on one pretense or another—a forgotten passport; a last-minute decision to wear a different pair of traveling shoes; a sudden desire to say good-bye to the head chef, who was even then preparing the sauces and soups for that evening's customers—but eventually Alex insisted she hurry lest they miss their train. Her delaying tactics were not caused by any worry about what would happen to the business in her absence; she trusted Mariko to manage the club efficiently and profitably. And she wasn't worried about Mariko's safety either, for there would be around-the-clock bodyguards. Her reluctance to depart was solely the result of a surprising homesickness that seized her even before she had left home. She had come to this country under mysterious circumstances, a stranger in a strange land, and she had prospered. Everywhere she went, these wonderful people had welcomed her in their own low-key way. She loved Japan and Kyoto and the Gion district and the Moonglow Lounge. She loved the musical sound of the language, the extravagant politeness of the people, the merry sound of fingerbells at worship services, the beauty of temple dances, the scattered ancient structures that had survived wars as well as the encroachment of Western-style architecture, loved the taste of sake and tempura, the delicious fragrance of hot brown *kamo yorshino-ni;* she was one with all of that, with this most ancient yet ever blossoming and growing culture. This was her world, the only place to which she had ever truly belonged, and she dreaded leaving it, even temporarily. However, she was determined not to let Alex go to England alone; therefore, she hugged Mariko one last time and followed Alex out the front door. When she got into the red-and-black taxi, her mood was melancholic.

The superexpress to Tokyo was a luxurious train with a buffet car, plush seats, and, considering the great speed it attained, surprisingly little rail noise and lateral motion. She wanted Alex to sit by the window, but he insisted she have the privilege, and the porter was amused by their argument. Alex was less persistent than she; he took the window seat, but neither of them spent much time looking at the scenery. They talked about Japan, about England, and about a dozen other things—although, by unspoken agreement, neither of them said a word about brainwashing, British-Continental Insurance, or Senator Thomas Chelgrin.

In the course of the four-hour trip, Joanna discovered that Alex was an effective medicine for melancholy. They had been so completely occupied with the unraveling of the mystery in which they had found themselves that she had quite forgotten what a charming conversationalist he was. For days they had talked about little else but the tangled skein of her past and the possible terrors that lay like knots in her future. Now once again she had the opportunity to notice and appreciate his sense of humor, compassion, wit, and intelligence—all of the qualities that had caused her to fall in love with him so easily. They held hands, and his touch thrilled her as if it had been her first romantic contact with a man. Several times, as they rocketed along the rails toward Tokyo, she wished she could lean over and kiss him, even if only on the cheek, but that sort of public display of affection would be shocking in Japan. Gradually she relaxed when she realized that, although Kyoto was her home, she could also feel almost equally at home with Alex, no matter where he led her. She wanted him more than she had ever wanted anything else in her life.

At the Western-style hotel in Tokyo, a two-bedroom suite was reserved for them. The employees at the front desk were unable to conceal their amazement at this brassy behavior. A man and a woman, with different last names, unmarried, using the same suite and making absolutely no effort to conceal their association, were considered terribly decadent, regardless of the number of bedrooms at their disposal. Alex didn't notice the raised eyebrows punctuating nearly every face in sight, but Joanna did and nudged him with her elbow until he realized that everyone was watching them surreptitiously. She was amused, and her unrepressed smile, taken to be an expression of lascivious anticipation, only made matters worse; the registration clerk would not look at her directly. But they were not turned away. That would be unthinkably impolite. Besides, in any Tokyo hotel that catered to Westerners, desk clerks and bellhops knew that almost any boldness could be expected of Americans. Two bellmen escorted her and Alex to the tenth floor, distributed their luggage between bedrooms, turned up the thermostat in the drawing room, opened the heavy drapes, and refused tips until Alex assured them that he offered the gratuities only in respect of their excellent service and fine manners; tipping had not yet taken hold most places in Japan, but Alex, so long accustomed to American expectations, felt guilty if he provided nothing. The accommodations looked pretty much like any good two-bedroom suite in Los Angeles or Dallas or Chicago or Boston; only the view from the windows firmly established the Japanese setting.

The moment she was alone with Alex, she moved closer to him. In a stage whisper she said, "Ah, at last we can do wonderfully wicked things to each other!"

He laughed.

"How does it feel to be totally depraved?" she asked.

He put his arms around her, and that seemed like the most natural thing in the world for him to do.

"Careful," she said teasingly. "They'll call the cops and have us thrown out."

"When I booked the suite," he said, "I forgot about Japanese propriety. I hope I didn't embarrass you."

She hugged him. It began as a show of affection, but it was swiftly transformed into a demand for something more. He was warm, solid, powerfully masculine. Her hands were on his back, and she could feel the muscles like ribbons of stone.

"Joanna—"

To hush him she stood on her toes and kissed the left corner of his mouth, then the right.

His hands moved slowly down her back until they parenthesized her waist.

Her kisses grew bolder. She suddenly became the uninhibited woman that everyone in the lobby thought she was. She licked Alex's lips, and the kiss became deeper, harder. Her hands were still on his back, but her fingers were raised and bent, poised like claws; she wanted to tear the clothes from him.

He squeezed until she thought he might break her, but then he slid his hands all the way down to her buttocks. An almost indetectable shudder of pleasure passed through him and was transmitted to her. Through the cool, silky fabric of her dress, he stroked and caressed and kneaded the firm flesh; and with his fingertips he lovingly traced and retraced the deep cleft of her bottom.

She interrupted the kiss only long enough to say his name, the breath of it expelled against his lips. She was certain that he had made the decision at last.

After a few seconds, however, he seemed to catch

himself on the brink of a long fall. He stiffened and pulled back from her.

He cleared his throat and said, "Let's not rush into it, Joanna."

Trying her best to hide her disappointment, she said, "Your depravity doesn't run very deep."

He smiled, but there was a troubled, haunted look in his eyes.

"You realize, of course, that this is ridiculous," she said. "I mean, you're playing the frail, virginal maiden, and *I'm* playing the young stud full of fire. Haven't we got this backwards?"

"I suppose we do," he said.

"I want you."

"And I want you, Joanna. More than anything."

"Then take me."

"I want to make love to you. Love, Joanna. Not just sex. I could take you to bed now and fuck you six ways from Sunday. But if I did that without being committed to you, then it would be like all the other times. You'd be like all the others. If I did that without being committed to us, to the future, to a future together . . . well, I might just be throwing away the best chance either of us has had for happiness." He shook his head sorrowfully. "I've got an awful lot to work out in my mind before I can tell you I love you and really mean it."

She opened her arms to him. "Let me hold you. Hold me. Let me help you."

He turned away from her, strode to the nearest window, and stared out at the city. He was angry; she could tell that much by the way he stood, by the way he drew up his shoulders. But he was angry with himself, not with her.

"My parents did a damned good job on me, didn't they?" he asked, his voice cold and bitter. "They screwed me up real good. They conditioned me to think of love as something treacherous, something that's always followed by pain—terrible, unexpected, disabling pain." He turned from the window and faced her. "I know why I feel this way. I know why I'm afraid to love you. I'm scared to death because there's this worm inside of me, this hideous black worm that keeps telling me that love means pain, that love and agony are synonymous. That worm is the only legacy my parents left me. I've figured it all out. I've psychoanalyzed myself. I know that when it comes to this subject, I behave irrationally. But I can't help it. I'm trying. God knows, I'm trying, Joanna. But it's going to take time."

She went to him. She took his hands in hers, and she pressed his fingers to her lips.

He pulled her close. They kissed, but not half as passionately as they had kissed before.

He had been patient with her. Now she must be patient with him.

Nevertheless, she was determined that the veil between them would be cast aside before their plane left for London in the morning. They were rushing headlong into dangerous times, into a confrontation with dangerous men. Joanna knew intuitively that they would be better off if they were bonded together, not just physically but emotionally as well, fast together in flesh and in spirit, together in every sense of the word. She was certain they would be safest if they could function almost as a single organism. Love had more power than hate and guns and all the governments in the world. She was convinced that love was the force that could move the immovable. Perhaps that conviction was silly; perhaps it was the result of her long-held, quietly desperate desire for a love that, until now, had been denied her, and perhaps she was exaggerating the importance of such an abstract concept in a modern world that put its faith only in that which was concrete. But she was convinced nonetheless. As lovers, physically entwined, they would find their strength more than doubled; it would be increased geometrically, a hundredfold, even a thousandfold. She *knew*—and, like the most dogmatic missionary, would not allow any argument or evidence to

convert her from her view—that they would have far
more courage and fortitude if they thought, worked,
and dreamed as one. In the days to come, love was
going to be the source of their power and, therefore,
a matter of survival.

"What about sushi for dinner?" she asked.

"Sounds good."

"At the Ozasa?"

"You know Tokyo better than I do. Wherever you
say."

She also sensed that Alex was struggling out of the
emotional straitjacket into which his parents had put
him, and that he did not have many more straps to
unbuckle before he would be free. With care she
might finesse him out of the tangled sleeves.

Tonight.

It had to be tonight.

It began with an early dinner.

The December evening was chilly, but the restaurant
was warm. And Alex, who could not take his eyes off
Joanna, was generating a lot of heat, too. Tonight
her hair seemed a more lustrous shade of gold, her
eyes bluer, her face more beautiful than ever. She
wore a clinging, forest-green knit suit with a scoop-
neck, white sweater; and every movement she made—
no matter whether she was walking, standing, or sitting—seemed calculated to present the full curves
of her breasts or the narrowness of her waist or the
sleek roundness of hips and bottom for his considera-
tion.

Joanna looked cool, tranquil, sublime.

The restaurant was the Ozasa, in the Ginza district,
around the corner from the Central Geisha Exchange.
It was upstairs, cramped, and noisy, but it was one of
the finest sushi shops in Japan. A scrubbed wood
counter ran the length of the place, and behind it
were the chefs, dressed all in white, their hands red
from continual washing. When Alex and Joanna entered, the chefs shouted the traditional greeting,

"Irasshai!" The room was virtually awash in wonderful odors—omelets sizzling in vegetable oil, soy sauce, various spicy mustards, vinegared rice, horseradish, mushrooms that had been cooked in a special aromatic broth, and more. But there was not the slightest whiff of fish, even though several varieties of raw fish were the primary ingredients in every dish in the house. The only seafood fresher than Ozasa's was that which still swam in the deeps.

Joanna knew one of the chefs from her days as a Tokyo performer. His name was Toshio. She made the introductions, and there was much bowing all around.

They sat at the counter, and Toshio put large mugs of tea in front of them. They each received an *oshibori,* with which they wiped their hands while examining the selection of fish that filled a long refrigerated glass case behind the counter.

Tonight the unique and exquisitely torturous tension between Alex and Joanna transmuted even the simple act of eating dinner into a rare experience charged with erotic energy. He ordered *tataki,* little chunks of raw bonito that had been singed in wet straw; each would come wrapped in a bright yellow strip of omelet. Joanna began with an order of *toro sushi,* which was served first. Toshio had trained and practiced for years before he was permitted to serve his first customer, and now his long apprenticeship was evident in the swift grace of his culinary art. He removed the *toro,* fatty marbled tuna fish, from the glass case, and his hands began to move like those of a master magician, quicker than the eye. With a huge knife, Toshio smoothly sliced off two pieces of tuna. From a large tub beside him, he grabbed a handful of vinegared rice and deftly kneaded it into two tiny loaves spiced with a dash of *wasabi.* Toshio pressed the bits of fish to the top of the loaves, and with a proud flourish he placed the twin morsels before Joanna. The entire preparation required less than thirty seconds from the moment the chef slid open the door of the refrigerated case. The brief ceremony, which ended with Toshio washing his hands before creating the *tataki,* reminded Alex of the posthypnotic code words that Omi Inamura had used with Joanna: Toshio's hands were like butterflies, capering through an airborne mating dance. Sushi could be a messy dish, especially for a novice; but Joanna was not a novice, and while consuming the *toro* she managed to be both neat and sensuous. She picked up one piece, dipped the rice part in a saucer of *shoyu,* turned it over to keep it from dripping, and placed the whole thing on her tongue. She closed her eyes and chewed, slowly at first, then more energetically. The sight of her enjoying the *toro* increased the pleasure that Alex took in his own food. She ate with that peculiar combination of dainty grace and avid hunger that he had seen in cats. Her slow, warm, pink tongue licked left and right, at the corners of her mouth, cleaning her lips; and she smiled as she opened her eyes, as she picked up the second piece of *toro.* He said, "Joanna . . ." She said, "Yes?" He hesitated, then said, "You're beautiful." It was not everything that he had intended to say, and it was not nearly as much as she wanted to hear him say, but she grinned. They drank tea and ordered other kinds of sushi—dark-red lean tuna, snow-white squid, blood-red *akagai* clams, octopus tentacles, pale shrimp, caviar, and abalone; and between servings they cleared their palates with sliced ginger. Each order of sushi contained only two pieces, but Alex and Joanna ate slowly and heartily, sampling every variety, then returning to their favorites. (In Japan, Joanna explained, the complex system of etiquette, the rigid code of manners, and the tradition of almost excessive politeness all contributed to the creating of a special sensitivity to the sometimes multiple meanings of language. The two-piece-and-only-two-piece method of serving sushi was an example of that sensitivity. Nothing that was sliced could ever be served singly or in threes, for one slice was *hito kire,*

which also meant *kill,* and three slices was *mi kire,*
which also meant *kill myself.* Therefore, if sliced food
were presented for consumption in either of those
quantities, it would be an insult to the customer as
well as a tasteless reminder of an unpleasant subject.)
So they ate sushi, and Alex thought about how much
he wanted Joanna. They drank tea, and Alex wanted
her more with each sip he watched her take. They
talked continuously, and they joked with Toshio, and
when they weren't eating they turned slightly toward
each other so that their knees rubbed together, and
they chewed bits of ginger, and Alex wanted her. He
was still sweating, and not all of his perspiration could
be attributed to the fiercely hot *wasabi* in the sushi
loaves; the want, the need, was like a fist inside him,
twisting his innards; but this heat, this pain was much
sought, much pursued, much trumpeted; delicious pain.

White faces. Bright lips. Eyes heavily outlined in black
mascara. Eerie. Erotic.

Ornate kimonos. The men wearing dark colors.
Other men dressed as women, in brilliant hues, be-
wigged, mincing, coy.

And the knife.

The lights dimmed. Suddenly a spotlight bored
through the gloom.

The knife appeared in the bright hole, trembled in a
pale fist, then plunged down.

Light exploded again, illuminating all.

The killer and his victim were attached by the blade,
an umbilical of death.

The killer twisted the knife once, twice, three times,
with gleeful ferocity, playing the midwife of the grave.

The onlookers watched in silence and in awe.

The victim shrieked, staggered backward. He spoke
a line, another, last words. Then the immense stage re-
sounded with his fall.

Joanna and Alex stood in the back of the auditorium,
in darkness.

Ordinarily, advance reservations were required by every kabuki theater in Tokyo, but Joanna knew the manager in this place.

The program had begun at eleven o'clock that morning and would not be finished until ten o'clock that night. Like the other patrons, Joanna and Alex had stopped in for just one act.

Kabuki was the distillation of Japanese culture; it was the essence of dramatic art. The acting was highly stylized; all emotions were exaggerated; the stage effects were elaborate, dazzling; but, Alex thought, the result was somehow both wildly colorful and subtle. In 1600, a woman named O-kuni, who was in the service of a shrine, organized a troupe of dancers and presented a show on the banks of the Kamo River, in Kyoto, and thus began kabuki. In 1630, in an attempt to control so-called immoral practices, the government prohibited women from appearing on stage. Consequently, there arose the Oyama, specialized and highly accomplished male actors who took the roles of female characters in the kabuki plays. Eventually women were permitted to appear on stage again, but the newer tradition of all-male kabuki was firmly established by that time and was considered inviolate. In spite of the archaic language, which most members of the audience could not understand, and in spite of the artificial restrictions imposed by the transvestism, the popularity of kabuki never waned. That was partly because of the gorgeous spectacle it presented, but the vitality of the art was mostly attributable to the themes it explored—comedy and tragedy, love and hate, forgiveness and revenge—which were all made bigger and brighter than life by the ancient playwrights.

Emotions ARE *universal,* Alex thought as he watched the play. He was aware that the idea was not new with him, but it was something he had never carefully considered; and he began to realize that the implications were stunning. Emotions varied not at all from city to city, country to country, year to year, and century to century. The stimuli to which the heart responded changed slightly as a man grew older; the child, the young man, and the elder did not perceive exactly the same causes of joy and sorrow; but the feelings were identical in all of them, for feelings were woven together to form the one true fabric of life, always and without exception, a fabric with but one master pattern.

Suddenly, through the medium of kabuki, Alex Hunter achieved two valuable insights:

First, if emotions were universal, then in one sense he was not alone, never had been alone, and never could be alone. As a child, cowering under the harsh hands of his drunken parents, he had existed in despair, for he had thought of himself as a boy in a bubble, sealed up and cast adrift, beyond the ken of society, floating outside of the normal flow of time. But now he realized that he had never really been alone. Every night that his father had beaten him, other children, in every corner of the world, had suffered with Alex, victims of their own sick parents or of strangers, and together they had all endured. They were a brotherhood. No pain or happiness was unique. All feelings were drawn from a common pool, a vast lake from which all of mankind drank; and (oh, he could see it, see it so clearly) throughout this lake were webs of common experience, invisible but nonetheless substantial fibers that linked one drinker to the next and every one to every other; so that all the races, religions, nationalities, and individuals became one, indivisible. Therefore, no matter what distance he put between himself and his friends, between himself and his lovers, perfect isolation would forever escape him. Whether he liked it or not, life meant emotional involvement, and involvement meant taking a lot of risks.

Secondly, he saw that if emotions were universal and timeless, they represented the greatest truths known to mankind. If millions upon millions of people in dozens of different cultures arrived independently at the same concept of love, then the reality of it could not be denied.

The loud, dramatic music that had accompanied the murder now began to subside.

On the huge stage one of the "women" stepped forward to address the audience.

The music fluttered and was extinguished by the Oyama's first words.

Joanna glanced at Alex. "Like it?"

"Yeah. It's wonderful. It's something. It's really something."

They went to a bar where the owner greeted them in English with three words: "Japanese only, please."

Joanna spoke rapidly in Japanese and convinced him that they were natives in mind and heart if not by birth, and he smilingly welcomed them.

They had sake, and Joanna said, "Don't drink it like that, dear."

"What am I doing wrong?"

"You shouldn't hold the cup in your right hand."

"Why not?"

"Because that's considered to be the sign of a gross, impatient drunkard."

"Maybe I am a gross, impatient drunkard."

"Ah, but do you wish everyone to know it?"

"So I hold the cup only in my left hand?"

"That's right."

"Like this?"

"That's right."

"I feel like such a barbarian."

She winked at him and grinned. "You can use both hands on me."

They went to the Nichigeki Music Hall for a one-hour show that smacked of vaudeville and burlesque. Comedians told low jokes, many of them very amusing, but Alex was cheered more by the sight of Joanna laughing than he was by anything the funnymen had to say. Between the variety acts, gorgeous young women in revealing costumes danced rather poorly but with faultless enthusiasm and energy. Most of the chorines were breathtaking beauties, but in Alex's eyes, at least, none of them was half as stunning as Joanna.

Back at the hotel, in their suite, Joanna called room service and ordered a bottle of French champagne. She also asked for appropriate pastries, things that were not too sweet, and these came packed in a pretty red lacquered wood box.

They changed into pajamas. She wore a pair made of black silk, with red stripes at the cuffs and collar.

At her suggestion, Alex opened the drapes, and they pulled the sofa in front of the low windows. They sat side by side and studied the Tokyo skyline while they drank the champagne and nibbled almond crusts and walnut crescents.

Shortly after midnight, some of the neon lights in the Ginza began to wink out.

"Japanese nightlife can be pretty frantic," Joanna said, "but they start to roll up the sidewalks early by Western standards."

"Shall we?" he asked.

"Shall we what?"

"Shall we roll up the sidewalks here?"

"I'm not sleepy."

"The champagne isn't working?"

"It's invigorating."

"You'll drink me under the table."

She grinned wickedly. "Yeah? Once we're under there, what'll we do?"

He wanted her, needed her. He was hungry for the taste of her mouth, starved for the feel of her skin and the soft tension of her flesh. He wanted to undress her and kiss her breasts and slip deep into her. But he said, "We *do* have to get up at six o'clock."

"No, we don't."

"We do if we want to catch the plane."

"We don't have to get up at six if we never go to sleep in the first place. We can sleep on the plane tomorrow."

"What'll we do now?" he asked.

"Sit here silently waiting for the dawn."

"Is that supposed to be romantic?"

"Don't you think it is?" she asked.

"Boring."

"We'll drink champagne all the while."

"We'll never make one bottle last that long."

"So we'll order another."

"Room service closed shop a few minutes ago."

"Then we'll just talk," she said.

"All right. About what?"

She turned sideways, facing him. Her eyes were very blue. "We'll talk about what we want to do."

"In England?"

"No."

"With our lives?"

"No."

"About the state of the world?"

"Who can do anything about that?"

"Then what?"

She slid against him. She was warm.

He put an arm around her.

"We'll talk about what we want to do with each other," she said.

She put her lips to his throat. She did not kiss him. Not exactly. She seemed to be feeling the passion in the artery that stood up and thumped in his neck.

He turned to her, moved to her, and they pressed hard together, belly to belly. Her breasts were squashed pleasantly against his chest. He kissed her forehead, her eyes.

"Please," she said.

Her soft mouth opened under his, and for a while the world was reduced to four lips, two tongues, and a warm moist sharing. She tasted like almonds and champagne.

His hands roved over her. She was marvelously smooth and firm beneath the silk.

"Please," she said. "Please, Alex."

He stood, bent down, and scooped her up in his arms. She seemed weightless, and he felt as if he could lift the earth.

She clung to him. In her clear eyes there was a vulnerability that touched his heart.

He carried her into his room and put her down on the bed. Slowly, lovingly, he undressed her.

The only light was that which came from the drawing room, through the open door. Pale as moonlight, it fell in a wide band across the bed. She lay naked in the ghostly glow, too beautiful to be real. Ethereal.

He stripped off his own pajamas, stretched out beside her, and took her in his arms.

For a moment the bedsprings sang in the cathedral silence; then a prayerlike hush settled once again through the shadows.

They kissed and touched, and his erection was like an iron staff between them.

After a while he could hear her heart pounding —or perhaps it was his own.

He explored and worshiped her with kisses. He pulled his mouth from hers, kissed her ears and throat, kissed her bare shoulders, kissed her slender arms and fingers, kissed her lovely breasts and licked gently at her nipples, which were very swollen, hard, and slightly salty. He kissed her taut, concave belly, kissed her thighs and her knees and each of her toes. He parted her long legs and kissed the insides of her perfect thighs, and finally he kissed the dewy center of her, kissed those tender folds again and again, kissed the button hidden in them, kissed and tasted.

She put her hands on the obeisant head, tangled her fingers in his hair, urged him on without speaking a word, arched her back, lifted herself to him.

Alex ached for her. She was so wonderfully warm. So fresh. So vibrant. This precious, precious body. This very precious woman. Her flesh trembled in his reverent hands. Delicate . . . as delicate as . . . dancing butterflies. He ached, but not just with lust; he ached with a pure crystalline desire to possess her and to be possessed by her, to know all there was to know about her and to be held up for her scrutiny as well, to trust and be trusted, to cherish and be cherished.

She began to groan softly, excitedly. Her breathing grew ragged and fast.

"Oh, Alex!"

He kissed, kissed.

Joanna whimpered with pleasure and called his name again and suddenly cried out and thrashed under the loving lash of his tongue.

As she partly raised herself from the bed, he slipped his hands beneath her, gripped her buttocks, held her to him, and relentlessly pursued the secret kiss. She shook in a wind that he stubbornly resisted; she shuddered and tossed and at last fell back, sighing with release.

He moved his mouth upward, across the triangular patch of crisp hair, across her belly, lingering at her breasts for a minute or two, then moving up again. He spoke her name against the hollow of her throat.

She was smiling. A Madonna smile.

He kissed her lips, which were sensuously moist and slack.

Her eyes gleamed darkly, and her hair looked silver in the phantom light.

She reached down between his legs and took him in her hand. "Feel it jump about. It's an eager beast, isn't it?"

He laughed. "Not a beast."

"Oh, yes. A real beast."

"Not in your hands."

"What is it in my hands?"

"A puppy anxious to nuzzle you."

She laughed, too. "No, a beast."

"If you say so."

"But I'll tame it."

"That's the fate of it," he said.

"To always be tamed."

"Yeah."

"Poor beast."

"Lucky beast."

"It likes to be tamed?"

"Loves to be tamed. Repeatedly."

He was poised above her, supported by his arms, and she guided him into her.

"Now," Joanna said. "Sweet Alex. Sweet, sweet, sweet Alex. Now . . ."

He closed his eyes because he was afraid that the sight of her would send him off like rockets too soon; but with his eyes shut he imagined he could see his penis moving within her, swimming within her, as if it were a mysterious fish gliding through a warm, dark, jellylike sea.

He filled her—emotionally as well as sexually. She had never felt so alive. She was exploding. She wrapped her legs around him and thought of the beast with two backs and had a crazy urge to howl.

He wanted to hold back until her own frenzy was as great as his, until he could carry her over the edge with him. But for once he found it almost impossible to restrain himself. He sensed that it was not just a couple of tablespoons of semen that wanted out of him. It was more than that, much more. A torrent of pent-up fears, terrible memories, and years of despair would burst from him with his seed; he would be clean for the first time in his life. This was not merely an act of sex; it was rejuvenation; more than that, rebirth; it was a kind of reincarnation.

Love existed.

Love was real.

And he had found it.

He searched for his new soul, which was within her.

Her hands traveled rapidly over him, testing the muscles that bulged in his arms and shoulders and back.

He drove into her with both power and tenderness, and she felt herself dissolving beneath him.

"I love you, Joanna."

She barely heard him. He made the declaration quietly, as if he were afraid for her to hear.

"I love you, darling," she said.

"I mean it. I can say it and mean it."

"I mean it, too," she said.

"I love you."

"I love you."

"Love you, love you."

She hugged him and writhed against him and wept with happiness and climaxed again, incredibly, the very moment that she felt him begin to loose himself in her.

Drained, he collapsed gently upon her breasts.

But they did not sleep at all. They wrapped the hours of the night around them, as if time were a brightly shining thread and they were a wildly spinning spool.

• 45 •

Pump, pump, pump . . .

"Nine," said Paz.

"Damn!" Carreras said explosively.

"Ten," said Paz.

"Shit!" said Carreras, exhaling violently.

The barbells dropped with a resounding crash.

The bodybuilder walked back and forth, swinging his arms, flexing his legs, allowing himself only a minute or two of rest before he continued.

In Switzerland, in Zurich, in the magnificent house above the lake, in the gymnasium that had been an elegant music room, Ignacio Carreras was working diligently on his calves, thighs, buttocks, hips, waist, lower back, and abdominal muscles. He had been lifting weights for two hours, with little time off to rest. After all, when he rested there was no pain; and he wanted the pain because it tested him, and because it was an indication of growth.

Seeking pain, he began his last exercise of the day —a set of Jefferson lifts. He straddled the barbell, keeping his feet twenty-four inches apart. He squatted, grasped the bar, right hand in front of him and left hand behind. He inhaled deeply, then exhaled as he rose to a standing position, bringing the bar up to his crotch. His calves and upper thighs throbbed painfully. He squatted, hesitated only a second, and rose with the bar again. His legs felt as if they were afire. He was gasping. Face red. Pumped-up muscles like ropes in his neck and shoulders. Blinking sweat out of his eyes. His royal-blue boxer shorts were soaked with perspiration; they clung to him. He squatted. Rose up. Buttocks clenched. Then down. Letting the weights touch the floor. But only for a second. Then up again. Legs stiff as wood. Muscles threatening to lock on him. All the way up, hold it, teeth clenched, then down. Pain like a spark, like a flame, like a roaring blaze.

Other men lifted weights for many reasons. Some did it to improve their health. Some wanted to look better. Others did it just to have their pick of the women who pursued bodybuilders. Some did it for reasons of self-defense; and some did it as a game, some as a sport, and some as an art.

To Ignacio Carreras, those were all secondary reasons.

"Seven," said Paz.

"Christ!" Carreras said.

"Eight," said Paz.

Carreras endured the torture because he was obsessed with power. He wanted to have power of all kinds over other people—financial, political, psychological, and physical power. To his way of thinking, it was no good at all to have great wealth if he were also physically weak. He was able to break his enemies with his bare hands as well as with his money, which he enjoyed immensely.

"Ten," said Paz.

Carreras put down the barbells and wiped his hands on a towel.

"Excellent," said Paz.

"No."

Carreras stepped in front of a full-length mirror and posed for himself, studying every visible muscle in his body, searching for improvement.

"Superb," said Paz.

"The older I get, the harder it becomes to build. In fact I don't think I'm growing at all. These days it's a battle just to stay even."

"Nonsense," said Paz. "You're in wonderful shape."

"Not good enough."

"Getting better."

"Never good enough."

"Madame Dumont is waiting in the front room," said Paz.

"And she can continue to wait," Carreras said.

He left Paz and went upstairs to the master bedroom suite on the third floor.

It was a classic eighteenth-century room. The ceiling was high and white. The molding was richly detailed, although the only curved lines were in the three fleurs-de-lis above the marble fireplace. All the woodwork was painted pale gray, and the walls were dressed in two-tone gold-stripe paper. The Louis XVI bed had a high headboard and a high footboard, both of which were upholstered in a red-and-gold leaf-pattern silk that matched the abbreviated canopy and the spread. Directly opposite the foot of the bed, against the wall, stood a matched pair of Louis XVI mahogany cabinets with painted tôle plaques on the drawers and doors. One corner was occupied by a large eighteenth-century harp; the instrument was intricately carved, gilded, and in perfect playing condition. The carpet was beige with faded red roses spaced widely upon it.

In that room Ignacio Carreras looked like an ape that had lumbered unexpectedly into the middle of a lady's tea party.

He stripped out of his damp boxer shorts, went into the enormous master bath, and spent ten minutes baking in the attached sauna room. He thought about Madame Marie Dumont, who was tapping her foot impatiently downstairs, and he smiled. For another half an hour he soaked in the big tub, massaging his legs beneath the water. Then he suffered through an icy cold shower; however, he stayed warm inside by picturing Marie, boiling mad, down there in the front room.

He toweled himself vigorously, put on a robe, and walked into the bedroom just as the telephone sounded. Paz answered it downstairs but rang through a moment later.

Carreras picked up the receiver. "Yes?"

"London calling on line one," said Paz.

"Marlowe?"

"No. The fat man."

"He's in London?"

"So he says."

"Put him through—and make sure Madame Dumont doesn't get a chance to pick up an extension."

"Yes, sir," said Paz.

A scrambler device was attached to the phone. Carreras switched it on.

Peterson said, "Ignacio?"

"Yes. Where are you?"

"Marlowe's office. Safe to talk?"

"As it ever is. What are you doing in London?"

"Hunter and the girl will arrive here tonight," Peterson said.

"Rotenhausen swore that she'd never be able to leave Japan."

"He was wrong. Can you move fast?"

"Sure."

"Go to Rotenhausen in St. Moritz."

"I'll leave this evening," said Carreras.

"We'll try to put Hunter on to the good doctor's trail, as planned."

"Are you directing the show in London now?"

"Not all of it," said the fat man. "Just this business with Hunter and the girl."

"Good enough. Marlowe isn't fit to handle it."

"I realize that."

"It's made him hypertense."

"I've noticed."

"He broke some rules. For one thing, he tried to pry her real name out of me."

"Out of me, too," said Peterson.

"He made some silly threats."

"Can't have been any sillier than the ones I've heard." said the fat man.

"I've recommended his removal," said Carreras.

"So have I."

"If approval comes through, I'll take care of him myself."

"Dear Ignacio, it won't be anything that drastic. Just a trip home."

"If it's approval for more than that, I want the job."

"Don't worry. No one's going to deny you your fun."

"See you in Moritz?" Carreras asked.

"Certainly," said the fat man. "I think I'll take a few skiing lessons."

Carreras laughed. "That would be an unforgettable sight."

"Wouldn't it?" Peterson laughed, too, and hung up.

The telephone doubled as an intercom. Carreras buzzed the front room.

"Yes, sir?" It was Paz.

"Madame Dumont may come up now."

"All right, sir."

"And you should pack a suitcase for yourself. We'll be going to St. Moritz in a few hours."

"Yes, sir."

Carreras put down the receiver and went to a closet door that concealed a fully equipped wet bar. He began to mix drinks: orange juice and a couple of raw eggs for himself; vodka and tonic for Marie Dumont.

She arrived before he finished preparing her vodka, and she slammed the bedroom door behind her. She strode up to him, confronted him. She was furious.

"Hello, Marie."

"Who the hell do you think you are?"

"I think I'm Ignacio Carreras."

"You bastard."

"I've made vodka and tonic for you."

"You can't keep *me* waiting like that!" she said angrily.

"Oh? I thought I just did."

"Bastard."

"Such a sweet-talking young lady."

"Stuff it."

She was beautiful. She was only twenty-six years old, but she was sophisticated and wise beyond her years—although not so wise as she thought. Her dark hair framed a cool face and darker eyes that contained strange hungers and more than a little pain. Her fine features and the elegant carriage that she had learned in expensive boarding schools combined to give her a haughty look. She was as thin as a fashion model, leggy, but with full round breasts.

She dressed beautifully, too. She wore a well-tailored two-piece beige suit, a thousand-dollar Paris original which she brightened with a pink blouse, just the right amount of jewelry, and a subtle perfume that cost two hundred dollars an ounce.

"I expect an apology," she said.

"Do you?"

"Yes."

"There's your drink."

"You can't treat me like this!"

She had been spoiled all her life. Her father was a wealthy Belgian merchant, and her husband was a far wealthier French industrialist. She had been denied nothing—even though her demands were often excessive.

"Apologize," she insisted.

"You wouldn't like it."

"Like it? I demand it!"

"You're a snotty kid. You know that?"

"I told you to apologize."

"But a beautiful snotty kid."

"Apologize, damn you!"

"Calm yourself, Marie."

"Apologize, you greasy ape!"

He slapped her lightly, but hard enough to sting.

"There's your drink," he said.

"Bastard."

"Bitch. Pick up your drink."

"Stuff it up your ass."

He slapped her so hard that she almost fell.

"Drink it," he said.

"You make me sick."

"Then why do you come here?"

"Slumming."

He slapped her again. Harder.

She bounced off the wall, wobbled, and put a hand to the red mark on her cheek.

"Pick up your drink," he said sternly.

She spat on him.

This time he did knock her down.

She sat on the floor, stunned, legs akimbo.

Carreras quickly pulled her to her feet. With one big hand on her throat, he slid her up the wall and pinned her there.

She was crying, but there was a perverse desire in her eyes.

"You're sick," he told her. "You're a sick, twisted little rich girl. You have your white Rolls Royce and your little Mercedes. You live in a mansion. You've got servants who do everything but crap for you. You spend money as if it were going out of style tomorrow, but you can't buy what you want. You want someone to say no to you. You've been pampered all your life, and now you want someone to push you around and hurt you. You feel guilty about all that money, and you'd probably be happiest if someone took it away from you. But that won't happen. And you can't give it away because most of it's tied up in trusts. So you settle for this, for being slapped and humiliated and debased. I understand. I think you're crazy. But I do understand. You're too shallow to realize what great good fortune you've had in life, too shallow to enjoy it, too shallow to find some way to use your money for a meaningful purpose. So you come to me. *You* come to *me*. Keep that in mind. You are in my house, and you will do what I say. Right now you'll shut up and drink your vodka and tonic."

She had saved up saliva while he'd been talking, and she spat at him again. The spittle landed on the side of his nose, dribbled down to the corner of his mouth.

He pressed her against the wall with his left hand, and with his right hand he grabbed the drink he had fixed for her. He held the glass to her lips, but she kept her mouth tightly shut.

"Take it," Carreras said.

She refused.

Finally he forced her head back and tried to pour the stuff into her nose. She tossed her head as much as she could in his firm grip, and at last she opened her mouth to keep from drowning. She snorted and gasped and choked, spraying vodka from her nostrils. He poured the rest of the drink between her lips and let go of her as she spluttered and gagged helplessly.

Carreras turned away from her and picked up the

mixture of orange juice and raw eggs that he had made for himself. He drank it in a few long swallows.

When he finished, she was still not recovered. She was doubled over, coughing, trying to clear her throat and get her breath.

Carreras seized her by the arm, dragged her to the bed, and pushed her face-down on the mattress. He shucked off his robe and stood naked behind her. He pushed up her skirt. She was wearing a garterbelt and stockings rather than pantyhose; she was prepared for something quite like this. He hooked his fingers in the elastic of her panties and jerked them down. The flimsy material tore. She began to struggle, as if she realized only at that moment what he intended to do. He fell upon her, held her down with his hips, and entered her roughly. He thrust with great force, thrust brutally, faster and deeper and harder with each stroke, eagerly pursuing his own pleasure but not at all concerned about hers.

"You're hurting me," she said weakly.

He knew that was true. But he also knew she liked it this way more than any other. Besides, this was the *only* way he liked it.

He used women. Abused them.

Pain was power.

Sexual power over other people was as vitally important to Ignacio Carreras as was financial, psychological, and sheer physical power. Before he finished with Marie Dumont, she would be his slave once more. He would take her every way possible—between her lovely breasts, in her vagina, as now, then in the anus, in her mouth with enough insistence to choke her, and always without tenderness. He would call her filthy names and force her to call herself by those names. He would squeeze her until she begged to be let go, pinch her until she squealed with pain. He would degrade and humiliate her. He would require the worst of her, and then demand things even more disgusting

than what had come before, until she felt totally worth-
less, until he felt godlike, and until they were both
thoroughly satisfied.

As Marie clawed at the bedspread, wept, and struggled beneath him, he thought of Lisa-Joanna. He
wondered if he would have the opportunity to do to
Joanna what he was now doing to Marie. The very
thought of it made him swell to impossible dimensions
within the Frenchwoman, and he drove even more
wildly, more viciously into her.

When he had first seen the Chelgrin girl, more than
a decade ago, she had been the most beautiful and
desirable creature he'd ever encountered, but he had
not been able to touch her. And judging by the
photographs taken in Kyoto, time had only improved
her.

Carreras ardently wished that Dr. Rotenhausen's
treatment would fail this time; then the girl, Lisa-
Joanna, might be passed to him for disposal. According
to Rotenhausen, she might be irreparably damaged if
she were put through the program a second time. In
fact, the doctor thought there was a better than even
chance that she would come out of it with the mental
faculties of a four-year-old, and be forever frozen at
that level of intellect. The thought of a four-year-old
child's mind in that lush body appealed to Carreras as
nothing else ever had. If Joanna were affected by the
treatment in precisely that way and then given to
Carreras for disposal, he would take her away, tell
them she was dead and buried, but keep her alive for
his own use. If he possessed her when she was in such
a retarded state, he would be able to dominate and use
her to an extent that he had never been able to dominate and use anyone, including Marie Dumont. She
would be his little animal, a loving kitten to lick his
boots. He would train her as if she were a dog, and—

Madame Marie Dumont was screaming.

"Shut up, bitch," he said.

"Hurting me. Hurting me so bad."

He reached out, pushed her face against the mattress, to muffle her crying.

—Joanna would learn the limits of joy, and she would be thrust beyond the limits of pain in order to learn total, unquestioning obedience. If Carreras commanded it, she would bring his slippers in her mouth. With a child's mind and a woman's body, she would have no purpose but to provide him with every conceivable sexual thrill; and he would bruise her mouth, her thighs, and the sweet inner regions of her, bruise her with constant violent use. In a tight collar, on a leash, naked, crawling at his side, eager to please him, terrified of him yet worshipping him, Joanna would be his pet. He would use her until he had explored every permutation of lust. Then he would share her with Paz; the two of them would use her together, in every normal and perverse act that they could imagine. Finally, when there was nothing left of Joanna that was secret, when she had endured every degradation, when she could no longer arouse him, Carreras would beat her to death with his hands. He was obsessed with power in all its variations, and the power of death was the greatest of them all. He could think of no license more valuable than the license to kill, no freedom more precious than the freedom to kill again, no pleasure more intense and exhilarating than that which he absorbed by some sort of mystical osmosis from the dying bodies of his victims. When he had his fill of the child-woman Joanna, he would take at least an entire day to murder her; slowly, slowly; he would draw out her final agony and thus extend his own monstrous joy.

Borne away by that fantasy of absolute dominance, he lost control of himself and spurted repeatedly, explosively into Madame Dumont. He hadn't intended to loose himself so quickly. He'd wanted to turn her upside down a few times, ravish her in every orifice, and leave her exhausted and defeated. But the sadistic image of Joanna in his mind's eye defeated him instead.

Power.

At the moment he felt drained of power.

Limp, he pulled away from Marie Dumont. He picked up his robe and put it on.

She rolled onto her back and looked quizzically at him. Her skirt was rucked up to her waist. Her hair and face were wet with vodka, tears, and sweat. Her expensive clothes were a mess.

Carreras went to the bar and began to crack eggs into a tall glass.

"What did I do?" she asked worriedly.

"Nothing."

"Tell me."

"You can leave."

She got up, shaky as a newborn colt.

"Tell me what I did wrong."

"Nothing. I just want you to go."

"But we've hardly—"

"Get the hell out of here!"

She was stunned.

She sat down on the edge of the bed.

"Get out. Didn't you hear me?"

"You don't mean it," she said, shaken.

He could only think of Joanna, of using her and then breaking her.

"I'm tired of you," he said. "Go."

She began to cry again.

He went to her, jerked her to her feet.

She clung to him.

He hustled her to the door.

"Can I come back?" she asked.

"Maybe."

"Say yes."

"Call me in a week."

He pushed her into the hall and closed the door.

He went back to the bar, mixed some juice with the raw eggs, and drank the viscous concoction.

He went to the closet, took a suitcase down from the shelf, put it on the bed, and began to pack.

He was anxious to get to St. Moritz.

PART THREE

A PUZZLE IN A PUZZLE

The winter tempest
Blows small stones
Onto the temple bell.
—Buson, 1715–1783

• 46 •

Neither Alex nor Joanna slept well on the flight from Tokyo. They were tense, excited about their new relationship, and worried about what awaited them in England. To make matters worse, the plane encountered heavy turbulence several times; they lolled in their seats like seasick landlubbers on their first ocean voyage.

When they landed in London, Thursday night, Alex felt as if he belonged in a hospital ward for terminally ill patients. His long legs were cramped, swollen, and heavy; sharp pains shot through his calves and thighs with each step. His buttocks pinched and burned as if he had been sitting on needles during the trip, and his back ached all the way from the base of his spine to the top of his neck. His eyes were bloodshot, grainy, and sore. His mouth was fuzzy and dry and tasted like sour yogurt.

From the look of her, Joanna had the same list of complaints. She promised to get down on her knees and kiss the earth—just as soon as she was certain she had enough strength to get up again.

At the hotel they unpacked none of his suitcases and only part of one of hers. She had brought two hand-held hair dryers. One of them was a light plastic model, and the other was a big old-fashioned metal blower with a ten-inch metal snout. There was also a small screwdriver in the suitcase, and Alex used it to dismantle the bulkiest of the two hair dryers. Before leaving Kyoto, he had stripped the insides from the machine and had carefully fitted a gun into the hollow shell; it was the silencer-equipped 7mm. automatic that he had taken off Shifty more than a week ago. It had passed through x-rays and customs inspection without detection. He took a large tin of body powder from the same suitcase, went into the bathroom, squatted beside the commode, put up the lid and the seat, and sifted the talc through his fingers. When there was no more powder in the can, two extra clips of ammunition remained.

"You'd make one hell of a criminal," Joanna said.

"Yeah. But I've done better being honest than I'd have done on the other side of the law."

"We could rob banks."

"Why don't we just buy control of one?"

"That's not as romantic."

"But safer."

"Oh, you're just not adventurous."

"I guess not."

"A regular stick-in-the-mud."

"Dull. That's me."

"Colorless."

"Bland."

"A wallflower."

"Withdrawn," she said.

"I'm painfully shy."

She laughed and hugged him.

They ate a light dinner in the main room of their three-room suite. At ten o'clock they crawled under the covers of the same bed; but before they slept, they shared nothing more than a chaste goodnight kiss.

Alex had a strange dream. He was lying in a soft bed in a white room, and three surgeons, all in white with white masks over their faces, stood above him. The first surgeon said, "Where does he think he is?" The second surgeon said, "South America. Rio." And the third said, "What happens if this doesn't work?" The first surgeon said, "Then he'll probably get himself killed without solving our problem." Alex lifted one hand to touch the nearest doctor, but his fingers suddenly changed into tiny replicas of buildings, then became five tall buildings seen at a great distance, and then the buildings grew larger, into skyscrapers, and they came nearer, and a city grew across the palm of his hand and up his arm, and the faces of the surgeons were replaced by a clear blue sky, and below him was Rio, the fantastic bay, and then his plane landed, and he got out, and he was in Rio, and a Spanish guitar surrounded him with mournful music.

When Joanna moved against him in the darkness and kissed the back of his neck, the travel clock on the nightstand showed four o'clock.

"Awake?" she asked.

"Am now."

"I heard you're shy."

"A wallflower."

He turned onto his back.

She straddled him, and he fondled her heavy breasts, and she rode him as if she were a cowgirl on a bronc.

"I tamed the beast again," she said.

"He'll be wild again by morning."

"I hope so."

Later, they slept.

At seven thirty Friday morning, Alex was awakened by a loud pounding noise. At first he thought it was inside his head, but that wasn't the case. It sounded like a man slamming his shoulder into a sturdy door.

Joanna sat up beside him, clutching the cover to her bare breasts. "What's that?"

Alex shook off the last shroud of sleep. He cocked his head, listened for a moment, and said, "Someone's at the door in the main room."

"Sounds like they're breaking it down," she said.

He reached for the loaded pistol that he had left on the nightstand.

He wanted Joanna to remain in bed, but she refused. She stayed close to him.

He didn't turn on the light when he got up, for he was afraid it would reveal them to the enemy rather than the other way around.

The furious thumping ceased when Alex reached the open door between the bedroom and the drawing room. The silence, having come so suddenly, now seemed more ominous than the thunderous pounding had been.

He took one step into the other room, and she stopped him. "Wait."

"It's all right," he said. "They won't try anything too serious in a hotel."

"But it won't be just a game either," she said.

Alex stood quite still, listening for footsteps. There were none.

The drapes were shut. The dim gray light that seeped in at the edges of the windows was not enough to illuminate the room. The writing desk and chairs and sofas resembled sleeping animals in the gloom. The purple-black shadows, which looked as dense as pudding, appeared to pulse and writhe malignantly in the corners.

Alex felt for the light switch, found it, flicked it on. He squinted against the sudden glare and held the gun in front of him.

"There's no one here," Joanna said.

He started toward the door that led to the hotel's eighteenth-floor corridor.

"Alex, maybe you shouldn't."

A blue envelope was on the carpet in the foyer. It had been slipped under the door.

"That's the reason for all the knocking," Alex said. "They wanted to roust us out of bed and get us out here so we'd see it."

He picked up the envelope.

"What is it?" she asked.

"A note from the senator."

"How do you know that?"

"I just do."

"How?" she persisted.

The envelope was clean, unmarked by typewriter or pen, and it was sealed.

Alex frowned. "I can't say how I know, but I'm sure of it." He tore open the envelope and unfolded the single sheet of blue paper that was inside.

Do not read this aloud. There are listening devices in your room. I must speak with you. Come to the British Museum at 10:00. You will be followed. I trust you to lose your tail. I am risking my life to send this note.

—Tom Chelgrin

• 48 •

London was rainy and cold. The bleak December sky was as low as the tallest building, and thin beards of mist trailed even lower.

The taxi driver who picked them up in front of their hotel was a burly man with a neatly trimmed white beard. He wore a rumpled hat and smelled of peppermint. "Where can I take you this morning?"

"Eventually, we want to go to the British Museum,"

Alex said. "But first you'll have to lose the people who're following us. Can you do that?"

The driver stared at him.

"He's perfectly serious," Joanna said.

"He seems to be," said the driver.

"And he's sober," she said.

"He seems to be," said the driver.

"And he isn't crazy," she said.

"That remains to be seen," said the driver.

Alex counted out four five-pound notes and gave them to the man. "I'll have the same for you, plus the fare, at the other end. Will you help us?"

"Well," the driver said, "they tell you to humor a madman if you meet one."

"That's good advice. Humor me."

"Only one thing bothers me," said the driver. "Is it coppers watching you?"

"No," Alex said.

"Is it coppers, young lady?"

"No," Joanna said. "They're not nice men."

"Neither are the coppers." He grinned, tucked the bills into his shirt pocket, stroked his white beard with one hand, and said, "Name's Nicholas. At your service. What should I be looking for? What sort of car might they be using?"

"I don't know," Alex said. "But they'll stay close behind us. If we keep an eye open, we'll spot them."

The morning traffic was heavy. Nicholas turned right at the first corner, left at the second, then right, left, left, right.

Alex kept a watch out the back window. "The brown Jaguar sedan."

Nicholas had been glancing at the rearview mirror. "Can't be anyone else."

"Lose them," Alex said.

Nicholas wasn't a master of evasive driving. He weaved from lane to lane, dodging between cars and buses, trying his best to put a lot of traffic between them and their tail; but none of his maneuvers was sufficiently dangerous to discourage pursuit. For the first ten minutes the brown Jaguar was always in sight. Nicholas turned corners without signaling his intent, but never at high speed and never from the wrong lane, which made it easy for the Jaguar to stay with him.

"Your daring does not exactly take my breath away," Alex said.

"Doin' my best, sir."

Joanna put one hand on Alex's arm. "Remember the story of the tortoise and the hare."

"Yeah. But I want to lose them quickly. At the rate we're going, we'll only lose them after eight or ten hours—when they're too damned tired to bother with us any more."

Alex knew that a London taxicab was not permitted to operate if it bore any mark of a collision—even a small dent or scrape. Obviously, Nicholas was thinking of that as he drove. The insurance company would pay for any repairs, of course; but the car might be in the garage for a week, which would be lost work time. That possibility inhibited the driver.

Nevertheless, before long, Nicholas managed to put three cars between them and the Jaguar. "We're going to lose them," he said happily.

To Alex, it looked as though Nicholas was being *allowed* to lose the tail. The driver of the Jaguar was not handling his car as well as he had at the start; in fact he, not their cab driver, was responsible for the growing separation, as if he wanted to let them get away.

Why?

Because they know where we're going, he told himself.

He fell into a conversation with himself, one of those debates that he would have carried out aloud if he had been alone.

They know we're going to meet the senator? he asked himself.

Yeah. And he's one of them, so they really don't have to tail us.

But if he's one of them, why did he approach us like this? Why did he tell us to lose our tail?

I don't know. But he must be one of them. How else did he find out we're in London?

Watch it. Just watch it. It's good to be a little bit paranoid. But if you're a whole lot paranoid, you won't be able to think clearly. Maybe you're seeing subtle layers of plot and counterplot where there are none. Maybe the driver of the Jaguar is just cautious, even more cautious than good old Nicholas. Could be as simple as that. Could be.

Still . . . He stared out the back window, unable to wipe the frown off his face.

They came to an intersection where the traffic signal had just gone from green to red, but Nicholas screwed up enough courage to round the corner illegally. The tires even squealed.

The cars behind them stopped, good citizens all, and the Jaguar was boxed in. It wouldn't be able to move until the light changed again.

They were on a narrow street, flanked by exclusive shops and theaters. There were only a few cars, not nearly so many as on the thoroughfare. Nicholas drove halfway down the block and turned into an alley before the Jaguar had a chance to round the corner after them. From that alley they went into another, then onto a main street once more.

As they continued to wind from avenue to avenue through the slanting gray rain, Nicholas glanced repeatedly at the rearview mirror. Gradually he broke into a smile, and at last he said, "I did it! I lost 'em. Just like in those American police shows on the telly."

"You were marvelous," Joanna said.

"You really think so?"

"Simply terrific," she said.

"I guess I was."

Alex stared out the back window.

At the British Museum, Joanna opened the door of

the cab, got out, and ran for the shelter of the main entrance.

As Alex paid the fare, Nicholas said, "Her husband, I suppose."

Alex blinked. "What?"

"Well, if it wasn't the coppers—"

"Oh. No. Not her husband."

Nicholas scratched his beard. "You aren't going to let me like this?"

"I'm afraid I am," Alex said.

He got out of the cab and slammed the door.

For a moment Nicholas stared at him curiously through the rain-streaked window; then he drove away.

Alex stood in the cold drizzle, shoulders hunched, hands in his coat pockets. He looked up and down the street, studying the traffic and paying especially close attention to the parked cars.

Nothing suspicious.

At last he joined Joanna in the doorway, out of the rain.

"You're soaked," she said.

"Yeah."

"What are you looking for?"

"I don't know," he said. He was still reluctant to go inside; he studied the street.

"Alex, what's wrong?"

"Getting rid of the Jaguar was too damned easy. Nothing's been easy so far. Why this?"

"Isn't it time our luck changed?"

"I don't believe in luck," he said. But finally he turned away from the street and followed her into the museum.

• 49 •

They were standing in front of an impressive array of Assyrian antiquities when they were finally contacted. It was not the senator; Chelgrin's representative was a small, wiry man in a peacoat and dark brown cap. He had a hard face with watchful little eyes, and his mouth appeared to be set in a permanent sneer. He stepped up beside Alex, pretended to appreciate a piece of Assyrian weaponry for a minute or two, but gave up the ruse when Alex faced him directly.

"Yer 'unter, ain't yer?"

The stranger's cockney accent was nearly impenetrable, but Alex understood him: *You're Hunter, aren't you?*

Occasionally Alex's interest in languages extended to especially colorful dialects. Cockney, richer in slang and more distorted in pronunciation than any other regional usage of the English tongue, was nothing if not colorful. It had evolved in the East End of London, but it had spread to many other parts of England. Originally it had been a means by which East End neighbors could talk to one another without making sense to the law or to other outsiders; but these days the law spoke it, too, when necessary.

The stranger squinted at Alex, then at Joanna. "Yer butchers like yer pitchers. Both of yer."

Alex translated for himself: *You look like your pictures. Both of you.* The word *butchers* meant *look* by virtue of cockney rhyming slang. A butchers hook rhymed with look; therefore, by the logic of the code, "butchers" meant "look" when used in the proper context.

"And yer butchers bent ter me," Alex said. "Wot

300

yer want?" *And you look like a less than honest man to me. What do you want?*

The stranger blinked, astonished to hear an American speaking the East End dialect with such confidence. "Yer s'pposed ter be a Yank."

" 'At's wot I am."

"Yer rabbit right good," said the stranger. *You talk very well.*

"Tar," said Alex. *Thanks.*

Joanna said, "I'm not following this."

"I'll explain later," Alex said.

"Yer rabbit so doddle . . . 'ell, nofink surprises me no more," said the stranger.

"Wot yer want?" Alex asked him.

"Got a message."

"Who from?"

"From a right pound-note geezer."

Alex translated: *From a man who speaks real fancy* (usually a man with a la-de-da Oxford accent, though not always).

" 'at don't tell me much," Alex said.

"Geezer wif a double of white barnet."

Alex deciphered it: *A man with a lot of white hair.* Barnet Fair was a famous carnival just outside London. Since Barnet Fair rhymed with hair, the single word *barnet* meant *hair.*

"Wot's 'ee call 'imself?"

"Nofink."

"Gotta call 'imself somfink."

"The geezer just gimme a poney ter bring yer a message."

A poney was twenty-five pounds.

"Wot message?"

"Seems 'ee's stayin' at the Churchill in Portman Square, and 'ee says 'ee wants to see yer."

It was Senator Thomas Chelgrin who was waiting in a room at the Churchill Hotel. It could be no one else.

"Wot else?" Alex asked.

The stranger scratched his chin and said, "Well, 'at's all der was."

"Not much of a message."

"All I got, mate." The stranger started to turn away, then stopped, looked back, licked his lips, seemed to make up his mind about something, and said, "One fing."

"Wot's 'at?" Alex asked.

"Be careful of 'im."

"I know 'ee's dodgey," Alex said. *I know he's no good.*

"Worse 'an 'at. 'ee's shnide." *Worse than that. He's slimey.*

"I'll be careful," Alex said. "Tar."

The stranger pulled down on his cap. "If it was me, I wouldn't touch 'im less 'ee was wearin' a durex from 'ead ter foot of 'imself."

Alex translated and laughed. *I wouldn't touch him unless he was wearing a contraceptive sheath from head to foot.* He held the same opinion of the senator from Illinois.

The man in the peacoat hurried away from the Assyrian antiquities and disappeared around the corner.

"What did he say?" Joanna asked.

Alex told her all of it, including the final comment.

She laughed weakly. "Unfortunately, he won't be wearing a durex."

And sure as bloody hell, Alex thought sourly, that goddamned pompous bastard's carrying a disease.

· 50 ·

From a public telephone at the museum, Alex called the Churchill Hotel in Portman Square.

Joanna fidgeted beside him. She was frightened. The prospect of meeting her father could not be expected to fill her with joy.

Alex asked the hotel operator for Mr. Chelgrin's room, and the senator answered on the first ring. "Hello?"

"This is Alex Hunter."

"Is . . . she with you?"

"Of course."

"I can't wait to see her. Come on up."

"We're not in the hotel," Alex said.

"Then where are you?"

"Still at the museum."

"I've got to see you soon. I don't know how much time I have."

"I think we should have a nice long chat on the phone before we get together."

"This is urgent! I—"

"We need to know a few things. Like what happened in Jamaica. And why Lisa became Joanna."

"It's too important to discuss on the phone," Chelgrin said. "Much more important that you can possibly have guessed."

Alex hesitated, glanced at Joanna. At last he said, "All right. Let's meet just inside the entrance to the National Gallery in half an hour."

"Oh, no. No. That's impossible."

"Why?"

"It has to be here. In my room at the Churchill."

"I don't like that. Too risky for us."

"I'm not here to harm you."

"I hope that's true."

"I want to help."

"I'd prefer we met on neutral ground."

"But I don't dare go out," Chelgrin said. A note of panic wavered in his voice, and that was completely out of character. "If I'm seen with you . . . if I'm even seen here in London . . . then I'm dead."

"Who would kill you?"

Chelgrin began to speak rapidly, excitedly, as if he thought Alex might hang up on him. "They would. They'd kill me. No doubt about it. If they saw me with you, they'd know I'd changed sides." His panic was increasingly evident. "I've taken every precaution to conceal this trip. My office is telling everyone that I've gone home to Illinois to meet with a few important constituents. I didn't fly out from Washington because I was afraid I'd be traced too easily if I did." He spoke faster, faster, running the words together. "So I drove to New York, flew from there to Toronto, caught another flight to Montreal, then a third from Montreal to London. I'm wiped out. Exhausted. I'm a nervous wreck." And he was getting more nervous by the minute. "I'm staying at the Churchill because it's not my usual hotel. I usually stay at Claridge's. But if they find out I'm not in Illinois, they'll know where I've gone, and they'll start looking for me. They'll find me sooner or later. Dammit, Hunter, I've risked my life! I've broken with them! I'm going to help you and my daughter. If she'll allow me to call her my daughter, after what I did. Together we can expose the whole thing. The whole damned thing. They're finished."

"Who are they?" Alex asked.

"The Russians."

"What have Russians got to do with this?"

"I simply can't talk about it on the phone. It's too damned big for that. You've got to come to me. I can't risk showing my face."

Alex thought about it for a while.

"Hunter?"

"I'm still here."

"My room number is four sixteen."

Alex didn't say anything.

"Please hurry. Before they find me."

Alex was silent.

"Hunter?"

"Yeah."

"You've got to come."

Alex sighed. "All right."

· 51 ·

They took a taxi to Harrods. Even that early in the day, the huge world-famous store was aswarm with shoppers, including a surprisingly large number of swarthy, hawk-nosed men in Arabian attire.

"You used to see a lot of wealthy Americans buying everything in sight," Alex said. "Then for a while there were more Japanese than Americans. Now the Arabs outnumber both the Americans and the Japanese. Who will it be twenty years from now? Black Africans spending uranium and chromium money? Maybe a bunch of Eskimos who've cornered the walrus tusk market."

Harrods' Telex address was "Everything, London," and that was not hyperbole. In two hundred departments, the great store carried everything from specialty foods to sporting goods, from chewing gum to Chinese art, from rare books to rubber boots, from faddish clothes to fine antiques, from hairpins and nail polish to expensive oriental rugs—a million and one delights.

Alex and Joanna ignored all of the exotic merchandise as well as most of the mundane stuff. They purchased only two sturdy umbrellas and a set of plain but well-made steel cutlery.

In the privacy of a toilet stall in the ladies' room, Joanna unwrapped the package of cutlery. She examined each piece and chose a wickedly sharp butcher's knife, which she concealed in her coat pocket. She left the other knives behind when she departed.

Now both she and Alex were armed. That was a far more serious offense in London than it would have been most anywhere else in the world, but they were not concerned about spending time in jail. Walking *unarmed* into Tom Chelgrin's hotel room would be by far the most dangerous course they could take.

From Harrods they took another taxi on a winding course through the rain-slick streets, until Alex was certain that they were not being followed. They got out of the cab three blocks from the Churchill.

They cautiously approached the least public aspect of the hotel, using the umbrellas to hide their faces as much as to shield them from the rain. Rather than barge through the front entrance and walk across the large regency-style lobby, where they were most likely to be spotted by a lookout, they used an unlocked rear door meant for certain hotel deliveries. They quickly found a service stairwell and darted into it before anyone spotted them.

"Better leave your bumbershoot here," Alex said. "We'll want our hands free when we get there."

She stood her umbrella beside his, in the corner, at the bottom of the steps.

"Scared?" he asked.

"Yeah."

"Want to back out?"

"Can't," she said.

Even though they were whispering, their voices echoed in the cold stairwell.

He kissed her cheek. "Love you."

"I love you, Alex."

He unbuttoned his coat and pulled out the 7 mm. automatic that had been jammed under his belt. He put it in his overcoat pocket and kept his hand on the butt.

She put her hand on the butcher's knife in her pocket.

"Ready?" he asked.

"As I'll ever be."

They climbed the stairs to the fourth floor.

The corridor was warm, brightly lit, and deserted. It was too silent—as if every guest on this level was holding his breath, waiting tensely for a trap to fall on a couple of unsuspecting mice.

They left the stairwell and scurried along the hallway, glancing at room numbers. In spite of the elegant decor, Alex couldn't shake the feeling that he was in a carnival funhouse and that some monster was going to spring at them suddenly from a door or out of the ceiling.

Just before they reached 416, he was stopped abruptly—not by a funhouse beast but by a vivid premonition, a vision like the brief but commanding burst of a camera's flashbulb. In his mind he saw Thomas Chelgrin spattered with blood.

Joanna stopped beside him, gripped his arm. "What's wrong?" she whispered.

Alex wiped one hand across his forehead. A moment ago he had been cold; but now he was dripping sweat.

"Alex?"

"He's dead."

"Who?"

"Tom Chelgrin."

"How do you know that?"

"I just do. I'm sure of it."

He took the pistol from his coat pocket and continued along the corridor.

The door to 416 was ajar.

She shuddered.

"Stand behind me," he said.

"Let's call the police."

"We can't. Not yet."

"It's their job."

"We've been through that."

"We have enough proof now."

"We don't have anything more than we had yesterday."

"If he's dead, that's proof of something."

"We don't know he's dead. Besides, even if he is, it's not proof of anything."

"Let's get out of here."

"We don't have anywhere to go."

He stepped forward and knocked on the door.

No one answered.

He stood to one side and used the silencer-extended barrel of the pistol to push the door all the way open.

Stillness.

The lights were on in there.

Alex called softly: "Senator?"

No answer.

He stepped across the threshold.

"No!" Joanna said, but she followed him.

Thomas Chelgrin was face-down on the sitting room floor, in a puddle of blood.

· 52 ·

Senator Chelgrin was wearing a blue bathrobe that had soaked up a great deal of blood. The back of the garment was marred by three bloody holes. He had been shot once at the base of the spine, once in the middle of the back, and once between the shoulders. His left arm was thrown out, fingers hooked into the carpet; and his right arm was folded under him. His head was turned to one side. Only half of his face was visible, and that was obscured by smears of blood and by a thick shock of white hair that had fallen across his eye.

Alex cautiously inspected the rest of the small suite, but the killers were not there.

When he returned to the main room, Joanna was kneeling beside the corpse.

"Don't touch him!" Alex said.

She looked up. "Why not?"

"It's not going to be easy to walk out of here and into our own hotel if you're covered with bloodstains."

"I'll be careful."

"You've already got blood on the hem of your coat."

She glanced down. "Oh, damn!"

He pulled her to her feet and away from the corpse. He took his handkerchief from his pocket and rubbed the stain on her coat.

After a while he said, "It doesn't look good, but it'll have to pass."

"Alex, shouldn't we check him over?"

"Why?"

"Maybe he's still alive."

"Alive?" he asked, incredulous. "Look at those wounds. Look at the size of those holes. They used a gun with a hell of a punch. They were professionals. Jesus. The bullets had to go straight through him. Had to tear open his chest as if it were just a piece of rotten fruit. Look at all that blood. Too much. Too much blood. Smashed his heart. Shattered his spine. He's as dead as a man can be, Joanna."

"How did you know he'd be here like this? Out there in the hall, how did you know what we'd find?"

"A premonition," he said uneasily.

"But how?"

He shrugged. "I wish I knew." His recent clair-voyance gave him the creeps.

She stared at the corpse and shook her head sadly. "I don't feel a thing."

"Why should you?"

"He *was* my father."

"No. He wasn't. He surrendered all those rights and privileges a long time ago."

"I guess he didn't mourn for Lisa," she said.

"That's right. You don't owe him any tears."

"Why?"

"We'll find out."

"Will we?"

"Sure."

"I don't think so. I think we're in some sort of gigantic Chinese puzzle. We'll just keep climbing into smaller and smaller boxes forever."

Alex watched her closely for a moment, wondering if she might go to pieces on him after all. She was surprisingly calm, but that could mean she was bottling up her feelings, suppressing them. Her eyes were steady; her lips were pressed tightly together, and they didn't tremble; but she was pale.

She realized he was worried about her, and she conjured up a ghost of a smile. "I'll be okay. Like I told you—I don't feel a thing. Let's get out of here."

"Not yet."

"But what if they come back and—"

"They won't be back," Alex said. "If they'd known the senator had made contact with us, and if they'd wanted to kill us, they'd have waited here. Come on. We've got to search this place."

The thought of a search didn't appeal to her. "That's ghoulish."

"But necessary."

"Search for what?"

"For anything. For everything. For whatever little scrap might help us solve this crazy goddamned puzzle."

Joanna glanced at the front door, which they had closed and locked.

"We won't be interrupted," he assured her, although he wasn't certain of that.

"If a maid walked in—"

"The maid's already been here this morning. The bed's freshly made."

Joanna took a deep breath. "Let's finish this as fast as we can."

"You follow me," Alex said. "Double-check me as I go through his things. I might overlook something. But I don't want you to touch anything, for the same reason I don't want you touching the corpse; we have to be careful not to leave fingerprints or any other clues that would point to us. If the police think we did it, that'll just add to the confusion."

"And we're confused enough."

"Exactly. We can't be running from the cops and working on this case at the same time."

In the bedroom Chelgrin's two calfskin suitcases were on a pair of folding luggage racks. One of them was open. Alex pawed through the clothes until he found a pair of the senator's black socks. He pulled these over his hands: makeshift gloves.

Chelgrin's billfold and credit card wallet were on the dresser. Alex went through them, with Joanna watching closely, but neither the billfold nor the wallet contained anything unusual.

The closet held two suits and a topcoat. The pockets were empty.

Two pair of freshly shined Gucci loafers were on the closet floor. Alex took the shoe trees out of them and searched inside. Nothing.

A Gucci shaving kit stood beside the sink in the bathroom. There was nothing in it but an electric razor, shaving powder, cologne, a comb, and a can of hairspray.

Alex returned to the open suitcase. It also proved to be a barren field.

The second suitcase was not locked. He opened it and tossed the clothes onto the floor, piece by piece, until he found a nine-by-twelve-inch manila envelope.

"Something?" Joanna asked.

"Let's hope to God it is," Alex said. " 'Cause if it's not, we're back on square one of this game."

The envelope contained several brittle yellow clippings from the *New York Times* and the *Washington Post*. There was also an unfinished letter, apparently in the senator's handwriting, which was addressed to Joanna. Alex didn't take time to read either the letter or the newspaper pieces, but from a quick scan of the clippings he saw that they were all twelve or thirteen years old and dealt with a German doctor named Franz Rotenhausen. One of the articles featured a photograph of the doctor: thin face, sharp features, balding, eyes so pale they seemed colorless.

Joanna gasped. "Oh, God!"

"What's wrong?"

"It's him."

"Who?"

"The man in my nightmare."

"With the mechanical hand?"

"Yes."

She was stunned.

"His name's Rotenhausen," Alex said.

"I've never heard it before."

She was shaking. Badly.

"Easy," Alex said.

"I never thought I'd see him again."

Her eyes were very wide.

"This is what we wanted—a name."

"Please," Joanna said. "Please, Alex, let's get out of here."

The face in the grainy photograph was hard, bony, somehow like the face of a vampire. The eyes seemed to be staring into a dimension other men could not see. They were cold eyes. Franz Rotenhausen had a maniacal look about him.

Alex felt the hairs standing up on the back of his own neck. Perhaps it *was* time to get moving.

"We'll read these later," he said, stuffing the clippings and the unfinished letter back into the envelope.

As they crossed the main room of the suite and stepped around the dead man, Alex expected the door to open in front of them. It didn't.

· 53 ·

In spite of the gore they'd seen at the Churchill, they were exceedingly hungry. Actually, Alex thought, they were probably so hungry precisely because of what they'd seen, rather than in spite of it. After confronting death, most people experienced a sudden rush of all the basic animal appetites; they got horny, hungry, and thirsty. By indulging themselves, they were making a loud, jubilant, defiant, but unconscious declaration to the universe: *I'm still alive, damn you!*

Alex and Joanna ate lunch in a busy coffee shop near Piccadilly Circus. Over too many thick sandwiches and too many cups of tea, they read the old clippings from the *New York Times* and the *Washington Post*.

Franz Rotenhausen was a genius in more than one field. He had degrees in biology, chemistry, medicine, and psychology, and he had written many widely recognized and important papers in all those areas. When he was twenty-four, he lost his hand in an automobile accident. Unimpressed with the prostheses that had been available at that time, he had invented a new device, a mechanical hand nearly as good as flesh and blood, controlled by nerve impulses from the stump and powered by a rechargeable battery pack. Rotenhausen had spent the first eighteen years of his working life as a seminar lecturer and research scientist at a major West German university. He was primarily interested in brain function and dysfunction; and especially in the electrical and chemical nature of thought and memory.

"Why would they let a man work on this sort of

thing?" Joanna asked angrily. "It's George Orwell. It's *1984*."

"It's also the route to ultimate power," Alex said. "And that's what all politicians are after."

Thirteen years ago, at the peak of a brilliant career, Rotenhausen had made a terrible mistake. He had written a book about the human brain, with emphasis on the most recent developments in behavioral engineering, brainwashing, and chemical-electrical methods of mind control; and he had structured the entire work to support his belief that even the most drastic forms of mind alteration should be used by "responsible" governments to create a dissension-free, crime-free, worry-free "perfect" society. His greatest error was not the writing of the book; it was his failure to be contrite that ruined him. The scientific and political communities can forgive any stupidity, indiscretion, or gross miscalculation so long as the public apologies are loud and long; the humble contrition does not even have to be sincere to earn an unconditional pardon from the establishment; it must only *appear* genuine, so that the citizenry is able to settle back into its usual stupor. However, as the controversy grew in the wake of publication, Rotenhausen had no second thoughts. He responded to his critics with increasing irritation. He showed the world a sneer instead of the embarrassed smile that it wanted to see. His public statements were colored by his harsh voice and by his unfortunate habit of making violent gestures with his hideous steel hand. The European newspapers were quick to give him nicknames—Dr. Strangelove and Dr. Frankenstein—but those soon gave way to another that stuck: the Zombie Doctor. He was accused of wanting to create a world of mindless slaves, obedient automatons. The furor increased. He complained that reporters and photographers were hounding him wherever he went, and he was intemperate enough to suggest that they would be his first choice for behavior modification if he were in charge of things. He steadfastly refused to back down from his position, seeing it as a matter of principle, and thus was unable to take the pressure off himself. By persevering, he surrendered every shred of privacy.

"I'm usually able to sympathize with the victim of press harassment," Alex said. "But not this time."

"He'd like to do to everyone what he did to me," Joanna said, amazed.

"Or worse."

"And what scared them was that his research was close to making it possible."

The waitress brought more tea and a plate of small cakes for dessert.

They continued to read about Franz Rotenhausen:

In Bonn, the West German government was painfully aware of its people's totalitarian past and conscious of the damaged future that could result from the unnecessary resurrection of long-buried memories and hatreds; therefore, the government was extraordinarily sensitive to the general world opinion, loudly and repeatedly expressed, that Rotenhausen was Adolf Hitler's spiritual descendant, heir to the greatest terror ever known. The brilliant doctor ceased to be a national treasure (solely because he had not been able to keep his mouth shut), ceased to be even a national asset, and became a terrible albatross around the neck of the German state and around the tender reputation of its citizens. A great deal of weight was brought to bear on the university that employed him. Eventually he was dismissed on a morals charge involving one of his undergraduate students. He denied all wrongdoing, branded the story a lie, and accused the administration and the girl of conspiring against him. Nevertheless, he knew what he was up against, and he was tired of wasting so much time on politics when infinite research awaited him. He departed gracelessly but without seriously challenging the power that had gone after him with such success. Eventually, the morals charge was dropped, as if it had never been.

"What they did to him wasn't wrong," Joanna said. "He might not have been guilty of molesting that girl, but he sure as hell was guilty of molesting others. I know him. I know him very well. Too well."

Alex could not endure the haunted expression in her beautiful eyes. He stared at the half-eaten cake that lay on the plate in front of him.

After a while they took another yellow clipping from the stack and read more about Franz Rotenhausen.

Six months after he was forced out of the university, the Zombie Doctor had liquidated all of his holdings in West Germany and had moved to St. Moritz, Switzerland. On his last day in his homeland, he denounced Germany, called it weak, and said that its people were for the most part a pack of sniveling cowards and imbeciles. The Swiss granted him permanent residency for two reasons, neither of which was his personality. First of all, Switzerland is a country with a very old and admirable tradition of providing asylum for the prominent (though seldom the ordinary) outcasts of other countries. Secondly, Rotenhausen was rich, a millionaire many times over. He had inherited a lot of money and had earned even more from his dozens of medical and chemical patents. He was able to reach an agreement with the Swiss tax authorities; and each year he paid a tithe, which seemed meager to him but which covered a substantial percentage of the government's expenses in the canton in which he lived. It was thought that he continued his research in the private laboratory in St. Moritz; but because he never wrote another word for publication and never spoke to newsmen, that suspicion could not be verified. In time, quite clearly, he had been forgotten.

The unfinished, handwritten letter from Tom Chelgrin to his daughter was two pages of half-baked apologia. The tone was pitiful: an ineffective whine. It didn't provide any new information, not even a single fresh clue.

"How does Rotenhausen connect with the senator and with Jamaica?" Joanna asked.

"I don't know. We'll find out."

"You said the senator mentioned Russians when you talked to him on the phone."

"Yeah. But I don't know what he meant by that."

"What would Rotenhausen be doing in a deal with the Russians? He sounds like a Nazi."

"Nazis and Communists have a lot in common," he said. "They want the same thing—absolute control, unqualified power. A man like Franz Rotenhausen can find sympathy in both camps."

"Now what?" Joanna asked.

"Now we go to Switzerland," Alex said.

• 54 •

Joanna leaned across the table. "Alex. Please, please, Alex. Listen, we don't have to go to Switzerland." She was trying to convince herself, not him.

"Yes, we do have to go," he said.

"We can turn this whole thing over to the police now."

"We still don't have enough proof."

She shook her head. "I disagree. We've got all these clippings, this letter, a dead body at the Churchill Hotel, and the fact that my fingerprints match Lisa's."

Alex spoke quietly but forcefully, determined that she would see things his way. "What police should we go to, then? The Jamaican police?"

"Of course not. We—"

"The American police? Maybe the FBI? Or the CIA? The Japanese police? The British police? Should we go to Scotland Yard? Or to the Swiss police?"

She opened her mouth, closed it without saying anything, and frowned.

Alex reached across the table and put his hand over hers.

"It's not simple, is it?" she said.

"If we go to the cops now, we'll be dead by morning. These people, whoever they are, have been hiding something big, really damned big, for a long, long time. Now the charade is over. The cover-up isn't working any more. The whole thing's falling apart. A regular house of cards. And they know it. That's why they killed the senator. They're trying to clean up the mess before anyone notices it. Right now they're looking for us."

She blinked. "You mean they're looking for us . . . so they can kill us? Yeah. Of course that's what you mean. Of course."

"Bet on it. Whatever immunity you had is gone. If we go public with the case now, we'll just be making targets of ourselves. Until we've got the entire story, until we understand the why of it, until we've figured out what it means from Jamaica to Japan to here, until we can blow them out of the water, we'll stay alive only so long as we stay out of sight."

Joanna seized on that. "But we'll be very visible if we go hunting Rotenhausen in Switzerland."

"We won't blunder straight over there. We'll go sort of roundabout," he said. "We'll fly from England to Belgium. Then we'll catch another flight from Belgium to Germany and take the train to St. Moritz. We'll sneak in as best we can."

She was not impressed. "The senator tried to sneak into London. It didn't work for him."

"But it'll work for us," he said. "It has to."

"What if it does? What will you do after we get to St. Moritz?"

He sipped his tea and thought about her question. He pulled on one end of his mustache.

"I'll find Rotenhausen's place," he said. "I'll look it over. If it isn't too heavily guarded—and I don't think it will be—I'll find a way into it. Once I'm inside, I'll prowl around until I locate his file room. If he's the careful, methodical man of science that he seems to be, he'll have a complete record of what he did to you, how he did it, and why. When we have that, we'll be ready to tell the world what happened to Lisa Jean Chelgrin."

"What about British-Continental Insurance?"

"What about it?"

"If we follow up on that lead," Joanna said, "maybe we won't have to go to St. Moritz."

"Now that we know where your brainwashing took place, we don't have to pry into British-Continental. Besides, that would be just as dangerous as going to Switzerland, but we wouldn't be likely to find as much there as we will at Franz Rotenhausen's place."

She slumped back in her chair, resigned to the trip. "When do we leave London?"

"As soon as possible," he said. "Within the hour, if we can manage it."

• 55 •

Alex and Joanna had to get their passports from the hotel. They would also pick up their tail again, and they would have to lose him one last time before leaving England from someplace other than London. If they departed for Europe quietly, from some other city, no one would be able to trace them easily. Then, after a roundabout trip to St. Moritz, they might be able to sneak up on Dr. Franz Rotenhausen.

When they returned to the hotel, they did not go to their suite alone. They stopped at the front desk, ordered a rental car, told the clerk that they were checking out sooner than expected, and took two bellmen upstairs with them.

Although the bellmen served as unwitting guards, and although the senator's killers were not likely to strike in front of witnesses, Alex paced nervously in the drawing room of the suite and watched the door, alert for the silent turning of the knob, while Joanna got their bags ready to go. Fortunately, when they'd arrived last night, they had been too tired to unpack more than the essentials; and this morning, awakened by Tom Chelgrin's noisy messenger, they'd had no time to hang up their clothes and transfer their things from suitcases to dresser drawers, so repacking required only a couple of minutes.

On the way downstairs, the elevator stopped to take on more riders. At the tenth floor, as the lift doors were about to slide open, Alex unhooked one button on his overcoat, reached inside, and put his hand on the butt of the pistol that was tucked under the waistband of his trousers. He was half convinced that the people waiting out there were not merely other hotel guests, that they would have machine guns, and that they would spray the interior of the lift with bullets. The doors slid all the way open. An elderly couple got aboard. They were having an animated discussion in rapid-fire Spanish, and they hardly seemed to be aware of their fellow passengers.

Joanna glanced at Alex and smiled grimly. She knew what he had been thinking.

He took his hand off the 7 mm. automatic and re-buttoned his overcoat.

In the lobby they waited for the hired car, which was delivered forty-five minutes after they ordered it. At three o'clock they drove away from the hotel, into the teeming, gray, rain-soaked city.

For five minutes they weaved through the Byzantine complexity of London. The streets branched off one another with no discernible logic. They were lost, but they didn't care. At the moment they did not have a destination in mind. They were making random turns, zigzagging through traffic, trying to determine which car was following them.

Joanna turned in her seat and stared out the back window. After a while she said, "You see him?"

Alex glanced at the rearview mirror again. "Another Jaguar, isn't it?"

"Yeah. A yellow one this time."

"All of these bastards seem to travel in style."

"Well, they knew the senator," Joanna said sarcastically, "and the senator always moved in the very best circles, didn't he?"

"That he surely did," Alex said wryly. "Now you better buckle up."

She faced front and engaged her seatbelt. "All right, let's lose the son of a bitch."

Alex swerved right, in front of a bus, into a gap in traffic. He tramped down hard on the accelerator. The tires squealed, and the car jumped forward. They shot ahead nearly a block. Then Alex braked abruptly as they came up much too fast on another car, swung left, directly in the way of a lorry that nearly took off their rear bumper. The truck driver blew his horn angrily. Alex tooted in reply, as if they were exchanging pleasant greetings, and accelerated again. He turned left at the corner, darted in front of a taxi with only centimeters to spare, and turned the wrong way into a one-way backstreet. He maintained a dangerous speed through the narrow alley. The building walls flashed past, less than two feet away on either side. The car bounced and shimmied on the rough cobblestones. He prayed that no one would enter the alley ahead of them, and his prayer was answered; a few seconds later they plunged out of the mouth of the cramped street, onto a main thoroughfare. He turned right and sped through a red light as it changed from yellow.

The Jaguar was no longer in sight.

"Terrific!" Joanna said.

"Not so terrific," he said worriedly.

"But we lost them!"

"And we shouldn't have. Not that easily."

"Easily? We nearly wrecked half a dozen times!"

"They kill like professionals, so they ought to be able to run a tail like professionals. And professionals would have kept on top of us every minute. They have a better car than we do. And they must be more familiar with these streets than we are. It's just like this morning. It's just like it was with the *brown* Jaguar. It's as if they wanted to let us get away."

"But why would they be playing a game like that?" she asked.

He scowled. "I don't know. I feel like we're being manipulated, and I don't like it. It scares me."

• 56 •

Joanna fiddled with the car radio until she located a station that was playing a two-hour program of Beethoven. Within a few minutes the beautiful music relieved some of her tension; and she saw that the hard lines of worry in Alex's face began to soften a bit.

Using the complimentary road maps provided by the car rental agency, they got lost only three times before they were headed safely south. They were going to Brighton, on the coast, where Alex intended to spend the night.

For many years Joanna had thought this was the highway on which Robert and Elizabeth Rand had lost their lives. But London had proved to be a new and strange place, and so had this outlying landscape. It was unknown to her, completely alien. Although she once thought she'd lived most of her childhood and adolescence in London, she knew now that this was her first visit. Robert and Elizabeth Rand had existed only on a few scraps of paper, in a handful of phony documents—and, of course, in her mind.

The windshield wipers thumped like a heartbeat.

She thought of her real father, Thomas Chelgrin, lying dead on the hotel room floor, and she wished that the image of the senator could reduce her to tears. Feeling grief was better than feeling nothing at all. But her heart was closed to him.

For a moment she perceived herself as a speck of ice adrift in a great lightless sea. For an instant she was lonely, achingly lonely, bitingly and unendurably lonely; then she looked at Alex, and the icy loneliness melted, evaporated. She put a hand on his shoulder. He glanced away from the road. She said she loved him, and he looked back at the road and said he loved her, too, loved her very much, and she was all right again.

Gradually, however, a new fear began to preoccupy her. What if they took Alex away from her? What if they killed him? Then she would be that speck of ice; as she had once been; but this time, forever.

The storm continued without surcease as the dark winter afternoon blended quickly into evening. Rain fell out of an ash-gray sky and puddled on the lead-gray land. The highway was a shiny black ribbon on which the headlights shimmered like the washed-out glow of the moon reflected from the glassy surface of a gently flowing river.

"Just west of Brighton," Alex said, "on the way to Worthing, there's a quaint little inn called The Bell and the Dragon. It's a couple of hundred years old but damned well kept, and the food's quite good."

"Won't we need a reservation?"

"Not this late in the year. The tourist season is long past. They ought to have several nice rooms available."

When they arrived at The Bell and the Dragon a short while later, Joanna saw that it was indeed quaint. The only sign was a large wooden billboard that hung from a crossbar between two posts near the highway. The Bell and the Dragon was tucked in a stand of ancient elms, and the parking lot was nearly as dark as it must have been in the days when guests arrived in horse-drawn coaches. It was a rambling structure, pleasing to the eye. The exterior was half brick and half plaster, with a crosswork of rugged, exposed beams. The doors were fashioned from oak timbers. In the lobby and public rooms, the soft electric lights, hidden in converted brass gas lamps, imparted a marvelous luster to the polished, richly inlaid paneling. Alex and Joanna were given spacious quarters on the second floor, rear, a place with white plaster walls, darkly stained beams, and a pegged oak floor that was protected by plush area rugs.

Joanna examined the griffin-head water spouts in the bathroom, was pleased to find that the stone fireplace in the bedroom would actually work if they chose to use it, and finally threw herself onto the four-poster bed. "Alex, it's absolutely delightful!"

"It belongs to another age," he said. "An age that was more hospitable than ours."

"It's charming. I love it. How often have you stayed here?"

The question appeared to surprise him. He stared at her but didn't speak.

She sat up. "What's wrong?"

Alex tugged at one corner of his mustache. His tawny skin went through pale to sallow. "I've never stayed here before."

"So?"

"I've never even been to Brighton before," he said. "I haven't the faintest idea how I knew about The Bell and the Dragon. This is the third time today, dammit!"

He went to the nearest window and studied the darkness beyond.

"The third time for what?" Joanna asked.

"It's the third time I've known about something that I shouldn't know about. The third time I've known without having any way of knowing. It's creepy. Before I opened that note this morning, I knew it was from the senator."

"That was just a good guess," Joanna said.

"And before we ever got to his hotel room, before I saw that his door was ajar, I knew that Tom Chelgrin was dead. Knew it!"

"Precognition."

"No."

"There are clairvoyants who can—"

"Don't believe in it."

"Then call it just plain intuition," she said uneasily. "You once told me that you sometimes have strong hunches and that you usually find they're right."

Alex turned away from the window. "This is more than a hunch, Joanna. I knew that name—The Bell and the Dragon. I knew exactly how the place looked, as if I'd seen it before."

"Maybe someone told you about it. Maybe someone said you should stay here if you were ever in Brighton."

He shook his head. "No. If someone had, I'd remember who it was."

"Well, maybe you read about it in a travel article—and saw a picture."

"I'd remember that, too."

"Not if it was a few years ago. Not if it was casual reading. Maybe a magazine in a doctor's office. Something you skimmed and forgot. But it stuck in your subconscious."

"Maybe," he said, clearly unconvinced.

"It's something like that," she said. "Something quite ordinary. There's nothing sinister about it. There's a very simple explanation."

"Simple? I'm not so sure," Alex said grimly. "I have that strange feeling again—that feeling that we're being manipulated."

He turned to the window, put his face close to the glass, and stared into the darkness, as if he was certain that someone out there was staring back at him.

· 57 ·

In London, with the coming of night, the temperature had dropped ten degrees. It now hovered at the freezing point. The wind had grown stronger, and the rain had become sleet.

On his way home from the Fielding Athison offices, Marlowe—the man in charge of all the Soviet operations that used the importing company as a front—drove slowly and cursed the weather. He kept his head tucked down and his shoulders drawn up in anticipation of a collision. His hands were tight on the wheel, and his knuckles were bloodless. In front, beside, and behind him, cars slid on the icy pavement. He used brakes and accelerator judiciously, holding the speedometer needle between twenty and twenty-five kilometers an hour. He was furious with the other drivers; so far as he could see, he was the only one who wasn't driving like a suicidal maniac.

Don't they want to live? he wondered.

He was tempted to roll down his window and shout at them: "What the hell's the matter with you crazy bastards? Don't you people want to live?"

Ahead, another driver stood on the brakes. Too hard. Too suddenly. The car fishtailed.

Marlowe tamped his brakes carefully and congratulated himself on having left enough room to stop.

Behind, the brakes of a third car squealed horribly.

Marlowe winced and gritted his teeth. He counted the seconds until impact.

Miraculously, nobody hit anybody else.

Marlowe wanted to live very much. He cherished life. He wanted to die no sooner than his hundredth birthday—and then in bed with a young woman. A very young woman. Two very young women.

At the moment his anxiety was exacerbated by his inability to concentrate on his driving as thoroughly as he would have liked. In spite of the constant fear that some lunatic would plow into him, his mind wandered. The past few days had been filled with signs and portents. Bad omens. He couldn't help thinking about them.

First there had been the confrontation with Ignacio Carreras. When Marlowe had demanded Joanna Rand's real name, he had been testing his strength against Ignacio's. He had not expected to find that he was more powerful than Carreras, but he *had* expected to reaffirm a long-held opinion that they were equals in the Soviet espionage system. Instead, he was slapped down. Hard. He could still feel the pain. Carreras was higher up the ladder than Marlowe—at least so far as the Joanna Rand business was concerned. When Carreras ordered him to leave her unharmed regardless of the difficulties she might create, he promised Marlowe confirmation from a higher source. The backup orders had come swiftly and had been phrased forcefully. Marlowe feared, at worst, a sharp rebuke from his immediate superior in the KGB, but the word came down from a much higher place than that—higher than the head of station in London, higher than the sectional chief in Moscow, and higher than the director of the entire KGB. The message was from the man at the pinnacle of the Russian government, and its meaning was unmistakable: back off, Marlowe; obey Carreras; stay out of the Rand operation; in fact, forget what little you know of it; mind your own business or else.

He was still smarting from that loss of face, when the grotesque fat man, Anson Peterson, swept in from America and began issuing commands with a royal arrogance. Marlowe was not permitted to see the Rand woman—not even a photograph of her. He was told not to speak to her if she should call the British-

Continental Insurance number again. He was not even supposed to think about her. Peterson was in charge of the operation, and Marlowe was instructed to go about his other work as if he knew nothing whatsoever about the crisis.

Marlowe was extremely reluctant to surrender even a single minor prerogative of his position. Every one of his privileges had been earned. He guarded them jealously. The fat man's cavalier usurpation of power worried and infuriated him.

He was jolted abruptly out of his reverie by the blast of an air horn. A lorry loaded with frozen poultry skidded and nearly sideswiped him. He glanced at the rearview mirror, saw that no one was close behind, and jammed his foot down on the brake pedal harder than he should have done—all in an instant. His car began to slide, but he let the wheel turn as it wished, and a moment later he was in control again. The lorry slid past him rather than into him. It swayed as if it would topple, then regained its equilibrium and rushed on.

Marlowe lived on the entire top floor of a large, three-story, eighteen-room townhouse that had been converted to apartments. When he parked at the curb in front of the building and switched off the car's engine, he sighed with relief.

As he ran toward the door, sleet pelted him and got under his coat collar. All the way across the warm foyer and up four flights of stairs, the sleet melted and cold water trickled down his back; he shivered violently.

Marlowe unlocked the apartment door and switched on the lights. He took two steps inside and stopped as if he had walked into a wall.

Gas!

The air was thick with acrid fumes.

He snatched a handkerchief from his pocket, held it over his nose and mouth, and hurried into the kitchen. He checked the knobs on the gas stove, but they were all turned off.

Something was wrong. Terribly wrong.

Even if every one of the pilot lights had gone out, even if they'd been out all day, that would not account for such a buildup of gas.

He began to cough into his handkerchief.

Suddenly he knew what the gas signified. He realized he had only a few seconds, and a great deal happened in that time:

He couldn't move. He tried to lift his feet. No use. He felt as if he had been nailed to the floor. Fear had frozen him.

One second gone. How many more?

He stared at the stove, morbidly fascinated.

"No," he said. "Please, Peterson. No!"

Another second gone.

Still couldn't move.

If you wanted to live to be a hundred, he told himself, *you should have chosen another line of work.*

He was dizzy.

They're going to kill me because I know too much about the Rand woman, he thought. *But for God's sake, I hardly know anything! Is she so important that they need to snuff me just because I know she exists? Can't be that important! Can't be!*

Four or five seconds after the first horrible glimmer of understanding, as Marlowe was finally turning away from the stove, he heard the beginning of the explosion. He never heard the end of it. He was pierced instantly by hundreds of shards of glass and metal; at least a dozen wickedly sharp splinters tore through his eyes and lodged deep in his brain. Dead already, he was catapulted backward, through the kitchen wall and into the bitter winter night.

The fat man was across the street from Marlowe's apartment, sitting alone in a parked car. He saw Marlowe get out of a small black Ford. He saw Marlowe go into the building. He saw the third-floor lights wink on. He saw the flash of fire, the bursting windows, and the exploding wall. He saw the corpse, too, as it was launched into the night. For the briefest of moments, the dead man appeared to be able to fly as well as any bird—but then he plummeted to the pavement.

A man and a woman ran from the front entrance of the building. No one was at home on the second floor, so Peterson figured those two were the first-floor residents. They rushed to Marlowe's crumpled body, but they drew back, sickened, when they got a close look at him.

The fat man popped a butter-rum Lifesaver into his mouth. He released the parking brake, put the car in gear, and drove away from that place.

Peterson had not yet received permission to eliminate Marlowe. In fact, he never had expected to receive it. Though Marlowe knew about the Rand case and was aware of its relative importance, the precise nature of it was a mystery to him; he did not know enough to endanger the operation. And although he had made several mistakes in the past week, he had not made enough of them to deserve termination. The directorate in Moscow frowned upon field men who tried constantly to widen their spheres of influence, as Marlowe had done; however, a killing was seldom ordered for that reason alone. At worst, Marlowe would have been sent home. More likely than that, because he was truly an effective agent, he merely would have been given a stern warning and put under closer observation.

But Marlowe had had to die. He was one of the six primary targets on the fat man's death list. Peterson had made several promises to a very powerful group of men, and if he failed to keep any of those promises, his own life would not be worth a penny. Peterson could not leave England until Marlowe was dead; and since he was scheduled to fly out to Zurich at eight o'clock, he was forced to act without Moscow's permission. He had worked for an hour to set up the gas stove explosion, so that it would appear to be an accident. The men in Moscow, who demanded absolute obedience from Anson Peterson, might be suspicious about such an "accident"; but they would blame the other side rather than one of their own agents. And the other men, those to whom Peterson had made so many commitments, would be satisfied that the first promise had been kept.

One man was dead. The first of many.

• 58 •

Alex and Joanna ate dinner in the cozy, oak-paneled main dining room at The Bell and the Dragon. The food was excellent, but Alex was unable to get a full measure of enjoyment from it. While he ate he watched the other customers surreptitiously, trying to determine if any of them was watching him.

Later, in their room, in bed, under the covers, in the dark, they made love. This time it was slow and tender. They finished like a pair of spoons in a drawer: she faced away from him; his chest was against her back; her buttocks were warm and smooth against his groin. Holding her, one hand on her firm breasts, held within the tight moist center of her, he lost the feeling of being watched and manipulated. He was overwhelmed by the exquisite texture of her skin, by the silkiness of her hair, and by the love that seemed to rise from her like a sweet fragrance from a flower. She blotted out all of his thoughts and filled his mind with herself as if she were a supernova expanded to the far reaches of a solar system and beyond.

That night Alex had the strange dream again. The soft bed. The white room. The three surgeons in white gowns and masks. They stared down at him. The first surgeon said, "Where does he think he is?" The second surgeon said, "South America. Rio." And the third surgeon said, "What happens if this doesn't work?" The first surgeon said, "Then he'll probably get himself killed without solving our problem." Alex lifted one hand to touch the nearest doctor; but, as before, his fingers changed magically into tiny replicas of buildings. He stared at them, amazed, and then his fingers ceased to be just replicas and became five tall buildings seen at a great distance, and then the buildings grew larger, into skyscrapers, and they came nearer, and a city grew across the palm of his hand and up his arm, and the faces of the surgeons were replaced by a clear blue sky, and below him was Rio, the fantastic bay, and then his plane landed, and he got out, and he was in Rio, and the mournful but beautiful music of a Spanish guitar surrounded him.

He mumbled and turned over in his sleep.

And he turned into a new dream. He was in a cool dark crypt. Candles flickered dimly. He walked to a black coffin that rested on a stone bier, took hold of the brass handles, and lifted the lid. Thomas Chelgrin lay inside—bloody and dead. He stared at the senator for a moment, finally started to lower the lid, and gasped as the eyes of the corpse popped open. Chelgrin grinned malevolently at Alex, grabbed him with fiercely strong gray hands, and tried to drag him down, into the coffin.

Alex sat straight up in bed.

A scream was stuck in his throat. He swallowed it.

Joanna was asleep.

He remained very still for a while, suspicious of the deep shadows in the corners. He had left the bathroom door ajar, with the light on behind it. Nevertheless, most of the room was shrouded in darkness. Gradually his eyes adjusted. At last he got out of bed and went to the nearest window.

Their room had a sea view, but at this time of night Alex could see nothing but a vast black emptiness marked only by the vague lights of a large ship that was almost concealed behind curtains of rain. He shifted his gaze to something closer at hand—the slate-shingled roof that slanted low over the window, creat-

ing a deep eave. Still closer: the windows were di-
amond-patterned leaded glass; each pane was beveled
at the edges. In the surface of the glass he saw himself
—his drawn face, transparent, haunted, eyes like twin
bottomless pools, mouth set in a tight grim line.

The case had begun with Joanna's repeating nightmare. Now, it appeared as if it might end with his
own recurring dream. He didn't believe in coincidence.
He was certain his dream contained a message that
they must interpret if they were to survive. His subconscious was trying to tell him something desperately
important.

But for God's sake, what did it mean?

He had been to Rio for three weeks last spring, but
he had not been in the hospital while he was there.
He hadn't met any doctors. The trip had been perfectly ordinary—just one of his many temporary escapes from a job that had begun to bore him.

His eyes shifted from his reflection, and he gazed
into the distance, into the darkness.

We're puppets, he thought. *Joanna and me. Puppets. And the puppet master is out there. Somewhere.
Who? Who are you? Where are you? What in the hell
do you want?*

Lightning slashed the soft flesh of the night.

• 59 •

The rain had stopped. The morning was clear and fear-
fully cold.

Joanna felt refreshed and more at ease than she
had been for quite some time. But she could see that
Alex had not benefited from the night at the inn. His
eyes were red and ringed by dark circles of slack
skin.

He returned the 7 mm. automatic to its hiding place in the hollowed-out hair dryer and packed the dryer in Joanna's largest suitcase.

They checked out of The Bell and the Dragon at nine o'clock. The clerk wished them a swift, safe trip.

They went to an apothecary and purchased a tin of body powder to replace the one that Alex had emptied into the toilet in London. In the car again, Alex slipped the extra magazines of ammunition into the talc. Joanna put the resealed can in her suitcase.

They drove from the outskirts of Brighton to Southampton. No one followed them.

At the Southampton airport, they abandoned the hired car in the parking lot. They had rented it for a week; it would not be missed for at least eight or nine days. If they returned it to a branch of the rental agency, Alex explained, they'd be leaving an easily followed trail.

Aurigny Airlines had a few unsold tickets for the Saturday morning flight to Cherbourg. Alex and Joanna sat behind the starboard wing; she had the window seat. The flight was uneventful; there wasn't even mild turbulence.

The French customs officials thoroughly inspected the luggage. However, they neither opened the can of body powder nor took a close look at the hair dryer.

Alex and Joanna took the express turbotrain from Cherbourg to Paris. Alex's spirits lifted a bit. Paris was one of his favorite cities. He usually stayed at the Hotel George V; indeed, he was so well known there that they might have gotten a room without a reservation. However, they stayed elsewhere, in less grand quarters, precisely because they did not want to go where Alex was well known.

From their hotel Alex telephoned a hotel in St. Moritz. Speaking fluent French and using the name Maurice Demuth, he inquired about the availability of a room for one week, beginning Monday, two days hence. Fortunately, there was a recent cancellation, and at the moment there was no waiting list for week-long accommodations.

When Alex put down the receiver, Joanna said, "Why Maurice Demuth?"

"So that if anyone connected with Rotenhausen should go around St. Moritz, checking advance bookings at the hotels, he won't find us."

"I mean why Maurice Demuth instead of some other name?"

He blinked. "I haven't the slightest idea."

"I thought maybe you knew someone with that name."

"No. I just plucked it out of the air."

"You lied so smoothly."

"It's a talent one acquires in my line of work."

"I'd better start taking everything you say with a grain of salt," she said coquettishly.

"Dammit, I've given myself away!" He smiled.

"Have you lied to me?"

"Shamelessly."

"You told me I was pretty."

"And you're not."

"I'm not?"

"You're not just pretty. You're beautiful, gorgeous, breathtaking."

"You told me you loved me."

"I didn't mean it."

"You villain," she said, grinning.

"The word *love* is inadequate. I meant more than that. I *treasure* you."

"Oh, you probably say the same thing to every woman you meet."

"I confess."

"Just to get them into bed."

"Can I get you into bed?"

"I thought you'd never ask."

For an hour they explored each other with hands and tongues, playfully and passionately. When Joanna finally urged him to take her, they were both as ready as they had ever been. He entered her tenderly but

deeply, and she clung to him. She gripped the unyielding muscles of his arms, his shoulders, and his back.
Her hands moved over him, testing, finding him to be
as hard as rock, everywhere. She was flying, shooting
up and up and up as if she were a rocket; and after a
long time she fell back, but slowly, floating, following currents of pleasure in much the same way that a
glider drifted on warm rivers of air high above the
earth.

They ate dinner in the upstairs room at Lapérouse.
The low ceiling, the murals on the crack-webbed walls,
the elegant appointments, and the gracious waiters
contributed to an atmosphere more romantic than any
Joanna had ever experienced in a restaurant. From
their table they had a view of the dark river, which
was speckled here and there with the lights of small
boats and the reflected glow of buildings that stood
along its banks.

As she nibbled flawless *oie rôtie aux pruneaux* and
listened to Alex's stories about Paris, she knew that
she could never allow anything or anyone to separate
her from him.

She would rather die.

• 60 •

In St. Moritz the fat man had a gray Mercedes at his
disposal. He drove himself, but he still managed to
peel a roll of Lifesavers and pop a circlet of butter-
rum into his mouth every now and then.

The sky looked nine months gone, bulging with
storm clouds that were about to deliver a lot of fine
dry snow. The peaks of the mountains were hidden in
beardlike gray mist.

During the afternoon Peterson played tourist. He

drove from one viewing point to another, enchanted by the scenic beauty.

The resort of St. Moritz is in three parts: St. Moritz-Dorf, which is on a mountain terrace more than two hundred feet above the lake; St. Moritz-Bad, which is a charming place at the end of the lake; and Champfèr-Suvretta. Until the end of the nineteenth century, St. Moritz-Bad was *the* spa, but thereafter it lost ground to St. Moritz-Dorf, which is perhaps the most sparkling winter playground in the world. Recently, St. Moritz-Bad had been making a concerted effort to recapture its lost position, but its ambitious recovery program had led to a most unlovely building boom.

An hour after nightfall, the fat man kept an appointment in St. Moritz-Bad. He left the Mercedes with a valet at one of the newer and uglier hotels. Inside, he crossed the lobby to the lakefront cocktail lounge. The room was crowded and noisy.

The hotel's day-registration clerk, Rudolph Ubersex, had gone off duty fifteen minutes ago and was waiting at a corner table. He was a thin man with long, slim hands that were seldom still. Peterson shrugged out of his overcoat, hung it across the back of a chair, and sat facing the clerk. Ubersex was nearly finished with a brandy and wanted another. The fat man ordered the same.

After they were served, Peterson said, "Any word?"

The clerk was nervous. He sipped his brandy, swallowed hard, and said, "Monsieur Maurice Demuth called four hours ago."

"Excellent."

"He will arrive Monday."

"Not alone, I trust?"

"With his wife."

Peterson took an envelope from his coat pocket. It contained five thousand Swiss francs. He passed it to Ubersex and said, "That's your second payment. If all goes well on Monday, you'll receive a third envelope."

The clerk glanced left, right, and quickly tucked the

envelope out of sight, as if anyone who saw it would know at once what it was. Actually, none of the other drinkers was the least bit interested in them.

"I would like some assurance," Ubersex said.

Peterson scowled. "Assurance?"

"I would like a guarantee that no one . . ."

"Yes?"

"That no one will be killed."

"Oh, of course. You have my word on that."

Ubersex studied him. "If anyone were killed in the hotel, I would have no choice but to go to the authorities and tell what I know."

Peterson kept his voice low, but he was sharp with the man. "That would be foolish. You are an accomplice, sir. The authorities would not deal lightly with you. And neither would my people."

Ubersex tossed back his brandy as if it were water. "Perhaps I should return the money."

"I wouldn't accept it," Peterson said. "And I would be terribly angry if you tried that. A deal is a deal, my dear sir."

"I guess I'm in over my head."

"That you are, sir. But relax. You have my word. No violence in the hotel." He smiled and said, "Now, tell me, is the restaurant here any good?"

Ubersex stared at him for a long time and finally sighed. "The food is terrible here."

"I suspected as much."

"Try Chesa Veglia."

"I'll do that."

"Or perhaps Corviglia, at the top of the funicular."

Peterson put enough money on the table to cover the bill, stood, struggled into his coat, and walked out of there.

· 61 ·

On Sunday they flew from Paris to Zurich. Their hotel, Baur Au Lac, was elegant. It stood in its own lakeside park near the end of Bahnhofstrasse.

In their room Alex dismantled the hair dryer and put the 7 mm. automatic under his belt. He took the spare clips of ammunition from the can of powder.

"I wish you didn't have to carry that," Joanna said.

"So do I. But we're getting too close to Rotenhausen for me to risk going without it."

They made love again. Twice. He could not get enough of her. He wasn't seeking sex so much as grasping for the emotional intimacy that accompanied sex. When they made love he felt that it was not merely his penis moving within her; he imagined that his heart and mind slipped into her as well; in passion, somehow, they were two souls within a single body.

That night he had a dream again.

He woke shortly before three o'clock, a scream caught in his throat. He made dry rasping sounds, choked the scream, and managed not to wake Joanna. He didn't go back to sleep. He sat in a chair beside the bed, the pistol in his lap, until the wake-up call came at six o'clock. For at least the one millionth time, he was thankful for his peculiar metabolism, which allowed him to function well on very little sleep.

Early Monday morning they boarded a train at Zurich's Hauptbahnhof and headed east.

As they pulled out of the station, Joanna said, "We certainly are going roundabout. No one'll be able to track us down easily."

"Maybe they don't need to track us down."

"What?"

"Maybe they knew our route long before we did," Alex said.

"What do you mean?"

"I'm not sure. But sometimes I feel . . . programmed. Like a robot."

"I don't understand."

"Neither do I," he said wearily. "Forget it. Let's enjoy the scenery."

At Chur they changed trains and followed the fertile Rhine Valley downstream. In summer the land would be green with vineyards, wheat fields, and orchards, but now it lay dormant under a blanket of snow. Moving into the towering Rhaetain Alps, they came to Landquart, passed through the dramatic Landquart Gorge, and followed a new river upstream. After a long, winding, but for the most part gentle ascent, past a handful of resort villages, they came to Klosters, which was nearly as famous as St. Moritz.

They debarked at Klosters and left their luggage at the station while they outfitted themselves in ski clothes. During the trip from Zurich, they had realized that nothing they'd packed was adequate for high-altitude December weather. Besides, dressed in the winter clothes of city dwellers, they were conspicuous, which was precisely what they did not want to be. They changed in the dressing rooms at the ski shop and threw away the clothes they had been wearing; the clerk was amazed.

After lunch they boarded a train to Davos. It was crowded with a large party of French skiers bound for St. Moritz. The Frenchmen were happy, noisy, drinking wine from bottles that were concealed in plain paper sacks.

A fine snow began to fall. The wind was surprisingly light.

The Rhaetain Railway crossed the Landquart River on a terrifyingly lofty bridge, climbed through magnificent pine forests, and chugged past a ski center called Wolfgang. Eventually the tracks dropped down again to the Davosersee and the town of Davos, which was composed of Davos-Dorf and Davos-Platz.

The snow was coming down fast and hard now. The wind had picked up.

From the train window Alex could see that the storm concealed the upper regions of Weissfluh, the mountain that most dominated the town. Up there, in the mists, behind the heavy drape of falling snow, skiers began the descent along the Parsenn run, from Weissfluhjoch, at the 9,000-foot level, down to the town at 5,500 feet.

In spite of the charming town beyond the train window, a sense of absolute isolation was unavoidable. That was one of the qualities that had attracted people to this place for more than a century. Sir Arthur Conan Doyle often had come here to escape London, and perhaps to think about Holmes. In 1881, Robert Louis Stevenson had sought the solitude and the healthful air of Davos in which to finish his masterpiece, *Treasure Island*.

"The top of the world," Alex said, for that was how it seemed to him.

"I get the strange feeling the rest of the earth was destroyed," Joanna said. "All of it gone . . . in a nuclear war . . . or some other sort of cataclysm. I get the feeling this is all that's left. It's so . . . separate . . . remote."

And if we were to disappear in this vastness, Alex thought uneasily, *no one would ever find us.*

From Davos the train went to Susch and Scuol. The Frenchmen were singing rather well; no one complained. In the early darkness the train moved up the Engandine Valley, past the lake, and into St. Moritz.

They were in the middle of a blizzard. The wind was coming off the mountains at thirty kilometers an hour, gusting to fifty kilometers at times. The incredibly dense snowfall reduced visibility to one block.

At the hotel Alex and Joanna used their own names when they checked in, but he asked that the Maurice Demuth *nom de guerre* be kept in the registration file.

In a town that was accustomed to playing host to privacy-conscious movie stars, dukes, duchesses, counts, countesses, and wealthy industrialists from every corner of the world, such a request was not unusual, and it was honored.

They were given a small but comfortable suite on the fifth floor. When the bellhops left, Alex tested the two locks and double-locked the door. He went into the bedroom to help Joanna with the unpacking.

"I'm exhausted," she said.

"Me too," he said, taking the 7 mm. automatic out of the waistband of his slacks. He put it on the nightstand.

"I'm too tired to stand up," she said, "but I'll be afraid to sleep."

"We'll be safe tonight."

"Do you still have that feeling?" she asked, handing him a bundle of socks.

He put the socks in a dresser drawer and said, "What feeling?"

"The feeling that we're somehow programmed to—"

"No," he lied. "It's gone. It was silly of me. Forget I ever said it. I was just depressed and nervous."

"What will we do tomorrow?"

"Scout around," he said.

"Find out where Rotenhausen lives?"

"Yeah."

"And then?"

Alex heard something behind them. He turned.

A tall, husky man was standing in the open doorway between the bedroom and living room.

They not only know we're here, Alex thought, *but they have keys to our room! So fast! They moved so fast!*

Joanna saw the intruder and cried out.

The man was holding an odd-looking gun and wearing a strange mask.

A very strange mask.

Gas mask!

Alex lunged for the pistol that he had left on the nightstand.

The man in the mask fired the gas gun. Soft, waxy bullets struck Alex and disintegrated on impact, exuding clouds of sweet fumes.

Alex picked up the 7 mm. automatic, but before he could use it the world went away.

· 62 ·

In the front room of the suite, Ignacio Carreras and Antonio Paz filled the bottoms of two large hotel laundry carts with the luggage that had been in the bedroom. Then they loaded Alex Hunter and Joanna Rand into the carts, on top of the suitcases.

To Carrera's eye the woman was even more beautiful than she appeared in the photographs. If the gas could have been counted upon to keep her unconscious more than just another half hour, he would have undressed her and raped her here, now. Helplessly asleep, she would be warm and exquisitely pliant. But there wasn't time.

Carreras had brought two pieces of Hermes leather luggage with him. They belonged to the fat man. He put them in the bedroom.

Tomorrow, the day clerk would alter the registration card. It would appear that Anson Peterson had checked in on Monday.

Hunter and Joanna would simply vanish.

Paz covered the unconscious man and woman with towels and rumpled bed linens.

They wheeled the carts to the service elevator on the fifth floor, rode down to ground level. They encountered no one.

When Alex regained consciousness he had a headache. His tongue felt furry. The taste in his mouth was like bile. His vision was blurry at first, but it gradually cleared.

At least I'm alive, he thought.

And then he thought: *But why am I? They don't need me alive. Should be dead.*

He was lying on his left side on a white-and-black tile floor. It was a kitchen. A single small light was on above the stove.

His back was against a row of cabinets, and his hands were tied behind him. Good, heavy cord. Clothesline or something like it. His feet were also bound together.

Joanna was not there. He called her name softly, but there was no reply. He hadn't really expected one.

He despised himself for letting them take her so easily.

He was alone. They had left him unguarded. He might still have a chance.

He listened for movement or voices in another room. Nothing. Silence.

Knowing that the rope would not break or come loose easily, nevertheless hoping it would happen, hoping for a bit of luck for a change, he tried to jerk his wrists away from each other. Incredibly, impossibly, the rope snapped on the second try.

Stunned, almost afraid to move, he lay motionless, listening and wondering.

Silence.

Fear sharpened his senses, and he was able to smell things that were shut away in the cupboards: a clove

344

of garlic, soap used for dish washing, a pungent cheese of some kind, and other stuff.

Finally he brought his hands out from behind his back. The rope was loosely draped around his wrists. He pulled it off.

He scooted around on the shiny floor until he was sitting up with his back to the cabinets. He untied his feet.

He stood, crouched, ready to run, hands fisted at his sides. He had made some noise getting loose. He waited for the sound of running feet. No one came.

He picked up the piece of rope that had been around his hands and took it to the stove. He examined it under the small fluorescent light.

He saw immediately why he had been able to snap it with a minimum of effort. While he had been unconscious, someone had cut most of the way through the rope, leaving only a fraction of the diameter intact. Where it had been cut, the break was clean; where it had pulled apart, it was frayed.

We're all functioning like robots, Alex thought. *We're programmed. Everything that's going to happen in the next few hours was decided a long time ago.*

But by whom?

And why?

And am I going to be the winner or the loser of the game? he wondered. *And Joanna? Are we programmed to live—or to die?*

• 64 •

Joanna woke in the white-walled room that stank of disinfectants, the familiar setting of her nightmare. She was in a hospital bed, head raised. The bed was flanked by a cardiac monitor and other machines, but she was not attached to any of them.

For a moment she thought she was dreaming, but the full horror of her situation became quickly apparent. Her heart began to pound, and she broke out in a cold sweat.

Rotenhausen.

The mechanical hand.

I've got to get out of here!

Her hands and ankles were secured by leather straps. She tried to pull free but could not.

"Ah," someone said from behind Joanna, "the patient's awake at last."

She had thought the head of the bed was against the wall and that she was alone in the room; but it was not, and she was not. She twisted her neck, trying to see who was back there, but the straps and the tilted mattress made that impossible.

After a teasing moment a woman in a white smock walked out where she could be seen. Brown hair. Brown eyes. Sharp features. Unsmiling. Cold. It was the other doctor, Franz Rotenhausen's assistant. Joanna remembered the face from one of the regression therapy sessions in Omi Inamura's office.

"I want to see Alex Hunter," Joanna said.

"That's not possible."

"Where is he?"

"Upstairs."

"Bring him to me."

The woman smiled thinly.

"Is he all right?" Joanna asked.

The woman picked up a sphygmomanometer from a tray of medical instruments.

"Is he all right?" Joanna asked again. "Damn you, tell me! Is he all right?"

"Yes," the woman said. "For now."

Joanna stared hard, trying to perceive the truth behind the woman's icy expression.

The doctor wrapped the pressure pad of the sphygmomanometer around Joanna's arm.

She tried to struggle. But with her wrists held down, she was helpless.

The doctor took her blood pressure. "Excellent." She unwound the pad and put it aside.

"Unbuckle these straps," Joanna said.

"You might as well give up, my dear."

The doctor tied a rubber tube around Joanna's arm. A vein rose up below the tubing. The doctor swabbed the skin with alcohol.

"I'll fight you," Joanna said.

"You can't win. Make it easy on yourself."

The woman had an accent, as Joanna had remembered in regression therapy. It wasn't German. Nor Scandinavian. Slavic accent of some sort? Russian? The senator had said something about Russians when he'd talked to Alex on the phone.

"Are you a Russian?" Joanna asked.

The woman gave her a sharp look.

"You are," Joanna said.

The woman shrugged. "What does it matter if you know. Yes, I'm Russian."

"What are you doing here?"

"Helping. Learning." She broke open a plastic packet that contained a hypodermic syringe.

Joanna's heart began to race. "Learning what?"

"Everything Franz Rotenhausen knows."

"He's a monster."

"You're wrong. He's a brilliant man."

"They threw him out of Germany."

"He left of his own free will."

"The Zombie Doctor."

"You know so much," the woman said coldly.

"Enough to put you in jail."

"Perhaps. But you've no one to tell it to."

"I'll tell the world. Somehow."

The doctor thrust the needle through the seal on the end of a tiny bottle that contained no more than 200 ccs of some colorless drug. She drew the fluid into the syringe.

"I won't let you give me that," Joanna said.

"It will only relax you."

"I won't let you."

"It isn't going to hurt."

"*No!*"

"It will just make you calm and cooperative."

When the woman took hold of her arm, Joanna was able to twist and jerk enough to make the vein a difficult target. Then suddenly, unexpectedly, the woman slapped her across the face, backhanded, very hard. In the instant Joanna needed to recover from the shock and pain, the doctor slipped the needle into her.

Tears ran down Joanna's cheeks. "Bitch."

"You'll feel better in a minute."

"Bitch."

"That is not my name."

"What *is* your name?"

"Ursula Zaitsev."

"I'll remember that," Joanna said bitterly. "I'll remember it forever."

Ursula Zaitsev smiled. "No, my dear. You won't remember it—or anything else."

• 65 •

Alex put one hand on the swinging door and carefully pushed it away from him. A dimly lit hallway lay beyond the kitchen. No one waited in it.

Five other doors opened off the corridor before it reached the head of the stairs. Three of the doors were closed. Two of them were open, showing dark rooms across those thresholds.

Alex went to the closed door directly across the hall, hesitated, turned the knob slowly, and pushed it open. He found a richly furnished bedroom. The lamp on the nightstand spread a warm circle of light on an Edward Fields carpet that had evidently been imported from the United States. There was a spacious master bath with sunken tub and sauna. No one was there.

He had no difficulty figuring out whose house it was. Beside the bed he found half a dozen books. Five of them dealt with new discoveries in the behavioral sciences. The sixth volume was a heavily illustrated, privately printed collection of pornography; the main subject was sadism, and the beautiful women in the pictures appeared to be suffering in earnest. The blood looked real. It turned Alex's stomach. In one of the bureau drawers there were three pair of fine leather gloves. Actually, there weren't three pair, but just three different gloves—all for the same hand. Franz Rotenhausen owned this house.

In the corridor Alex stepped through one of the open doors. He found the light switch, flipped it on and off in a second. It was a dining room, and it was deserted.

The next open door led to a living room with low modern furniture and two Dali originals. The casement windows framed a splendid view of St. Moritz at night, aswirl with snow. This house was slightly above the town, at the edge of the forest.

The second of the three closed doors opened on a large guest bedchamber with its own bath. The room had not been used in quite some time; it exuded a vague musty odor.

Alex was impressed with the size of the buliding. If Rotenhausen live here on the top floor, what filled the two levels below?

The final door opened on the library. A single Tiffany desk lamp was on, casting multicolored light.

When he saw the shelves of books, Alex experienced a case of déjà vu. He stopped, afraid as he had never been, trembling.

I've seen this room before, he thought. *But I know I've never been here until now. What is going on?*

He entered the library with the firm conviction that he would find something there that he needed. He saw books, a rack filled with pipes, a selection of magazines, and a huge globe. None of that interested him.

He started opening desk drawers. In the second one he found the 7 mm. automatic and spare magazines of ammunition.

When he saw the pistol he realized that he had known it would be there.

• 66 •

After she administered the injection, Ursula Zaitsev left the room. Joanna was alone.

The winter storm pounded on the windows.

Joanna strained against the straps once more. It was useless. She finally fell back, gasping for breath.

What now?

She decided that she could do nothing but wait.

A minute passed. Two. Three. Five.

She expected the drug to take hold of her. Ursula Zaitsev had implied that it was a sedative, a depressant of some sort. She should be more relaxed than she was. She should be getting a bit drowsy, but instead she was thinking faster and clearer by the minute.

It's an adrenaline rush, she told herself. That's what it has to be. It'll fade in a minute or two, and I'll calm down.

But it didn't fade.

She was ready to struggle with the straps again when the door opened. Rotenhausen came in and smiled at her. He closed the door after himself and locked it.

Alex sat at the desk for a couple of minutes and carefully, thoroughly, examined the gun. He was suspicious. They could have done something to it to keep it from firing.

Wind rattled a pane of glass behind him. A cool draft occasionally chilled the back of his neck.

The gun appeared to be untouched, but he wondered if the ammunition had been replaced with blanks. He felt as if he was being suckered into something. Something deadly.

Finally he decided that he couldn't sit there all night. He had to find Joanna and get her out of this place. He stood up, pointed the silenced pistol at a row of books on the far side of the room, and squeezed the trigger.

Pfffffttt!

One of the books jumped in its place, and the spine cracked with a sound louder than that which the gun had made.

They weren't blanks.

"All right, then," he said softly. "All right. Let's find out what the hell this is all about."

He walked out of the library and went to the head of the stairs.

· 68 ·

The Hand.

Now she had a name for him: Franz Rotenhausen.

He looked much the same as he had in her nightmares. He was tall and thin. His clothes hung loosely on him. He was balder than he had been a decade ago, but there was no gray in his hair. His eyes were light brown, pale, almost yellow; and in those eyes a perfectly controlled madness shone like arctic sun flickering on strange configurations of ice.

The mechanical hand was as terrifying as it had ever been in her dreams—more terrifying now, in fact, because this time she knew she would not wake up and find that it was gone. The shiny, chitinous, jointed steel fingers worked like the grasping legs of certain carnivorous insects, and the purring mechanisms produced a sinister sound. She had forgotten that the hand was commanded by the nerve endings in Rotenhausen's stump but not powered by them. The energy to operate it came from a battery case that was strapped to his upper arm; it was no bigger than two packs of cigarettes.

Mariko had assured her that she would find this man less frightening in reality than he was in her nightmares. That was not true. The sight of him left her weak with terror. She felt a scream building in her, even though she knew it would relieve none of the pain that was to come.

As he approached the bed he said, "Are you sleepy, my little girl?"

She was wide awake. And that was odd. Zaitsev had said that the drug would relax her. Rotenhausen expected her to be drowsy. She wondered if Zaitsev had made a mistake. Perhaps the woman had used the wrong drug.

"Are you sleepy, little lady? Are you?"

Joanna suddenly realized that fate, or someone in its employ, had given her a last chance. Not much of one. A very slim chance. But perhaps she could escape. If she made him believe that she was heavily doped, he might release the straps. Then, at the first opportunity, she would surprise him and flee.

Dear God, please let it happen that way! she prayed silently but fervently.

"Sleepy?" Rotenhausen asked again as he reached the side of her bed.

She forced down the scream and half closed her eyes. She yawned.

"That's fine," he said.

She smiled at him stupidly, groggily. "Who're you?"

"I'm the doctor." His eyes were almost transparent, the very image of death.

"Everythin's fuzzy," she said.

"That's the way it's supposed to be."

"Real, real fuzzy," she said thickly.

"Good."

The metal fingers clicked as he reached for her. He grasped the sheet in his mechanical hand and pulled it down.

She was wearing a flimsy hospital gown that was tied in back.

"Pretty," he said.

She needed all of her courage to smile.

The steel fingers gripped the neckline of the gown and tore the garment from her.

She almost gasped.

He watched her closely.

She grinned at him and yawned.

The steel hand settled on her breasts.

The house was solidly built. Not even one of the steps creaked.

Alex paused at the second-floor landing. The hallway was bathed in pale, yellow light. It was deserted. A combination of odors, various antiseptics and disinfectants, reminded him of Joanna's recurring nightmare. Evidently, this part of the house was used for Rotenhausen's research.

Alex was about to investigate the first of the six closed doors when he heard voices. He crouched, prepared to run or shoot. Then he realized that the conversation was in progress downstairs and that no one was coming his way. Attracted by the voices, he decided to leave the second floor unexplored for the time being, and he continued down.

The ground-level hallway looked like the two corridors above it: exceptionally clean and dimly lighted. There were six doors. One of them was ajar, and people were talking loudly—arguing?—in the room beyond it.

Alex came to the door and listened. They were talking about him and Joanna.

He risked a peek through the three-inch-wide crack between the door and the jamb. It was a conference room. Three men were sitting at a large round table, and a fourth stood at a window, his back to the others.

The nearest man was extremely fat. He overflowed his chair. He was unwrapping the end of a roll of Lifesavers.

Anson Peterson.

The name came to Alex unbidden. To the best of

354

his knowledge he had never seen the fat man before,
yet he knew the name.

The next man was unnaturally large but not fat.
Even sitting down he looked tall. He had a bull's neck
and truly massive shoulders. His face was broad and
flat beneath a low brow.

Antonio Paz.

The second name came to Alex as if someone had
gotten inside him, inside his head, and had whispered
it. It made him feel as if he had been born and had
lived for the sole purpose of arriving in this place
at this time.

Predestination.

Fate.

I don't believe in that, Alex thought.

But he had no other explanation.

He was scared.

The third man at the table had coarse black hair,
a prominent nose, deeply set dark eyes, and a swarthy
complexion. He looked dangerous. He was shorter than
Paz but even more powerfully built. Worse than that,
he had the subtly peculiar, intense appearance of a
psychopath.

Ignacio Carreras.

The fourth man turned away from the window and
faced the others.

Alex almost cried out in disbelief.

The fourth man was Senator Thomas Chelgrin.

• 70 •

The fat man popped a butter-rum Lifesaver into his
mouth and savored it for a moment. Then he looked
at Carreras and said, "So it's decided. You'll kill
Hunter tonight, strip him, and dump the body into the
lake."

Carreras nodded. "I'll cut off the tips of his fingers so the police won't be able to print the body, and I'll smash out his teeth to prevent identification from dental records."

Peterson winced. "Isn't that excessive? By the time the lake thaws and they find him—next summer, perhaps the summer after that—the fishes will have left nothing but bare bones."

"The fish have often served us well in that respect," Carreras said. "But what if they don't get a chance to do their work? What if Hunter's body is found tomorrow or the day after?"

"It won't be," Peterson said. "No one will miss him for a while. And he hasn't reported in to his Chicago office for a few days. No one knows he came to Switzerland. When they finally track him this far, they'll find he vanished without a trace. They won't want to drag the lake. Why would they? They'll figure he's just as likely to be dead in the mountains, dead in some other town—or even living a new life in the South Seas."

"He'll be another Judge Crater," said the usually taciturn Antonio Paz.

"Exactly," said the fat man. "He'll be an eternal mystery."

Carreras shook his head impatiently. "I don't believe in taking chances. Not even little ones. I'll play it safe. I'll chop off the fingertips, knock out the teeth, and maybe even disfigure his face."

And you'd enjoy every minute of it, Peterson thought sourly.

Chelgrin hadn't said much in the past half an hour. Now he walked to the table and faced Peterson. "You told me I'd be allowed to see my daughter as soon as they brought her here."

"Yes, dear Tom. But Rotenhausen must examine her first."

"Why?"

"I don't know. But he felt it was necessary, and he's the boss in this place."

"Not when you're around," Chelgrin said.

"Well, of course he is. It's his home and his clinic," Peterson said.

"When you're here it doesn't matter who owns the place," Chelgrin said. "You're the boss type. You're the boss wherever you go. It's in your genes. You'll be in charge of hell an hour after you get there."

"How very kind of you to say so, dear Tom."

"I want to see Lisa."

Carreras interrupted, and Peterson was thankful for that. "And there you have another problem," Carreras said. "The girl. What do we do about the girl if—"

"That's been settled," the senator said sharply. "The Joanna Rand memories will be erased. Another identity will be implanted. She'll be set up in a brand new life in West Germany."

"That's what'll happen if everything goes as planned," Carreras agreed. "But what if she can't survive the treatment a second time? What if her mind snaps? What if there's brain damage? We might end up with a vegetable on our hands, and we have got to be prepared for that."

"It won't happen!" Chelgrin said.

"Dear Tom, I warned you that it might end up just like that," the fat man said. "In Washington, last week, I warned you."

"You're still trying to trick me," Chelgrin said.

"No, dear Tom."

Chelgrin was working up to an apoplectic rage. "You want me to think the treatment will destroy her," he said angrily. "You want me to believe it because *if* I believe it I might agree to send her home instead of taking that risk."

"But it's true, dear Tom."

"It isn't! It isn't true. And this game of yours won't work. I will not—" Chelgrin stopped, looked past Peterson, and frowned. "Who's that? There's someone at the door. Someone's been eavesdropping."

The instant he knew that he had been seen, Alex pushed the door all the way open and stepped into the room.

"Welcome," said the fat man.

Alex stared at Chelgrin. "You're dead."

The senator didn't respond.

Alex was suddenly furious. He was tired of being lied to, tricked, and used. He waved the gun at Chelgrin. "Tell me why you're not dead. You stinking, rotten bastard! Tell me why!"

Nervously patting his silver hair with one hand, the senator said, "Officially, I'm on a skiing holiday."

"Why aren't you dead?"

"It was faked," Chelgrin said shakily. "I pretended to be dead. It was all engineered for you. We wanted you to find those newspaper clippings about Rotenhausen so you'd come here where we could handle you."

"And the unfinished letter to Lisa—?"

"A nice touch, wasn't it?" Peterson said.

Alex was confused. His next question was for himself more than for any of these men. "But why didn't I examine you when I found you lying there? Why didn't I check for a pulse? That's what I should have done. That's what I would have done any other time."

Chelgrin cleared his throat. "You were convinced I was dead. We did our best to make it look real. The bullet holes in the robe, some wounds made of putty and rabbit blood, so much blood, the hair over my eyes so you wouldn't notice any involuntary muscle spasms . . . I wore only the robe and left my wallet on the dresser so you wouldn't have any reason to search me."

Alex glanced at each of the men. He thought about what Chelgrin had said. Finally he shook his head. "No. That doesn't wash. I'm a professional. The first thing I should have done was check your pulse. But I avoided you. And when I caught Joanna kneeling beside you, I made her get away fast. I used some excuse about not getting blood on her. But in fact I didn't touch you because I was programmed to keep my distance. I was programmed not to shatter the illusion. Isn't that right?"

Chelgrin blinked. "Programmed?"

"Don't lie to me!"

"What are you talking about?"

"You tell me."

The senator was genuinely perplexed.

Alex turned to the fat man. "It's true, isn't it?"

"What's that?"

"I've been running around like some goddamned robot, operating on a program, like a machine!"

Peterson smiled. He knew.

Alex thrust the pistol at him. "Last spring, when I went to Rio for a vacation—what in the name of God happened to me there?"

Before the fat man could answer, Antonio Paz reached inside his jacket. Alex saw the movement from the corner of his eye. Paz started to bring out a gun.

Alex was quick. He swung away from the fat man. He fired twice.

The bullets ripped into the big man's face. Blood puffed into the air like perfume from an atomizer. Paz and his chair went backward with a great crash.

Carreras shouted and started to get up.

A voice in Alex's head whispered: *Kill him*. Before he could think about that, he obeyed. He squeezed the trigger.

Carreras was hit. He fell.

Shocked, wide-eyed, terrified, the senator backed away. His hands were out in front of him, palms toward Alex, fingers spread, as if he thought death was a solid object that could be held at arm's length.

Kill him.

Alex heard the voice inside his head, but he hesitated. He was bewildered. He was shaking.

He tried to think through to another, less violent solution: Paz and Carreras were dangerous men, but they were dead now, gone, no longer a threat; and the senator was no longer a threat either; he was a broken man, begging for his life; whatever he was trying to hide would come into the open now; no need to kill him; no need to kill.

Kill him.

He couldn't resist. He pulled the trigger twice.

The bullets thumped into the senator's chest. He toppled backward, into the window. His head struck the glass. One of the thick panes cracked. He dropped to the floor with a very final sound.

"Jesus," Alex said. "What have I done? What am I doing? *What in the hell am I doing?*"

The fat man was still sitting in his chair. "The terrible angel of vengeance," he said. He smiled at Alex. He appeared to be delighted.

Carreras got up. He was bloody, but he was only grazed. He moved fast, picked up a chair and threw it.

Alex fired and missed.

The chair struck him as he tried to turn away from it. Pain speared through his right arm.

The pistol was knocked out of his hand. It flew across the room.

He staggered backward. He came up hard against the door jamb.

Carreras started toward him.

• 72 •

The Hand. It caressed her. It squeezed her. It patted and stroked and pinched her. It gleamed. It was cold. It hummed. It purred. It clicked, clicked, clicked.

Her own courage amazed her. She did not flinch. She endured Rotenhausen's obscene explorations and pretended to be doped. She mumbled, murmured with feigned pleasure as he touched her, occasionally warned him off as if she had briefly surfaced from the drug, but followed each scowl with a stupid smile and more murmuring.

She had just about decided that he was never going to stop petting her with those steel fingers, had just about made up her mind to spit at him—when he unbuckled the strap that held down her left hand. She froze, afraid to breathe or move. She didn't want to do anything that would make him stop what he was doing. In the same instant she realized that any change in her behavior would alert him; and with a tremendous effort she managed to murmur and smile at him again. He reached across her and loosened the strap on her right hand. She didn't move her arms. She tried to appear content, stuporous. He went to the other end of the bed and freed her left foot, then her right. She was unbound.

"Such a lovely little girl," Rotenhausen said, more to himself than to her.

He returned to the head of the bed.

She still did not make a break for freedom.

Rotenhausen took off his white smock and draped it across the instrument cart that held the syringes and the sphygmomanometer.

"I remember you," he said. "I remember how you felt."

He began to unbutton his shirt.

Through half-closed eyes Joanna studied the mechanical hand. A flexible steel-ring cable, half an inch in diameter, came out of the metal wrist and led up the arm. In the last two inches of its length, the cable split in two and terminated in a pair of male jacks, which were plugged into a set of female slots on the battery pack.

He took off his shirt and tossed it on top of the smock.

"It will be interesting, considering that your father is just downstairs," he said.

Joanna imitated lightning. Her hand flashed out and seized the ring cable. She tore the jacks out of the battery pack. The hand stopped purring, and the steel fingers froze as if time had stopped while he was making a fox in a game of silhouettes. As the astonished doctor watched, she rolled away from him. Naked, she dropped off the bed on the other side and ran for the door.

He caught her with his real hand just as she touched the lock. He gripped a handful of her long hair and swung her around.

Starbursts of pain flared behind her eyes. She flailed at him and screamed.

Rotenhausen cursed her. He dragged her from the door, then shoved her away from him.

She staggered backward and collided with the bed. She swayed, grabbed at the footrail, and managed to stay on her feet.

He plugged the jacks into the battery pack again.

The hand purred.

The steel fingers moved: *click, click, click.*

· 73 ·

Alex saw Ignacio Carreras coming like a human locomotive, and he knew that the loss of the pistol had left him virtually no chance of survival. He was moderately well skilled in the martial arts—jujitsu, karate, suvate—but he didn't doubt that Carreras was also familiar with those disciplines; therefore, the weightlifter's extra pounds of muscle would be a deadly advantage.

Alex chose retreat. He stepped out of the room and slammed the door between them. There was no way for him to lock it.

He ran to the rear of the ground-floor corridor. The door opened behind him. He heard running footsteps in his wake, but he didn't look back.

He opened the last door on the right and went into the dark room beyond. He shut the door and felt frantically, desperately, for a latch. He found a lock button in the center of the knob and pushed it.

A second later Carreras reached the other side and tried to get in. The door wouldn't open.

Alex played blindman's bluff until he located the light switch. He had hoped to find something that could be used as a weapon. He was out of luck. The single overhead light showed him an empty storeroom.

Joanna, I'm not going to let you down, he thought. *I'm going to find you and get you out of here.*

Of course, Rotenhausen might already have begun work on her. If he had started the treatment, she might not be Joanna anymore.

How long would it take to erase more than a decade of memories? An hour? Surely longer. A day? A week? A month?

He might have plenty of time—or perhaps he was already too late to save her.

In any event he had to escape. He needed to find a hiding place where he could gain time to think. He couldn't plan well with Carreras breathing down his neck.

Alex crossed the storeroom to a window and put up the blind. A fierce gust of wind showered snow against the glass.

Carreras hit the door again. And again. Something cracked.

With trembling fingers Alex unlatched the casement window and pushed the halves outward. Cold wind exploded into the room.

Carreras rammed the door. The impact was accompanied by the sound of splintering wood.

The man's a goddamned bull!

Alex climbed over the window ledge and stepped into a foot of snow. The wind whistled along the walls of the valley at something more than fifty kilometers an hour; it bit his face, made his eyes water, and instantly numbed his bare hands. He was thankful for the insulated ski clothes he was wearing.

Carreras hit the door.

Alex shuffled into the darkness, kicking up clouds of snow as he went. He had not gone far when he heard the door collapse with a *boom* in the room he had just left. He ran.

• 74 •

By the time the fat man reached the end of the hall, Ignacio Carreras had broken down the door and was climbing out the window of the storeroom, in pursuit of Alex Hunter. Peterson started after him, thought better of it, and went back into the hall.

"Ursula! Ursula, where are you?"

She didn't answer.

He walked up the hall, toward the conference room. "Dr. Zaitsev! It's me. Anson."

She opened the door on his right and peered warily at him. "What's all the noise? I was afraid to come out. What's gone wrong?"

"Everything. We must get out of here."

"Leave?"

"Hurry," the fat man said urgently. "There's no time to waste."

She regarded him through the partly opened door. "But where will we go?"

"Someplace safe."

"I don't understand."

"Come on, come on, my dear. If we don't move quickly, we'll be caught."

"Caught? By whom?"

"The police, of course!"

Bewildered, she stepped into the hall.

Peterson was wearing a silenced pistol in a shoulder holster. He pulled the gun and shot her twice.

Ursula Zaitsev died almost prettily. The bullets spun her around as if she were twirling to show a new skirt to her boyfriend. There was not much blood. She sagged against the wall, looked at the fat man without seeing him, allowed a delicate thread of blood to escape one corner of her mouth, let go of her icy expression for the first time since Peterson had known her, and slid down into death.

Four of the six people on the fat man's list had been eliminated. Marlowe. Antonio Paz. Thomas Chelgrin. Ursula Zaitsev. Only two awaited disposal.

Peterson ran to the rear of the house. He had that peculiar grace that certain very fat men could summon on occasion. He dashed into the storeroom, levered himself through the window, and groaned when the bitter night air slapped his face.

The wind was scouring the footprints from the newly fallen snow, but he was still able to follow Hunter and Carreras.

· 75 ·

For a couple of minutes there was a lot of shouting and other noise in a distant part of the house. At first she hoped it was Alex coming for her—or someone from outside coming for both her and Alex. But Rotenhausen ignored it, and after a while she gave up all hope of being rescued.

He backed her into a corner. He pinned her there with his body.

There was no escape.

The nightmare had become real.

Rotenhausen spread his steel fingers and took hold of her throat. He placed his real hand over the battery pack to prevent her from pulling out the jacks.

She could not look away from his extraordinary eyes. They were exceedingly pale. Yellowish. Cat's eyes. Demonic eyes. They didn't look human.

He cocked his head and watched her quizzically while he squeezed her throat. He looked as if he were observing a laboratory animal through the wire walls of its cage.

She spluttered, choked.

He squeezed harder. He was smiling now.

Joanna couldn't get her breath, and she panicked. She twisted, squirmed, kicked ineffectually with her bare feet, and tried to wrench loose of those awful fingers.

Rotenhausen was unimpressed with her spirited resistance. His grip was unbreakable.

She had expected him to call for help and put the straps on her again. But it was obvious that he had another idea. She could guess what it was. He was going to half strangle her. He was going to choke her unconscious, and then he was going to rape her.

Black spots swam in front of her eyes. They grew larger by the second, blotting out more and more of her vision.

• 76 •

Millions of billions of flakes of snow poured out of the Swiss night. They frosted Alex's hair. They got under the collar of his jacket. They melted on his face and clung like paste to the shiny fabric of his ski clothes.

The darkness and the storm reduced visibility to ten or fifteen yards in open country. Fortunately the snow took what little light was there and refracted it in an infinity of tiny prisms, increased it twofold, and cast it back; the resultant, eerie phosphorescence made it possible for Alex to distinguish shapes if not details.

He crossed a hundred yards of open land before he reached the shelter of the forest. The mammoth pines grew close together, but a great deal of snow still found its way through. The trees did provide considerable relief from the banshee wind.

Alex entered the forest on a path that he found quite by accident, a narrow but well-established trail that might have been made by deer. He ran twenty or thirty feet under the imperfect canopy of branches before he stumbled and fell over rocks that were hidden by snow. The fall knocked his breath out of him.

Afraid that Carreras would come upon him at any second, he rolled onto his back and threw up his arms. He was prepared to kick and fight for his life as best he could.

Carreras was not yet in sight.

Alex struggled to his feet. He slipped, slid, and scrabbled in the snow.

In the process of getting up, he found a weapon. He got hold of a loose rock the size of an orange. It had a few rough spots, a couple of jagged edges. It wasn't as good as a gun, but it was better than nothing.

Alex hurried deeper into the woods.

Thirty feet from the spot where he had fallen, the trail bent sharply to the right, curved around an especially dense stand of shoulder-high brush. He stopped there and considered the potential for an ambush. The terrain looked perfect for it. Here, the darkness was almost complete. His eyes continued to adjust to the conditions of the night; but although he squinted down at the snow, he could barely discern the disturbance that his own feet had made in the smooth skin of white powder. He weighed the rock in his hand, backed against the wall of brush until it poked him painfully, and hunched down. He became a shadow among shadows.

Above the roof of pine and fir needles, the raging wind howled incessantly. It sounded like a distant pack of hungry wolves.

Snow sifted over him.

His hands were cold, almost numb. He was afraid he would soon be unable to hold onto the stone.

Within a minute he heard Carreras. The man evidently had no fear of his quarry; he was not making an effort to be quiet. He barged through the forest, crashing and cursing as if he were a drunk in transit between two taverns.

Alex tensed. He kept his eyes on the bend in the trail, four feet away.

Carreras appeared and started past. He was bent forward, intent on the vague footprints he was following.

Alex leapt up as if propelled by a spring, startling the other man. He swung his arm high and brought the rock down fast with all of his strength. It caught Carreras alongside the head, and the big man dropped.

Alex looked at him and saw that he was very still and stepped across him.

Carreras grabbed his ankle.

· 77 ·

Joanna rammed her knee into Rotenhausen's crotch.

He sensed it coming and deflected most of the force with his thigh. Nevertheless, the blow made him gasp in pain, and he bent forward reflexively, protectively.

His mechanical hand slid along her throat. The cold, clicking fingers loosened their grip on her.

Joanna slipped out of his grasp and started toward the door, and he scurried after her. The pain caused him to hobble, crablike, but he moved fast.

She abandoned the idea of reaching the door in time to throw the lock and get out. Instead, she put the wheeled cart between them. His shirt and smock were draped across the cart, and she threw them on the floor. In addition to syringes, the sphygmomanometer, a bottle of glucose for the IV tree, a packet of tongue depressors, a penlight, a device for examining the eye, and many small bottles of drugs, the instrument tray held a pair of surgical scissors. Joanna picked them up and brandished them at Rotenhausen as if they were a great magical sword.

He glared at her. He was red-faced, furious.

"I won't let you do it to me again," Joanna said. "I won't let you tamper with my mind. You'll either have to let me go or kill me."

With his mechanical hand he reached across the cart and seized the scissors. He wrenched them away from her and squeezed them in his steel fingers until the blades snapped with a two-beat *clink-clink.*

"I could do the same to you," he said.

He threw the broken scissors aside.

Her heartbeat exploded, and her breathing grew very rapid, and her skin was suddenly ruddy and warm; she could almost feel the adrenaline gushing into her system. The governor on the engine of time seemed to burn out; suddenly everything happened very fast. She plucked the container of glucose from the tray, and Rotenhausen swung his metal hand, smashing the bottle before she could throw it, and she was left with just the neck of it in her hand, and he violently shoved the cart out of the way, came at her, his pale eyes murderous, and she stepped back, and she saw that he was too confident and that there was an opening for her, a real chance to triumph, because she realized that she had a weapon, a damned good weapon, and as he grabbed her she thrust the jagged neck of the broken bottle deep into his throat, and he stopped, shocked, and blood spurted, and she let go of the bottle, and he staggered back and raised his hands to his throat and tried to pull the glass from his flesh and began to gag horribly and finally collapsed.

Carreras grabbed Alex's ankle. He fell, jerked free of the weightlifter, and rolled.

By the time Alex got to his feet, Carreras was on all fours in the middle of the path. He looked at Alex and shook his head as if to clear his mind.

Alex took advantage of the situation. He stepped forward quickly and kicked Carreras squarely under the chin.

The weightlifter's head snapped back. He fell over, into the brush.

Alex was sure the kick had broken Carrera's neck, but after a moment the big man moved. He started to get up on his hands and knees again.

The son of a bitch is indestructible! Alex thought.

He still had the rock in his right hand. He raised it and moved toward Carreras.

The big man threw an arm up and blocked the blow. He also caught Alex's wrist. His fingers were like talons.

Alex cried out when it felt as if his wrist bones were being ground to powder against each other, and he dropped the jagged stone. He tried to pull away, slipped in the snow, and fell.

Carreras clambered on top of him. He was growling like an animal. He swung one huge fist.

Alex wasn't able to duck it. The punch landed in his face, split his lips, and broke a couple of teeth. He almost choked on a tooth that slid down his throat, and he tasted blood.

He knew he was no match for Carreras in hand-to-hand combat. He had to get on his feet and be able to maneuver. As Carreras swung his fist again, Alex heaved and thrashed and bucked like a bronco. The fist missed him. He kept bucking, and the weightlifter fell sideways. The instant that Carreras was off him, Alex scrambled upslope, clutched at a tree for support, and stood.

Carreras was halfway to his feet.

Alex kicked him in the stomach, which gave about as much as a board wall would have done.

Carreras skidded in the snow and went down on his hands and knees again.

Alex kicked him in the face.

The weightlifter sprawled in the snow, on his back, arms extended like wings. He didn't move.

Cautiously, as if he were a priest approaching the coffin in which a vampire slept, Alex crept up on Carreras. He knelt at the man's side. The eyes were open wide, but they saw nothing. Alex tried to find a pulse. There was no need to fetch a wooden stake or a crucifix or a necklace of garlic, for this time the monster was definitely dead.

He thought of Joanna in the house with Rotenhausen, and he did not pause to catch his breath. He got up at once and started back down the trail, back the way he had come.

Anson Peterson was waiting for him in the open land just beyond the perimeter of the forest. The fat man had a gun.

· 79 ·

Rotenhausen was dead.

Joanna felt no remorse for having killed him. She was not frightened any more either. She was just worried about Alex.

She went to the wheeled cart and found the drug

that Ursula Zaitsev had given her. The bottle still contained a small amount of colorless fluid. She pulled the seal from it and shook a couple of drops onto her hand. She sniffed it, then tasted it. She was pretty sure it was nothing but water. Someone had switched bottles on Zaitsev.

But who? And why?

She found her ski clothes in a closet. She dressed and left the room.

The house was silent. She cautiously inspected the other five rooms on that floor and found no one. For almost a minute she stood on the second-floor landing, looking alternately up and down the steps, listening, but she heard only the wind in the eaves.

She quietly descended to the ground floor, where there was an entrance foyer, a long hallway—and a corpse. Ursula Zaitsev lay in her own blood.

Don't think about it, Joanna told herself. *Don't think who. Don't think why. Just keep moving.*

Six doors led off the long hall. Joanna didn't want to open any of those doors, but she knew that she must investigate all of them in order to find Alex.

She stepped past the dead woman and saw that the first two doors were ajar. She went to the one on her right and slowly pushed it all the way open.

"You!" she said.

Senator Thomas Chelgrin stood before her. He was ashen. His face was spattered with blood. His silver hair was spotted and streaked with blood. His left hand was pressed over what appeared to be a bullet wound in his chest, and his shirt was soaked with blood. He swayed and almost fell and took one step toward her. He put his bloody hand on her shoulder.

On the snowy slope, one hundred yards from the house, above the lights of St. Moritz, Alex and the fat man stared at each other for a long, uncertain moment. Only the wind spoke.

Finally Alex said, "Why didn't I kill you?"

"You weren't supposed to," the fat man said. "Where is he?"

"Carreras? He's dead," Alex said weakly.

"He's what?"

Alex could not speak clearly. His mouth was sore and swollen. "Dead. He's dead."

"You killed him?"

"Yeah."

"But you didn't have a gun."

Alex said, "No gun." He was weary. His eyes were watering from the cold; the fat man shimmered like a mirage.

"It's hard to believe that you could kill him without a gun," said the fat man.

"I didn't say it was easy."

Peterson gaped at him, grinned, and suddenly began to laugh.

"All right," Alex said. "All right. Get it over with. I killed him. Now you kill me."

"Oh, my heavens, no! No, no," Peterson said. "You've got it all wrong, all backwards, dear boy. You and me—we're on the same team."

· 81 ·

The sight of the blood-smeared specter—her true
father, the man who had somehow started all of this,
a man now risen from the grave—immobilized Joanna.
She stood still, as if rooted, every muscle locked, while
the senator clung weakly to her shoulder. She did not
understand how he could be here, dying all over again,
and she couldn't help wondering about her sanity.

"I'm weak," he said thickly. "Too weak. I can't
stand up anymore. Don't let me fall down. Please. Help
me down easy. Let's go down easy. Real easy."

Joanna put one hand on the door jamb to brace
herself. She went slowly to her knees, and the senator
used her for support. At last he was sitting with his
back against the wall, pressing the palm of his left
hand against the chest wound; and she was kneeling
at his side.

"Daughter," he said, looking at her wonderingly.
"My daughter."

She could not accept him as her father. She thought
of all that he was responsible for: the years of programmed loneliness, the programmed claustrophobia,
the nightmares, the fear that might have been defeated
if it could have been defined. She thought of how
Rotenhausen had raped her the first time she'd been
to this place—and of how he had tried to use her
again, tonight. Worse than all of that was the possibility that Alex was dead; and if he was, Thomas
Chelgrin was the man who had directly or indirectly
pulled the trigger. In her heart there was no room for
the senator. Perhaps it was unfair of her to freeze him
out before she knew his reasons; perhaps her inability
to forgive her own father was an awful thing, an

infinitely sad thing; however, she felt no guilt about it and knew she never would. She despised this man.

"My little girl," he said.

"No."

"You are. You're my daughter."

"No."

"Lisa."

"Joanna. My name's Joanna Rand."

He wheezed and cleared his throat. His speech was slurred. "You hate me, don't you?"

"Yes."

"But you don't understand."

"I understand enough."

"No, you don't. You've got to listen to me."

"Nothing you say will make me want to be your daughter again. Lisa Chelgrin is dead. Forever."

The senator closed his eyes. A fierce wave of pain swept over him. He grimaced and bent forward.

She made no move to comfort him.

When the attack passed he sat up straight, opened his eyes, and said, "I've got to tell you about it. You've got to give me a chance to explain. You have to listen to me."

"I'm listening," she said, "but not because I have to."

His breath rattled in his throat; it sounded worse by the minute. "Everyone thinks I was a war hero. They think I escaped from that North Korean prison camp and made my way back to the United Nations lines. I built my entire political career on that story, but it's a lie. I didn't spend weeks in the wilderness, inching my way out of enemy territory. A North Korean officer drove me to within a mile of the United States forces, and I walked the rest of the way. I never escaped from a prison camp because I was never in one. Tom Chelgrin was a prisoner, but not me."

"You *are* Thomas Chelgrin."

"No. My real name is Ilya Timoshenko," he said. "I am a Russian."

Haltingly, often pausing to cough or wheeze or spit blood, he told her how Ilya Timoshenko had become the Honorable United States Senator from Illinois, the well-known and widely respected potential candidate for the Presidency, Thomas Chelgrin. He was convincing. But then she supposed that a dying man's confession was always convincing.

She listened, amazed and fascinated.

• 82 •

In 1950, in every North Korean concentration camp that was used for the detention of captured United Nations soldiers, the commandant was looking for certain special prisoners. He was searching for United States citizens who shared a list of characteristics with a dozen men whose photographs had been secretly but widely distributed among high-ranking Communist prison officials. The photographs were of young Russian intelligence trainees who had volunteered for a project code named Mirror.

When Thomas Chelgrin was brought in chains to the camp near Hyesan, the commandant saw at once that he vaguely resembled Ilya Timoshenko, one of the Russians in the Mirror group. The two men were the same height and build. They had the same color hair and eyes. Their basic facial bone structures were nearly identical. The day he arrived at Hyesan, Chelgrin was taken away from the other prisoners; and for the rest of his life he spent mornings and afternoons with North Korean interrogators, evenings and nights in solitary confinement. A Red Army photographer took more than a hundred and fifty photographs of Chelgrin, of his entire body, naked and clothed, but mostly of his face, from every angle, in every kind of light, close-ups, medium shots, long shots to show how he stood and held his shoulders. The film was developed under top security conditions at a nearby military base, and both the prints and the negatives were sent by special courier to the Kremlin, where the men in charge of the Mirror group anxiously waited for them.

Military doctors in Moscow studied the pictures of Thomas Chelgrin for two days and finally reported that he was a reasonably good match for Timoshenko. One week later, Ilya underwent the first of many operations to make him into Chelgrin's double. His hairline was too low; they destroyed hair follicles and moved the line back half an inch. His eyelids drooped slightly, the result of a Mongolian great-great-great grandmother; they lifted the lids, made them look Western. They operated on his nose, made it smaller and took out a bump on the bridge. His earlobes were too large; they cut some of that flesh away. His mouth was right, but his teeth were entirely different from Chelgrin's. A dentist ground and drilled and filed his teeth until they were just thin splinters, then capped them so that they matched photographs of Thomas Chelgrin's dental structure. Timoshenko's chin was round, which was no good for this masquerade; therefore, they made it square. He had a great deal of hair on his chest, but the American did not. They permanently removed most of it. Finally the chief surgeon circumcised Ilya and said that the transformation was not merely complete but perfect as well.

While Timoshenko was enduring seven months of plastic surgery, Thomas Chelgrin was sweating out a long series of brutal inquisitions at the Hyesan camp. He was in the hands of North Korea's best interrogators. They used drugs, threats, promises, hypnosis, humor, anger, and even torture to learn everything there was to know about him. They compiled an immense dossier about both the important and mundane things in his life, a dossier about: the foods he liked least and the foods he liked most; his brand of beer; his public and his private religious beliefs; his favorite cigarettes; his friends, their likes and dislikes, their habits, their virtues and weaknesses, their peculiarities; his political convictions; his favorite sports; forms of entertainment he most enjoyed; his racial prejudices; his fears; his hopes; his poor mathematical ability; his talent for essay composition; his inability to tolerate ignorant people; his sexual techniques; preferences in women; and thousands upon thousands of other things. They squeezed as if he were an orange, and they did not intend to leave one drop of juice in him.

Once a week, transcripts of the sessions with Chelgrin were flown to Moscow, where they were edited down to lists of data. Ilya Timoshenko studied them while convalescing between operations. He had to commit literally hundreds of thousands of bits of information to memory, and it was the most difficult job he had ever undertaken. He was assisted by two psychologists who worked in memory research programs under the auspices of the KGB. At their direction, Timoshenko read every list three times, then had it read to him again while he was in a hypnotic trance. While he slept, recordings of the lists played softly in the room, sending their messages directly to his subconscious.

After twelve years of English studies, which began when he was ten years old, Timoshenko had come to speak the language without a Russian accent. In fact, he spoke with the clear but colorless diction of television newsmen in the Middle Atlantic States. Now he listened to recordings of Chelgrin's voice and attempted to imprint a Midwest accent over the bland English he spoke. By the time the final operation was performed, he sounded as if he had been born and raised on an Illinois farm.

When Timoshenko was halfway through his metamorphosis, the men in charge of Mirror began to worry

about Tom Chelgrin's mother. They believed that Timoshenko would fool Chelgrin's friends and casual ac-
quaintances, but they were afraid that anyone especially
close—such as mother, father, or wife—would notice
changes in him or lapses of memory, and would become suspicious. Fortunately for the Mirror plan,
Chelgrin had never been engaged or married. He was
handsome and popular, which meant he had the opportunity to keep a lot of girls on the string; he played
the field; he didn't have one steady girlfriend back
home. His father had died when Tom was a child. So
far as the KGB was concerned, that left only one
serious threat to the success of the masquerade—Tom's
mother. But that problem was easily remedied, for the
KGB had a long arm. Orders were sent to an agent in
New York on January 5, 1951. Ten days later Tom's
mother was killed in an automobile accident on her way
home from a bridge party. The night was dark and the
narrow road was icy in patches; it was a tragedy that
could befall anyone. When the men in charge of
Mirror heard about it, they didn't grieve, even though
a couple of them had read John Donne's most famous
bit of wisdom and, therefore, knew for whom the bell
tolls.

In the spring of 1951, eight months after Chelgrin
had been captured, Ilya Timoshenko arrived by night
at the Hyesan camp. He was in the company of the
KGB director who had conceived the scheme, a man
named Emil Gorov. He waited with Gorov in the
camp commandant's private quarters while Chelgrin
was brought from his cell. When the American walked
into the room, he looked at Timoshenko and knew
immediately that he was not destined to live. "Mirror,"
Gorov said, astounded. "A mirror image."

That night the real Thomas Chelgrin was taken
quietly out of the prison. They shot him in the back
of the head, cremated him, and scattered the ashes.

Within a week the new Thomas Chelgrin "escaped"
from the Hyesan camp. He made his way back to

friendly territory, connected with his own division, eventually went home to Illinois, wrote a book, and became a war hero.

Thomas Chelgrin's mother had not been a wealthy woman, but she had managed to keep up the premiums on a $25,000 life insurance policy that named her son, her only child, as sole beneficiary. That money came to him when he returned from the war. He used it and the earnings from his book to purchase a Volkswagen dealership just before the buyer's rush began. He got married and fathered a daughter. The business flourished beyond his wildest expectations, and he put his profits into other investments that also did well.

His orders from Mirror had been simple. He was expected to become a small-business man. He was expected to prosper; and if he could not do well on his own, KGB money would be carefully funneled to him through third parties. In his late thirties, when his community knew him to be a respectable family man and at least a moderately successful entrepreneur, he would run for public office. At that point the KGB would definitely but indirectly contribute substantial funds to his campaign.

He followed the plan, but with one important change. By the time he was prepared to seek elective office, he was an extremely wealthy man. He had become rich on his own, without the help of the KGB. When he sought a seat in the United States House of Representatives, he received all of the legitimate financial backing he needed to complement his own money, and the KGB did not have to open its purse.

In Moscow the highest hope was that he would become a member of the lower house of Congress and that he would win reelection for three or four more terms. During those eight or ten years he would be able to pass along incredible quantities of vital secret information.

He lost his first election, primarily because he had never remarried after the death of his first wife. There was a prejudice against bachelors in American politics at that time. Two years later, when he tried again, he used his cute daughter, Lisa Jean, to win voters; and he gained considerable sympathy by playing upon the tragic loss of his wife when his child was so young. He won. He swiftly rose from the lower house to the upper, and now he was considered the prime Presidential candidate in his party. His success was a thousandfold greater than Moscow's expectations.

Eventually his success became the central problem of his life. By his late thirties Thomas Chelgrin, who had once been Ilya Timoshenko, had lost faith in the principles of communism. As a United States congressman, and later as a senator, his soul secretly in hock to the KGB, he was called upon to betray the country that he had learned to love. He didn't want to pass the information, but he could not think of any way to refuse. The KGB owned him.

He was trapped.

· 83 ·

"But why was my past taken from me?" Joanna asked. "Stolen from me. I don't understand. Why did you send me to Rotenhausen?"

"Had to."

"*Why?*"

The senator bent forward, wracked by an especially vicious burst of pain. His breath bubbled wetly, hideously, in his throat. After a while he found the strength to sit up straight again. He spat dark blood on the carpet and licked his red lips.

"Why did the bastard tamper with my mind?" Joanna demanded.

"Jamaica," said Chelgrin-Timoshenko. "You and I were going to spend a whole week together at the vacation house in Jamaica."

"You and Lisa," she said.

"Yes. I was going to fly down from Washington on a Thursday night. You were at school in New York. You said there was a project you had to finish. You said you couldn't get away until Friday."

He closed his eyes and was perfectly still for so long that she might have thought he was dead if his breathing hadn't been so labored. Finally he continued:

"You changed your plans without telling me. You flew to Jamaica on Thursday morning. You got there hours ahead of me. When I arrived late at night, I thought the house was deserted, but you were napping upstairs."

His voice was growing fainter. He was striving mightily to stay alive long enough to explain himself, in hopes of receiving her absolution.

"I had arranged to meet with some men . . . Russian agents . . . to hand over a suitcase full of reports . . . very important stuff . . . most of it labeled secret. You woke up . . . heard us downstairs . . . started down . . . heard just enough to know that I was a traitor. You barged into the middle . . . of the meeting. You were shocked . . . indignant . . . angry as hell. You tried to leave . . . but of course they wouldn't let you. The KGB gave me a simple choice. Either you had to be killed . . . or sent to Rotenhausen . . . for the treatment."

"But why did Lisa's entire life have to be eradicated?" Joanna asked. "Why couldn't Rotenhausen just remove all her memories about what she'd overheard—and leave the rest of her untouched?"

Chelgrin spat blood again; there was more of it than he had coughed up the last time. "It's comparatively easy . . . for Rotenhausen to scour away . . . huge blocks of memory. It's far more difficult . . . for him to reach into a mind . . . and pinch off just a few select pieces. He refused to guarantee his work . . . unless he was permitted . . . to erase all of Lisa . . . and create . . . an entirely new person. You were put in Japan . . . because you knew the language . . . and because they felt it was unlikely . . . that anyone would spot you there . . . and realize you were Lisa."

"Jesus!" Joanna said.

"I had no choice."

"You could have refused."

"Impossible."

"You could have broken with them. You could have stopped working for them."

"They would have killed you."

"Would you have worked for them after they killed me?" she asked.

"No!"

"Then they wouldn't have touched me," she said. "They wouldn't have had anything to gain."

"But I couldn't go up against them," Chelgrin said weakly, miserably. "The only way I could have gotten free . . . was to walk into FBI headquarters . . . and expose myself. Then I would have been thrown in jail. I'd have been treated like a spy. I would have lost everything . . . my business . . . the investments . . . all the houses . . . every one of the cars . . . the Steuben glass . . . I would have lost everything!"

"Not everything," Joanna said.

"What?"

"You wouldn't have lost your daughter."

"You're . . . not . . . even . . . trying . . . to understand," he said. Then he sighed. It was a long sigh, and it ended in a rattle.

"I understand all too well," Joanna said. "You went from one extreme to the other. You went from being a rigid, unbending, dogmatic communist to being a rigid, unbending, dogmatic capitalist. There wasn't room for humanity in either position."

He did not reply.

She realized that he hadn't heard.

He was dead. For real this time.

She looked at him for a moment, thinking about what might have been.

At last she got up and went back into the ground-floor corridor.

Alex was there, at the end of the hall.

He was alive!

He called her name.

Weeping happily, she ran to him.

• 84 •

The fat man insisted on a brandy to warm their souls and bodies. He led Alex and Joanna to the third floor. They sat on the living room sofa and held hands while he poured three double measures of Remy Martin from a crystal decanter. He sat in a huge chair, which accommodated him with no room to spare, and he clasped the brandy snifter in both pudgy hands, warming the liquor with his body heat.

After a while the fat man said, "A toast." He lifted his glass to them. "Here's to the living."

Alex and Joanna didn't bother to raise their glasses. They just drank the brandy—fast.

The fat man smiled contentedly.

"Who are you?" Joanna asked.

"As I told Alex, my name's Anson Peterson. I'm from Maryland. I'm in real estate there."

"If you're trying to be funny—"

"It's true," the fat man said. "But of course I'm more than that."

"Of course."

"I'm also a Russian."

"Isn't everyone?"

"My name was once Anton Brokawski. I was thin when that was my name. Positively svelte. Oh, you should have seen me then, my dear! I started getting fat the day that I went to the States from Korea, the day I began impersonating Anson Peterson in front of his friends and relatives. Eating is my way of coping with the terrible pressures."

Joanna sipped more brandy. "The senator told me all about the Mirror group before he died. You're one of them?"

"There were twelve of us," said the fat man. "They made us into mirror images of American prisoners of war. They transformed us, not unlike the way in which you were transformed."

"Bullshit!" Alex said angrily. "You didn't endure pain. She did. You weren't raped. She was. You always knew who you really were and where you came from. But Joanna lived in the dark."

She patted Alex's hand. "It's all right. I'm fine. You're here with me, and I'm fine."

Peterson sighed. "The idea was that all twelve of us would come to the United States, start independent businesses, and get rich—with the help of the KGB's bankroll. Some of us needed that help, and some of us didn't. We all made it to the top—except for two who died young, one in an accident and the other of cancer. Moscow figured that the perfect cover for a communist agent was wealth. Who'd ever suspect that a millionaire would plot to overthrow the system that made him what he is?"

"But you've told us that you're on our team," Joanna said.

"I am."

"We're not Russians."

"I've gone over to the other side," Peterson said. "Did it fourteen years ago. I'm not the only one. It was a possibility the Mirror plan didn't consider carefully enough. If you let a man make his mark in a capitalistic society, if you let him achieve everything he wants in that society, then after a while he's likely to feel obligated to the system. Four of the others have switched. Dear Tom would have gone over, too, if he could have overcome his fear of having his millions stripped from him."

"The other side," she said thoughtfully. "You mean you're working for the . . . United States?"

"I'm working for the CIA," Peterson said. "No need to be afraid to say it. The CIA. I told them about dear Tom and the others. They hoped Tom would turn double like I did, of his own free will. But he didn't, and rather than try to turn him, they decided to use him without his knowledge. For fourteen years they fed subtly twisted information to dear Tom, and he passed it on to Moscow. We've been quietly misleading them on several issues for fourteen years. Too bad it couldn't continue."

"Why couldn't it?" Alex asked.

"Dear Tom was going too far in politics. Much too far. He had a better than even chance of becoming the next president. With him in the Oval Office, we couldn't continue to fool the KGB. You see, if intelligence analysts in the Kremlin somehow discovered a mistake in the information sent to them by *Senator* Chelgrin, they would figure it was because he wasn't in a sufficiently high position to acquire the entire unvarnished story. But they wouldn't lose faith in him. They would continue to trust him. However, if they uncovered inaccuracies in reports sent to them by *President* Chelgrin, they would know something was rotten. They'd have to figure he'd purposefully included some false data. They'd painstakingly reexamine everything he'd ever given them, and gradually they'd realize that it was all doctored, slightly and subtly but thoroughly doctored. They'd discount everything they'd gotten from him—scientific data, diplomatic and military information—and they'd be able to repair a lot of the damage we'd done to them. We didn't want that. So dear Tom had to be removed before he became a Presidential candidate and received secret service protection."

"Why did *I* have to do the removing?" Alex asked.

Peterson finished his brandy and, incredibly, took a roll of butter-rum Lifesavers from his pocket. He offered them to Alex and Joanna, then popped one into his own mouth. "The CIA determined that maximum propaganda value should be gotten from the senator's death. They decided his status as a Russian operative should be revealed to the world—but in such a way that the KGB would think the Mirror plan itself had not been uncovered. We don't want to damage my position or that of the other remaining eight Mirror agents. If the CIA itself tore the mask off Tom Chelgrin, the KGB would be certain that he had been made to tell the entire Mirror plan. But if a civilian stumbled across Chelgrin's double identity through a chance encounter with his long-lost daughter, and if Chelgrin were killed before the CIA could question him, the KGB might believe that Mirror was still safe."

"But the senator told me all about it," Joanna said.

"Merely pretend that he didn't," the fat man said. "In a few minutes I will leave. You'll wait half an hour, giving me time to make myself scarce, and then you'll call the Swiss police."

"We'll be arrested for murder," Alex said.

"No. Not when the whole story comes out. You shot these people in self-defense." The fat man smiled at Joanna. "You'll tell the press that your father was a Soviet agent. He told you his story as he lay dying. But you'll make no mention of Mirror or of other Doppelgängers like him."

"What if I do?" she asked.

The fat man scowled. "Now, that would be most unwise. You would destroy one of the most spectacular counterintelligence operations of the cold war. There are people who would not take that lightly."

"The CIA."

"That's right."

"You mean they'd kill me if I told it all?"

"Let's just say they wouldn't take it lightly."

Alex said, "Don't threaten her."

"I didn't make a threat," said the fat man. "I merely stated a fact."

"What happened to me in Rio?" Alex asked.

"We stole a week of your vacation. The CIA has sponsored a few behavioral psychologists and biochemists who have been expanding on Rotenhausen's research. We used some of Franz's techniques to implant a program in you."

"That's why I went to Japan for a vacation," Alex said.

"Yes. You were programmed to go."

"That's why I stopped in Kyoto."

"Yes."

"And at the Moonglow Lounge."

"Yes. We implanted that and a lot of other things, and you performed perfectly."

Joanna slid forward on the couch. She was filled with a new fear. "How . . . detailed was the program?"

"What do you mean?" the fat man asked.

"Was Alex . . . ?" She bit her lip, took a deep breath. "Was Alex programmed to fall in love with me?"

Peterson smiled. "No. I assure you. No. But by God, I wish I'd thought of that! It would have been like a guarantee that he would follow the program."

Alex stood, went to the bar, and poured more brandy for himself. "Moscow will wonder why you weren't killed, too."

"You'll tell the police and the press that there was a fat man who got away. That's the only description you'll be able to give. You'll say I shot at you. You returned my fire. I ran out of ammunition. You chased me, but I got away in the darkness."

"How do I explain Ursula Zaitsev?" Alex asked. "She wasn't armed, was she? Don't the Swiss frown on killing unarmed women?"

"We'll put the seven millimeter automatic in her hand," the fat man said. "Believe me, Alex, you won't wind up in jail. The CIA has friends here. It'll use them in your behalf if necessary. But that won't even be called for. All of this killing was self-defense."

They spent the next fifteen minutes constructing and memorizing a story that would explain everything that had transpired without mentioning Mirror or the fat man's role in Chelgrin's downfall.

Finally Peterson stood up and stretched. "I'd better get out of here. Remember—wait half an hour before you call the police."

• 85 •

They stood at the open door and watched the fat man shuffle out of sight, into the night and the snow, down toward the lights of St. Moritz. In a minute he was out of sight.

Alex closed the door. He looked at Joanna. "Well?"

"I suppose we have to do what he said. If we talk about the Mirror plan, if we spoil the CIA's fun and games, they'll kill us. I don't doubt that. You know they will."

"They'll kill us anyway," Alex said. "They'll kill us even if we do what they want."

She blinked. "Why?"

"It'll happen like this," Alex said. "We'll call the Swiss police. We'll tell them our story. They won't believe us at first. They'll detain us. But in a day or two days or three, they'll match your fingerprints to Lisa's. And other things will fall into place. Then they'll accept what we've told them. They'll let us go. We'll tell the story to the press, just the way that Peterson wants us to tell it. Newspapers all over the world will front-page it. The Russians will be terribly embarrassed. Everything will quiet down eventually. We'll start to lead normal lives. Then someone in the CIA will start to worry about us, about a couple of civilians walking around with this big secret. They'll send someone after us, sure as hell."

"But what can we do?"

He had been thinking about that while the fat man had been helping them create a slightly altered version of the truth for the police. "It's a cliché, but it'll work. This is what we'll do. It's the only thing we *can* do. We're not going to call the cops. We're going to walk out of here. They'll find the bodies eventually. We'll go to Zurich tonight or tomorrow and hole up in a hotel. We'll write a complete account of this, all of it, including the Mirror plan and everything Peterson just told us. We'll make a hundred copies of it. We'll spread them out among a hundred attorneys and banks in ten or twenty countries. With each sealed copy we'll leave instructions that it be sent to a major newspaper, each to a *different* major newspaper, in the event that we are killed—or in the event that we simply disappear. Then we'll send a copy to Peterson in Maryland and another copy to the CIA, along with notes explaining what we've done."

"Will it work?"

"It better."

For twenty minutes they moved down through the house, wiping everything they might have touched.

They found the van that had brought them from the hotel. Their luggage was still in the back of it.

Exactly half an hour after Peterson left, they drove away from Rotenhausen's clinic and the carnage within it. The wipers thumped metronomically, and snow caked on them, turned to ice.

"We can't drive out of these mountains tonight," Joanna said. "The roads won't be passable. Where will we go?"

"To the depot," Alex said. "Maybe there'll be a last train out to somewhere."

There was.

They sat in a nearly empty car, holding hands, as the train clattered toward midnight and then, finally, beyond.